THERE WILL BE PIRATES

Also by STACEY HORAN

OLD CITY MYSTERIES

A Place for Good and Evil

City of Innocent Monsters

———

STANDALONES (Young Adult)

Inland

Sycamore Lane

THE ELIXIR VITAE ADVENTURES SERIES (Young Adult)

Book One: *Ortus*

Book Two: *Juvenis*

Book Three: *Adultus*

Book Four: *Senectus*

Book Five: *Mortem*

THERE WILL BE PIRATES

An Old City Mystery

STACEY HORAN

Ghost Bridge Press LLC

Cover Design by James T. Egan of Bookfly Design

ISBN: 978-1-964473-08-6

For Mom

THERE WILL BE PIRATES

Where there is a sea, there are pirates.

—Attributed to an ancient Greek proverb

Prologue

I t's funny how life can go from peaceful to apocalyptic in the time it takes for a tourist trolley to pass by you while you're standing on the sidewalk. That is exactly what happened to Violet Rizzo.

It was a glorious February day in St. Augustine, with bright sunshine in a cloudless sky, blessedly low humidity, and an ever-so-slight crispness to the air. Or, at least, it was glorious until one of those red trolleys rumbled past Violet as she waited to cross King Street. The Old City was teeming with tourists from northern climes, all of them escaping their dreary, snowed-under lives for a few days of sun, fun, and sightseeing. One of those elderly, pasty-white, Hawaiian-shirt-clad, Bermuda-shorts-wearing tourists sat on the end of the bench seat with his legs spread wide and one arm draped over the seat back. That man, Violet knew, was the stuff of nightmares. Her nightmares, to be exact.

She recognized him instantly. How could she not? The man was the human embodiment of a pit bull, with wide-set, golden-brown eyes; brutal cheekbones; and a jawline so sharp it looked like it had been chiseled from stone. And even though he stood at only five feet, ten inches tall, he was built like a professional linebacker. He had wide shoulders, thick arms and legs, and a natural speed that was terrifying. He was sitting next to his wife. Violet was pretty sure she was the same wife he'd had all those years ago, except now the woman had dyed-blonde hair covering all the gray and a face so full of Botox that it had ironed out not only her wrinkles but her ability to convey expression.

While he might look like a tourist on vacation, soaking up the warmer weather while learning a little North Florida history, Gio Segreti was no doubt on the job. He was always on the job.

Violet knew for certain that Gio wasn't retired; no one ever really retired from his organization. It was guaranteed lifetime employment for someone like him. Even if you were merely a subcontractor or hired help like herself, you were still considered part of the family. And you never, ever fully quit the family. No matter how hard you begged or how far you ran.

Anyone who had ever met Gio Segreti in his prime didn't live long enough to speak about it. Gio Segreti was the enforcer. He was the man called in to clean up the mess, to take out the trash. If Gio turned up on your doorstep, it was inevitable that you would end up rolled up in your living room rug and dumped in a landfill or adorned with a couple of cinderblocks and sunk to the bottom of the East River. Either way, it wouldn't have mattered to you; you would already be dead from any one of a half dozen different means that Gio liked to use to do his job. There was a good reason everyone called him "da Vinci." The man was nothing if not creative and prolific.

As soon as Violet saw Gio on the trolley, she ducked behind a group of Flagler College students, two boys and two girls who were all mercifully taller and broader than she was. She also began praying to every saint she could think of because her clock was now running. She should begin counting her remaining time in days, if not minutes, because she likely had precious few left.

Violet had spent forty years hiding in the Old City, and Gio Segreti had finally come for her. If he was here, it meant that they'd figured it out, learned of her deceit. The discreet and precarious retirement she'd been granted all those years ago was about to be terminated in every sense of the word.

Gio Segreti's presence in the Old City could mean only one thing: da Vinci had been commissioned to use his artistic talents once again. This time, he'd use them on her.

Chapter One

Leo Roberts glanced over his shoulder and saw the man, the same one who had been following him and his boss, Sidney Stone, since they'd left the office on this warm, sunny October evening and walked the two blocks south to Valencia Street to meet Sid's newest client. The air smelled of freshly mown grass, and a few fallen leaves, the first of the season, crunched under foot. The man was keeping his distance but hardly hiding his presence. Then again, he didn't need to hide. No one except Leo could see him.

"Is he still there?" Sid asked from her position next to Leo, facing the front door of the two-story Mediterranean-style house. She reached out and brushed her fingertips over an exposed bit of coquina stone, where the cream-colored plaster had flaked off. The house was old, probably late nineteenth century, but it had been updated and expanded over the years in a manner so seamless that the elegant property managed to look both historic and modern at the same time.

Leo nodded. "Yep. He's still there."

Sid stole a glance over her shoulder, too, and Leo tried not to smile. "Why am I bothering to look?" Sid asked. "I can't see him." She turned back around, shaking her head. "What do you think he wants?"

"Don't know." Leo shrugged.

"Maybe you should ask him," Sid suggested.

Leo glared at her. "Are you crazy? I am not going to walk across the street and ask a real- life pirate why he's stalking us."

"But he's not a real, *live* pirate, is he?" Sid grinned.

Leo huffed. "He may not be alive, but he's definitely a pirate. Trust me."

The spirit across the street crossed his arms over his broad chest and grinned. Even from this distance, Leo could see the poor state of his dental hygiene as well as the sword sheathed at his hip, the pistol tucked into the front of his belt, and the large bloodstain on his torn, white shirt.

"There's no way I'm talking to him."

"What do you think he's going to do?" Sid elbowed him in the ribs. "Run you through with his sword? Wait, does he have a sword?" Her eyes grew wide as she began to turn toward the street.

"Yes, and a pistol." Leo jabbed his boss with his elbow, returning the favor. "Stop trying to look. Besides, we don't know that he can't kill me with his weapons." Leo tugged at the brim of his baseball cap. "Or did you forget the bruises I got from those two ghosts on the Oakmire golf course after they beat me with their clubs?"

"Oh, right." Sid nodded. "Okay, so no talking to pirate ghosts."

"Spirit," Leo corrected her. "I think this one is a spirit, not a ghost."

Sid shifted her bag to her other shoulder, growing restless. "How can you tell?"

Leo shrugged again. "He knows he's dead, first of all. Second, he's not haunting any particular place. I've seen him at Bonney's Bar and walking around downtown, so he's not stuck anywhere. I think he just likes hanging out around here."

"Yeah, well, who wouldn't?" Tired of waiting, Sid reached out and rang the doorbell again. "The Old City is full of pirates. Living and dead ones."

"You mean, there are real pirates here? Right now?" Leo's eyebrows shot up. "Living ones?"

"There are real pirates everywhere, kid." Sid sighed. "Some folks who will do anything to get what they want. And wherever there is an opportunity, there is always someone around willing to take advantage of it. You'd be amazed at what people will do for the chance to exploit someone or something for their own benefit." She shook her head. "Pirates, every last one of them."

She had reached out to ring the bell a third time when the door swung open. A man stood in the doorway. The spirit of an old woman stood right behind him.

"Sorry about that. I was in the carriage house out back. Took me a little while to get to the front door." The man stepped back, gesturing for them both to enter. "Come in, come in."

Sid and Leo stepped into the impressive foyer. Terracotta tiles covered the floor, which ran from the front door to the kitchen about thirty feet away. The kitchen could be viewed through a wrought iron gate that hung in an arched doorway positioned under the second-floor mezzanine. The second floor was accessed by the stone staircase to their left, which had a small landing about one-third of the way up.

The spirit of the old woman floated up to the landing and hovered there, staring down at Leo. He fought the urge to tug on the brim of his Jacksonville Jaguars baseball cap and utter the words Mad Hattie had taught him. Instead, he pulled off his cap and braced for what would inevitably come. After all, this was why he was here. While Sid and their host exchanged pleasantries, Leo stared at the spirit, swallowed hard, and waited for the woman to speak. But there was only silence in his head as they stared at each other, one live fifteen-year-old boy and one dead octogenarian.

Leo gave the woman a small smile, and she smiled at him in return. Then, she patted her bouffant-style hairdo, which was dyed such a dark brown it looked almost like jet against her pale, blue-veined skin. She wore a tailored, slate-blue dress and matching short-heeled pumps, and her hand drifted to a large, sparkling necklace at her throat. The woman's wrinkled yet elegant fingers brushed over the intricate setting of diamonds and rubies before she raised one finger to her lips and winked at Leo. Then she vanished.

"This is my assistant, Leo," Sid was saying.

Leo turned away from the staircase to face Sid and their host. Thanks to Sid's quick briefing on their walk over, he knew the man was Buddy Rizzo, the property appraiser for St. Johns County. Buddy was a skeletal man of about Sid's height, who looked like his bones would break if you so much as stared at him too hard. He was balding, and what little hair he had left was thin, dark brown, and trimmed so short that you could see his freckled scalp. Despite the thinning hair on his head, the man sported thick eyebrows over his dark brown eyes. He had a long, straight nose; cheekbones that could cut glass; and the same pale, paper-thin, blue-veined skin that Leo had seen on the spirit of the dead woman.

Buddy extended his right hand, which was plagued by a slight tremor. "Nice to meet you, young man."

"You, too, sir." Leo shook his hand, being very careful to keep his grip light so as not to crush the man's fingers.

Buddy led them into the home's sunken living room. Sid and Leo chose seats on the sofa while Buddy sat down in a chair opposite them.

"Thank you for coming," he said. He pointed with his shaking hand to a blue-and-white-tiled serving tray that had been set out on the glass and wrought iron coffee table. Then he quickly covered his right hand with his left, trying to hide the tremor. "Please help yourself."

Sid smiled and poured herself a glass of water from the hand-painted pitcher.

Leo declined a glass and sat back on the well-worn sofa. The chocolate-brown leather groaned softly with his shifting weight. He studied the living room, which was painted the same light cream color as Sid's office, a color that always reminded Leo of French vanilla ice cream. The room was filled with dark, heavy, elaborately carved, wooden furniture as well as wrought iron end tables; ceramic lamps; and various colorful throw pillows and knickknacks in primary shades of red, yellow, and blue. Terracotta tiles covered the floor, and dark wood featured prominently in the overhead beams, windowsills, and shutters. The stone fireplace was empty, darkened from decades of fires but currently cleared of soot. Off of the living room, directly behind Buddy Rizzo, was the dining room, complete with a solid oak table and ten chairs in the same dark stain as everything else. Beyond the dining room, visible through a double set of French doors, was a paved courtyard bursting with potted palms; climbing, hot-pink bougainvillea; and a three-tiered stone fountain that was currently bubbling away.

Sid took a sip of water and set her glass down on a tile coaster. "We are very sorry for your loss, Mr. Rizzo."

The man nodded. "Thank you." He heaved a sigh. "It still hasn't sunk in yet." He shook his head. "We held the vigil last night. Not too many people came. Mom tended to keep to herself." He tried to smile, but the effort seemed too great. "Her funeral Mass was this morning, and we laid her to rest this afternoon." He looked around the room. "Everyone else is gathered at my house, but I just needed a few quiet moments . . . alone."

He shook his head again. "I keep thinking she's still here. In her bedroom upstairs or back there in the kitchen. You know what I mean?"

Leo glanced over at the empty staircase.

Buddy chuckled. "Oh, I don't mean literally, Leo. I just mean that I expect to see her shuffling across the floor in her slippers or to hear her scolding me for not taking off my shoes and tracking dirt into the house. If she were still with us, she'd be so mad right now because we are all wearing our shoes indoors."

"We can take them off, if you'd like," Sid offered.

Buddy waved the notion away with his shaky hand. "Not necessary . . . at least not anymore." He sighed, leaned back in his leather armchair, and ran both hands down his face. "There's so much to do. It's all so . . . so overwhelming." He gripped the arms of his chair and fixed his gaze on Sid. "That's why you're here, Sidney."

Sid nodded. "Yes, about that," she began as she sat forward and folded her hands in her lap. "As I mentioned when you called yesterday, this is not the sort of thing I'm usually hired to do. It's not typical PI work, so I'm not sure you need a PI for it. Perhaps your lawyer would be better suited for this type of job. Or even a trusted family member or friend? Maybe someone with some extra time on their hands?"

"No, no, no." Buddy shook his head. "I appreciate your concern, Sidney, I really do, but I simply can't engage our lawyer." He sighed. "Mostly because it would be much too expensive, given the amount of hours it will likely take. No offense to you, but your rates are much more reasonable than hers."

Sid smiled. "I'm not surprised."

Buddy tried to return her smile but couldn't quite manage it. "And I'm not sure I trust any of our friends." He cleared his throat. "What I mean to say is that this is a big job, and there is a lot at stake. It's not something I feel comfortable asking our friends to do."

"And you? Your wife and daughter?" Sid asked. "It's not something you're able to do as a family?"

Buddy rubbed his right hand with his left and glanced between Sid and Leo. "It's too much. Mom was a bit of a pack rat, as you'll see. And it's just too much for me. Too much work and, well, it's just too hard . . . emotionally." He blinked rapidly and cleared his throat again. "As for my family, my daughter is in her first semester at Flagler, and I'd like her to concentrate on her studies. She doesn't need to be spending her days here." He shook his head. "And my wife is very busy with the Women's Advancement Guild and her other charity work. She couldn't possibly take this on. And . . . and I wouldn't want her to." Buddy stared down at his shaking hand. "She's very distraught about it all, and, to be honest with you, I fear she would probably tear the place apart." He looked back up at Sid. "So, no. It has to be someone else, I'm afraid. That's why I called you."

Sid and Leo exchanged a quick glance. "Okay, Mr. Rizzo. I understand. We'll be glad to help you."

"Please, call me Buddy." His shoulders seemed to relax upon hearing Sid's assent. "You know, you come highly recommended. My wife and I have heard excellent things about you."

"Oh?" Sid cocked an eyebrow.

Leo fought to keep the smirk from his face and said nothing.

Buddy nodded. "Yes. Our lawyer recommended you. Carleigh Sutton. I believe you know her? She said you'd helped out her sister recently."

Sid nodded, recalling Carleigh's request for help for her sister, Lorelai Sutton, a budding social media influencer whose pro golfer ex-boyfriend, Cameron Chase, was brutally murdered on the Oakmire golf course several weeks ago. Sid and Leo had been working for the Oakmire Golf and Country Club at the time, investigating suspected alligator poaching, and, with the help of two ghosts who haunted the golf course, ended up solving the mystery of Cameron Chase's murder. Lorelei Sutton had nothing to do with his death, and Carleigh had been so grateful that she'd given Sid a nice bonus. Sid had earmarked the money for some new office furniture but hadn't yet had the time to spend it.

"It was nice of Carleigh to recommend me," Sid replied with a smile.

"And Emmaline Colquitt raved about you to my wife. We've known the Colquitts a long time. Terrible business about the sheriff"—Buddy shook his head—"but Emmaline said you were a great help to her."

Sid smiled again. "I'm glad she thought so," she said, though Sid wasn't so sure. The Colquitt case, her first big one, had ended with the St. Johns County sheriff being arrested and his wife, Emmaline, filing for divorce and fleeing the state with her children. The Colquitt family had been dragged through the mud by the media, which had only recently quieted down because of the murder of Cameron Chase. Thanks to the Colquitt case, Sid had finally found closure for the untimely deaths of her husband and daughter, but that closure had come at the expense of knowing that the former sheriff, who had been her husband's boss at the time, was directly responsible for both of their deaths and the cataclysmic destruction of the life she once knew.

Sid pulled her pink notebook from her bag. "While I'm happy to take your case, Buddy, I want to be clear on exactly what it is you want us to do. You mentioned when you called last night that you want us to go through the contents of your mother's home—"

"And the carriage house," Buddy interrupted.

Sid nodded. "And the carriage house, of course."

"Yes, I'd like you to itemize what's here. Eventually, I'll have to sell everything or give it to charity, but I'd like to know what I'm dealing with. There's just so much." Buddy shook his head. "My mother was a very private person. I was never allowed in her bedroom or her office. And now, I . . ." He shook his head again. "It just doesn't feel right for me to go through her things, so it will be easier for me to handle matters later on if I have itemized lists. Then I can make the necessary decisions and arrange for things to be taken care of in the proper manner."

"We can do that for you." Sid tapped her pen on her notebook. "And if I understood you correctly on the phone, you also want us to search for your mother's jewelry. Is that right?"

Buddy nodded. "Yes. We found what she kept in her safe deposit box at the bank. A few pieces—a necklace, a bracelet, and a couple of rings—but there is one piece that's gone missing. It's a rather valuable one, I'm afraid." Buddy rubbed his shaking hand with his steady one. "My wife is rather desperate to find it."

Sid nodded and made some notes. "And what exactly is this missing piece of jewelry? What does it look like?"

Leo watched as the spirit of the old woman floated across the dining room behind Buddy Rizzo. She placed one finger to her lips as she headed toward the kitchen and disappeared from view. Leo knew exactly what Buddy would say next.

The frail man leaned forward, his elbows coming to rest on his bony knees, and answered: "It is a rather elaborate diamond and ruby necklace."

Chapter Two

"What do you mean you saw it?" asked Sid as she shut her office door an hour later.

Buddy had given them an extensive tour of both the main house and the carriage house. The amount of stuff his mother had accumulated over the years, and subsequently hidden away in closets, in drawers, and under beds, was enough to make Sid's head explode. She and Leo would be inventorying reams of paperwork, scores of mementoes, and who knew what else for days, if not weeks. Finding a necklace buried somewhere in the midst of all those effects was not going to be as easy as she'd hoped.

Leo made a beeline for the mini fridge and removed a cold soda. "Want one?" He held out the can for Sid.

She waved the can away. "No, thank you. And stop avoiding the question. What do you mean you saw the necklace?"

Leo took two huge gulps before answering. "The old woman was wearing it."

Sid felt her jaw drop open. "Have a seat, kid, and start from the beginning." She took her seat behind her desk, the old metal chair squealing its usual appeal for a good oiling, while Leo plucked a bag of chips from the basket on top of the fridge and sat down opposite her in the sagging, green velvet guest chair.

"I saw Violet Rizzo's ghost. She was there when we arrived." He popped a chip into his mouth and chased it with a swig of soda. Sid waited as patiently as she could, drumming her fingers on the desktop. Leo swallowed and continued. "She was wearing this grayish-blue dress, and her hair was all big and fluffy." He mimed Violet's bouffant hairdo while still holding a chip. "And she was wearing this really fancy necklace. Lots of diamonds and rubies."

"You're sure?" Sid opened the Rizzo file that was sitting on top of the short stack on her desk.

"I'm sure." Leo frowned at her. "You couldn't miss it. It practically glowed, it was so sparkly."

Sid made some notes. "So, what does that mean? The fact that her spirit is wearing the necklace must mean something. Was it her favorite necklace? Is there a message hidden in it? Does it somehow factor into the way she died?" She looked up, waiting for Leo to respond.

"I think she's wearing it," he answered. Sid opened her mouth to protest, but he cut her off. "In the ground. I think she's wearing it in her coffin. She was buried with it."

Sid shook her head. "She can't be wearing it. Buddy hired us to find that necklace, and I'm pretty sure he wouldn't have done so if his mother was buried with it."

He shrugged. "I'm just telling you what I saw."

Sid leaned back, the movement eliciting more squeaks of protest from her chair. "Well, that's unfortunate." She blew out a breath as Leo nodded and popped a chip into his mouth. "Are you sure, Leo? Are you certain about this?"

"No. It's just a guess," he answered with his mouth full. He swallowed and added, "She kept floating past and putting her finger to her lips." He mimed the gesture. "She was smiling, like she was having fun with it. Like it was a big secret, and she was happy no one had figured it out."

"That's just great," Sid said, rubbing her temples. "Well, we're going to have to look around and do some investigating. Maybe the necklace is hidden somewhere in the house. Or maybe there's a note saying where she put it. We'll have to rule out other possibilities first before we . . . you know." She picked up her pen and scratched some more notes in the file.

"Before we what?" Leo asked, eyebrows raised.

Sid sighed. "Before we tell Buddy Rizzo that we think his dead mother is wearing the ruby necklace, and he'll have to dig her up if he wants to get it back."

Sid spent the rest of Saturday and most of Sunday doing research, tidying her office, and twiddling her thumbs. She should have used her time wisely and gone shopping for new office furniture—real, proper pieces that were new and professional-looking, not the beat-up, eclectic mix of previously owned junk that she'd inherited from her mentor, Trip Murdock, or thrifted from the local charity shop—but she didn't have the energy. She was tired, and the last day and a half had been a welcome change of pace.

The last couple of weeks had seen an uptick in her caseload. After her success with the Oakmire alligator poaching case and Cameron Chase's murder, she'd enjoyed a steady stream of work. Almost all of it had involved cheating spouses, and Sid was beginning to wonder if anyone in the Old City still remained faithful to their partner.

She was just printing off the last bit of her research

regarding Buddy Rizzo's mother when Leo opened her office door and stepped inside.

"Band practice is over now, and Grandpa's firing up the grill," he announced. "He wants to know if you're joining us for dinner."

"Sure, kid," Sid answered as she pulled the small stack of papers off the printer. "I'll be there in five." She looked down at her stained tee and cutoff shorts. "Make that ten."

Leo pointed to the papers in her hand. "Whatcha working on? Is that for the Rizzo case?" He frowned and tilted his head to the side. "Is it even a case? I mean, we're just gonna be rummaging through an old lady's belongings. Doesn't seem like an actual PI case. It seems more like housecleaning."

"In a way it is." Sid dropped the stack of papers on the open file in front of her and sat back in her chair. She understood Buddy Rizzo's need to have someone else deal with his mother's possessions. When she lost her husband and daughter, she hadn't been able to touch either one's clothes or Iris's toys or Wes's fishing gear. She'd ignored it all, stepped over it or walked around it, for months afterward. It had taken help from others—Leo's grandfather, Burt; their neighbor, Kitty Lonigan; and the other members of Burt's band, Recent Geezer—to get Wes and Iris's possessions sorted, boxed, and taken away. She understood Buddy's inability to deal with this task on his own, but she wasn't really looking forward to it herself. She would do it—*someone* had to help him, and she *was* getting paid—but she didn't relish the idea.

"Have a seat, kid, and I'll tell you what I've found." She pointed to one of the guest chairs, and Leo did as he was told, though one leg bounced up and down with pent-up energy. "I've found out a bit more about our new client." Sid pulled the file closer to her so she could read her notes. "Buddy was actually born Charles Albert Rizzo. He is forty-eight years old.

Widowed from his first wife. Remarried a year and a half later to a woman named Penelope, maiden name Draper. He's still married to her, three years later. He has one daughter from the first marriage, whom he told us is a freshman at Flagler College. He's had no arrests or public scandals, a rarity for the public officials around here." Leo snorted a laugh, and Sid couldn't help but smile. "And prior to his election as the county's property appraiser, he was a partner in a local three-man appraisal firm."

"What's a property appraiser, anyway?" Leo asked. He removed his ball cap and ran his hand through his mop of messy, brown curls.

"Well, the county property appraiser is responsible for making sure all the property in the county is given a yearly valuation. Those valuations are then used to calculate the property taxes owed by the property owners." Sid picked up her pen and twirled it through her fingers. "An appraisal firm, unlike the government, does valuations of commercial and residential properties for purposes of sales and loans and stuff like that."

"Oh," Leo said, frowning. "Sounds boring."

"I'm sure it is." Sid tapped the folder in front of her with her pen. "As for Buddy's mother, her name was Violet Rizzo. I put in a call to Detective Davis to get the details on her death, and he told me that she was found dead in her home last Tuesday morning. Apparently, she'd fallen down the stairs the night before and broke her neck. Violet's daughter-in-law, Buddy's wife, Penelope, found her when she arrived to take her to a hair appointment. It seems the two of them had a standing appointment every Tuesday morning at the Cielo Spa so that Violet could get her hair done."

"I saw her hair." Leo wrinkled his nose. "She paid someone to do that to it?"

"It's called a bouffant." Sid smirked. "And yes, she probably paid a lot of money to have that done. Anyway, I found out she bought that house about fifty years ago for a song. Must have been in bad shape. It's worth a small fortune now."

"I bet." The bouncing in Leo's leg increased.

Sid sighed. "You got a hot date or something?"

Leo froze. "No. Why are you asking?"

Sid pointed to his leg, which had resumed its bouncing almost immediately. "Because you look like you've got somewhere else you need to be."

"I do." Leo held his arms out wide. "It's dinnertime, or did you forget why I came in here in the first place?"

Sid had forgotten. "All right, all right." She held up her hands in surrender. "Go help your grandfather. I'll join you in a few minutes."

Leo shot up out of the chair and bounded for the door. Before exiting, he turned back. "Did you find out anything about the fancy necklace? You know, the diamond and ruby one that she was probably buried with?"

Sid shook her head. "No, kid. Nothing. But it's still early in the game."

Leo nodded and opened the door to leave. The heavenly scent of steaks on the grill wafted in, and Sid's stomach growled. She straightened the papers in front of her and closed the file. What she didn't tell Leo was that she'd been unable to find out much more about the recently deceased Violet Rizzo despite the fact that the woman had lived a mere two blocks away for the last fifty years or so.

There had been no photos of Violet Rizzo online, at least none that Sid had been able to find, and she had searched for hours. There were none in the various photo spreads of the WAG's charity events, even though her daughter-in-law, Penelope, reigned supreme as this year's chairperson. Nor were there any photos of her at past events at the Lightner Museum, located in the Old City's historic downtown, where Violet was credited as being one of the museum's many volunteers. She was also absent from Penelope Rizzo's carefully curated social media pages. The complete lack of any photographic evidence of her existence fascinated Sid.

It appeared that Violet Rizzo liked to keep a much lower profile than anyone else she'd encountered in her limited experience as a private investigator. And, in Sid's opinion, that made her all the more interesting.

Chapter Three

Dinner with the members of Recent Geezer, and their oldest groupie, Kitty Lonigan, was always entertaining. Kitty insisted that the superlative of "oldest" groupie meant "longest standing" and was in no way a reflection on her age. Leo sat through dinner listening to the Geezers tell stories, some of which he'd heard before but none of which would ever get old, and he laughed until he nearly cried. Kitty had made them a four-layered coconut cake with buttercream frosting, and it was possibly one of the best things Leo had ever tasted. He had had no idea he liked coconut so much.

When dinner was over, Sid and Kitty cleared the table, Burt went outside to tend to the grill, and all the Geezers except for Eli packed up their instruments and loaded them in their cars. Leo sat in the living room with Eli, the gentle giant who played guitar and sang lead vocals for the band. It was time for his lesson on the bass guitar. He was getting two lessons per week now: one with Eli on Sundays after dinner with the band and one on Thursday nights with his grandfather, unless the band was playing a set at Granny Oak's

Music Park. He felt like he was in good hands. Burt was Recent Geezer's bass guitarist, and his skills on the instrument outshone Eli's, which were already more than proficient.

Leo liked both lessons for very different reasons. At Thursday's lesson, Burt would share memories of Leo's father, Gunner, including tales of Gunner's own bass guitar lessons. These were stories Leo had never heard from his father when he was alive. And it was no wonder; the man had spent most of Leo's formative years on deployment with the navy. These lessons with Burt were becoming precious to Leo, especially now that Leo had made peace with his father's passing.

Sunday night lessons, on the other hand, were altogether different. Whereas Burt spent time teaching technique and precision, Eli was teaching Leo to jam, to feel the music and to let it take him wherever it wanted to lead him. Eli would play something on his guitar, and Leo would try to follow along despite not really knowing what he was doing. Most of the time, Leo was not making music. He was making something more akin to a disharmonic whale song or the sounds cats make when they're in heat, which probably explained why everyone cleared out or went home as soon as possible.

But every once in a while, Leo would get it, and the result was something so special that Eli would nod and smile and start scatting, making up short lyrical phrases on the spot. It made Leo feel alive, and he didn't mind at all that Kitty's dead husband, Jerry, stuck around to listen instead of following her home like usual.

As they wrapped up this particular session and were putting away their instruments, Eli reached over and gave Leo's shoulder a gentle squeeze. "How you doin', Leo?"

Leo was taken aback. They'd been playing for nearly an hour, and this seemed like a question Eli should have asked when they greeted each other earlier in the afternoon, not something to end the night with. "Fine. You?"

Eli laughed, a deep, booming sound that filled the room. "I'm fine as well. Thank you for askin'. But I was meanin' how you're doin' with your gift. You okay? You havin' any problems with spirits these days?"

Leo blushed with embarrassment. Eli knew about his ability to communicate with the dead because Mad Hattie was his cousin and she'd told him. Eli knew that Hattie had helped Leo speak with Gunner's spirit a few weeks ago, an episode that had started out horrifically but ended in tears of joy and love. "I'm fine, sir. No problems." Leo bent over and snapped the guitar case shut, trying to avoid the big man's dark, soulful gaze.

"Did I ever tell you how I learned about ol' Hattie's gift?" Eli sat back and draped one arm over the back of the sofa. Leo sat bolt upright and shook his head. "She kept it a secret from me when we were little. She's a couple years older'n me, and she didn't want me gettin' scared. She knew I couldn't see what she could see. None of the men in our family can. It's just the women who've got the gift. Not all of 'em, but a fair few." His gaze drifted off toward the corner of the room, toward his memories of the past. "I caught her talkin' to herself in her room one day. When I asked her what she was doin', she said that she was talking to our great-granddaddy and that he'd given her a message for me. He said I needed to be singin', not just fishin'."

Leo gave him a lopsided grin. "He said that?"

Eli nodded. "Hattie told me Great-Granddaddy said I'd do a lot of fishin' in life, and it's true. I have. But he said I needed to do a lot of singin' as well." He wagged his finger in the air. "He said, 'Tell him not to stop singin'.'" Eli shrugged. "So I kept on singin'. And look at me now." He chuckled again, and Leo grinned widely at the big man. "That's when Hattie told me that she could see the dead." He whistled low and soft. "And Hattie's gift? Boy, it was somethin'. Stronger than any of the others' in the family. She didn't tell anyone else the truth of it all for a long time, kept actin' like her gift was just like everyone else's." He shook his head. "But it wasn't. And when she finally told people about what she was seein' and feelin' and hearin', well, a lot of the family didn't believe her."

"Really?" Leo's voice cracked, and he cleared his throat. "They didn't believe her? Even though they knew she could see spirits?"

"Even though they knew." Eli nodded slowly. "They were scared, some of 'em. A few of 'em were jealous."

"Did you believe her?"

"I did."

"Why?"

Eli smiled. "Because she asked me to. Simple as that. She was"—he chuckled—"and still is my big cousin." Leo smiled at the image of the diminutive Mad Hattie next to the hulking Eli Williams. Eli nodded, as if reading Leo's thoughts. "And she'd never lied to me before." He cocked his head to the side. "She might not've told me the whole truth about her gift, but she never did lie. So I believed her, even when the others didn't."

Leo stared down at the hem of his Collective Soul T-shirt. It had been his father's back in the day and was faded and soft with wear. Leo's finger had found a small hole in the hem, and he made a mental note to stitch it closed before the shirt found its way into the wash. "Did she tell anyone other than her family?"

"She did." Eli paused, waiting for Leo to look at him before continuing. "And it went about as you'd expect it to. Just like with family, some folks were scared, some were jealous, but most didn't believe her." He shrugged. "You should ask her 'bout it sometime. I know it wasn't easy for her, and she told me there were times when she was scared of what people might do to her. Not everyone is as kind and understandin' as you and me." He placed his big hand on Leo's shoulder again. "Some people tried to take advantage of her, tried to hurt her, use her." He sighed. "But she learned to read people, learned who to trust and who to run away from." He squeezed Leo's shoulder gently. "You got to be careful, son."

Leo nodded. "I will."

Eli gave him a sad smile. "You know what got ol' Hattie through those hard times?" Leo shook his head, so the big man replied, "Leanin' on the people she found who believed her, the ones she knew she could trust."

He heaved himself up from the sofa and picked up his guitar case. "I think Hattie'd be the first one to tell you that holdin' it all in, keepin' it all to yourself ain't the best thing for you. Keepin' a secret like yours is hard. Real hard. Now, I'm not sayin' you need to go shoutin' from the rooftops that you can see spirits walkin' around, but maybe you don't need to be so afraid of sharin' your gift a little . . . when it seems like the right time, of course."

He headed toward the front door, and Leo followed. "Leo, sometimes buryin' the truth way down deep ain't much different than lyin' about it. And there'll be times when you may wanna dig up those secrets and share 'em with people. Don't be afraid of doin' that. It can be a good thing, a real good thing. Just watch out for those people who want to take advantage of you for doin' it." He smiled. "And don't be afraid to ask for help when you need it." He raised his eyebrows at Leo.

"I will." Leo nodded. "Promise."

"Good man." Eli opened the door and strode out into the balmy Florida night. "Keep practicin' now. We'll jam again next Sunday."

Leo stood on the front porch, waited for Eli to climb into his truck, and waved to him as he pulled out of the drive. Once again, his finger found the hole in the hem of his dad's T-shirt. As he watched Eli drive past the front of the house and head for home, his gaze snagged on a figure standing across the street. In front of Kitty Lonigan's bright yellow house stood the pirate with the bloodstained shirt, his sword and pistol stowed in their usual places. Leo swallowed hard, quickly ducked back into the house, and locked the front door, not that a lock would do any good against the spirit of a dead pirate.

Chapter Four

On Monday morning, Sid opened the door to Violet Rizzo's house using the old woman's own set of keys, which Buddy had given her, and turned off the alarm. She stood in the foyer, jingling the keys in her hand, and surveyed the ground floor. The plan of attack she'd developed late last night—to start at the bottom and work her way up—still seemed like a good idea. The house was quite large, with four bedrooms and three bathrooms on the second floor, plus living space on the second floor of the carriage house. The prospect of combing every square inch of the property was daunting.

"Better get started," Sid muttered to herself. Then she cleared her throat and said in a louder voice, "Please don't be mad, Mrs. Rizzo, but I've been hired to do a job, and I'm just going to get on with it."

Without Leo here, Sid had no idea if the spirit of the dead woman was looming nearby. It was probably best to act as if she was and proceed as respectfully as possible. There was no way the spirit wouldn't realize what Sid was doing. The dead woman might already know, given her cheeky behavior when they were here on Saturday evening, and it was unlikely that Violet Rizzo would be too happy about Sid wading through her private documents and personal items. Sid waited in the silence of the empty house for a few moments, but nothing happened, so she took a deep breath and steeled herself for the task ahead.

The house smelled faintly of flowers and was blessedly cool, the air conditioner clearly working well in the Florida heat. Even in early autumn, the temperatures in St. Augustine were high, and the humidity was even higher. Sid swallowed audibly as she felt a cold breeze on her arm, knowing full well that it was not the air-conditioning that she was feeling. Shivering, she dropped her bag by the front door and got to work.

She started in the foyer and eventually moved into the living room, checking behind the artwork on the walls; studying each floor tile on her hands and knees; and knocking against all of the baseboards, windowsills, and doorframes. She opened every drawer, squeezed every pillow and cushion, and checked under and behind every piece of furniture. She felt like Nancy Drew in the mystery books she used to read as a little girl, looking for secret passageways and hidden compartments.

She lay down on her back in the fireplace and shined the flashlight on her phone up at the damper and into the smoke chamber. She couldn't reach into the flue, but then, if she couldn't, Violet couldn't either. Her efforts turned up nothing of interest, but she itemized every piece of furniture, every photograph, every knickknack. Her search continued into the dining room where she crawled over every square inch of the floor. No loose tiles, no secret hiding places. The long table, the ten chairs, and the sturdy buffet unit revealed nothing sparkly and made of rubies, but Sid added each and every napkin, candlestick, and serving platter to her growing list of inventory.

After finishing the dining room, she sat down and rested

her forehead on the dining table, feeling fairly certain that Nancy Drew never complained about bruised knees and a sore back in any of her adventures. She had just closed her eyes when her phone at the other end of the table began ringing. She reached for it, almost knocking it to the floor.

"I'm done with school now, so I'll come and help you. You're at the house, right? I'll be right over." The words poured out of Leo before Sid even had a chance to say hello. "And Grandpa wants to know if you've eaten lunch yet. If not, he's going to make you a sandwich, and I'll bring it with me."

Sid smiled, marveling again at the fact that this fifteen-year-old boy wanted to spend time helping her with her PI business. Even more amazing was the fact that she looked forward to spending time with him. He was a good kid, and it was nice having him around, even though he could be quite snarky. "Thanks, kid. Tell Burt I'd love a sandwich."

"Got it," Leo said. She heard him clomping down the stairs in Burt's house, yelling to his grandfather that Sid did, indeed, want a sandwich. "I'll be there soon." Before Sid could say anything more, he hung up.

About twenty minutes later, Sid was awakened by a knock at the front door. She'd fallen asleep at the dining table and could now add a stiff neck to today's tally of bodily aches and pains. She shuffled to the door, checking her watch to see that it was past three o'clock in the afternoon, and found Leo standing on the stoop with a soft-sided cooler in hand.

"Here's your sandwich." He held up the cooler. "Grandpa thought we might get hungry this afternoon, so he packed a bunch of stuff for us, too."

Sid smirked. "You mean he thought *you* might get hungry this afternoon."

Leo shrugged. "We, me, same thing."

They sat at the dining table and ate in companionable

silence for several minutes. Burt had packed three ham and cheese sandwiches, one for Sid and two for Leo, despite the fact that the boy had already eaten lunch. Leo glanced over the lists Sid had made of the contents of the foyer, living room, and dining room. "So, what's next?"

"Kitchen," Sid replied before taking a bite of her sandwich.

Leo wadded up his sandwich wrapper and opened a bag of chips. "That's it?" When she raised an eyebrow at him, he shrugged. "Shouldn't take too long, should it?"

They began by moving the half dozen floral arrangements that were lined up on the kitchen counter into the dining room so they'd be out of the way. An hour later, after they'd finished searching and cataloging the upper kitchen cabinets, Leo grumbled, "Why does anyone need so many glasses?"

Sid groaned as she got down on sore knees and opened the lower cabinet closest to the dining room. It was chock full of pans of every shape and size, and it was only one of several. "I don't know, kid. Some people like to entertain." She began pulling out the cookware piece by piece and rattling off their names so Leo could note it in their log. It was after six o'clock before they finished up, returned the floral arrangements to the kitchen, locked the front door, and headed home.

"You didn't mention seeing Violet today," Sid noted as they walked side by side along the sidewalk. "Was she not around?"

He shook his head. "Nope. Didn't see her."

"Really?" Sid asked. "I'm surprised because I felt her when I first arrived."

"You did?" Leo blinked in surprise.

Sid smiled. "I may not be able to see dead people, but I've gotten pretty good at feeling them. And she was definitely there this morning."

Leo shrugged. "Well, she wasn't there this afternoon, at least not anywhere I could see her."

"Let's hope she stays away," said Sid, "because tomorrow I'm going to have to paw through her underwear drawer."

"Eww," groaned Leo. "Please don't ever say anything like that to me again."

Sid laughed as they strolled across Saragossa Street toward Burt's house and her office-apartment combination in the garage around back. When they reached the driveway, they heard knocking and saw a petite, young woman with shoulder-length, pink hair standing in front of Sid's office door.

"Can I help you?" Sid called out, causing the young woman to jump and spin around.

"Oh my gosh, you scared me!" She laughed breathlessly. Her gold nose ring glinted in the fading sunlight. "Sorry to bother you, but I'm not sure I'm in the right place." She smiled shyly. "Are you Sidney Stone?"

"I am." Sid nodded.

The young woman sighed with visible relief. "Oh, good. I thought I had it wrong. When I looked up your address online, it looked like this was just a garage."

"It used to be, once upon a time, but it's my office now." Sid smiled at the young woman. "This is Leo. He lives there." She pointed over her shoulder at the house.

The young woman's gaze landed on Leo, and her smile broadened. "Hello."

"Hi," said Leo. Sid watched as he straightened his posture and smoothed his T-shirt. Today he was wearing his father's old Black Crowes tee. The once-black shirt was now a faded gray, and the cartoonish dual-crow design had seen better days, so no amount of smoothing was going to make it look good, but Leo was trying anyway.

Sid cleared her throat. "How can I help you?"

"Oh, sorry." The young woman blushed. "I'm Joey Rizzo. My dad said he hired you to help him with my grandmother's estate. She died recently. Her name's Violet Rizzo." Each sentence ended with a lilt and sounded like a question.

Sid smiled. "Yes, that's right. We're helping your father." She fished her keys out of her bag. "Let's all go inside, whaddya say?"

She unlocked the door and stepped inside, the young woman and Leo following closely behind. Joey glanced around the office, taking in the ramshackle, thrift-store aesthetic. Sid motioned for her to have a seat, patting the tall back of the Queen Anne dining room chair that served as one of the two guest chairs. "Have a seat. Would you like a drink? I have soda and water."

"Um . . ." The woman glanced between Sid and Leo before answering, "Soda, I guess?" Again, it sounded like a question.

Sid removed two sodas from the mini fridge and handed one to Joey Rizzo, who dropped her backpack on the floor and sat in the chair Sid had designated, and the other to Leo, who remained standing. Sid worked to suppress her grin when she realized that he had probably chosen to stand rather than risk embarrassment by sinking into the other guest chair, which sagged comically under anyone's weight. Remembering Violet Rizzo's elegantly appointed home office in the carriage house, which she'd glimpsed on Buddy's tour, Sid mentally kicked herself for not going out and shopping for better office furniture.

She watched Joey Rizzo tentatively open the soda can and take a sip. From what she remembered from her research, this girl was barely eighteen and was in her first semester at Flagler College. The pink hair was new. In most of Joey's social media posts, she'd been a brunette, like her father. The hair dying had started after her high school graduation. Since then, her shoulder-length locks had been blue, purple, and pink, in that order. Her black nail polish was chipped on the tips of several fingers, and she wore a black tank top, black jeans with artfully placed rips and tears, and black combat boots. A small diamond solitaire sat at the base of her throat, suspended there by a fine, gold chain. The young woman's warm, brown eyes were lined with kohl, and her lips were bare but for a shiny, clear gloss.

"We're very sorry for your loss," Sid said.

Joey lowered her gaze. "I'm gonna miss her. My grandma was really special. She was an artist." She looked back up at Sid. "Did you know that?"

"I did." Nothing in the research had revealed Violet to be an artist, but Buddy's tour of the carriage house had included Violet's studio. Dozens of painted canvases had littered the space, all of them signed with the deceased's artist mark—a stylized VR. Sid guessed that Violet had probably displayed and sold paintings under a pseudonym, which was why she'd not found anything online.

Joey smiled. "She's got paintings hanging in some of the galleries around town. And several restaurants, too. She even has one in the Lightner Museum."

"Are you an artist as well?" Sid asked.

Joey laughed nervously. "No. I didn't inherit her gift. My dad's a pretty good artist, but I take after my mom. She could barely draw a straight line." She picked at the frayed edges of one of the holes in her jeans. "I'm in a band, though. I play piano and keyboards, and I sing a little. Not lead. Just backup vocals, but I can carry a tune." She shrugged.

"Really?" Sid pointed to Leo. "Leo here is learning bass guitar." She looked up at him and saw his cheeks and ears beginning to turn pink. "His grandfather plays in Recent Geezer. Have you heard them?"

"Oh, my gosh! I love the Geezers!" Joey sat up straight and smiled at Leo. "They are so awesome. You're so lucky."

Leo lowered his eyes and nodded. "Yeah, they're really good. My grandpa plays bass."

"Ah, so it's in your genes then," Joey added. "Lucky you."

Leo nodded again but said nothing. His face and ears were now scarlet.

Sid folded her hands in front of her on the desk and leaned forward. "So, what can we help you with, Joey?"

"Oh, right." Joey's leg began to bounce, much like Leo's did when he was nervous or anxious. "I want to hire you."

Sid blinked in surprise. "I . . . I don't understand. Your father already hired us."

Joey held up her hands. "Oh, I know. You're sorting through everything and helping Dad with the estate. I get that. That's not what I mean. I want to hire you myself." She reached into her backpack—a beat-up, olive-green, canvas bag with more pins and patches on it than Sid could count—and pulled out a wallet. "I'm eighteen. See?" She held up her driver's license and then placed it on the desk in front of Sid. "And I can pay you. I'm not sure how much you charge, but I can pay. I have some money in my account, and Grandma left me some, too, but I have to wait for the probate stuff to end before I can access any of it. So there may be a delay in paying for the whole thing, but I promise I will pay you. Every cent. As long as it's not more than fifty thousand dollars." She chewed on her thumbnail and shifted in her seat.

"Joey," Sid began as she slid the driver's license back toward the young woman, "I can assure you that nothing you might hire me to do should cost fifty thousand dollars." She smiled and sat back. "And before we discuss rates and payment schedules, I think we should talk about why you want to hire me in the first place."

"Right, okay, yeah." Joey's knee began to bounce again, and she glanced back and forth between Sid and Leo.

"Leo helps me on cases. He's my . . . intern." Sid smiled up at Leo who frowned at her in return. "If it is something personal, he's happy to step out of the room. And I promise that whatever you discuss with me will be kept in the strictest confidence."

Joey nodded. "Good, okay, good." She began to chew her thumbnail again but stopped herself and sat on her hands to keep herself from doing it again. "And it's okay if Leo stays. It's not personal." She dropped her chin to her chest. "It's nothing like that."

Sid noticed Leo blushing an even deeper shade of red. "Okay then," she replied. "Why do you believe you need to hire a private investigator?"

Joey looked up and held Sid's gaze. "I want you to find out who killed my grandmother."

Chapter Five

S id blinked in surprise. Out of the corner of her eye, she saw Leo's mouth drop open. "Perhaps we should start at the beginning," she suggested as she picked up her pen, pulled a fresh legal pad from her top drawer, and got ready to take notes. "Tell me everything you know about your grandmother's death."

Joey nodded. "Right, okay, right." She scooted up to the edge of her chair, hands on her knees. "Grandma had this rule. I knew it. Dad knew it. I think everyone knew it: No shoes in the house."

"Your dad said something about that when we met with him." Sid smirked. "I'm afraid we didn't follow that particular rule today."

Joey let slip a nervous laugh. "I don't think it matters now. Anyway, there are two baskets by the door. Have you seen them? Do you know the ones I'm talking about?" Both Sid and Leo nodded, and Joey continued. "Whenever I visited, I had to put my shoes in the first basket and take my slippers out of the second basket. We all had slippers at Grandma's house. She bought us new ones for Christmas every year. Me, Dad, and Penny. We had to keep them there. We weren't allowed to take them home." She shook her head at the memory. "Whenever we went over there, she made us remove our shoes and put on our slippers, and then we were allowed into the rest of the house." She held up a finger. "But there was no going past the entryway until we put our slippers on."

Sid nodded as she took notes. "Okay, so what does that have to do with your grandmother's death?"

"Well, here's the thing." Joey tugged at the loose threads around the knees of her jeans. "Grandma never wore her slippers on the stairs. She would remove them at the bottom and put them in the basket by the door. Then, she would climb the stairs in her bare feet and put on a different pair of slippers that she kept upstairs." Both Sid and Leo raised their eyebrows, and Joey laughed nervously again. "She was a bit unusual, but I swear she wasn't crazy."

Sid smiled. "No one is saying that she was. Clearly, she had a . . . ritual. She liked to do things the way she liked to do them. There's nothing wrong with that."

Joey nodded. "Yeah, she did like things to be a certain way. I was used to it growing up, but Penny always thought it was weird."

"And when you say Penny," Sid began but was interrupted.

"My stepmom, Penelope." Joey's fingers wrapped around the small diamond at the base of her throat, and she began to slide it back and forth along the thin chain. "She married my dad a few years ago. Mom had only been dead about a year before they started dating, and they got married just six months after that. It was all rather . . . sudden." She hung her head. "I guess Dad just didn't want to be alone." She looked back up at Sid. "Which is weird, because he had me. He had Grandma. He wasn't alone."

"I'm sure your dad knows that, Joey, but, speaking from experience, it's not exactly the same thing." Sid shrugged. "I lost my husband a few years ago, and being without him does feel a lot like being alone, regardless of how many other people I have in my life."

Joey's lips twitched to one side as she bit the inside of her cheek and thought for a moment before commenting. "I guess."

Sid studied the girl. "Do you like your stepmom?"

Joey's knee began to bounce again. "She's okay." The girl shrugged. "She's always been nice to me. And she's good with my dad. I guess that's what matters, right?"

"I guess so." Sid nodded slowly. "You were telling us about the slippers," she prompted.

"Right." Joey sat up straight again. "Grandma wore one pair of slippers downstairs and a different pair of slippers upstairs, and she only ever climbed up and down the stairs in her bare feet. She used to say all the time that those stairs were slippery 'cause they were so worn and smooth and that she was afraid she might fall. That's why she wouldn't wear the slippers. She didn't trust them not to slip on the stone." She gave Sid a small smile. "She would make me take off my slippers and walk barefoot up and down the stairs, too. And then I'd have to put my slippers back on again. You see, I only had one pair, not two like her." She shivered. "That stone was so cold, even on the hottest days in summer."

"Joey, your dad told me that your grandmother slipped on the stairs," Sid noted.

"No, she didn't. I'm sure of it." The young woman shook her head.

Sid raised an eyebrow. "Why is that?"

"'Cause she was wearing her upstairs slippers when she fell." Joey's voice hitched. "I saw the police report. Dad doesn't know I saw it, so please don't tell him." Her eyes grew wide, and it was only after Sid nodded to her that she continued. "It said she was found in her bathrobe and slippers."

"Okay, well," Sid began slowly, "you just told us that she thought her slippers might make her slip on the stairs."

"But she wouldn't have had them on!" Joey blurted. "If she had been coming down the stairs, she wouldn't have had any slippers on at all."

Sid took a breath, trying to give the young woman a moment to calm down. "Maybe she slipped as she was trying to take them off."

Joey shook her head again, even more forcefully this time. "No. Definitely not. There was a little chest at the top of the stairs in the hallway. She would sit on the chest, take off the slippers, put the slippers in the chest, and *then* she would go downstairs. She never stood at the top of the stairs with her slippers on. Never!"

"Okay, okay, Joey. I believe you." Sid held up her hands. "But I'm not sure what I can do to help you. The police—"

"The police ruled it an accident," Joey interrupted. "And they're wrong. I want you to find out what happened."

Sid sat back and stared at the notes she'd taken. Then she looked up at Leo, who was staring at Joey with narrowed eyes and a crease pinched between his brows. Without allowing herself time to second-guess her decision, Sid pulled a form from her desk drawer and filled in some information.

Sliding the form across the desk and holding out her pen to Joey, she said, "Fill in your information. I'll do this for a flat fee. I'll give you two weeks of time for this rate"—she tapped the form—"and if I don't find an answer for you by then, we'll call an end to it. But if I figure it out sooner than that, this is the amount you'll still owe." Sid had quoted the girl a ridiculously low amount, which probably wouldn't even cover her time for more than a few days, but since Buddy Rizzo was paying handsomely for the work being done to sort through Violet's belongings, she could afford to give Joey Rizzo a huge discount.

Joey took the pen and filled in her information. "That's more than I can pay right now, but I can give you some of it now and the rest when Grandma's probate is done."

"Don't worry about it," Sid said with a wave of her hand. "We'll work it out at the end of the two weeks. Or sooner, if that's the way things turn out."

Joey nodded. "Okay, yeah, okay." She grabbed her ratty backpack, stood up, and held out her hand to Sid. "Thank you for this."

Sid shook the proffered hand, which Joey then offered to Leo. He shook the girl's hand as his cheeks began to fill with color once again. Joey left the office, closing the door softly behind her.

Leo blew out a breath. "So, what do you think?" He pulled off his baseball cap and ran his hand through his sweaty curls.

"I don't know." Sid sat back down and leaned back in her chair, ignoring its squeaks and squeals. "What do *you* think? Did you get any feeling from Violet that she might have met her end by foul play?"

"Nope." Leo shoved his hands into his pockets and shook his head. "Then again, she and I haven't exactly had a conversation."

"Not yet." Sid smiled. "But I bet you can guess what you're going to be doing the next time you see her."

Chapter Six

Sid didn't arrive at Violet Rizzo's house until almost noon on Tuesday. She had forgotten to set her alarm and woke up late, and her body was so sore from her scavenger hunt on Monday that she went for a long, slow jog to help work out the kinks. The run had also done wonders for her mental state. She'd tossed and turned a fair bit during the night, replaying the conversation with Joey Rizzo about her grandmother's death. In fact, she'd dreamed of slippers. Lots and lots of slippers—silvery ones, fur-lined ones, and ones that looked like floppy-eared rabbits.

As she stepped into the foyer, she was assailed by a blast of cold wind. "I'm sorry, Mrs. Rizzo, but I have a job to do. You know that." She rubbed her arms. "Your son has asked for my help, and I'm going to give it to him. I'm only here to inventory the contents of your home. That's it." She felt silly talking out loud in an empty house. She couldn't see Violet Rizzo, wasn't even certain that the cold she was feeling was the presence of the deceased's spirit, but she had nothing to lose by trying to be nice to the dead. "I'm not here to steal anything. I promise."

The cold persisted, and Sid pulled a sweatshirt from her bag. Since working with Leo, she'd learned to prepare for the drop in temperature that accompanied the presence of spirits. "By the way," Sid said as she slipped the sweatshirt over her head, "I met your granddaughter, Josephine, last night." She used Joey's full given name, presuming that Violet's persnickety temperament probably preferred the formal to the casual. "She doesn't think your death was an accident."

And just like that the cold vanished, and the air returned to the same familiar temperature it had been the day before. Sid had managed to get only her head and one arm into her sweatshirt. "Mrs. Rizzo? Are you still here?" Nothing but conditioned air enveloped her. "Was it something I said?" she muttered to herself as she pulled off her sweatshirt and stuffed it back in her bag.

Sid noted the two baskets by the door, both of them large, squat, lidded, and made of a tightly woven seagrass. She'd looked inside them yesterday and noted their contents in her log. One contained a few pairs of shoes: two pairs of low-heeled pumps, a pair of thick-soled walking shoes, and a pair of beaded sandals. The other contained four pairs of slippers, which tallied with Joey's story that this was the slipper receptacle. Another peek inside confirmed what she'd seen yesterday. The smallest pair of slippers, a silky, champagne-colored pair in the same size as the shoes in the other basket, was well-worn.

Sid left the baskets where they stood and began to climb the staircase. She checked each stone step as she ascended, running her fingers along the edges and seams, looking for cracks and worn spots, hoping to find something—anything— that could serve as a hiding spot for Violet's jewels, but nothing revealed itself. The stone was unforgiving on her bruised knees, and she noted that Joey had been correct. Even on a hot Florida day, the stone staircase seemed unnaturally cold to the touch. Pausing at the landing where Violet Rizzo's body had been found, she avoided the dark spot in the center. While the blood from the old woman's head wound had been cleaned up, the stone would be forever scarred, a reminder of the tragedy.

She called out, "Mrs. Rizzo? Are you here?" The temperature remained the same. Violet Rizzo had apparently left the building.

Sid continued to inspect the stairs until she reached the mezzanine. At the top, she found the chest that Joey had described. It was positioned against the wall a few feet away from the top of the stairs. Lifting the lid, she found nothing inside. The upstairs slippers were missing, which made sense, given that Violet had been found dead with her slippers on her feet.

She inspected the rest of the hallway, checking the wooden floorboards and baseboards and looking behind each photograph and framed piece of art that hung on the walls. Working her way to the end of the hall, she noted the location of each of the bedrooms. The front room, facing the street, was Buddy's childhood bedroom with its own bath. Next in line were two small guest bedrooms separated by a modest guest bath. Finally, at the end of the hall with large windows providing a view of the courtyard and carriage house, was Violet's bedroom and en suite bath.

Sid placed her bag by the door and looked around the expansive space that ran the entire width of the back of the house. The four-poster bed, long dresser, and tall chest of drawers were bulky pieces in the same dark wood stain as the downstairs furniture. Everything was neat and tidy—the bed crisply made, the pillows fluffed, the closet door closed. She peered into the en suite bathroom and found a large clawfoot tub and a sink and countertop made of pearlized white marble.

White fluffy towels hung from the towel racks, but the hook on the back of the bathroom door was empty.

At first glance, Violet's bedroom appeared to be well organized. Half a dozen perfume bottles and a boar bristle hairbrush sat on an etched, silver tray atop the dresser. A few framed photos were neatly arranged on the top of the chest of drawers: two childhood photos of Buddy; one of Joey; and a family photo of Buddy, Joey, and a woman who must have been Joey's mother and Buddy's first wife. Conspicuously absent from the small collection were any photos of Penelope. Sid was beginning to feel confident that her search might not take as long as she feared, given the orderly and somewhat sparse nature of the contents of Violet's bedroom.

Upon opening the closet door, however, her spirits plummeted. The closet was packed floor to ceiling with shoeboxes, vacuum-sealed bags, and multi-tiered hangers packed with clothing. She stepped back, stunned by the volume of clothes and shoes, and reached to open one of the drawers in the chest. It stuck fast. After several attempts and quite a bit of jostling, including shoving her hand inside to try to flatten the contents, the drawer finally opened to reveal more than a dozen vacuum-sealed bags of colorful garments. She wouldn't know for certain until she opened the bags and checked inside, but they appeared to contain scarves. Well over a hundred scarves.

"Who needs so many scarves?" muttered Sid. "It's Florida, for crying out loud. I don't think I've ever worn a scarf here." She shook her head. "Ever."

Sid left the drawer open, not wanting to fight with it to get it closed again, and went and sat on the bed. "Where do I even begin?" she whispered. No one answered her, not that she was expecting that to happen, but she wished that someone else would take charge and tell her what to do. The project now seemed overwhelming, and Leo wouldn't be able to help until he finished with his day of online homeschooling later this afternoon. Why had she agreed to this? It was madness. All of this well-ordered, well-hidden hoarding was enough to do her head in. She would have preferred a meager pigsty to this craftily concealed bedlam.

Sid stood up, bounced on the balls of her feet, gave her arms a shake and her neck a stretch, and then pulled the vacuum-packed bags from the open drawer and dumped them on the bed. Then, she pulled her notebook and pen from her bag and set them on the nightstand. Before doing anything else, she went in search of the vacuum cleaner; there was no way she was opening any of those bags without being able to seal them up again immediately after completing her inventory. If she didn't, the room would soon devolve into complete chaos.

———

It was a little after three o'clock when Sid shut off the vacuum cleaner and heard her phone ringing. She pressed one hand to the wrinkled, compressed plastic bag filled with wool sweaters, making sure that there was no more air to remove, and answered the call.

"What are you doing in there?!" Leo barked into the phone. "I've been standing out here, pounding on the door, for forever. How can you not hear me?"

Sid sighed and arched her back to try to loosen the stiffness created by hours spent bending over the bed, refolding clothes and resealing them in their bags. "You haven't been out there forever."

"Yes, I have!"

"No, you haven't. A couple of minutes maybe. Five at most."

"Forever!"

She shook her head. "I'll be right down." She left the room, a stack of bags yet to be unsealed and catalogued piled high on the bed, and went downstairs to open the front door.

Leo was standing on the stoop, tapping one foot, with his arms folded across his chest. The soft-sided cooler dangled from one hand.

"Good afternoon. Welcome to Insanity Central." Sid stepped back and made a sweeping gesture with her arm. "Please come inside and be prepared to lose your mind."

Leo dropped his arms. "What's gotten into you?"

"Violet Rizzo has gotten into me." She ran her hands down her face. "And I'm not sure how much more of this I can take."

Leo hesitated in the doorway, his gaze darting around the foyer behind Sid. "Has she . . . has she been trying to hurt you?"

Sid's shoulders slumped as she realized that she'd just amped up the kid's anxiety. "No, Leo. Nothing like that." She slid an arm around his back and ushered him inside, steering him toward the dining room. "I'm upstairs inventorying her bedroom, and it's, well, a lot." He looked at her sideways, and she smiled. "You'll see."

Leo unpacked the cooler, and they ate two of the three sandwiches that Burt had packed for them. Sid was glad for the break. As she opened a snack pack of chocolate chip cookies and laid it out for them to share, she asked, "Do you see Violet around? Sense her in the house at all?"

Leo leaned forward to see into the kitchen and glanced back over his shoulder to check the living room. "Nope. Don't see her. She might be upstairs, though. I can't tell." He grinned and pointed to the ceiling. "I can't see through walls or ceilings, you know. I'm not Superman."

Sid smiled. "Well, I'm pretty sure she was here this morning. I came in and felt the temperature drop immediately. But when I mentioned that I met Joey—"

"You talked to her?" Leo's grin widened.

"Yes, I talked to her." Sid plucked a cookie from the open bag. "As I was saying, when I told her that Joey thought her death wasn't an accident, she vanished. The cold went away. The temperature returned to normal. And I don't think she's been back since then."

"Hmm." Leo reached for the cookies. "Sounds like she didn't like what you said."

"What do you mean?"

"You said that Joey thinks she was murdered, and then she immediately vanished." Leo shrugged. "Seems like she doesn't want to talk about it. At least not with you."

"Well, I was hoping she'd be around so that *you* could talk to her about it." Sid wadded up their empty sandwich wrappers and put them back in the cooler to dispose of later.

"Wonderful." Leo rolled his eyes. "Can't wait."

He took his time getting up from the table, and Sid placed her hands on his shoulders and steered him back toward the staircase. "I want you to tackle Buddy's old bedroom. Make a list of everything just in case he doesn't remember what's in there. Check under the bed, under the mattress, behind all the furniture, and check the floorboards and the baseboards and the windowsills, just like I showed you yesterday. Look for hiding places and secret compartments. Basically, anything unusual. Do the same in his bathroom—every drawer, every cabinet, every tile, all of it. And make a note of anything that looks unusual."

"You keep saying *unusual*, but what do you mean exactly?"

"I don't know," Sid answered. "Unusual. You know, out of the ordinary."

"We're in a dead woman's house, searching through all of her stuff, and looking for a stash of hidden jewelry. All of this is out of the ordinary."

"Fair point, kid." Sid nodded. "All I can say is that you should trust your instincts. If it seems weird, then flag it." She lowered her voice. "And if Violet comes back and starts acting funny . . ." Leo opened his mouth to comment, but Sid cut him off. "Funnier than she has been so far, let me know."

Leo nodded, and together they climbed the stairs to the second floor. He entered Buddy Rizzo's old bedroom to begin his search and inventory, and Sid returned to Violet's bedroom to pick up where she'd left off. It was tedious work for them both.

A few hours later, Sid shut off the vacuum cleaner and heard Leo rap on the open bedroom door.

"How's it going?" He leaned against the doorframe, crossing his legs at the ankles.

"Slow." Sid moved aside the latest resealed bag of clothes and sat down on the bed. "How about you?"

"Same, but I'm done." He held out several pages of notebook paper covered in his clear, compact printing.

"Already?!" Sid held out her hand and wiggled her fingers, hoping Leo would come to her. She was too tired to get up and walk the dozen or so feet over to him.

He obliged. "I just did the bedroom. Did you want me to do the bathroom, too?"

"Yes, obviously. We have to do the whole house." She shook her head at him at the same time as he rolled his eyes at her.

While she studied his list from Buddy's childhood bedroom, Leo inspected the vacuum-sealed bags of clothes, picking one up and turning it over in his hands. "What is this?"

"Underwear."

He dropped it immediately, and Sid released a laugh. "They're clean. They smell like lavender, in case you're wondering."

"I wasn't," he mumbled.

"I'm going to have to find out what kind of laundry detergent she used. It's nice." She stifled a yawn and moved the bag back to the top of the pile next to her on the bed. "Besides, the bag is hermetically sealed. You're not in any danger of actually touching an old lady's panties."

"Eww." He groaned and backed away from the bed and the piles of bags. "Please stop saying things like that. It's gross."

Sid shook her head again and glanced at her watch. It was nearly half past six. "You better head home, kid, before Burt calls, wondering why you're not home for dinner. And thanks for this." She waved his lists in the air and then placed them on the nightstand under her notebook. "I appreciate the help."

"Are you sure you don't want me to stay?" he asked, glancing around the room at the open drawers and stacks of bags.

"Well, if you're offering," Sid stood with a slight groan and pressed a hand to her aching back, "there's another drawer of underwear still to be—"

Leo was gone before Sid could finish the sentence.

It was another two hours of more of the same before Sid finally called it quits, locked the front door behind her, and headed for home. She had just stuck her key in the lock of her office door, feeling mentally and physically dead on her feet, when a pair of headlights caught her in its beam as it pulled into Burt's driveway. Sid shielded her eyes with her hand.

The engine shut off moments later, and Detective Tony Davis stepped out of the car.

"Good evening, Detective."

"Sid."

"Working late?"

"Yeah. Just finished my shift. Long day." He reached back into the vehicle, grabbed his blazer, and fished his notebook out of the inside pocket. Holding up the notebook for Sid to see, he said, "I looked up that matter you called me about last night."

Sid smiled. "Usually you bring donuts, too."

"It's nine o'clock at night, Sid. Who eats donuts at nine o'clock at night?"

She shrugged. "Who doesn't? Come on in. Wanna join me for a beer?"

He ran his hand over the back of his neck. "I really shouldn't. I need to get home to Naomi. Get some sleep."

"Half a beer?"

He grinned, revealing dazzling, white teeth beneath tired eyes. "Sold."

Chapter Seven

Tony sat in Sid's guest chair, the wooden frame creaking under his hulking form, and crossed one long leg over the other. He flipped through his notebook while Sid went upstairs to her apartment and came back down a minute later with two beers and two pint glasses.

"I thought we were going to split one," said Tony, watching as Sid poured half of one of the beers into a glass.

"We are." She handed him the half-filled glass. "I plan on drinking the other one by myself." She sat down at her desk, poured the rest of the bottle into the other glass, and lifted it in salute. "Cheers."

Tony set his glass down on the dinged and scarred side table next to him. "So you wanted to know about Violet Rizzo."

Sid nodded. "Anything you can tell me, particularly about how she died."

"There's not much to tell." He shrugged and checked his notebook. "She was eighty-six. Lived alone. One son, Buddy. He's the county property appraiser."

"Yeah, we've met. He hired me to help him sort through his mother's stuff."

"Is that the kind of thing you usually do?"

"No." Sid took a sip of her beer.

"Care to expound on that?"

"Not really." Sid set her beer down on the desk and leaned forward on her elbows. "Buddy told me Violet's body was found by his wife, Penelope, last Tuesday morning when Penelope arrived at the house to take Violet to a salon appointment. She was found dead on the staircase landing. She was wearing her bathrobe and slippers, and Buddy was told that it appeared she merely slipped and fell and died where she landed."

"Right," Tony agreed. "It was investigated but determined not to be suspicious. Ruled an accident and case closed."

Sid pinched the bridge of her nose. "Anything else?"

"I'm not sure what I can tell you that you don't already know." Tony flipped a couple of pages in his notebook. "She was wearing slippers like you said. Dressed for bed. Wasn't wearing any jewelry except for an emerald ring. Nothing in the house appeared to be missing. No indication that she disturbed a burglar or anything like that. She had a bit of paint on her hands, but officers found a partially painted canvas on an easel in her studio behind the house. Her family said it wasn't unusual for her to paint at night, so again, not suspicious." He shrugged. "The theory was that she had been painting in her studio that night, came back into the house, and went upstairs to get ready for bed. Before going to sleep, however, she must have decided to go downstairs. Maybe she needed a drink of water. Who knows. But she slipped and fell." He reached for his beer.

"Time of death?" Sid asked.

"Estimated between nine and eleven." He glanced down at

his notes. "The alarm was activated at 9:27, so that tracks with time of death."

"Injuries? Marks on the body?"

"Consistent with a fall down the stairs. Nothing out of the ordinary. Certainly not for an eighty-six-year-old woman." He took a sip of his beer and studied her pinched expression. "What's up, Sid? Why are you asking about her death? Has Buddy asked you to investigate?"

"Buddy? No." She shook her head slowly. "Let's just say not everyone in the family is convinced it was an accident."

Tony sighed. "Well, the detectives assigned to the case found nothing suspicious. The medical examiner found nothing suspicious." He drained the last of his beer and set his glass down. "I think someone may be wasting your time and their money."

"Perhaps." She smiled at him. "But I'll let you know if I find anything of interest."

He ran his hand down his face, looking spent from the long day. "I swear, Sid, if you call me to let me know you've found another dead body or uncovered another murder plot"—he shook his head and got to his feet—"I may have to quit the department and come work with you."

"Wouldn't that be fun?" She sat back and put her feet up on the desk. "I should warn you, though: There's no pension plan, the hours are miserable, and the pay is shit. But you're welcome to join me anytime."

He laughed again and headed for the door. "'Night, Sid. Stay safe."

"You, too, Detective."

By midmorning the next day, after a short run and a quick shower, Sid was back in Violet Rizzo's bedroom, continuing to sort through her possessions. She'd finished the dresser and chest of drawers the night before but called it quits about a third of the way through the closet. She began where she left off, with the mindboggling number of shoeboxes. Inside each box, Violet had stashed more stuff: pantyhose, socks, trinkets, photographs, you name it. Sid itemized the contents of each one and placed it back where she found it. The woman's handbags were no different, each containing its own wallet and cosmetics bag and various other detritus.

At half past three, her stomach rumbled loudly, and she realized that she hadn't heard from Leo. He should have finished with homeschool by now and arrived to help her. She reached into her bag, pulled out her phone and a granola bar, and fired off a text to him while she ate her snack. She finished cataloging the hanging clothes about forty minutes later and checked her phone. No response. She sent him another message, slid the phone into her back pocket, and made a start on the nightstands. Small as they were, it still took her nearly an hour to finish logging their contents, and still there was no response from Leo.

Sid checked the bedding, lifted the mattress, and lay down on the floor to inspect under the bed, where she found six plastic storage bins. Four of them contained vacuum-sealed bags of clothing, and Sid tackled each of them in turn. Her system of opening, inspecting, cataloguing, and resealing was now so efficient that she finished all four boxes in just over an hour. After inspecting the floorboards and baseboards under the bed, she returned the four bins to their hiding places.

The final two bins, intriguingly, contained what looked to be love letters. They were sorted into bunches of ten to fifteen letters each and tied with satin ribbons of various colors. In total, there were forty-eight bundles. The oldest was dated shortly after Violet moved to St. Augustine; the most recent letter was dated four years ago. All of them had return addresses and postmarks from New York City. Sid stacked the bins by the door so she could take them home and sort through them in the comfort of her own apartment, and then she set about putting the room back in order, just like she had found it. When all the lights were turned off, the alarm reset, and the door locked, Sid headed for home, wishing the entire time that Leo was there to carry the bulky bins for her.

She hated to remove the storage bins from the house, but she couldn't spend one more minute in there with all that organized clutter. Besides, the idea of reading some other woman's love letters made her feel a bit queasy, and she'd rather undertake the task in her comfy pajamas with a glass of wine in hand. While she was used to spying on people—watching men check into motels with their mistresses, photographing women sneaking off for dalliances with their lovers—reading someone else's love letters seemed a much more intimate violation than the job usually required. That being said, she was curious to learn what exactly went into a love letter. Her own husband had never written any to her. Who wrote such things, anyway? It was an antiquated exercise, particularly in these days of shorthand texts and social media blasts.

Violet Rizzo, who was well into her eighties, had been keeping up a romantic correspondence with someone for nearly half a century. Sid had never done more than write a line or two in Wes's birthday cards. She found the idea of a long-distance, long-standing romantic relationship to be both charming and tragic, and while she wasn't exactly looking forward to spending her evening reading the firsthand account of another woman's love affair, she was sincerely hoping that the letters would reveal the name of the person who gave Violet the ruby necklace as well as the reason she had decided to be buried with it.

Bleary-eyed, stiff and sore, and punch-drunk with fatigue, Sid stumbled into her office and set the storage bins down next to her desk. As she reached for the giant bottle of ibuprofen from the shelf in her makeshift kitchenette, there was a knock at the door.

Expecting it to be Leo with an explanation of why he'd been missing in action this afternoon, Sid called out, "Come on in." She swallowed the ibuprofen with a sip of soda just as the door opened.

"Hi. You must be Sid. I've heard a lot about you," said the woman in her doorway. Frowning slightly as she glanced around the office, the woman ran a hand through her blonde hair, a gesture that seemed familiar to Sid.

Sid waited a beat for the woman to say more. When she didn't, Sid asked, "Can I help you?"

"I've come to invite you to dinner. We were just about to sit down and eat when I noticed your lights were on." She pointed to the overhead lights. "Lucky timing."

Sid shook her head a little, trying to clear out the fuzziness accumulated from a day of drudgery. "That's a lovely offer, but who are you?"

The woman smiled, revealing bleached, slightly crooked teeth. "I'm Paizley. Leo's mom."

Chapter Eight

Sid damn near dropped the can of soda she was holding. The two women stared at each other for a long, awkward moment, the blonde forcing a smile and the brunette trying to keep her jaw from hitting the floor.

"Would you like to join us?" Paizley tilted her head slightly. "For dinner? Tonight? As in right now?"

Paizley's tone was light, and her smile was still in place, but Sid detected a current of annoyance, possibly anger, running through her words.

Sid forced a smile of her own. "I'd love to. Let's go." She set her soda can down on top of the mini fridge with slightly more force than was necessary and gestured for Paizley to lead the way.

They walked together in silence across the yard to the kitchen door. Neither woman said a word until they entered the dining room and Paizley announced, "Look who decided to join us." Again, her tone was bright, but the underlying message was anything but. It was obvious that Paizley was not happy to meet Sid, not happy for her to join their dinner party, and, most likely, not happy for Leo to be spending so much time with her.

Too damn bad, thought Sid.

Burt rose from his chair at the head of the table as they walked into the room, and, fumbling with his napkin, Leo followed suit a couple of seconds later. Burt moved around the table, past Leo and Paizley, to pull out the empty chair at the other end. "Glad you could join us, Sid. I'll get you a plate."

Sid moved toward the chair and placed a hand on Burt's forearm. "Wouldn't have missed it." Burt raised an eyebrow at her, but Sid simply patted his arm and sat down. "No Geezers tonight?"

"Practice was cancelled."

Sid noticed his tone was flat. She hadn't known Leo's mom was coming into town today, so she guessed Burt had been surprised as well. That's just what everyone needed, she thought. An ambush.

"Go ahead and start, everyone," Burt urged. "I'll be right back."

Sid reached for the wine, some black-labeled bottle from a winery in Georgia she'd never heard of, and poured herself a glass.

"I'm Brooklyn, by the way," said another blonde woman sitting across from Leo at the far end of the table. She was built like a swimmer, with broad shoulders and lean limbs, and her hair was cut in a severe, chin-length, white-blonde bob. Her nails were filed to long, talon-like points and painted cherry red. She raised her wineglass to Sid. "Cheers."

"Nice to meet you," Sid replied and took a sip of the tepid wine. It was both flavorless and sour at the same time.

"Good, right?" Brooklyn's eyes lit up. "It's from this darling little winery we found in the Georgia highlands. So cute! Wasn't it, Paiz?"

Paizley nodded but said nothing as she sipped her wine.

"It's nice." Sid put her glass down and hoped she could finish dinner without needing to drink any more.

Leo glanced around the table, his gaze finally settling on Sid. She wished she could decipher what he was thinking, but his expression was a mix of too many emotions for Sid to get a clear read.

Burt came back into the dining room with a plate, napkin, and cutlery for Sid, and everyone began to help themselves to the food. Burt had made burgers, which Sid thought was a curious choice given that he usually grilled steaks for the Geezers. He'd also bought potato salad and coleslaw from the grocery store, a noticeable change from Kitty Lonigan's home-made dishes. Everyone ate, accompanied by a retelling of the latest and greatest adventures of the dynamic trio known as PB&J—Paizley, Brooklyn, and Jezebel, Brooklyn's teacup something or other. Narration was provided mostly by Brooklyn in her annoyingly nasal voice.

When Brooklyn paused to take a breath after detailing their night in a jazz club in New Orleans, Sid took the opportunity to ask, "Where's Jezebel?"

"Asleep in her crate," Brooklyn explained. "Poor little sausage was just worn out from all the travel and playing with this one all afternoon." She pointed to Leo and laughed.

Leo, for his part, kept his head down and continued eating, but Sid saw his nostrils flare.

Sid took a sip of her wine before remembering that it was terrible and forcing herself not to spit it back out. "So, what's next for you two? Sorry! I mean, you three. Can't leave out Jezebel, now, can we?" Burt shot her a look from the other end of the table, but Sid ignored it and shifted her gaze to Paizley. "Any big travel plans?"

"Well—" Brooklyn began with a big, excited breath, but Paizley interjected before she could continue.

"We have a few ideas, but nothing definite yet." She flicked her gaze to Brooklyn, as if warning her to shut up, and then reached an arm around Leo's shoulders and pulled him toward her. He shifted awkwardly in his chair, almost dropping his forkful of coleslaw. "For right now, though, we're going to stick around here."

"Really?" Leo asked.

The look on his face almost broke Sid's heart. Paizley smiled back at him, and for a moment Sid could almost picture what the two of them might have been like as mother and son, before all the travel blogging and child abandonment.

"Really." Paizley nodded. "We want to go to the beach and to the fort and to St. George Street. And we want to head down to Port Canaveral and Daytona Beach since we're so close. And . . ."

Sid stopped listening to anything Paizley said after the words "we want to go to." Because nowhere in that PB&J itinerary, jam-packed full of tourist sites and exciting things to do, was any mention of Paizley spending quality, one-on-one time with her only son. The worst part was that Leo's reaction was the same. His smile fell, his gaze returned to his plate, and he fell silent for the rest of the evening.

Sid excused herself before dessert was served, citing lots of work still to do and an oncoming headache. Both the workload and headache were true, the latter likely brought on by the cheap wine and the not-so-dulcet tones of Brooklyn's speaking voice, but mostly Sid just wanted to be away from Paizley Roberts. She thanked Burt for dinner, told Paizley and

Brooklyn it was nice to meet them, and said good night to Leo. He'd glanced up at her with a pained expression, and she had to fight against the urge to pull him into a hug.

She calmly exited the dining room and quietly shut the kitchen door, impressed with herself for not storming off and slamming the door behind her. As she walked across the yard, she noticed for the first time that evening that Brooklyn's white Jeep and the little PB&J camper, painted turquoise with white polka dots, were sitting in the driveway. How had she not noticed either vehicle when she returned from work or when she walked with Paizley from the garage to the house? In the first instance, she'd been mentally exhausted. In the second, she'd been seething with rage.

Sid had spent the last two months trying hard not to hate the woman who had abandoned her fifteen-year-old son on his grandfather's doorstep to run away with her best friend on some harebrained scheme to become a travel blogger. Most days, Sid failed in her efforts not to judge Paizley too harshly. She had also failed to keep Leo at arm's length, coming to care about him much more than she wanted to admit. Right now, she hated the sight of Paizley's bleached-blonde hair and hot-pink manicure and sun-kissed glow. And she couldn't wait for PB&J to pack up their clown camper and hit the road for more of their low-budget, heavily choreographed, overly edited, once-in-a-lifetime brand of fun.

Sid slammed the door shut after entering her office, not caring if those back in the house heard the noise, and traipsed upstairs to her apartment. She changed into sweatpants and an oversize tee and plucked a bottle of good wine, hers and Wes's favorite, from the small wine rack on the kitchen counter. She didn't bother to grab a glass before descending to her office, bottle in hand.

Half an hour later, Sid had made her way through a third of

the bottle and the first three stacks of Violet Rizzo's love letters —written in cramped cursive handwriting; signed with a unique, calligraphic single initial *P*; and making for unusual reading, to say the least—when Burt knocked on the unlocked door and opened it. She hadn't even had a chance to say, "Come in," before he closed the door behind him, marched across the room, and placed a cupcake on her desk.

"Dessert," he announced.

"Thanks." She stared up at him. "Why are you mad at me?"

He ran a calloused hand down his face and rubbed the day's growth of gray stubble on his chin. "Because I need you to be my ally, Sid." He slumped down into the floral-printed Queen Anne dining chair opposite her. "I need you to help me get through this."

She leaned back, and her chair squealed in protest.

"Remind me to oil that for you tomorrow," Burt said softly, all fight leaving him at that moment.

She waved the comment away, feeling sorry for him. He was tired and upset and more than a little worried, all of it evident in his weary expression and watery eyes. "What do you need me to do, Burt?"

"I need you to be civil." He fixed her with his stare. "I know it's probably too much to ask for you to be nice to them, especially Trisha—"

"Paizley," Sid corrected. "She's not Trisha anymore. Remember the branding. It's all about the branding."

Burt sighed. "Please, Sid."

She held up her hands in surrender. "Civil. I got it. I'll even try to be nice, painful as that might be."

"Thank you." He tried to smile, but it fell flat. "Our primary concern is making sure Leo knows that we love him and support him no matter what."

Sid's brow furrowed. "What do you mean, no matter what? What do you think is going to happen?"

He shrugged. "He'll decide to go with her."

Sid shot forward in her chair. "He's leaving?! Has he told you that? Has she said she's taking him?"

"No, Sid. Not in so many words." He shook his head and heaved a sigh. "I don't know. It's just things they've said. Comments that Brooklyn has made. I don't know. It might be nothing. They may pack up next week and head out, and Leo will be right here with us just like before." He rubbed his jaw again. "But something in my gut tells me they're planning something, and I wouldn't be surprised if it includes Leo."

"Fuck," Sid hissed under her breath. She reached for the wine bottle and took a good, long swig. When Burt raised an eyebrow, Sid held up a hand. "Don't judge. This merely saves me having to wash a glass."

Burt rose slowly and shuffled to the door, looking older than his sixty-five years. It was as if he'd aged a decade in the past twelve hours.

"Hang in there, Burt," Sid called after him. He nodded, and she added, "If you need me—you or Leo, call me."

After he left, Sid didn't have the energy to continue reading the old love letters. She grabbed the half-empty wine bottle, locked the door, and climbed up the spiral staircase to her apartment. She wanted this long, miserable day to be over. She wanted to put the madness of Violet Rizzo's hoarding and the frustration of that awful dinner behind her and fall into a deep sleep, dreaming of absolutely nothing.

And yet, at the same time, she wanted the world to stop spinning and for time to grind to a halt. She wanted to hug Leo and tell him everything was going to be okay, that he was wanted and cared for, and that people loved him. Lots of people. Including her. But that wasn't going to happen, not tonight, and definitely not the part about time standing still.

The realization that he might choose to leave the Old City with Paizley felt like a punch to the gut. For Sid, it felt like she was losing another child.

But that was ridiculous, and she shook her head at the notion. After all, Leo wasn't her child. He was someone else's kid. And she needed to remember that.

Chapter Nine

On Thursday morning, Leo woke early and shuffled downstairs. He found Burt sitting at the kitchen table, buttering a slice of toast. The scent of strong coffee filled the air, and, on mornings like this, Leo wished he liked the taste of it. He stood staring at the pot, not sure whether to bite the bullet and pour himself a cup.

"Don't do it," Burt said without looking up from his toast. "That way madness lies, my boy."

"Huh?" Leo turned to him, a look of confusion scrunching up his features.

Burt chuckled. "I started drinking coffee when I was about your age. Wasn't long before I was completely addicted to the stuff. Get raging headaches now if I don't have at least two cups a day."

Leo stepped away from the pot and retrieved the orange juice out of the refrigerator instead. He took a long swig from the container and then poured a tall glass while he toasted two slices of bread. Unable to wait for the toaster to finish, he stood at the counter, smeared peanut butter on a third slice of bread, and then grabbed the box of cereal. A couple of minutes later, he slid onto the seat across from Burt with his bread, toast, cereal, and juice.

"Hungry?" Burt asked as he sipped his coffee.

Leo stared at his food and nodded, his mouth full of sticky peanut butter.

"You didn't eat much last night."

Leo shook his head. He'd had only one burger and a couple of spoonfuls of coleslaw, less than half of what he'd normally eat. He hadn't even bothered to have a cupcake for dessert.

"How'd you sleep?"

He shook his head again.

Burt sighed. "Look, Leo. I know this is hard. A lot has happened in the last couple of months—to you and your mom. You've both been dealing with a lot. She's still grieving, you know." Leo finally looked up at his grandfather, and Burt nodded. "She didn't have the same opportunity that you did to say goodbye."

Leo swallowed hard, the bread and peanut butter getting stuck inside his throat as it constricted with the memory of seeing his father's spirit. His grandfather was right. Leo had been able to say goodbye—and so many other things he'd wanted to say for a long time—thanks to Mad Hattie's help. Sid's, too, for that matter, but his mom hadn't had that opportunity.

"Just give her a chance, that's all I'm saying. Things will get easier, calmer. You two just need to spend some time together, get to know each other again. That's all I'm sayin'." Burt took a bite of his toast.

"Okay," muttered Leo.

He went back to his breakfast, and the two men didn't speak again for ten minutes, until Burt announced he was leaving for work.

"What do you mean, you're leaving?!"

"I got a job to finish, Leo." Burt got up, put his plate and coffee cup in the dishwasher, and grabbed his lunch box off the counter. "The restaurant is reopening next week, and I've still got a lot of work to do."

Leo knew Burt liked to finish all of his renovation jobs on time, early even. He prided himself on it, and word was spreading that he could be relied on to meet his deadlines. But when he'd left the restaurant job early yesterday, after Leo called to tell him Paizley and Brooklyn had arrived unannounced, Leo had seen the specks of paint on his hand. Painting was usually one of the last parts of any job for Burt, so Leo knew his grandfather probably didn't have as much work still left to do as he claimed. But he let the issue drop.

"I hid Dad's T-shirts under your bed," Leo said, staring at his bowl of cereal.

When his mom had dropped him off in St. Augustine all those weeks ago, Burt had told Paizley that he'd gotten rid of Gunner's old concert tees. The truth was, he'd actually saved them for Leo, and Leo had been wearing them nonstop ever since. By some stroke of good fortune, he'd been wearing a plain black tee when his mom arrived yesterday. He'd darted upstairs, grabbed the entire stash of his dad's old shirts, even the dirty ones in the hamper, and shoved them under Burt's bed. There was no way his mom would go snooping in Burt's room, so the T-shirts were safe there.

"Hope you don't mind." He glanced up at his grandfather. "Don't tell Mom, okay?"

"Your secret's safe with me." Burt ruffled his hair and left via the back door.

Two hours later, Leo was in his room completing his geometry lesson when he heard the door to the guest room open on its squeaky hinges. His mother shuffled past his closed door and headed downstairs. An hour after that, he heard voices in the kitchen. Brooklyn, who had offered to sleep in the camper instead of roughing it on the sofa in the living room, had finally joined Paizley in the kitchen for breakfast. It was almost lunchtime before both women were showered, dressed, and ready to start the day.

A knock on his door meant they had finally come looking for him. He'd squirreled himself away in his bedroom all morning, working on his lessons, waiting for someone to notice he wasn't around. Apparently, that realization had finally hit.

The knob turned, and the door opened a crack. "You decent?"

"Yeah." Leo put his pencil down and turned to find Paizley standing in the doorway in a floral minidress. She wore strappy, high-heeled sandals; a pink headband; and more makeup than he'd ever seen her wear in his life. The woman standing in the doorway was definitely not his mother.

His mother wore faded jeans and sweatshirts when she wasn't wearing her waitress or cleaner uniforms for the various jobs she'd held over the years. She tied her hair up in a knot on the top of her head because she barely had time to wash it. And the only makeup she wore was lip balm from the dollar store. She'd also been rail-thin from always working two jobs and there never seeming to be enough to eat.

But the woman in front of him now was tanned, rosy-lipped, shiny-haired, and healthy-looking. Her limbs weren't bony, her clothes weren't faded and worn, and the dark circles under her eyes had either vanished or been covered up by all the makeup she was wearing. She also flipped her hair and talked in a slightly higher pitch than he'd remembered.

And she giggled. She'd giggled when she'd first arrived at the house and all afternoon while she unpacked the camper, started some laundry, and chatted with Burt in the living room.

She even giggled while showing him the souvenirs she'd bought —only two of which, a Disney T-shirt and a ball cap from the Savannah Bananas minor league baseball team—were for him. Leo couldn't recall his mom ever giggling. She tended to laugh loudly, snorting often, and it was a funny, wonderful sound. But the giggling? It was awful, like an instrument in desperate need of tuning.

Leo forced himself to smile at her, trying desperately to see the woman he remembered from just a couple of months ago. "Are you going out?"

"Of course, silly." More giggling. "And you're coming, too." She held out her hand to him and wiggled her fingers.

"Really?" He stood and crossed the room cautiously. When he reached her, she wrapped her arms around him in a bear hug, and he rested his forehead on her shoulder. He'd missed this. He'd missed it so much that tears began to sting the corners of his eyes.

"Absolutely. You're going to be my date for lunch." She released him, grabbed his hand, and tugged him toward the stairs. He followed, eager to spend time alone with her. Just the two of them, like it had been when his dad was at sea and then again after he died.

But waiting at the bottom of the stairs was Brooklyn Montecito, wearing a red minidress and carrying a large straw bag in one hand and tiny Jezebel in the other. She lifted Jezebel and rubbed her cheek against the dog's cottony head.

The fluffy, teacup-size, purebred something-or-other was the pair's usual third wheel, as evidenced by the countless photos of the dog posted on their social media accounts. Leo sighed, knowing that this meant the lunch date with Paizley wasn't going to be just the two of them like he'd hoped. No, he was now relegated to the status of fourth wheel.

"Hello, handsome." Brooklyn smiled and held out Jezebel for him to take. "Coming with us?"

Leo glared at the platinum-haired woman. Paizley gently transferred Jezebel from Brooklyn's outstretched hand into Leo's arms. The dog never made a sound but simply looked up at Leo with a blank and dispassionate stare.

"Of course he is." Paizley ruffled Leo's hair, smiling at him.

"Great." Brooklyn's tone made it clear that Leo's presence was anything but wonderful. "Well, hon, since you're practically a local, maybe you can show us around a little." She slid her sunglasses off the top of her head and down to the bridge of her nose before turning and strutting out the front door.

Paizley trotted after her, and Leo, still holding the placid dog, grabbed his keys from the hall table and locked the door behind them.

Chapter Ten

"Make sure you get the whole lion, not just part of it."

Paizley fluffed her hair and leaned against the concrete plinth. Brooklyn struck a pose next to her, one arm bent and resting on Paizley's shoulder. They smiled widely and waited for Leo to snap the photo of the two of them standing under one of the eponymous marble statues at the foot of the Bridge of Lions.

The two women had been at it since they all left the house, and at this point in the late afternoon, Leo was no longer embarrassed. He'd passed embarrassment a couple of hours ago, then reached mortified, and was now completely numb to it all. His mother and her friend had stopped to pose with, under, or in front of everything that didn't move and even a few things that did, much to the delight of a middle-aged man in full pirate regalia waiting to give his next guided tour of the Old City's historic district. And they didn't want just one photo at each and every landmark, tree, shop, and decommissioned cannon; they wanted at least a dozen.

He'd been designated their photographer and dog wrangler. To be fair to Jezebel, the dog didn't bark or fuss. She simply sat in the straw bag, which Leo carried over his shoulder, and watched the world around her with seemingly no interest. As for his other job as photographer, Brooklyn had shoved her expensive new phone into his hand before they'd barely made it off the front porch and given him a lesson in how to use it, including detailed instructions on lenses, lighting, and filters. He'd been forced to practice taking several dozen photos of them in front of Kitty Lonigan's pretty front yard and white picket fence before Brooklyn had been satisfied that his skills with a camera were adequate to meet PB&J's publicity needs.

Now, he stood precariously perched on the curb of busy A1A, the scenic coastal highway that spanned the Matanzas River at this point via the Bridge of Lions. Jezebel was asleep in the bag on his shoulder, and he was trying to frame the shot of his mother and Brooklyn standing in front of the marble lion with a view of Matanzas Bay in the background, all while taking into account the too-bright afternoon sun, the shadows falling across the women's faces, and the whoosh of vehicles close behind him.

He snapped a couple dozen photos as the two women struck different poses before lowering the phone and announcing, "Got it." About an hour ago, he'd stopped asking them whether they could be done with all the photos and finally do something fun, so there was no use bothering to ask again now.

"I certainly hope so," Brooklyn barked in that annoying voice of hers, as if it was Leo's fault that she had to pose for pictures. She snatched the phone from him and began inspecting his work. "Yeah, okay. These are fine." She handed the phone back to him and sighed, turning to Paizley. "I still don't understand why we can't go to the fort. I mean, we came all this way. And the fort is right there!" She pointed furiously toward the Castillo de San Marcos, the giant, coquina-stone structure at the end of the seawall that was the oldest masonry fort in the continental United States. "What's the point in coming to St. Augustine and not getting photos of us at the fort?!" She was shouting now to be heard over the roar of traffic at the busy intersection of A1A and Avenida Menendez, and, for Leo, the sound was akin to being jabbed in the eardrum with a sharp stick.

"We can't today. Leo doesn't like the fort. It makes him uncomfortable." Paizley explained for the tenth time that day.

Leo ground his teeth at her comment. It wasn't that the fort made him uncomfortable. Rather, it was all the spirits that hung out there. In his experience, spirits usually stayed away from places like churches and graveyards and other locations that reminded them of death. Castillo de San Marcos seemed to be an exception to that general rule. A lot of people had died there, many of whose spirits were roaming around the grounds right now, but the fort's location was spitting distance to St. Augustine's lively and vibrant historic district. Spirits liked to congregate wherever there was life, and there was a lot of life in the Old City's downtown.

But Leo was adamantly opposed to touring the fort. Until recently, it had reminded him of his father, of running with his dad across the sloping expanse of lawn and stalking through the fort's inner rooms on their one and only vacation to St. Augustine when he was a little kid. Those had been wonderful memories. But a few weeks ago, he'd stood on the fort's seawall and been frightened by his father's spirit, which had been masked as a dark shadow figure. The result of that encounter was a fall into the bay, an entanglement with a seabed bristling with razor-sharp oyster shells, and a trip to the emergency room.

When you combined that painful experience with the gang of spirits roaming the fort and the fact that he'd forgotten to bring his baseball cap with him when he left the house, there was no way he was going anywhere near that monument or its grounds. He'd managed to avoid the dozen or so spirits he'd seen so far on their walking photo shoot tour, but he knew his luck would run out eventually. It always did. And he was too hot and too tired to be able to deal with the hoard of spirits at the fort this late in the day, or at any time of any day, to be honest. So he shook his head when his mother glanced his way and held firm to his prohibition on a fort visit.

"Let's head over there." Paizley pointed across the street to the municipal marina. "We can get some shots in front of the boats. Look, there's even a pirate ship. That'll make a good post, won't it?" She linked her arm around Brooklyn's, trying to appease her sulking friend.

"Fine." Brooklyn huffed and marched over to the crosswalk to wait for the light to change. Leo glanced into the straw bag, checked to make sure Jezebel was still sleeping, and tagged along after the women, dragging his feet and hanging his head as they crossed the road.

When they made it to the other side, Brooklyn took her phone and the straw bag containing Jezebel from Leo and stormed off to scout a location for their next photo shoot. Paizley linked her arm with Leo's and guided him to a bench in Harbormaster Park, situated between the Bridge of Lions and the marina. They sat looking out at the water, letting the shade and sea breeze cool them a little. Leo slumped down and rested his head on his mother's shoulder. He used to do the same thing when he was a kid, but now that he was half a foot taller than she was, he needed to slouch in order to achieve the proper angle.

"How much longer, Mom?"

"I don't know, kiddo." She rested her cheek against his sweaty curls. "How are you doin'? You okay?" He nodded but said nothing. "When you called me last week, sayin' you wanted me to come get you, you sounded awful." She kissed the top of his head. "Are you sure?"

"Yeah, I'm okay." He didn't bother to correct her. That call had been nearly three weeks ago, and she'd told him then that she'd be arriving in St. Augustine in just a few days. But, as usually happened, those few days turned into a few more, and here she was, finally, almost three weeks later. He'd made that call to her when he was at one of his lowest points: being haunted by his father's spirit disguised as a dark shadow; fired from the Oakmire case by both Sid and Burt; and ghosted by Ellie, the pretty girl in the ice cream shop who had given him his first real kiss. Since then, however, he'd made peace with his father's spirit, solved two murders with Sid, and was learning to play bass guitar. And girls loved bass guitar players, or so his grandfather kept telling him.

He sat up slowly and turned sideways on the bench to face his mother. "Are you okay, Mom?"

She looked out at the water, sparkling like an expanse of sequins in the Florida sun, and smiled. "I am. I mean"—she shrugged and reached for his hand without turning to look at him—"I still miss your dad." She closed her eyes tightly. "So, so much." Opening them, she looked back out at the river. "But I'm finding my way. And for the first time in a long time, I feel like I can breathe deeply without crying, like I can smile without feeling guilty. Like I'm living. Really living." She glanced sideways at him. "You know what I mean?"

The truth was, he did. He felt the same way. Here in St. Augustine, living with Burt, working with Sid, playing guitar with Eli, and being mentored by Mad Hattie, Leo felt like he was finally living, too.

And it broke his heart that he and his mom had each found peace without the other.

Chapter Eleven

Thirty minutes later, after a lengthy photo shoot in front of nearly every boat in the quaint marina, Paizley kissed Leo on the cheek and told him he'd done enough for them for one day. Brooklyn pressed him to take Jezebel home with him, and he'd really had no choice but to agree once his mother handed him the dog, the leash, and a couple of plastic poop bags. The ladies headed off toward the Castillo de San Marcos, much to Brooklyn's exasperating delight, and Leo watched them go.

"Hey, kid!"

Leo turned to see a man jogging down the dock toward him.

"Kid, you from around here?"

Leo nodded. "Sort of."

The man came to a halt in front of him. "Sort of, huh? Well"—he paused to take off his mirrored sunglasses—"that might work."

He was middle-aged as far as Leo could guess, looking older

than his mom but younger than Burt, with sun-weathered skin and thick, wavy, caramel-colored hair that was graying at the temples. Shorter than Leo by about an inch, the man's lean build reminded him of Sid. Probably a runner, he thought, although the palm-tree-and-flamingo-patterned shirt, cargo shorts, and flip-flops made him look like he belonged at a beachside tiki bar with a beer in his hand.

"I'm looking for someone. My dad used to work with her." He pointed over his shoulder to the boats behind him. "I just got to town, and I tried calling the number my dad gave me, but it's not working." As he reached into the side pocket of his shorts and pulled out a folded piece of paper, he nodded to Leo. "Nice dog, by the way."

Leo looked down at Jezebel, momentarily forgetting that he was holding the little ball of fluff. Jezebel blinked up at him, then snuggled against his chest. "Thanks."

"What's her name? I'm assuming it's a girl. Rhinestone collar and all."

"Jezebel." Leo sighed, picturing in his mind what he must look like holding the tiny white dog with the blinged-out, hot-pink collar and leash.

"Cute." The man stared at the dog for a moment with a confused look on his face, as if he wasn't certain the creature in Leo's arms even was a dog, and then he unfolded his paper and checked the information. "My mom could only find her home number, and, honestly, I didn't bother to look her up online, so I don't even know if she still lives in St. Augustine. I figured I'd . . . I don't know . . . that I'd just figure it out when I got here." He rubbed the back of his neck with his free hand as he squinted at the piece of paper. "Things have been a bit hectic, and, well, shit. You don't really care, do you?" He looked up at Leo with a lopsided grin. "Sorry. Never mind." He shook his head and refolded the paper.

"It's okay." Leo shrugged. "I don't know a lot of people. But my grandpa's lived here forever. And my neighbor, too. They might know your friend."

"Yeah, well . . ." He scratched at the rough stubble on his cheek. "That's the thing. She's not my friend. I've never met her. My dad knew her. She was *his* friend, apparently." He shook his head again.

Jezebel began to squirm, so Leo put her down. She took half a dozen tiny steps away from him, squatted, and peed. He wrinkled his nose at the sight. Looking up, he saw the man was grinning. "What's your dad's friend's name?" Leo asked.

The man glanced up from watching the dog urinate on the dock. "Never mind, kid. It's okay. I'll find her myself."

"Are you sure?" He bent to pick up Jezebel, careful to keep her backside away from his shirt. The man shook his head, but Leo offered again. "I can ask my grandpa and let you know."

"All right." The man sighed and then said, "Sidney Stone. Do you know her?"

———

Sid turned onto Saragossa Street around half past eight and found the lights in Burt's house, as well as the PB&J camper, were all dark. Just as well, she thought. She had stayed late at Violet Rizzo's house to avoid having to join everyone for dinner, but it looked like she needn't have worried. They were clearly out somewhere, having fun without her. Sid smirked at the idea, finding it unlikely that any of them were actually having any fun, especially if last night's gathering was anything to go by.

She had missed having Leo around today to help with the workload, especially since much of it had involved inventorying washcloths, decorative soaps, and bottles of shampoo in the three upstairs bathrooms. More than that, however, she had missed his company. For the last two days, she'd gone without his snarky humor and his teenage attitude, without his smile and laughter, without seeing him blush whenever he was around a pretty girl or someone mentioned underwear. But she would have to get used to him not being around. This was likely how it was going to be for the next however many days while Paizley was in town. Leo would be spending his time with his mom, and that was exactly how it should be. The kid needed his mom. Sid just wasn't sure he needed this particular version of her.

Arriving home, she found an envelope taped to her office door. She yanked it off, unlocked the door, and went inside. Violet Rizzo's love letters were still sitting on her desk, waiting to be read. That was her plan for this evening, especially since she didn't have to worry about socializing with Clan Roberts and the obnoxious Brooklyn.

Sid dropped her bag at the bottom of the spiral staircase and climbed up to her apartment to change into something more appropriate for her evening of wine, romantic correspondence, and frozen pizza. Sid kicked off her shoes and opened the envelope that had been taped to her door to find a torn sheet of folded notebook paper. As she opened the note, a business card slid out and fluttered to the floor. Sid left it where it landed and walked over to the kitchen to pour herself some wine. Glass in hand, she finally read the note, written in Leo's familiar print, which invited her to join the gang at Granny Oak's Music Park to see a new band from Fernandina Beach.

"Thanks, but no, thanks, kid," Sid muttered as she lifted the glass to her lips and took a sip.

The rest of his note was a convoluted ramble about a man at the marina who used to work with her. If she understood correctly, the man had asked Leo to ask her to call him. Sid tossed the note on the counter and took another sip. Why was Leo at the marina? And why was he talking to strange men about her? Where had his mother been while all that was going on?

She walked back across the room, taking another sip of wine on the way and enjoying the feel of the low-pile, low-budget carpet under her bare feet. Searching around for the fallen card, she finally found a corner of it sticking out from under the bed she'd failed to make that morning.

Sid picked it up, read the front, then flipped it over, read the note scrawled on the back, and promptly spilled wine all over her comforter.

———

Twenty minutes later, Sid stood on the dock at the municipal marina, inhaling the familiar scent of salty sea air mixed with a hint of diesel fumes that always reminded her of Wes, and searched for the boat. She was still in the olive-green shorts and black tee she'd worn all day, but at least she'd brushed her teeth and retied her ponytail holder. He wouldn't care what she looked like anyway. Lord knows, he'd certainly seen her looking worse.

The boat was a handsome, forty-two-foot sloop painted navy blue and white with gorgeous wood trim. It was docked stern-to, and Sid smiled at the name written in bold, black letters outlined in shiny gold paint across the stern: *Hook, Line & Sprinter*.

"Hello?" Sid noted that the cabin was dark. It was late, and she should have called first, but she'd wanted to surprise him and had run down here without thinking. Her watch indicated that it was after nine. Perhaps he was asleep. Or maybe he was out visiting friends.

"Hi." The voice came from her left. "Any chance you're Sidney Stone?"

Sid turned to see a man strolling up the dock toward her, hands in his shorts pockets and in no hurry, judging by his pace. As he approached, she noticed his wavy, brown hair was graying at the temples, and he had the slim build and toned legs of a longtime runner. "I am." She pointed to the boat. "This yours?"

He smiled broadly, revealing rows of straight, white teeth, and came to a stop about a yard from her, much closer than Sid expected, but she didn't back away. He nodded toward the boat. "She is."

Up close, Sid noticed that his eyes were pale blue and framed with fine lines at the outer corners. She pulled the business card from her back pocket and held it up. "Yours?"

"It is." He rocked back on his heels, hands still in his pockets.

When he didn't elaborate, Sid placed her hands on her hips and stared him down. "And why did you hit up a teenage boy to deliver this to me? Do you know him?"

The man shook his head. "Met him today. I asked if he knew you. He said he did. I asked him to give you the card."

Sid's nostrils flared. "So, how do you know Trip?"

"Trip Murdock?" The man rocked back on his heels again, hands still in his pockets, but a ghost of some emotion crossed his face. Sid couldn't quite place what it was before it was gone again in an instant. "I understand you worked with him for a bit."

"You didn't answer my question." Sid crossed her arms in front of her and widened her stance a little. The man standing in front of her was really starting to annoy her. She didn't care if he was moderately attractive in a rugged, outdoorsy, devil-may-care sort of way. She'd have no problem telling him off, loudly and colorfully, if it came to that.

He removed his hands from his pockets and folded his arms in front of him, mimicking her posture. "I'm his son."

Sid blinked in surprise and took a half step backward. "You're Danny?"

She'd never met Trip's son, Danny. In the two years she'd worked with Edwin Lewis Murdock III, known to everyone as Trip, Sid had heard all sorts of stories about Danny—from high school track star to UPenn magna cum laude graduate to New York City high-flying financial something-or-other. Trip was enormously proud of everything his son did, including quitting his lucrative big-city job and moving to Key West to start a fishing charter, but Sid had never met him. During those two years she was being mentored by Trip, there had been half a dozen trips made by Danny to the Old City to see his father. Trip had always extended Sid an invitation to join them for dinner, but she'd always declined.

She'd been in no fit state to have dinner with a stranger during that time, when she was at her lowest low. The deaths of Wes and Iris were too recent, her grief too sharp and painful, for her to make polite dinner conversation with anyone. She could barely manage more than a few words to Trip at any given time, let alone getting herself showered and dressed up and using proper table manners. She'd been an absolute train-wreck of a human being until very recently.

At that very moment, as she stood before Danny Murdock, she was extremely grateful that her life was in some reasonable state of order. But that relief lasted no more than a second, when she realized what she must look like after a day spent at Violet Rizzo's house, much of it on her hands and knees, looking for secret hiding places.

"It's Dan. Only my dad ever called me Danny." He held out his hand, and Sid shook it. His grip was firm, his skin calloused and warm. "Nice to meet you, Sidney."

"Sid." Dan released her hand, and she was suddenly hyper-aware of having no idea what she should do with it. Or her other hand. Or her arms for that matter. She cleared her throat, trying to snap out of it, and managed a smile. "So, where's Trip? Is he asleep already?" She pointed to the boat.

"Oh." Dan's face fell. "You don't know, do you? Sorry, I just assumed you knew. Dad died about two and a half months ago."

Sid felt the whole world tilt. Perhaps it did because Dan reached out and grabbed her arms to steady her.

"You okay?"

She nodded, unable to manage any words, and forced herself to focus on his face—a face that now resembled Trip's so strongly that she couldn't believe she hadn't noticed it sooner.

"I have something for you." He left her standing on the dock and boarded the boat, disappearing below deck. A minute later, he was back with a small cardboard box in hand. "Mom and I have been slowly clearing out Dad's old stuff, and we found a few things of his that she thought you might want."

The box in his hands held a magnifying glass, an ancient camera, several used notebooks, and a coffee mug with the words "Licensed Stalker" written on the side in bold typeface. She picked up one of the notebooks and immediately recognized Trip's nearly illegible handwriting. Tears stung her eyes as she flipped through the pages, and it dawned on her that this little book contained his notes from the missing child case he'd successfully solved early in his career, the case that brought him fleeting nationwide fame and put his name on the map.

"Thank you." The words caught in her throat. Unable to look up for fear that she would fall apart if she had to look into a pair of eyes that reminded her too much of Trip's, Sid took the box from Dan and said, "I'm very sorry for your loss."

Without giving him a chance to say anything further, she turned on her heels and quickly walked away. The tears began to fall before she'd even reached the end of the dock.

Chapter Twelve

Even with her dark sunglasses, Sid squinted against the bright, late morning sun as she shuffled along the sidewalk toward Violet Rizzo's house. Her head still hurt despite the two ibuprofen pills and the half pot of coffee she'd had so far this morning. She wasn't hungover. In fact, she didn't drink a drop last night after returning from her meeting with Dan Murdock. Instead, she'd shoved the box with Trip's old things into the bottom of her closet and crawled into bed.

The sobbing didn't cease until sometime around two o'clock when she'd finally fallen asleep, but the dawn of a new day hadn't caused Sid's grief to fade. Nor had it lessened her guilt.

Trip Murdock had retired on the exact same day that Sid had sat for her state PI license exam, which had taken place at the end of May earlier this year. Then he'd shuttered his office, and he and his wife, Margaret, had packed up their house and moved to Key West before Sid had even received her exam score.

Now, she had to live with the cruel reality that she was the reason his retirement had been so short. His plan had been to retire two years earlier, but Burt had convinced him to take Sid on and teach her the ropes. The only reason he'd stayed in St. Augustine as long as he had was to see her through her two-year apprenticeship as a favor to Burt. When she and Trip began working together, Sid had been drowning in grief, and Trip had become her lifeline. She hadn't realized it back then, though. In fact, she'd been completely indifferent to learning the business. The job was simply a means to get Burt off her back, nothing more. But by the time she took her exam two years later, she had an appreciation for all that Trip had done for her, even though she was still reluctant to hang out her own shingle and become a fully licensed private investigator.

Trip Murdock had been a kind, charming, and patient man, and Sid would be forever grateful to him for his mentorship. She'd been sorry to see him close his doors and drive off toward the sweet-and-salty life of the Florida Keys. Now, only months after achieving that sun-drenched retirement he'd always wanted, he was dead.

In the bright sunlight, Sid's eyes felt dry and scratchy. Rightfully so. She also deserved the headache, the effect of heart-rending grief and lack of sleep. Unfortunately but not unreasonably, her sorrow hadn't lessened as the morning progressed, nor had the remorse subsided. The truth was that she'd robbed Trip of two years of retirement in the sun, with all those gorgeous days at sea and precious time with his family.

Sid fumbled with the key before finally unlocking the door and stepping into the blessedly cool foyer of Violet Rizzo's house. Trying to dam the flood of memories, Sid hoisted her bag higher up on her shoulder and headed toward the back of the house.

A noise upstairs stopped her dead in her tracks, and she waited for the temperature to drop. But it didn't. That's not Violet then, thought Sid, careful not to utter the words aloud.

More noises came from upstairs, and it dawned on Sid that she hadn't turned off the alarm system when she entered. Had she turned it on last night when she left? Of course she had. Hadn't she?

Sid fished her phone and the small can of pepper spray out of her bag, which she set down quietly by the iron gate that served as the kitchen door. She crept up the stairs, grateful that the stone steps made no creaking sounds, and followed the noises down the hall to Violet's bedroom. Scraping noises and mumbled curse words filtered out of the open bedroom door, and Sid carefully peeked around the doorframe.

She heaved a sigh of relief, shoved her phone and pepper spray into her back pockets, and knocked on the doorframe as she entered the room. "Good morning." She plastered a smile on her face and braced herself to play nice.

The blonde woman jumped and spun away from the chest of drawers. She'd been manhandling the poor piece of furniture, calling it a string of derogatory names while trying to move it back to its usual place near the bathroom door.

"Oh, you scared me!" Her hand flew to her throat. A breath later, she reached up and brushed a golden lock of hair out of her eyes and tucked it behind her ear. Sid noticed a large diamond solitaire dangling from a thin chain around her neck. "You must be Sidney," the woman said. Her voice was breathy, and Sid wasn't sure if it always sounded like that or if it was due to the shock of seeing her and the exertion from rearranging the furniture. The woman dusted off her hands and then slid them down her sides, checking to make sure the lines of her tailored linen dress weren't askew. "I didn't think you were coming today."

"Really?" Sid's smile faltered. "Why's that?"

"Because I've been waiting for over an hour." Her breathy

voice took on a slightly sharper edge. "I assumed you weren't working today."

"Nope. I'm working today." Sid held out her hand. "Nice to meet you, Mrs. Rizzo."

The woman shook Sid's hand, and Sid detected the cloying scent of Chanel No. 5. "You may call me Penny."

"Penny," Sid said flatly, "can I help you move that back?" She pointed to the chest.

"Yes, thank you." Penny patted her hair and stepped back toward the chest. They moved it back, and Penny cleared her throat. "Well, then"—she paused to walk quickly around Sid and over to the door—"have you been able to find anything?"

Sid clasped her hands in front of her and took a deep breath, stilling her features. This woman was rubbing her the wrong way, or perhaps Sid's nerves were too raw to get a good read on her. Either way, it wouldn't do to piss off the client's wife. "I've found a lot of things, but none of it has been what you and your husband are looking for, I'm afraid." She reached for the closet door and opened it. "As I'm sure you know, your mother-in-law has a lot of . . . stuff." She passed a hand in front of the open closet as if presenting the contents on a game show. "It is taking quite a while to go through everything." She shut the closet door and pointed to the floor. "And I'm checking every square inch of every room, just in case something is hidden out of sight." She shook her head. "So far, nothing of note."

Penny's nostrils flared. "I see." Her eyes darted around the room, as if trying to see something obvious that Sid had not. "Well, how much longer do you think you'll be?"

Sid clasped her hands in front of her again and took another breath. "Probably another week."

"Another week?!" The breathy voice was gone, replaced by something much closer to a cat's screech after someone stepped on the poor animal's tail. Penny's left eye twitched ever so slightly.

"I'm afraid so, yes." Sid gave the woman a slight smile. "I told your husband it was likely to take two weeks when he hired me. I'm hoping that will be the case. But I must confess, this job is much more involved than I originally anticipated."

"Well." Penny straightened herself up to her full height of no more than five foot two. "That is simply not acceptable." She flailed her arms out by her sides and then slapped them against her thighs. "I have to have the estate agents in. It's going to take an absolute age for them to go through everything and get the house ready to sell."

Sid kept smiling. "If it helps, I'm making itemized lists of every item in every room. I'm sure your estate agents will be able to use them to move the process along more quickly."

"I don't need lists," Penny hissed. "I need you to work faster and finish the job and find my mother-in-law's jewelry. We can't have people traipsing through here, nor can we sell the house, until we find it. It is absolutely imperative. I'm sure you understand."

"I do indeed, Penny." Sid nodded. "And I will do everything I can to find *your* missing jewels."

Chapter Thirteen

P enny's nostrils flared, and her left eye twitched again. Upon seeing that reaction, Sid felt she had Penny's number. She'd guessed that Violet's daughter-in-law didn't care much about getting the house ready to sell. What she cared about was getting her hands on what she believed was rightfully hers—that diamond and ruby necklace.

Penny spun away and marched off, and Sid followed her to the front door, making sure to lock it after she left. The scent of Chanel No. 5 lingered, and Sid was happy not to have to spend the day in the house smelling it.

She grabbed her bag and passed through the kitchen on her way to the courtyard. The half dozen vases still lined up on the counter, leftover from the funeral events this past weekend, now contained wilted flowers in fetid water. Someone would have to throw them out, and Sid wondered if Buddy expected her to do it. For now, she left them where they were, exited the kitchen using the French doors, and crossed the paved courtyard, which was partially shaded by a large oak.

The door to the carriage house required a different key

from the main house, and Sid wondered if that was to prevent her family from having access without an invitation. The building was long and narrow, running along the back side of the property and painted the same color as the house. Inside, on the ground floor, was a tarp-covered black Cadillac, probably twenty years old judging by the body style. Other than the car, there were some yard tools, a few storage boxes, and not much else. A small powder room had been built under the steep staircase that led to the second floor.

Sid climbed the stairs, which opened at the top into a large room with a small kitchenette at one end and a closed door at the other. A bank of tall windows ran the length of the room and offered a view of the pretty courtyard with its blooming bougainvillea, tiered fountain, and overhanging oak. The carriage house's air-conditioning wasn't as efficient as that of the main house, and the large room was warm and slightly humid. Sid reached for the thermostat and turned it down two degrees, hearing the telltale whoosh of the system kicking into high gear.

This room had been Violet Rizzo's art studio. If the stacks of painted canvases leaning against every vertical surface hadn't given it away, the stale smell of dried paint certainly did. Shelves ran the length of the room opposite the windows and housed pots of paint, jars of brushes, and various other tools and supplies. An unfinished painting sat on an easel in the middle of the room, lit by the sunlight streaming in through the windows. It was a street scene being painted from the photograph clipped to the top of the easel. Sid recognized it as Cuna Street, with the ugly, flamingo-pink trim of the Muy Local shop clearly visible in the background. A quick scan of the other canvases revealed that they were all scenes from the Old City.

On the far wall, opposite the kitchenette, was the locked door that lead to Violet Rizzo's private office. Sid unlocked it and peeked inside, finding everything just as she remembered it from Buddy's tour a week ago. The room was decorated in much the same fashion as the main house—cream-colored walls and a large desk and numerous bookcases stained a dark walnut. She closed the door, not bothering to lock it again, and turned back to face the art studio. She'd start in here, hoping to finish by the end of the day, and leave the office for last.

The kitchenette would be tackled first. She had just opened the first cabinet when her phone rang.

"Sidney, it's Buddy Rizzo. So glad I caught you." The man began speaking before Sid could even utter hello. "I just spoke with my wife, and she sounded very upset."

Sid listened patiently to Buddy as he summarized Penny's selective retelling of their meeting in Violet's bedroom, all the while staring out at the courtyard and the hot-pink bougainvillea. When she couldn't take it anymore, she interrupted him. "Buddy, let me stop you right there. First of all, I am not dragging my feet. You and I had a conversation before I began in which I was very clear that this job would take a minimum of two weeks."

Buddy sputtered something unintelligible, and Sid felt sorry for him. After meeting Penny in person, she thought the meek and mild man probably spent most of his time placating his wife.

"Buddy, I have to ask." Sid chewed her bottom lip for a moment, contemplating how best to pose her next question. "Are you certain that Violet wasn't buried with the necklace?"

Buddy barked a laugh. "I am quite certain. Both the vigil and the funeral Mass were open casket, so I know what my mother was wearing when we buried her, and I can assure you that she was not wearing the necklace." He huffed. "I'd be wasting my money if that were the case, wouldn't I?"

"Okay, okay." Sid held up her free hand in surrender,

despite knowing he couldn't see the gesture through the phone. "I just needed to make sure." She pinched the bridge of her nose and shut her eyes, shaking her head at the absurdity of having asked him such a thing. "Listen, I've finished my inventory of the house and will scan the pages and send them over to you tonight. I'm just beginning to tackle the coach house, and I expect to be another week going through everything in here."

More sputtering from Buddy followed.

"The moment I find the necklace, or anything else like it, I will call you." She took a deep breath to calm herself. "I understand your wife is impatient to move quickly on the sale of your mother's house"—this brought on another round of unintelligible blustering from Buddy, much as Sid had known it would —"but I ask that I be allowed to do the job you hired me to do and to be able to do it without having to navigate around real estate agents and whoever else Penny has lined up and waiting. One more week, that's all I should need."

After putting up a few more minutes of half-hearted resistance, Buddy Rizzo finally consented to giving Sid another week by herself at the house, and Sid thought his reluctance to do so probably had a lot to do with his unwillingness to upset his wife. Nevertheless, he agreed to keep Penny away from the house for one more week. After that, he warned, he wouldn't be able to hold her back.

Message received, thought Sid, and she turned her attention back to the kitchenette. Tiny as it was, it still contained two dozen coffee mugs, two full sets of dishes, enough cutlery for a banquet hall, and a dozen bags of ground coffee. And that was just the upper cabinets and the two drawers. The lower cabinets were chock full of drop cloths and various painting supplies. Each item was noted in the log and put back in its place.

Sid moved into the studio space and slowly surveyed the

canvases. A rough count tallied more than eighty paintings, but she could tell that some of the larger ones hid multiple smaller ones from view. She moved slowly around the room, carefully inspecting each and every painting, recognizing street after street, building after building, scene after scene. Violet must have spent half her life painting all of these, methodically working her way around the Old City.

After touring the entire room once, Sid made another slow pass and discovered a pattern beginning to emerge. The paintings appeared to be organized. Hard to believe, Sid conceded, given the way they were crammed into the space, but it appeared that Violet had stacked her canvases like a map of the Old City. The room ran lengthwise from east to west, with the windows set into the north wall. The paintings followed a similar pattern. Paintings of streets and landmarks on the east side of the historic district were on the east side of the room; the more westerly locales were on the west side of the room. Paintings of sites on the southside of downtown were closer to the room's southern wall. Those canvases with sites at the northern end of downtown were in front of the others, closer to the windows.

Hours later, Sid's phone buzzed with incoming texts, and she fished it out of her bag.

Finished school early.

Coming over to help.

Do you want grandpa to make you lunch?

Sid checked her watch. It was almost two o'clock. She hastily typed out a response.

Sid began a third survey of the room. This led to another discovery: Some locations had been painted more than once. In fact, there were a few locales, maybe half a dozen in total, that had been treated to greater study and garnered anywhere from five to ten canvases each. Sid sketched out some notes of her discoveries.

Forty-five minutes later, Sid heard a knock on the carriage house door and went downstairs to find Leo waiting in the courtyard with an insulated cooler in one hand and Jezebel in the other.

"You locked me out," he said with a frown.

"Sorry, Leo. I didn't realize." She smiled at him. "Nothing personal."

He smirked. "Yeah, right." He held the cooler bag out to her. "From Grandpa."

"Thanks, kid." She ushered him over to a small café table and chairs under the shade of the oak tree. "Dog-sitting duty, I take it?" She nodded at Jezebel. The little dog stood there, waiting patiently while Leo unhooked the leash from her collar.

"Yeah."

"Not spending time with your mom today?"

He shook his head.

"Why not?"

Leo shrugged.

Sid sighed. "Good talk, kid." She bit into the turkey sandwich Burt had packed for her and cracked open a cold soda.

Leo stayed silent and watched Jezebel wander around. After Jezebel finished her survey of the courtyard, he scooped up the little dog, set her on his lap, and finally looked up at Sid.

"She and Brooklyn went to the beach." Then, he reached for a bag of potato chips.

"I see." And she did. Paizley and her friend had likely donned their bikinis and floppy sunhats and driven to the beach in the Jeep with the top down for a day of sunbathing and photo shoots. Leo was a convenient dog minder, one Paizley didn't have to pay and could order around at will. Sid watched him pet the little dog as he shoveled chips into his mouth. He sat slumped in his chair, his shoulders hunched, and stared blankly at the fountain in the center of the courtyard. He had yet to ask her about the investigation and had said very little since arriving. The change in him was disappointing to see.

Sid wadded up her sandwich wrapper and zipped the cooler shut. "We should get to it then." She pointed to Jezebel. "You'll need to keep her on her leash, and don't say anything to the client. I have no idea if we're allowed to have her here, but I won't tell if you won't." She poked Leo in the arm. "Just don't let her make a mess."

"I won't," he grumbled, and he refastened the leash to the dog's collar.

They entered the carriage house and climbed the stairs to the second floor. As soon as they stepped into the open space of the studio, Jezebel began barking and snarling. It was a high-pitched, eardrum-splitting ruckus that no amount of cooing and petting seemed to be able to silence.

"What's her problem?" Sid asked, having to practically yell to be heard.

Leo leaned close to Sid's ear so she could hear him. "She must see Violet." He nodded toward the far end of the room and then leaned in again. "She's standing in front of that door."

"Really?" Sid glanced at the office door and then down at the apoplectic dog. "Let's go downstairs." She nudged the teen back toward the stairs and followed him down. It was only once they were outside again that Jezebel finally quieted down. "She can't stay, Leo. You'll have to take her home."

"But—"

"No, Leo. She can't stay. I have to work, and I can't think, much less get anything done, with her making that racket." Sid placed a hand on his shoulder. "I'm sorry. Maybe Burt will watch the dog."

He shook his head. "He had errands to run before the Geezers' concert tonight."

Sid shrugged. "You'll have to babysit until your mom gets home then." He began to protest, but she held up her hands. "If she expects you to watch the dog, then that's what you have to do. And I'm sorry, but you can't do it here."

He stomped through the courtyard toward the front yard without saying anything more, and Sid watched him slam the wrought iron gate closed with a loud clang. Moments later, he was back at the gate, waving Sid over. The dog was barking up a storm once again.

"He's here," Leo murmured. "He must have followed me."

"Who?" Sid's gaze darted around the front yard.

"The pirate." Leo's eyes were wide and unblinking.

"Did you see him when you arrived?"

Leo shook his head.

"Okay, kid. I'm sure you're fine, but I'll come with you just to be safe." She jogged back to the carriage house, locked the door, and rejoined Leo at the gate. She put her arm around his shoulder and walked with him across the lawn to the street. They walked that way—Sid's arm around Leo, Leo clutching Jezebel to his chest, Jezebel yipping and snarling with earsplitting shrillness—to the corner of Valencia and Sevilla streets. The pirate, however, remained firmly planted in front of Violet's house.

"I'm not sure what you think you're going to be able to do against a pirate," Leo said.

"Probably nothing," Sid admitted, "but, you know, safety in numbers and all that."

"Huh," muttered Leo as he looked back over his shoulder. The pirate watched his every move but made no move of his own. "He's not following."

"Maybe he's not here for us?" Sid offered, patting his shoulder. "Go on home. You should be fine." Leo walked about ten yards away from Sid, and Jezebel suddenly quieted. The teenager nodded to Sid and then broke into a run, heading for home.

Sid watched him until he turned and disappeared from view and then walked back to Violet Rizzo's house. As she crossed the front yard to return to the carriage house, she felt a blast of cold air and picked up her pace.

But the cold air didn't follow her into the carriage house. As far as Sid could tell, she was all alone in Violet's studio. The air was cool but not cold. Air-conditioned, not spirit-chilled. Still, she wished Leo was here to confirm that fact.

She resumed her investigation of the art studio and discovered that, on the back of each canvas, Violet had scratched a code. It was undecipherable at first, but Sid finally cracked it after checking several dozen canvases. The code included initials for the street, the direction from which the scene was viewed, and the time of day. More than one painting of the same scene was sequenced with Roman numerals.

Sid made a list of every canvas, its respective code, her interpretation of that code, any other details that might be helpful—size, orientation, dominant color—as well as a notation of the location of the canvas within the room based on a map that she drew herself. She was no artist like Violet Rizzo, but her own map wasn't half bad, if she did say so herself.

By the end of the day, she had a list of five sites in the Old City's historic district that had captured Violet Rizzo's attention so profoundly that she'd dedicated at least half a dozen canvases, and countless hours, to their study in oil paint. Sid snapped photos of the paintings Violet had done for each of these locations.

When all of that was complete, Sid sat on the stool in front of the easel and surveyed the room. She'd put everything back where she'd found it. The mess, cleverly organized as it was, was still a mess, in her opinion. She cast her gaze over the canvases, all of them stacked in a manner that, at first blush, seemed completely random but, in reality, resembled a map of the Old City.

"What are you trying to tell me, Violet Rizzo?" Sid felt a cold breeze brush over her arms for no more than a second before vanishing again. "Or, should I ask, what are you trying to hide?"

Chapter Fourteen

By seven thirty that evening, Sid strolled down St. George Street toward Granny Oak's Music Park, freshly showered and clad in a new sundress, ready to spend the evening watching Recent Geezer rock out and trying her best to play nice with Paizley and Brooklyn.

At the entrance to the music park, she stood in the doorway, took a few deep breaths, and steeled herself before heading into battle. That's how she thought of time spent with Leo's mother—as a battle. Was she vying for the boy's affection? No, that wasn't it. More likely, she was battling with herself, fighting to keep her anger, judgment, and tongue in check.

"Hello."

Sid turned to find Dan Murdock standing next to her. Some detective she was turning out to be, not to realize someone—him, of all people—had strolled up and now occupied the space right next to her.

"Hi." She could feel her cheeks flush with the embarrassment of having gotten so emotional in his presence last night and with the realization that she'd forgotten all about Trip's death once she'd arrived at Violet Rizzo's house. The guilt of momentarily forgetting pricked her heart. "Look, I'm sorry for my behavior last night."

He gave her another sad, lopsided smile. "You've got nothing to apologize for. In fact, I should apologize to you. I should have realized that you wouldn't have known about Dad. Mom told me that you and he were close, that he thought the world of you." He shrugged. "I didn't think. I'm sorry."

Sid nodded. "It caught me by surprise, that's all. I thought it was Trip who'd left me the card and asked me to meet him."

Dan's smile fell and his brow furrowed. "But I asked the kid to ask you to call me, to tell you that I was looking for you, not my dad. I only mentioned that you used to work with him."

"Leo's note said that a man at the marina was looking for me and that I needed to call him. The card was yours, but the writing on the back of it had Trip's name and a phone number." She smiled. "I assumed it was from Trip."

Dan ran a hand down his face and rubbed at the stubble on his chin. "Sorry about that. I didn't think . . . I should have been clearer when I spoke with the kid. Leo, was it?" He blew out a breath. "I really am sorry."

"Let's start over." Sid held out her hand. "I'm Sid. I used to work with your father. He was a wonderful man, and I am truly sorry for your loss."

Dan took her hand. "Nice to meet you, Sid. I'm Dan. Thank you for your condolences. Sounds like it was your loss, too." She nodded, and his smile returned. He nodded toward the band on stage. "Care to join me?"

"I'm friends with the band," she smirked. "I might be able to get you a backstage pass."

Dan frowned as he looked at the small wooden stage. "Correct me if I'm wrong, but there is no backstage."

Sid felt her grin widen. "Then, you'll have to settle for me buying you a drink."

———

At intermission, Leo ran between the stage and the little tiki bar, shuttling beers and waters to the band members. Leo had told his mom that he was Recent Geezer's roadie and didn't have time to be her photographer. One of Cesar Hernandez's regular groupies, a middle-aged woman with dyed-blonde hair and generous cleavage, had offered to help, and the band was kindly posing for photos with the Paizley and Brooklyn. Those photos would no doubt be splashed across the PB&J social media pages before the night was over.

Leo saw Sid in the back of the venue, standing next to the man from the marina. The two of them were deep in conversation, facing each other and oblivious to everyone else around them. He felt a bit annoyed, if he was honest. Annoyed that she hadn't come to sit next to him like she usually did at the Geezers' concerts. Annoyed that she wasn't coming over now to help save him from the public embarrassment of a PB&J photo shoot. And annoyed that her attention was elsewhere when it should be . . . where? On him?

Leo shook his head. He was being silly. His mom was here. Finally. He should be spending his time with her, not wishing he could just hang out with Sid, eating fried shrimp and listening to the Geezers play.

A tap on his shoulder had him spinning around and nearly dropping the two cups of ice water he was holding.

"Hi." Joey Rizzo stood smiling at him. Her hair was still pink, and her outfit was still black, although tonight she was wearing black shorts and fishnet stockings with her combat boots.

"Hi." He couldn't think of anything else to say but considered it a personal triumph that he wasn't standing there with his mouth hanging open.

"Are you their roadie?" Her eyes sparkled at the notion.

Leo nodded, feeling his cheeks heat and knowing they were turning bright red.

"You are so lucky." She bit her lip and tugged at the hem of her shorts. "They sound really good tonight."

Leo nodded again. The condensation from the ice was starting to make his hands slip on the plastic cups.

"Is there any chance I could meet the band?"

His face broke into a wide grin. He put the cups down on the edge of the stage and wiped his hands on the hem of his T-shirt. "Sure," he croaked. Clearing his throat, he tried again. "Sure, come on."

Less than a minute later, the band had stopped posing for photos, and all of the Geezers were giving Leo and Joey their undivided attention. Paizley and Brooklyn were forced to go find other sources of entertainment, which they did at the nearby tiki bar in the form of a couple of men clad in business casual attire. Standing next to Joey as they chatted with the Geezers, Leo glanced toward the tiki bar and locked eyes with his mom. She waggled her eyebrows at him and gestured toward Joey, nodding enthusiastically. Mortified, he immediately broke eye contact, stared at his sneakers, and inched away from Joey. Burt reached out, draped an arm over his grandson's shoulders, and gave him a squeeze. Leo could feel the blush heating his cheeks; he kept his gaze down, unwilling to risk meeting anyone else's eye and enduring further embarrassment.

Recent Geezer retook the stage ten minutes later than scheduled, after chatting with Joey and extending an invitation for her to join them and Leo for band practice and dinner on Sunday. The first song in the second half of their set list was

"American Woman" by The Guess Who. It was one of Paizley's favorites. She and Brooklyn immediately started dancing, and Leo wondered if his mom was paying any attention to the lyrics.

On Saturday morning, Sid returned from a run with Dan Murdock to find Leo sitting in the backyard in the shade of the neighbor's overhanging oak, watching Jezebel sniff her way around the small patch of grass. After shaking Leo's hand, Dan jogged off to try to squeeze in another few miles before it got too hot. Sid, however, was done for the day.

"What are your plans for the day, kid?" She sat down in the chair next to Leo and smiled as she caught him frowning at Dan's retreating form.

He shrugged. "Nothing."

"Nothing? No sightseeing?"

She'd witnessed Paizley and Brooklyn's obnoxious display with the Geezers last night at Granny Oak's. Brooklyn had practically draped herself all over Cesar and Guppy, but Sid knew both men well enough to know that neither man was especially thrilled with the attention. Dan, meanwhile, had offered to buy Sid a late dinner, and she had taken him up on it. They'd left before the Geezers retook the stage, so she had no idea how the rest of Leo's evening ended up. It was obvious when she left, though, that he wasn't really enjoying himself. She felt a little guilty for not saving him from the embarrassment of his mother's photo shoot, but the boy was going to have to learn to deal with his mother on his own if she was going to be hanging around here for a while.

"They're going shopping," he mumbled. "To the outlet mall."

Sid feigned shock, pressing a hand to her chest. "And you don't want to go? Shopping is your absolute favorite!"

He shot her a sideways scowl but couldn't completely hide his amusement. "No, it's not."

Sid stood and pulled her sweaty ponytail away from her neck. "Well, I'm going on a treasure hunt. You're welcome to join me, if you want."

"Really?!" He shot to his feet so quickly that Jezebel jumped and let out a high-pitched yip.

"Yes, really." Sid headed toward the garage, calling back over her shoulder. "You need to tell your mom and Burt that you're coming with me. It's work. For the Rizzo case. We'll be gone all day, so you can't bring the dog. We leave in twenty minutes."

Out of the corner of her eye, she saw Leo scoop up Jezebel and make a dash for the house. Yanking open the kitchen door, he shouted, "Mom, Grandpa, I have to go to work!"

———

Leo sat in Sid's desk chair waiting, for her to finish getting ready. Bundles of old letters, most of them tied with satin ribbons, were stacked on the desk. One letter was open, and he slid it toward himself with one finger and began to read. Two sentences in, he slid it away. It was a love letter, mushy, sentimental, and filled with embarrassing professions of love. An image of Ellie Owen flashed through his mind: strawberry-blonde hair, long legs, beat-up Chuck Taylors, and the Rolling Stones tee. That image was immediately followed by the memory of seeing her through the window of the N'Ice Day Ice Cream Shop, flirting with the behemoths from her high school football team.

He shook his head to clear the thought, which did the trick, but an image of Joey Rizzo appeared in place of Ellie. Pink-haired, goth-attired Joey Rizzo, who would be arriving at the house tomorrow to watch the Geezers' rehearsal and join them all for dinner afterward. Leo slid the letter back toward himself and began to read again.

"Learning anything?"

Leo jumped up, banging his thighs on the metal desk and causing the chair to shoot backward into one of the filing cabinets. Several bundles of letters tumbled to the floor. "I wasn't . . . I was just—"

"Relax, kid." Sid descended the staircase, a wide grin on her face. "Those letters don't make for very exciting reading."

Leo crouched down, glad to be momentarily blocked from Sid's view as he felt his face flush, and gathered the bundles that had toppled off the desk.

"You okay down there?" Sid's face peered down at him from the other side of the desk.

"I'm fine." Some of the loose letters had landed under the desk, so he had to stretch to retrieve them.

Sid picked up the letter he'd been reading. "I'm not much of a romance novel reader, but these seem pretty chaste to me."

He tried to look up at her but banged his head instead. "Shit," he muttered under his breath before asking, "what does 'chaste' mean?"

"Rated G. Nothing explicit. Sweet, not steamy."

"Eww," he grumbled.

She chuckled. "But I admit I don't understand all the references to baseball. Maybe that's some sort of sexual code."

"Please stop talking," he pleaded, avoiding eye contact with her as he finished gathering the scattered letters. As his fingers closed around a faded blue, satin bow tied around one bundle, an image flashed in his mind. Leo dropped the bundle and lost his balance, falling against one of the other file cabinets.

"Leo?"

He pointed to the bundle of letters. "That one." He pointed. "There's something wrong with it."

"What do you mean, 'wrong with it'?" Sid came around the desk and kneeled next to him. She picked up the bundle, running her fingers all over, around, and in between the letters and the ribbon. "This one?" she asked as she stood up, still examining the bundle.

He nodded again, and Sid held out a hand to help him to his feet. "I saw something when I touched it."

She raised an eyebrow and waited for him to elaborate.

With tentative fingers, he reached out and touched the ribbon, which was old and frayed in places and had probably been a deep, robin's-egg-blue back in the day. At contact, Leo's face went slack, and he appeared to be staring at the ribbon. In his head, however, he saw a little girl wearing a white cotton dress, white socks, and black patent leather shoes that gleamed in the sunlight. She was standing in front of a black door, partially blocking the shiny gold mail slot behind her. The ribbon was tied as a headband in the girl's thick, chocolate-brown hair.

Leo blinked and pulled his hand back. "This ribbon belonged to a little girl." He rubbed his hand down the front of his shirt, trying to wipe away any residual effects of the ribbon. "She wore it in her hair."

"I think it belonged to Violet Rizzo." Sid ran her fingers over the ribbon.

Leo frowned and shook his head. "But it's . . . I mean, it's wrapped around"—he paused and swallowed audibly—"love letters."

Sid smiled. "Yes it is, kid. Apparently, Violet had a long-distance love affair that spanned nearly forty-five years." She checked the date of the letter on top. "This bundle contains the oldest letters. She must have used an old hair ribbon to tie them up." She placed the bundle on the desk next to the others. "I found all of these in some storage bins under her bed."

Leo glanced at his hand and then wiped it on his shirt again. "That doesn't happen very often. In fact, it hasn't happened in a long time. It just took me by surprise, that's all."

"So you've seen people's pasts before when you've touched their things?"

"Sometimes." He shrugged. "Images. Feelings. Messages for people." He shoved his hands in his pocket. "You think I'm weird."

Sid smiled and patted his shoulder. "Kid, I've always thought you were weird, long before I knew you could talk to dead people and give psychic readings."

He smirked. "I don't give psychic readings."

"Maybe you should." She untied the ribbon and held it out to him. "Wanna give it a try?" His eyes flicked between Sid's face and the ribbon in her hand. "You don't have to, Leo." She dropped the ribbon on the desk and pulled her bag out of the bottom drawer of the desk.

As she headed for the door, Leo stayed where he was behind the desk. He gently picked up the ribbon and positioned it across his open palms. Images of Violet, snapshots of her life through the years, began flashing in his mind. The sensation was like flipping through a photo album—a little girl running, a teenager carrying schoolbooks, a young woman drawing something on a sketchpad, a woman holding a baby. Time sped up, decades passing in fractions of a second. Finally, he saw Violet as an old woman in her house, shuffling across her bedroom in her bathrobe and slippers.

The next image was of the second-floor mezzanine in Violet's house. It was a view from below, as if it was being viewed by someone falling backward down the stairs. The house was dark, and there were few details that he could see clearly. But one detail was unmistakable: a flash of pink.

Leo felt his breath leave his lungs, and the world went black for no more than a second. The sensation had him dropping the ribbon as if it were on fire and stumbling backward into the same file cabinet he'd collided with earlier.

"Leo?!" Sid raced toward him and grabbed him by the shoulders. "Leo!"

"I'm okay," he replied, trying to shrug her off. He slumped down in the desk chair, which squeaked in protest. "I saw Violet. I know how she died."

"She fell down the stairs." Sid leaned back against the desk and crossed her arms. "Right?"

"She fell, all right." Leo sighed. "After she was pushed." He felt hollowed out inside after what he'd just seen. "And I know who pushed her."

Chapter Fifteen

"That doesn't make any sense." Sid sat across from Leo in the sagging guest chair and rubbed her temples.

"Which part?" Leo stuck his arms out for exaggerated effect, shaking one hand. "The part where I held a piece of ribbon and saw an old woman's life flash before my eyes?" He shook the other hand. "Or the part where I saw the person who killed Violet Rizzo?"

"All of it, I guess." Sid continued to rub her temples. "That latter part in particular." She stood up and began pacing the room, back and forth, twisting her wet ponytail around her fingers. "You're sure it was Joey Rizzo standing at the top of the stairs? And I mean, absolutely certain?"

Leo nodded.

"Joey killed her own grandmother. That's what you're telling me?"

"Yes."

"And then she hired us to find the killer."

He shrugged. "I'll admit that's a bit weird, but I know what I saw."

"Tell me again." Her voice was strained, and her pacing sped up.

"I was Violet, and I was looking up at the hallway at the top of the stairs. It was a weird angle, like I was falling headfirst, but on my back facing up—"

"So, she was pushed from the front." Sid mimed a shove. "Her shoulders or her chest."

"I guess." Leo shrugged. "There was someone standing at the top of the stairs wearing all black. She had pink hair."

"You saw Joey's face?"

Leo frowned. "Well, no . . . not exactly. It was dark, too dark to make out her face. But she was wearing black and had pink hair."

"And you're sure it was a woman?"

Leo rolled his eyes at her. When she stopped pacing and scowled at him, he closed his eyes and recalled the image he'd seen. "Pretty sure it's a woman. Looks too small to be a man."

"Too small as in too short or too skinny? What do you mean by that?"

"I mean not huge," Leo replied, opening his eyes. "Not broad or bulky. Small, not big."

"And you didn't see the face clearly."

"No." He crossed his arms, mimicking his boss. "But I saw the pink hair. Definitely saw that."

"Shit," hissed Sid. She resumed her pacing.

"You know, she's coming back here." When Sid didn't respond, he raised his voice a little. "Joey's coming here tomorrow." That got Sid's attention, and she froze in her tracks. "Grandpa and the Geezers invited her to the house to watch band practice and then have dinner with all of us."

"Shit!" She began pacing once more, and Leo sat silently in the chair, staring at the ribbon and waiting for Sid to decide what to do.

After a couple of minutes, she threw up her hands. "I can't deal with this right now." She snatched up her bag from where she'd dropped it on the floor and flung open the door. "Come on. Let's get going."

"But—"

"But what?" She motioned for him to get up and move. "We have two clients. One has hired us to find a dead woman's missing jewelry. The other has hired us to find the dead woman's killer. That second client appears to actually be the killer." She threw her hands up. "I have no idea what to do about that right now, so we're going to park it." She patted the air to her side. "Just leave it here for now and come back to it later." She pointed to the open door. "So let's go take care of business for the first client, okay?"

Leo held up his hands in surrender. "All right, geez." He shuffled across the carpet and exited the office. Sid hit the switch, and as the lights turned off, her gaze landed on Violet's faded blue ribbon. Acting purely on gut instinct, Sid walked over, picked up the ribbon, and shoved it into her bag. You never knew when a length of old ribbon might come in handy, and this particular ribbon seemed handier than most.

———

"Tell me why we're here again?"

Leo stood next to Sid in the middle of St. George Street. The pair stared at the aged, wooden façade of a plain, diminutive building that time clearly forgot. Most of the tourists streaming around them weren't bothering to notice it either. "Oldest Wooden School House in the U.S.A.," Leo read from the sign nailed to the front of the dilapidated structure. "Seriously?"

Sid handed him her phone, a photo of Violet's painting

depicting this modest structure visible on the screen. "She painted this place six different times. Different hours of the day, slightly different angles, but six canvases with this little schoolhouse on them." She took the phone back and dropped it in her bag. "It has to mean something."

"What could it possibly mean?" Leo stared at the planks of weathered, gray wood.

"Maybe it's a clue."

"A clue to what? To where the necklace is?" He huffed. "I already told you where it is. She's buried with it."

"Be that as it may," said Sid through gritted teeth, "I can't go back to Buddy Rizzo and tell him he needs to dig up his mother's grave because her spirit is roaming around her old house wearing the rubies around her neck. We have to exhaust all other avenues first."

Out of the corner of his eye, Leo saw a familiar figure standing about fifty feet away in the middle of St. George Street. He was hard to miss, frankly, what with the pistol and sword and bloodstained shirt. Tourists passed right by the spirit, some even passed through him, but he didn't move.

"Our friend is here," Leo whispered, continuing to stare at the pirate in his peripheral vision.

"Violet?"

"No, the pirate."

"Oh." Sid sounded disappointed. "I was hoping it was Violet, come to tell us we were on the right track."

"Sorry to disappoint," Leo mumbled.

"Not surprising really," Sid offered. "I mean, he's not always standing outside the house or following us to Violet's, right? You said yourself you've seen him around town on occasion."

"Yeah." He sighed. "I guess."

"Forget about him." She tugged on his sleeve. "Come on."

They paid the admission fee and strolled around the small sliver of property that fronted busy St. George Street and claimed to house the oldest wooden school building in the United States, dating from the early 1700s. The little house, with its animatronic depiction of the schoolroom, as well as the separate kitchen and outdoor privy were tiny, ancient, and surprisingly interesting. Leo read the various tour notes and historical summaries tacked on the walls and placed next to artifacts, but nothing jumped out at either him or Sid as making this a place that might be connected in any way to Violet Rizzo.

After their brief tour of the buildings, they stood in the rustic garden behind the schoolhouse, and Sid pulled Violet's faded blue ribbon from her bag. "See what you can get from this?"

Leo flinched at the sight of the ribbon. "No."

"Please, kid. It's the only connection we have to Violet." She dangled the ribbon in front of him. "Unless you see her around here and can ask her yourself?"

He shook his head. Sid looked worn out and sounded exasperated, and it was only midmorning. He began to wonder whether shopping with his mom at the outlet mall would have been more fun than this. "Fine."

He took the ribbon, holding it loosely in his upturned palm. Only one image popped into his mind: Violet Rizzo snapping photos of the schoolhouse with a small camera. She was smiling. There was no fear, no sadness—only a peaceful joy, much like Leo felt when bass practice was going well.

Leo gave the ribbon back to Sid. "I saw her take photos of this place. She seemed happy. That's it. Nothing weird."

"Photos of anything in particular?"

"No. No one thing." He waved his arms around. "Just everything."

Sid wrapped the ribbon around her fingers. "Sounds like

Violet was scouting this location for her paintings. She painted from photographs, so the photos you saw her taking were probably used as inspiration and reference for her artwork. Today's expedition might turn out to be nothing but a wild goose chase." She sighed and tucked the ribbon back into her bag. "I hope not. We could definitely use a break." She headed for the exit. "Come on, Leo. We've got more sights to see."

Chapter Sixteen

"I don't see nothin'," Hattie said. "Sorry."

Sid took Violet's ribbon from the old woman and returned it to her bag. "That's okay. Thanks for trying."

The three of them were sitting on the grass in the Plaza de la Constitución. The historic downtown park was the second stop on the list of treasure hunt sites inspired by Violet Rizzo's original artwork. Sid and Leo had combed the park from St. George Street to Avenida Menendez, including Ponce de Leon Circle at the easternmost end but found nothing connected to Violet Rizzo. Leo's own turn with the ribbon had revealed the same type of image he'd seen at the Oldest Wooden School House—a smiling Violet Rizzo taking photographs.

When they came upon Mad Hattie sitting in her usual spot under one of the park's giant oaks, Leo had taken a seat in front of her and explained what they were doing. He'd asked her to try holding the ribbon to see if she could pick up something that he couldn't, and she'd agreed.

"It don't work the same for everyone, holdin' on to stuff," Hattie explained, leaning forward a little and speaking directly to Leo. "Not everyone can do it, not every object will let you see." She shrugged. "Sometimes it's just pure luck." She leaned sideways, trying to see around Sid, and paused for a long moment. "Hmm."

Leo nodded. "He's been following us."

"Really?" Hattie's eyebrows shot up so far that they were visible over the top of her large sunglasses. "What've you two been doin'?"

"Who? Who are we talking about" Sid asked, glancing between the two of them and then back over her shoulder. "Is it the pirate?"

"Shhh!" Leo and Hattie hissed in unison.

Sid held up her hands in surrender. "Sorry."

Hattie shook her arthritic finger at them both. "Don't know what you two did to pique that one's interest, but I would seriously consider lettin' it go, if I were you."

"Is he dangerous?" Sid asked, clearly fighting the urge to look back over her shoulder again.

Leo rolled his eyes at his boss.

"He's a pirate, ain't he?" Hattie leaned sideways again to get another look. "He could probably write a book on *dangerous*."

Hattie shooed Sid away in order for her to have some privacy to chat with Leo, so Sid found a bench on one of the many sidewalks that crisscrossed the park and made some notes about the search thus far. About ten minutes later, Leo rejoined Sid.

"Everything okay?" Sid asked as she stood and slung her bag over her shoulder.

Leo nodded. "She just wanted to make sure I was okay. Wanted to know if I'd seen my dad again." It had been several weeks since the encounter with his father's spirit in which

Hattie had served as his psychic intermediary and Sid as his moral, and sometimes physical, support system.

"And?"

"No. Haven't seen him." He shoved his hands in his pockets and kept pace with Sid.

Spirits of the dead passed them as they walked toward the bay. Plaza de la Constitución always had a few, sometimes more than a few, but today it wasn't an exceedingly popular hangout for the uncanny. Nevertheless, upon entering the shady park, Leo had tugged on the brim of his ball cap and uttered the command for the spirits to stay away, just like Hattie had taught him. So far, none had ventured near enough to bother him, including the pirate.

He repeated the words again in his head now, no longer needing to say them out loud, and wondered, not for the first time, whether saying those words was keeping his father's spirit away, too. The mental command hadn't worked at keeping Gunner at bay last time, and the spirit had haunted him for a couple of weeks as a dark shadow figure before finally revealing itself. Would his dad's spirit ever return for a visit? Ever speak to Leo directly? There was no telling. Even the friendliest spirits were finicky, inscrutable, and notoriously unreliable.

Sid and Leo crossed Avenida Menendez and walked up onto the Bridge of Lions. They huddled in a small alcove just past one of the marble lion statues, and Sid scrolled through the photos of Violet's paintings. The woman had painted a panorama of Matanzas Bay, as seen from the bridge. On the north side of the bridge, four canvases depicted the Castillo de San Marcos in the background and various sailboats moored to buoys in the foreground.

On the south side of the bridge, Violet had painted the public marina with its myriad sailboats and powerboats. One depiction even included a pirate ship. Leo recognized the vessel as the black-and-red replica he'd seen occasionally sailing up and down the bay. The replica ship's local advertising boasted live, onboard pirate shows and booze cruises. His mom and Brooklyn talked of booking a cruise at sunset in order to take full photographic advantage of the experience. This morning, however, the vessel sat docked at the marina, barely bobbing in the calm water.

Leo held the ribbon again and saw nothing but an image of Violet taking photographs on a sun-drenched day. "Sorry, Sid. It's still the same thing. She's just taking photos."

She took the ribbon from him, her posture slumping a little. "Is our pirate friend still with us?"

Leo nodded. "He's still in the park, but he's been watching us the whole time."

"Great," Sid muttered. "Apart from giving a dead pirate a guided tour of downtown, this little adventure is turning out to be a big waste of time."

"That's okay," Leo offered. "What else were we gonna do today?"

"Laundry," she replied and walked back down the bridge.

Their next stop was a tidy, two-story, white building with green shutters at the southern end of the Old City's historic district. A little green sign with white lettering, sticking up out of the ground between a set of shutter-framed windows, read, "The Oldest House."

"Why is everything so old around here?" Leo whined.

"You mean here, in the Old City?" When he nodded, Sid simply shook her head at him and then turned away, heading into the gift shop to pay the admission fee for the tour.

An elderly woman gave them a tour of the property,

detailing its history from the oldest parts of the house dating back to the early 1700s, through the various modifications made by its numerous owners, to the restoration and furnishing of its rooms based on the periods of the house's history. The tour ended in the walled garden, which was mercifully shaded by an enormous oak and several smaller trees. Their tour guide left them to wander around the garden, and Sid and Leo followed the brick path to a spot away from any eavesdroppers.

"Let's try this again." She handed Leo the ribbon.

He held it in his hand, closed his eyes for several seconds, and opened them again. "Same."

"Give me a break!" Sid hissed, kicking at the neatly trimmed grass bordering the path. "You're telling me she's just taking photos?"

"Yep," Leo shrugged. "Just taking photos."

Sid snatched back the ribbon and shoved it into her bag, not bothering to wind it with any sort of care. "Let's go." She stormed out of the house, through the gift shop, and turned down Charlotte Street, heading back toward the center of the historic downtown.

Leo followed, and so did the pirate. The spirit had been waiting for them outside the Old House, and now he followed at a distance that was still too close for Leo's comfort. Leo kept pace with Sid but let her march slightly ahead of him for several blocks. "Maybe we should stop for lunch," he offered.

Sid practically growled at him as she flipped her hand over to check her watch.

"It's just a suggestion, but maybe you're all cranky because you need to eat something, not because we can't find any clues."

Sid slowed as they approached the intersection with King Street. It was half past noon already. "Yeah, all right." She looked up and down King Street, then jerked her head to the left. "We can get something at the next stop."

Leo followed a couple of paces behind his boss as they passed the various art galleries, wine bars, and trinket shops along King. They had to wait for a silver Bentley to exit the porte cochere of the Casa Monica before continuing west on King for one more block. Next to the hotel, perched on a city block all its own, stood the Lightner Museum, a four-story, cream-colored building with the same red roof tiles and trim that also decorated the Casa Monica, Flagler College, and numerous other downtown structures built in the Old City's familiar blend of Spanish Renaissance and Moorish architecture. Leo had no time to admire the carefully manicured hedgerows and multi-tiered, stone fountain in front of the building as they darted around tourists and headed for the museum's front entrance.

On the other side of the red-trimmed archways at the front of the building, the world became quiet and cool. An inner courtyard stood like a secret oasis, filled with lush, tropical plants; a koi pond; and a quaint stone bridge leading from one side of the cloistered area to the other. A few tourists posed for pictures, speaking in hushed voices. The arcade around the courtyard amplified the sound of the pond's gurgling fountain. Leo inhaled the cool, moist air and sighed with relief. Perhaps they could stay here for the rest of the day. After they ate lunch, of course.

"This way," Sid ordered. She darted left and then right, venturing around the covered arcade to the south side of the courtyard. She yanked open a glass door and motioned for Leo to enter the small shop tucked into the corner of the cloisters. Written across the glass windows in fussy script was the shop's name, Peace and Tranquili-tea.

Leo stepped inside and was immediately assailed by the

scents of vanilla, cinnamon, and sugar. His mouth watered as Sid tugged him toward the only empty table, a two-top in front of a window on the building's east wall facing Cordova Street. The owner, a woman with frizzy, brown hair loosely gathered in a ponytail at the base of her neck, took their order while the only other employee, a skinny, teenage girl with angry acne covering her cheeks, ran between tables with pots of tea and plates of sandwiches.

Even though they were short-staffed, they served Leo and Sid quickly, and in less than twenty minutes, Sid had returned to her usual level of ornery. Leo had been right. She'd needed food and caffeine. If he'd learned anything these last couple of months, it was how to read the signs of Sid's various moods. Today's grumpiness had been one part frustration and two parts low blood sugar and caffeine deprivation.

After finishing their sandwiches, she ordered two slices of cake and a second pot of tea. He ate all of his cake and half of hers. Leo sipped a cup of tea, which tasted a little like chocolate, and watched the traffic on Cordova Street while Sid made notes in her pink notebook. The door to the tea shop opened with a jingle of bells, and an older woman entered. She was short, with dark skin; even darker eyes; and a halo of closely cropped, gray curls. She wore a navy-blue cardigan draped over her shoulders and sensible, black walking shoes. Her face was familiar, but Leo couldn't place her. Upon seeing them sitting by the window, however, she broke into a wide grin.

"Sidney," the woman called out as she approached their table. "I thought that was you."

Sid looked up and smiled. "Virginia. This is a nice surprise." She stood and gave the woman a hug. "This is my intern, Leo. He's Burt Roberts's grandson." The woman smiled at him. "Leo, this is Virginia Davis. She's Detective Davis's mom."

Leo blinked in surprise. He'd never considered the fact that the hulking detective and one-time college football superstar actually had a mother, let alone one as diminutive as Virginia Davis. But now that she stood so close, it was easy to see the resemblance. They had the same high cheekbones, same wide mouth, and same dark eyes that seemed to take the measure of you without you needing to utter a word.

Leo stood to shake her hand, bumping the table with his thigh and jostling the teacups in the process. "Nice to meet you, ma'am."

"Oh, aren't you the handsome one?" Virginia cooed. She smelled like gardenias and patted his hand with her other one before releasing it.

"Join us?" Sid asked.

Virginia glanced at the empty plates on the table. "But it looks like you're already finished."

Sid waved the idea away. "We still have some more tea in the pot, and I'm willing to bet that Leo could eat a little something else."

"Can I order more?" His eyes lit up as he surveyed the display case of pastries and cakes.

"Sure, kid, go ahead." She pulled over a chair from a nearby table that had recently been vacated. "Virginia, what'll you have? My treat."

"I just came in for a cup of tea before my next tour."

Virginia sat down, and Sid piled up the used dishes to make room. After their order was placed, the two women made polite conversation, mostly about the antics of Virginia's adorable grandson, Dante. They also discussed her time as a volunteer museum docent, something she'd been doing for more than eight years.

Sid set her teacup down in its saucer. "Virginia, since you're a docent, I wonder if you know anything about a local artist who is supposed to have a painting or two on display here at the Lightner. Her name's Violet Rizzo?"

Virginia's smile fell from her face so quickly that both Sid and Leo froze at the sight.

"What's wrong?" Sid asked, reaching for the woman's hand. "Did I say something wrong?"

The older woman shook her head and dabbed at her eyes with a napkin. "No, no. It's just hard to hear that name. Guess it will be for a while yet."

"Did you know her?" Sid asked.

Virginia nodded. "She was one of my best friends." She dabbed at her eyes again before lowering the napkin to her lap and glancing back and forth between Sid and Leo. "What do you want to know about her?"

Chapter Seventeen

"How long were the two of you friends?" Sid asked, scooting forward in her chair and leaning in to make sure she didn't miss a word.

"Nearly ten years." She smoothed the damp napkin in her lap. "Isaac and I moved here after Tony graduated college. We thought this was a lovely little town to retire in"—she shook her head—"but Isaac died two years later. Heart attack. I told him not to eat so much fried food, but he never did listen to me." She shook her head again. "After he was gone, I needed something to fill my time, so I began volunteering everywhere I could. At church, at the library, at the elementary school. But then I saw a notice in the paper that the museum was looking for volunteers." Her face brightened into a smile, and she clasped her hands to her chest. "And I loved it! All that lovely art. And all that cool air-conditioning." She winked at Leo, and he grinned back. "I volunteered as often as they would have me. After a while, they made me a docent, and I've been doing it ever since."

She nodded to Sid. "That's where I met Violet. She'd been

volunteering there even longer than me. We became friends instantly. She's such a good artist. Since you asked, yes, one of her paintings is hanging in there." She hooked a thumb over her shoulder at the museum entrance, visible through the tea shop window. "I can show you, if you'd like. She knew so much about art. We'd talk about all the paintings and the sculptures, everything. She was a real help to me, 'cause I knew nothing about art when I started here." She chuckled to herself before growing quiet and staring at her lap.

"I'm very sorry for your loss, Virginia." Sid had been saying that phrase much too often these days, and every time she did, she was reminded of all the times people had said the exact same thing to her. It was a useless phrase, the only one people could think to give when nothing else seemed appropriate. She glanced over at Leo, who had finally finished his triple chocolate brownie, and nodded toward the door.

Reaching out to pat Virginia's arm, Sid asked, "Can you show us Violet's painting? We'd love to see it."

Virginia's smile returned, but its wattage was no longer very bright. "Of course."

Sid paid for lunch, and she and Leo followed Virginia into the Lightner Museum. Virginia waved them past the admissions window and ushered them up to the third floor, guiding them directly to Violet Rizzo's painting.

The canvas looked to be eighteen by twenty-four inches, an average size based on the stash in Violet's home studio, and it hung in an elaborate, gilded frame. The scene was a beautiful depiction of the Castillo de San Marcos in early morning, with the sun rising over Matanzas Bay, bathing the background in golden hues. In the foreground, the west side of the building and its expanse of lawn were swathed in shadow.

"It's the fort," Leo whispered. "That wasn't on your list."

Sid nodded once and frowned. She'd found only three

paintings of the old fort in Violet's studio—one extra-large canvas and two small ones, all of them scenes of the old fort under moonlight. There'd been no paintings of the fort in the daytime, let alone anything as glorious as this sunrise spectacle hanging on the wall of the Lightner.

"It's beautiful," Sid said, giving Virginia a broad smile. "I can see why the Lightner displays it."

"Isn't it?" The older woman stood with her arms hugging her midsection, staring up at the oil painting.

"Tell me," Sid began, returning her gaze to Violet's artwork, "was Violet a baseball fan?"

Leo began coughing and sputtering as if he'd swallowed wrong, and Sid reached out and slapped him hard on the back.

"I don't think so." Virginia shook her head. "Don't remember her ever mentioning it. Why?"

Sid shrugged. "Just wondering. Was she married?"

"No. She never married."

"What about Buddy's father?"

"Oh, well." Virginia sighed. "Poor boy. As I understood it, he never met his father. Violet once said it had been a short affair. The man died. She didn't even know she was pregnant at the time. And that was all she ever said about it."

"Did she have a boyfriend? Maybe an old flame that she kept in touch with?"

The older woman shook her head. "She never mentioned anyone, and I never asked. Violet was a very private person, and I knew enough not to pry into things like that. If she didn't want to talk about something, then she didn't talk about it. If someone brought up something she found unpleasant, she shut them down like that"—a snap of her fingers to illustrate the point—"and if she didn't bring up a topic herself, then it was to be considered off-limits." She nodded to the painting. "I think that's why she and I got along so well. We didn't pry into each other's business. I would have done anything I could to help her if she asked, and she felt the same. I know she did. But we weren't all up in each other's business."

Sid nodded. "Sounds like an ideal friendship."

"Yes, it was." Virginia sighed and checked her watch. "I have a tour starting in ten minutes. You're welcome to join me. Otherwise, I'm afraid I'll have to leave you on your own."

Sid smiled. "Thank you, but I think we'll stay with Violet's painting for a little while longer, if that's okay."

The older woman smiled up at the canvas in its thick frame. "Of course it is." She gave Sid a hug and Leo a pat on the cheek and then hurried off to meet her tour group.

Once she was out of sight, Sid handed Leo the faded blue ribbon. "See if you, well, *see* anything."

Leo sighed and took the ribbon. The image he saw was confusing. Rubbing the satin in his fingers, he stared at the scene playing out. "This wasn't supposed to be the painting."

"What?!" Sid glanced between Leo and the painting on the wall.

"No." He shook his head. "It was supposed to be a small one of the fort at night. She was wrapping it up, but then she tore the paper off and picked this one instead. This is the one she wrapped and carried out of the studio." He handed Sid the ribbon when the images in his head went dark.

"What does that mean?" Sid chewed her bottom lip, and the two of them stood staring at the painting for a long moment. "You said it was a small one. Was it the same scene, only at night? Or was it from a different angle?"

"Different." Leo nodded. "Like, if you were standing on that walkway along the bay and heading toward the fort, that's the scene. Fort on the left, bay on the right. Moon at the top."

Sid shoved the ribbon into her bag. "Okay, let's go."

Twenty minutes later, they were standing in Violet's art studio in the carriage house, and Leo was holding the painting.

"I just see her sitting on her stool and painting it." He shrugged and held the small canvas out for Sid to take it. "That's all, like I said." He pointed to the stool and easel. "She's sitting there painting it. She seems happy, if that helps."

"It doesn't." Sid sighed and turned the canvas over for the twentieth time, looking for any other marks or writing besides Violet's weird code. This one was marked with the Roman numeral III. The other two nighttime paintings of the fort, one small and one extra-large, were marked I and II, respectively. That meant the painting in the Lightner Museum should be IV. But what did that mean? Was IV a magic number for Violet? And why choose it over III, the one in her hand?

"I like the other one better," Leo said. "The one in the museum. In case we're voting."

Sid nodded. "Me too." She looked around, noting that the temperature had not changed since they'd arrived in the studio. "Is she here?"

Leo nodded. "Over there, in front of that door." His voice was barely a whisper. "Please don't make me talk to her."

Sid set the painting down in the spot where she'd found it and turned to face Leo. "Don't you want to know if you're right? You know, about who did you-know-what to her?" She raised an eyebrow. "After all, she's coming to dinner tomorrow at your house."

Leo's shoulders sagged. "All right." He shuffled over toward the door, stopping about ten feet away from the spirit, just far enough to feel the slight tingling of cold air that always surrounded the dead.

Violet Rizzo put a finger to her lips and smiled that same sly smile she'd given him on previous visits to the house.

Leo cleared his throat and removed his ball cap, running his hand through his sweaty curls. "Mrs. Rizzo," began Leo as he squeezed the cap in his hands, "I'd like to talk to you about something." He glanced over his shoulder at Sid, who nodded in return. Turning back, he said, "You didn't slip and fall down the stairs, did you?"

The spirit's eyes widened, and she lowered the finger from her lips.

"You were pushed, weren't—"

But before Leo could finish his question, Violet Rizzo vanished.

Chapter Eighteen

"And you're sure she said nothing to you?" Sid asked as they stood on the bayfront walk a short time later. Matanzas Bay glistened to their right; traffic rolled by on Avenida Menendez to their left; and ahead of them was the Castillo de San Marcos, looking just as it did in Violet's painting.

"For the millionth time, no! She said nothing." Leo blew out an exasperated breath. "And I'm not seeing anything but Violet taking photos. Just like at all the other sites you've dragged me to today."

"Oh, well, I'm so sorry that I ruined your perfectly good day of shopping at the outlet mall." Sid snatched back the ribbon. "Or dog-sitting Beelzebub."

"Jezebel," Leo snarled.

"Whatever."

"And I wasn't planning on doing either of those things."

Sid bit her tongue, forcing down questions she wanted to ask about why he and his mom weren't spending the day together doing something that he wanted to do. Instead, she shoved the ribbon into her bag and counted to ten. And then counted to ten again.

"Hello!"

Sid recognized the voice without needing to turn around.

"Fancy meeting you two here." Dan Murdock stood less than six feet away, an amused smile on his face. "Am I interrupting?"

"Nope." Sid shook her head. "Not at all."

Leo pursed his lips and shook his head.

"I see." He glanced between them, the smile on his lips clearly indicating that he didn't believe them. "I know it's a little early for dinner, but I'm famished." He turned to Leo. "Any chance you know where a man can get a good burger around here?"

Leo fought the urge to smile, and Sid recognized that look on his face. It was the same look he wore whenever Detective Davis or any of the Geezers addressed him directly—the look of pure joy at being treated like he was a grown man, not a little kid. Sid's heart squeezed with sorrow and guilt for this teenager who'd already lost his father and appeared to be losing his mother now, too. Although, truth be told, he sort of lost her when she abandoned him here and took off in that stupid, polka-dotted camper, but whatever. The point was this kid deserved better—from everyone.

"Yeah, there's a couple of places." Leo straightened his posture, which brought him to standing a bit taller than Dan's height, and nodded.

Dan smiled. "Your favorite one. My treat." He glanced over at Sid. "You're invited, too, of course."

Leo grinned. "Well, my favorite is the Red Lion. It's sort of a pub, but the burgers are awesome."

"Sounds perfect." He stood back and made a sweeping gesture with his arm. "After you, mate." Glancing at Sid again, he asked, "Care to join us?"

Sid bit her lip and nodded.

They sat on the porch of the Red Lion under the whirling overhead fans for nearly two hours, eating burgers and drinking beer and soda. Leo told Dan about moving to St. Augustine, living with Burt, and taking bass guitar lessons with Eli Williams. He also entertained Dan with tales of their two big cases—the one involving the county commissioner who was cheating on his wife, which ultimately led them to discover the sheriff's decades-long false identity, and the alligator-poaching case at the Oakmire Golf and Country Club that turned up two dead bodies. To Dan's credit, he was most amused by Leo's stories of the lost pet cases he'd worked by himself, and he asked the teen a ton of questions about one particularly elusive hedgehog that had Leo running all around the neighborhood for four whole days.

Much to Sid's relief, Leo left out all mention of spirits and ghosts and things that go bump in the night. She didn't know Dan well enough to know whether he was open to such things, nor did she want the boy to feel the sting of prejudice or ridicule. Not on her watch. Not when much of the kid's para-normal experiences had been the direct result of working with her. She watched Dan carefully, picking up no signs of a bullying nature, but she couldn't be too careful. She had no qualms about cutting the man down to size if he so much as looked at Leo the wrong way.

So far, Dan had done nothing to garner ill feelings from her. All she felt was goodwill toward him, the stirrings of friendship, and possibly the very smallest hint of attraction. It was that last one that made her nervous. She'd not felt anything like it since Wes, with whom the attraction had been instantaneous and overwhelming. This was different, albeit not unpleasant, but it was too soon, much too soon, to even think of moving on from Wes. After all, he'd only been dead for three years. Three? Had it really been that long?

It was nearly eight o'clock when Sid, Leo, and Dan arrived at the house after stopping for ice cream. Leo said his goodbyes with a fist bump for Dan and a cheeky grin for Sid and jogged into the house. Sid hoped Paizley was waiting for him inside, eager to ask him about his day, but she doubted it. Leo hadn't checked his phone once during their treasure hunt through the Old City or dinner with Dan, and that meant that Paizley hadn't texted him at all while she was out shopping. Sid gritted her teeth and turned to Dan.

"I'd like to see your office," he said quickly. "May I?"

"Um, sure." Sid's mind whirled, trying to remember in what state of disarray she'd left it. More importantly, what state was her apartment in upstairs? Not that she'd be inviting him upstairs, of course. She unlocked the door and stood back.

Dan Murdock's reaction was unlike that of anyone else who had ever stepped foot inside her office. He smiled as he ran his hands over his father's old desk and file cabinets. "Is this his chair?"

"It is." Sid couldn't help but smile.

He sat down and leaned back. "It still squeaks!" He rocked back and forth, the sound akin to someone dragging their fingernails down a chalkboard. Repeatedly. He laughed, and Sid laughed right along with him. He finally stopped rocking and stood up. "Dad could never get that stupid chair to stop squeaking. No matter how much WD-40 he sprayed on it." He spun the chair and let his fingertips glide over the back of it.

"Your office looks nicer than his." Dan looked around at the makeshift kitchenette, the mismatched guest chairs, and Trip's old artificial palm standing in the corner next to the file cabinets. "A lot less mess. And it smells much better, too."

Sid smiled at the compliment. Trip's office always had an odor to it—a mix of burnt coffee, faint body odor, stale cigarette smoke, and a hint of something else she'd never been able to identify. The memory tugged at her heart. "Thanks."

He picked up the open letter on the desk and began to read it.

"Sorry." Sid shot forward, scooping up the bundles of letters and dropping them into the storage bin next to the desk. Then she plucked the letter from Dan's hand. "This is for a case I'm working on."

"Someone was a big baseball fan, huh?" He wore a frown.

"Apparently." She folded the letter and returned it to its envelope. "Seems like a weird thing to include in a love letter, but what do I know?"

"It's definitely weird." Dan held out his hand. "Can I see that again?"

"I don't—"

"I just want to see the date on it. I won't look at the names. Promise."

Sid slid the letter out and read the date on the top. "May 11, 1986."

His frown deepened. "That really is weird."

"Why? Other than the obvious, of course, that baseball references don't belong in love letters." She shrugged. "Except maybe bases and home runs."

"Exactly. Why mention owners and managers and players?" Dan nodded and rubbed absent-mindedly at his chin, staring into the middle distance.

Sid thought he looked so much like his father as he did so. She could practically see the thoughts forming in his head, the connections being made, the same way she had with Trip.

"The writer mentions Billy Martin. He was the manager of the New York Yankees for the latter half of the 1970s. Took the team to a World Series title in 1977. He was fired in '79, came back in '83, was fired again, returned in '85, and was fired once more." Dan pointed to the letter. "Billy Martin wasn't managing the Yankees in 1986. In fact, he didn't return to the Yankees until 1988."

Sid's eyebrows shot up. "Someone's a baseball fan. Maybe you wrote these letters."

A slow grin crossed his face. "I wouldn't have wasted precious space in a love letter discussing baseball."

She dropped her gaze, her pulse now audible in her own ears, and put the letter back into the envelope. It took three attempts before the letter finally slid inside. "So it's weird, then."

He was still grinning at her when she looked up. "Very," he said. "I think it means something."

Undoubtedly, she thought. She was unsure of what to do with this new information, so she simply nodded and stared down at the letter and then over at the two storage bins filled with more like it.

Dan folded his arms. "I'd like to take a crack at it." He nodded to the storage bins. "May I?"

Sid blinked in surprise. "Take a crack at what?"

"At the code. I'd like to try to crack it."

"You think Billy Martin is code for something?"

"I do."

"Code for what?"

He shrugged. "I won't know until I crack it."

She frowned. "What if it's something . . . weird?"

His grin returned. "You mean something X-rated?"

Her pulse quickened. "I don't know."

"Me neither. Let's find out." He picked up one of the bundles of letters. "Worst case, I waste my time, and it's all for nothing. All we learn is that the author was a baseball fan. But" —he held up the letters—"there's a chance we might learn something." He waggled his eyebrows. "Maybe even something . . . how did you put it?" He paused, grinning wider. "Weird."

Chapter Nineteen

Sid and Dan began reading the letters, finishing six or seven each, before Dan announced that he would need to spread out, make some notes, possibly begin a spreadsheet. Sid rolled her eyes, thrust a nondisclosure agreement in front of him, and told him he could take the letters with him if he promised not to lose any. He signed the NDA without protest or mockery, and they stuffed the letters back into the bins.

They then spent another two hours in her office, splitting a bottle of wine and chatting. During their quick dinner the night before, they'd talked about Trip. Dan had told tales of fishing vacations with his dad in the Florida Keys, and Sid recounted funny stories of Trip's saintly patience with her as he taught her the tradecraft of a private investigator. They also talked about running, an interest they had in common, but they'd been careful to keep the conversation light and not venture into anything sad or overly personal. The dinner was pleasant enough that Dan had invited Sid to join him on a run this morning, which she'd enjoyed more than she thought she would.

Tonight, however, the training wheels were off, and the conversation turned more personal, more poignant. He told her about Trip's all too short battle with lung cancer brought on by years of smoking, and she told him about Trip's help in the years after Wes and Iris died. Dan's mother, Margaret, was still alive in Key West, grieving the loss of her husband but otherwise happily ensconced in her local bridge club, book club, and knitting circle. From Dan's description, it sounded more like three avenues for gossip rather than three organized hobbies, but she was happy that Margaret, whom Trip had always referred to as "my darling Maggie," was doing well.

Sid also learned Dan's story. She'd only ever half listened when Trip used to brag about his son. This evening, however, she found herself paying very close attention. He was divorced, after his two-year marriage ended acrimoniously nearly a decade ago, and he survived a "near miss," as he called it, with a woman he'd proposed to before learning she was a grifter living under a stolen identity. Trip had been the one to discover her scheme, and Dan had never been so grateful for his father's PI expertise. After that experience, he swore off women for a long time, and Sid was left wondering if he was still sticking to a monastic lifestyle.

Dan had worked for six years as a quant, short for quantitative analyst, in a Wall Street firm, the name of which she knew she'd never remember. He'd tried to explain financial modeling and forecasting to her, but she'd had to make him stop. Unlike him, she didn't have dual degrees in mathematics and statistics from an Ivy League school, nor a master's degree in financial engineering from Carnegie Mellon, and she was convinced that such an education was needed just to understand the job's description, let alone to actually perform it.

But the job, along with the long hours and insane lifestyle, had been slowly killing him, so he saved his year-end bonuses, paid off the majority of his student loans, and finally packed it in and moved to Key West, a place he'd loved ever since his father took him there at the age of five for his first experience with deep sea fishing. He got a job crewing for a fishing charter, scrimped and saved, and eventually took out a small loan to purchase a modest ten-year-old sportfishing yacht, with which he started his own charter business. All these years later, that one-man operation had grown to a fleet of four boats with a roster of six captains and eight crew.

Less than a week ago, he'd left the business in the capable hands of a long-time business partner and set sail to mourn the loss of his dad and figure out what his next move should be. He'd been feeling restless before his parents migrated to the Keys to be closer to him during their retirement years, and Trip's presence every day at work seemed like the fresh start he'd been hoping for. But Trip had died, and his grief unmoored him so much that his mother finally ordered him to take a vacation. Thus, plans had been made for a monthlong solo sail up the East Coast, which included a stop in St. Augustine in order to deliver to Sid the box containing Trip's old coffee mug and PI notebooks.

Sid listened intently, asked very few questions, and marveled at how much Dan reminded her of Trip. And yet he was so different from her old mentor: Dan was fit and healthy and ambitious, so unlike Trip's unhealthy habits of smoking and drinking and his complete disinterest in growing his business beyond a small, one-man firm that brought in just enough money to pay the mortgage.

For her part, she shared some of the details of her own tragedy. The information that was available in the public domain—the crash and the allegations of the sheriff's involvement—were things she could share, and Dan had heard bits and pieces of it from his parents. But the private parts, like Leo's mediumistic channeling of Wes's spirit, she could not.

Dan was the first person she'd ever discussed her grief with who didn't already know the whole story themselves. Everyone else she knew had been a spectator with a front-row seat to her tragedy, her subsequent breakdown, and her inability to pick herself up and function again as a normal, healthy human being. In fact, he looked at her now and saw a woman who was put together. Well, one who was at least showered and dressed in something other than grubby yoga pants and a stained T-shirt. He hadn't known her when she was at her absolute lowest. Nor did he know the Sidney Stone she'd been before that horrible night three years ago. He only knew the Sidney Stone who existed right now—a single woman, a private eye, a human being finally capable of caring for other people again, and someone who was just starting to dream for herself.

Sid sipped her wine and shared her stories, without tears and without regret. By the time Dan left her office carrying the two bins full of Violet's letters, she found herself looking forward to seeing him again. Unfortunately for Dan, their next meeting would be tomorrow night at dinner with Leo, the Geezers, Kitty Lonigan, Paizley and Brooklyn, and the suspected murderer of Violet Rizzo.

Chapter Twenty

Dinner was pretty much how Sid had expected it to be: awkward, chaotic, an experience she hoped she'd never have to repeat. The Geezers were doing their best to keep everyone entertained, but the stories of their musical heydays could only do so much. Paizley and Brooklyn had drunk too much too early and were clearly buzzed. Before dinner even started, Paizley managed to insult Kitty's potato salad recipe, which embarrassed Leo and put Kitty in the foulest, snippiest mood Sid had ever seen. Brooklyn began flirting mercilessly with Dan as soon as she learned he owned a sailboat and a fishing charter business in Key West. Dan remained fairly quiet, not contributing much, and politely but firmly rebuked Brooklyn's multiple advances. Joey Rizzo managed to ask the band members a few questions about songwriting and cover arrangements whenever there was a brief lull in conversation, which wasn't often, but after a while, she, too, gave up on trying to participate in the evening's circus.

Leo had spent much of the dinner staring at his plate or shoveling food into his mouth so he wouldn't have to engage in conversation. In fact, he looked like an ostrich trying desperately to find enough sand to hide his head in. Every once in a while, he shot a sideways glance at Joey, who sat next to him, but any questions she asked him were answered with no more than a couple of words, a few grunts, and some shrugging.

Sid did her best to stay out of the conversation entirely. Best not to open her mouth at all, she thought, as there was no telling what would come out. Likely it would be harsh and critical and aimed at Paizley, Brooklyn, or both. That would only serve to embarrass Leo further, which was something Sid wanted to avoid at all costs.

By the time dessert was over, the Geezers packed up their instruments and beat feet out of Burt's house in record time. Even Eli left early, canceling Leo's guitar lesson. Burt went immediately to the backyard to scrub the grill within an inch of its life. Kitty departed for her own house across the street, not bothering to take her serving bowls and cake stand with her.

And Dan took his leave as soon as he was able. Sid walked him out of the house and across the lawn to the sidewalk on Saragossa Street, leaving those who remained to either clean up or continue drinking.

"Well, that was interesting." Dan leaned against the jasmine-covered fence that skirted the sidewalk along the front edge of Burt's property.

"Sorry about that," Sid said as she plucked green leaves off the jasmine vines. "I knew it was going to be a disaster, but they managed to exceed even my expectations. And there's still something I need to do in there. For work." She grimaced and looked back at the house.

"Don't envy you having to go back in there."

Sid shrugged. "At least I'm not in danger of Brooklyn throwing herself at *me*."

"You saw that, did you?" He grinned and folded his arms.

"Only the first half a dozen times," she admitted. "After that I stopped paying attention."

"Thanks for coming to my rescue," he said sarcastically.

Sid smiled. "You looked like you were holding your own. She just wasn't getting the message."

He rubbed his hand across his cheek, scratching at the stubble. "I read those letters today, and I'm beginning to develop a theory about them."

"Oh?" Sid dropped the leaves she'd pulled from the vines and dusted off her hands. "Care to share?"

He shook his head. "Not yet. I still have some work to do. Give me a couple of days." He pushed off the fence and stood in front of her. Right in front of her. "I'll call you. Maybe we can discuss it over dinner." He glanced quickly at the house and smirked. "A quiet dinner. Just us. On the boat."

Sid nodded. "Sounds—"

Before she could finish her comment, he leaned in and kissed her cheek. Then he turned and walked away.

"Good," Sid whispered. "Sounds good."

———

Half an hour later, Sid and Leo escorted Joey Rizzo out to the porch. The girl had stuck around, like Sid asked her to, and had even helped Leo wash and dry dishes while Paizley packed up leftovers and Brooklyn sat in the living room nursing her umpteenth glass of wine. Sid thought that said a lot about Joey, willing to help out when asked, willing to endure uncomfortable situations for a chance to meet the Geezers and discuss music. She didn't seem like a bad kid at all. Polite, inquisitive, accommodating. She stood on the porch with them now, still smiling even after that shit show of an evening.

"Thank you so much for inviting me over and letting me

stay for dinner," Joey said, addressing Leo. "Please tell Burt that I had a great time tonight. He and the other Geezers didn't have to spend so much time with me, answering my questions, but they did. And it was awesome! I'm really grateful." Even at this late hour, her eyes were still sparkling, and she was bouncing on her toes.

Oh, what I wouldn't give for even a tenth of that energy, thought Sid. Youth was definitely wasted on the young. "Joey, I need to ask you a couple of questions about the night your grandmother died. I'm sure you've already answered a lot of these questions for the detectives."

Joey shook her head. "No one's asked me anything."

"Really?" Sid's eyebrows shot up. She was going to have to have a chat with Detective Davis about that. "We know that Penny found your grandmother when she arrived at the house for their usual Tuesday morning salon appointment. And we know your grandmother passed away the night before."

Joey wrapped her arms around herself in a self-soothing hug and nodded. "That's right."

"I need to ask where you were on Monday and Tuesday." Sid held up her hands. "Just routine. I need a clear picture of where everyone was when Violet fell."

Joey nodded again. "I understand. Um"—she glanced out at the street and kept talking—"I was at school both days. On Monday, I had class like normal, ate dinner in the dining hall, and studied in my room until I fell asleep around midnight."

"Was anyone with you?"

"My roommate, Jen."

"The whole time?"

"Yeah. She was studying for an exam, and I was working on a paper. We didn't talk much." Joey smirked. "We never talk much." She glanced over at Leo. "She and I don't get along very well. I mean, we don't fight or anything. We're just not . . . friends. You know what I mean?"

Leo nodded.

So did Sid. "And what about Tuesday?"

Joey's gaze dropped to her combat boots as she rocked back and forth. "I was in class when Dad started calling me, but I didn't pick up. I just switched off my phone so I wouldn't be interrupted." She squinted as if she was in pain. "And then I forgot to turn it on again. Penny came and found me in the dining hall during lunch. She was so mad at me. She yelled at me in front of everyone for ignoring Dad's calls. But I didn't know. I swear I didn't know what had happened. I would have picked up if I'd known." She shook her head, and tears spilled down her cheeks. "And Penny just announced right there in front of everyone that Grandma was dead and that I needed to come with her right then." She swiped at her tears and sniffled. "That's how I found out. Penny yelled it at me in the dining hall."

Sid reached out and rubbed the girl's arm. "I'm so sorry, Joey."

She sniffled again. "It's okay. I know now that she was just upset and stressed out. She'd been the one to find Grandma. She was just freaking out about it all. And Dad was a mess. He went with the police to take care of things; that's why Penny had to come get me." She shrugged. "It was just a bad time for everyone."

Sid exchanged a quick look with Leo. "How was your relationship with your grandmother?"

Joey began crying again. "She was my favorite person. I'm gonna miss her so much."

Sid waved at Leo to go back inside. He did and came back moments later with the box of tissues from the downstairs bathroom.

"Here you go," he mumbled as he held out the tissue box. Joey nodded and pulled a few tissues to wipe her eyes and nose. Leo stood there holding the box, looking like he'd rather be anywhere else.

"How about your mom and dad?" Sid asked. "Did they get along with your grandmother?"

Joey nodded. "Grandma could be a bit hard on Dad sometimes, but she loved him. As for Penny"—she shrugged—"I think Grandma liked her well enough. They weren't best friends or anything, but I think she appreciated Penny taking care of Dad after Mom died. So I think they got along okay."

Sid nodded. "No fights among any of them?"

"No, nothing like that. Not that I ever saw."

"How about anyone else? Did your grandmother have any arguments with anyone else? Was there anyone she didn't like?"

She shook her head again. "Not that I know of. Grandma didn't have many friends. Liked to keep to herself. Just painted and volunteered at the museum and went to Mass. We had lunch at her house every Sunday after church." She shrugged again. "That's about it. She led a pretty quiet life."

"Okay, Joey. Thanks a lot." She rubbed the girl's arm again. "And thanks for sticking around. I appreciate it. I'll be in touch when I have something for you."

Joey nodded to Sid, gave Leo a quick wave, and left them on the porch as she headed home.

"What do you think?" asked Leo as they stood side by side and watched her walk away.

Sid sighed. "I don't think she did it."

Leo shook his head. "Me neither. If I hadn't seen her in my visions, standing there at the top of the stairs when Violet fell, I would never, ever suspect her."

"I think her grief is genuine," Sid added, "and she seems to have really loved her grandmother. I don't think she'd push her down the stairs."

"But—"

"I don't know, kid." Sid crossed her arms. "I don't know what happened. You saw what you saw, and we both just heard what we heard. But neither of those things line up." She rubbed her eyes. "I don't know where we go from here."

"Maybe we should go back in the house," Leo suggested, his voice suddenly low and quiet.

Sid looked over at him. "Why? What's up?"

"The pirate's back," he muttered softly. "He's standing in front of Kitty's house, staring at us."

Sid let out an exasperated sigh. "Oh, for crying out loud."

"I'm going inside." Leo blanched and turned, lunging for the door. "He just pulled out his sword, and I don't want to stick around to see if he'll try to use it."

Chapter Twenty-One

On Monday morning, Sid stood in the doorway of Violet Rizzo's office in the carriage house and rubbed her eyes. She hadn't slept well, too much tossing and turning and replaying her conversation with Joey Rizzo. She'd had no epiphanies, no new ideas about how to proceed with finding Violet's killer, despite obsessing about it half the night. But Joey wasn't her only client, and right now she had a job to do for Buddy. She took another sip of coffee from her travel mug and decided to just get on with it, much as she was dreading the day.

Sid crossed to the desk and sat down in the buttery-soft leather chair. It rocked easily with no squeals of protest, unlike her own desk chair. She set her bag down on the floor next to her, ran her fingers over the desk's smooth surface, and glanced out the window at the bougainvillea blooms.

On the wall behind her was a large painting of a tidy, yellow house surrounded by a white picket fence. Its front yard was full to bursting with rosebushes, all of which bloomed in a riot of color. Roses spilled over the fence, climbed up the front porch, and filled in every square inch of the yard. In the lower corner of the canvas was a stylized mark that Sid recognized as Violet Rizzo's artist signature.

Sid smiled at the painting, recognizing the scene as the house of her neighbor, Kitty Lonigan. The scene on the canvas was so vivid that Sid could almost smell the heady perfume of the roses. She knew that scent well. It often wafted across Saragossa Street and found its way into her garage apartment. Violet Rizzo's brushstrokes had captured Kitty's house on its best day, when it looked like something out of a fairytale.

"Kitty would love that painting," she mumbled to herself, making a mental note to ask if Buddy would be willing to part with it.

Sid spun the chair slowly, admiring the dead woman's office. It made her own look exactly like what it was—a room put together with thrift-store furniture by someone who didn't really care what it looked like. Sid had decorated her office with minimal expense and even less effort and enthusiasm, but that was back when she was still strangled by the grief of losing her husband, Wes, and daughter, Iris. Things were different now, and she was beginning to think that an office makeover was in order, especially seeing the elegant, sophisticated state of Violet Rizzo's.

And that begged the question of why someone, who had been a stay-at-home mom and never held a paying job outside the home since moving to the Old City nearly fifty years ago, needed such a fancy home office, especially one with so much paperwork, as evidenced by the contents of the desk and all the file boxes stuffed into the bookcases. Buddy Rizzo had been unable to offer any reasonable explanation as to why the office was needed, and Sid wondered whether this was yet another mystery she might not be able to solve.

According to Buddy, he'd never been allowed in his mother's office, and he had no idea what she did in here. Even during the tour he had given her when she'd visited the house the first time, he had stood in the doorway of the office and refused to enter. He'd admitted that Violet had once taken a belt to his hide when he was six years old for the seemingly innocent offense of playing with his toy cars on the rug in the office. Buddy had never stepped foot in the room after that day.

A cold breeze brushed her arm, and Sid pulled out the sweatshirt she'd stuffed into her bag that morning. "Sorry, Mrs. Rizzo, but I have a job to do," she said aloud as she tugged the sweatshirt over her head. "You're dead now, so none of this stuff is of any use to you anymore. I'm sorry to be so harsh, but that's the truth." Sid opened one of the drawers of the desk and began pulling out the contents, studying each item as she did so.

Another cold breeze brushed against her cheek.

"I understand that you don't want anyone going through your things, but it has to be done. You left a lot of stuff behind, and I mean *a lot*. Look at this place!" She held her arms wide and spun slowly in the chair. "What did you think would happen when you died? What did you think would happen to all this stuff?" She shook her head and scooted the chair closer to the desk. "Someone has to go through it all, and your son is too bereaved to do it himself. Now, if you don't mind"—she swatted at another cold breeze whispering against the other side of her face—"I have a job to do, and that means I'm going to go over every square inch of this place. If you don't want to watch, I suggest you leave."

A blast of cold air hit her in the face.

Sid shot up from her chair and slammed her hands down on the desk. "Look! You don't scare me. You can buzz around here all you want, but I'm going to do the job I was hired to do." She leaned forward and narrowed her eyes, scanning the room for any signs of movement. "I know you have the ruby necklace.

I know you found a way to have it buried with you, so if you want to keep it buried, you better let me get on with my work. Got it?"

The room instantly warmed, and Sid's skin prickled at the sudden change in temperature.

"Thank you," she muttered as she slumped back down in the chair. Never in a million years would she have thought she'd be yelling at the spirits of dead people. Until a couple of months ago, she wasn't even sure she believed in ghosts and spirits. It was all nonsense, nothing more than paranormal hocus-pocus meant to scare tourists and fill the pages of novels. But here she was, telling off a dead woman for getting in the way of her doing her job as a private investigator.

Sid sighed at the realization that her world had completely turned upside down since her days as a wife, mother, and first-grade teacher, and while she'd give anything to go back to the life she had before, she had to admit that her life, as it was right now, wasn't half bad. It had a lot more supernatural elements in it than she would have liked, but it certainly wasn't dull.

Sid combed through every drawer in the desk, turning up nothing but pens, boxes of staples and paper clips, reams of printer paper, and numerous envelopes bulging with receipts. Apparently, Violet Rizzo kept every receipt she'd ever received from every grocery store, restaurant, clothing shop, and drugstore. Every single receipt. They were stacked neatly in manila envelopes, each one labeled for the last five calendar years. After shuffling through three years' worth of receipts, Sid gave up and closed the drawers of the desk.

The bookcases were next. The first box she opened contained more manila envelopes chock full of receipts. The next box contained more of the same. Violet had saved all of her receipts for the last forty-eight years. Sid made a note of each year in her log but didn't bother to catalog the individual receipts. She hadn't quoted Buddy Rizzo nearly enough for that amount of work, so if he wanted it done, he could damn well do it himself.

She flipped through every book in the office but found nothing. No notes, no hidden messages, not even a bookmark.

There were several boxes of photographs, most of which were old and faded. The black-and-white photos had yellowed; the color photos had faded; and some of them had stuck together, further damaging the images. Sid found one box labeled "Josephina," which contained dozens of photos of Joey Rizzo growing up. Another was labeled "Charles Albert," and it contained photos of Buddy in various stages of youth: a young father with a small girl on his knee; a college graduate in a cap and gown; a high school student in a tuxedo next to his prom date; a grade-schooler in his T-ball uniform; a kindergartener with a smile full of baby teeth. There were baby pictures, too. Some of them featured a stunning brunette that Sid recognized as a very young Violet Rizzo. What didn't feature in any of Buddy's photos was a man. It appeared that Buddy's father hadn't been around at all, not since the very beginning, if these photos were to be believed. Feeling a pang of sympathy for her new client, Sid put the photo boxes back on the shelf where she'd found them.

She pulled another file box from a shelf and placed it on the desk. As Sid opened the lid, her phone rang, causing her to nearly jump out of her skin. She hadn't realized how quiet the carriage house was until its silence was broken. She fumbled in her bag and answered the call.

"I'm done with school, and I'm coming over. Don't say no."

Sid smiled upon hearing Leo's voice. "I wasn't going to."

"Grandpa wants to know if you want roast beef or turkey."

"Turkey, please." She heard Leo cover the phone and shout

to his grandfather to relay Sid's sandwich preference, and then the line went dead. Sid shook her head and typed out a text:

> When you get here, come around back to the carriage house. I'm upstairs in the office.

Teenagers. She would have to teach that boy some phone etiquette if he was going to continue working for her. With that thought, her heart skipped a beat. If Paizley stayed in St. Augustine, would she and Leo continue living with Burt, or would they find their own place? Would Paizley let Leo keep working with her? Did she know that Leo used his mediumistic talents to help her with her cases? If she did, would she approve?

Sid shook herself, trying to vanquish her mounting anxiety, and turned her attention back to the file box in front of her. Inside was an assortment of report cards, book reports, test papers marked with A's and A+'s, and various other bits and pieces of Buddy Rizzo's academic career, from his earliest years through to his university days. The remaining file boxes on the bookshelves, save for one reserved for Joey, held similar contents. Violet Rizzo had saved every art project, every home-made card, every scrap of paper that documented her son's childhood. She smiled at the assortment of math papers; finger-paint masterpieces; and notes from his teachers informing Violet that her son was an excellent student, a hard worker, and a joy to have in the classroom. Joey's file box contained similar items, just fewer of them. Once again, Sid logged the boxes with a general note regarding their contents but didn't itemize each and every item. None of them contained any jewelry, and she wasn't about to spend her time writing out descriptions of graded homework pages and wonky, hand-painted pottery.

Sid replaced the last file box on its shelf and surveyed the room. This was an office filled with Violet Rizzo's family photos, keepsakes, and memories. She was a proud mother and grandmother, that much was evident. No one kept decades' worth of coloring pages, homework papers, and hand-drawn Mother's Day cards if they didn't love and cherish their children and grandchildren.

Standing with her hands on her hips, she spun around slowly, taking in the elegantly furnished office. Violet Rizzo was a pack rat to be sure, but nothing she'd seen so far pointed to a stash of hidden jewelry. Nor did any of it seem so secret or precious that it warranted beating your kid with a belt simply because he'd snuck in here to play with his toys.

So, what was she missing?

Chapter Twenty-Two

S id was still contemplating Violet Rizzo's seemingly innocuous home office when she heard the knock on the front door of the carriage house. Picking up her bag, she shut off the lights and headed downstairs to meet Leo.

"You locked me out again." He stood with his arms folded, the cooler bag dangling from one hand.

Sid smirked. "It's a rough neighborhood, kid. Can't be too careful."

He rolled his eyes and held out the cooler. She took it and led him over to the little café table. It was half past two in the afternoon, and Sid had been working for a solid six hours with nothing to show for it. As they ate their sandwiches, Sid tried to engage Leo in conversation, but he was not in the mood. In fact, she hadn't seen him this melancholy in weeks.

"How was school today?"

A roll of the eyes.

"What are your mom and Brooklyn up to today?"

"They went to Cape Canaveral."

"And you didn't want to go with them?"

A shrug.

So that wasn't a no. He probably had wanted to go but wasn't invited. Sid ground her teeth to avoid saying something she'd regret; any criticism of Paizley would likely upset Leo.

"Well, that's a long drive," she offered. The camper had been in the drive when she'd left her office this morning, so they were only gone for the day. "Two hours down, two hours back. And that's if you don't get stuck on I-95 because of an accident or construction or whatever."

Another shrug.

"Did they take Zsa Zsa?" When Leo frowned in confusion, she added, "The dog?"

"Jezebel," he growled. "I'm supposed to watch her, but Grandpa said she'd be okay for a few hours by herself."

He shoved the last bite of his sandwich into his mouth, and Sid took that as her cue to cease her line of questioning. For the next few minutes, they sat in silence. She stared up at the carriage house, watching a tiny Carolina wren dart in and out of the bougainvillea that climbed up the walls and framed the windows of Violet's office.

"She's up there now, you know." He balled up his empty sandwich wrapper and tossed it back in the cooler. "She's watching us from the window."

"Which one?" Sid asked.

Leo snuck a quick glance, careful to look away before Violet locked eyes with him. "Second from the right. She's pacing back and forth, but she keeps stopping at that one to look down at us. Then she begins pacing again."

Sid studied the windows. The second one from the right was the middle window in the office. The dead woman was probably upset that her possessions had been disturbed but pleased that Sid had finally vacated the room. "Is she still wearing the ruby necklace?"

"Yep."

"Hmm," Sid muttered. "Not sure what we're going to do about that."

Leo shrugged and opened a snack pack of chocolate chip cookies. "Dig her up, I guess. Bet she's not gonna like it."

"Let's hope it doesn't come to that." Sid shivered at the thought. "But if we can't find any trace of it, I'll have to mention to Buddy that it might be buried with her." She bit her bottom lip. "I just have no idea how I'm going to explain my reason for thinking that. It's not like I can tell him his mother's spirit is parading around the house in her finest jewels."

Leo snorted, and Sid smiled as she stared up at the windows of the carriage house. She looked for movement in the three main windows of Violet's office, the ones that faced the courtyard, and the single window on the side of the building. Frowning, she stood up and walked away from the table toward the side of the carriage house.

The building was only one room deep, with no windows along its back side. Violet's office occupied one-third of the second floor; her art studio and kitchenette made up the other two-thirds. Sid studied the line of windows on the second floor, noting the space between each window as well as the distance between the windows on each end and the corners of the building.

"I'm going back inside," she said to Leo, crossing the courtyard and stuffing the remnants of her lunch back in the cooler. "I need to check something." She picked up her bag and headed for the carriage house door. Leo grabbed the cooler and followed, popping the last cookie into his mouth.

Back inside the art studio, Sid glanced around the space. There were six windows that faced the courtyard and one on the side of the building over the sink in the kitchenette. It was exactly what she expected to find. Marching across the studio to the office, she dropped her bag at the door and took two steps into the room. Three windows faced the courtyard, but there was no window on the side of the building. The side wall was solid, with four freestanding bookcases positioned in front of it.

"Huh?" Sid folded her arms.

"Um, Sid," whispered Leo as he came up behind her and stood in the doorway. "I don't know if you want to hear this, but Violet Rizzo is standing in front of the bookcases, glaring at you."

"Is she now?" Sid smiled. "That's very interesting." Sid marched across the room and began removing items from the shelves, placing knickknacks on the desk and boxes on the floor. She could feel the temperature drop as she worked. "Give me a hand, Leo."

"Do I have to?" He remained in the doorway, standing exactly where Buddy Rizzo had stood when he'd given her the tour of the property.

"She's angry, isn't she?" Sid asked.

Leo nodded. "Very." Nevertheless, he stepped into the room and slowly made his way over to Sid. "What are you doing?" he hissed.

"I have a hunch," she whispered back. "Now, help me move this bookcase out of the way." Leo sighed and did as he was told. Emptied of its contents, the bookcase was just light enough for the two of them to wrangle it. After they'd moved all four bookcases out of the office and into the art studio, they stood in front of the empty wall. There was no window; there were no electrical outlets; nothing. Sid ran her hands over the smooth surface, then knocked on it in various places. "Just as I thought."

She pulled her phone from her bag and made two phone calls. The first was to Buddy Rizzo, and the second was to Burt Roberts.

Chapter Twenty-Three

While they waited, Sid sat in the desk chair and reviewed the pages and pages of itemized lists she'd made thus far, and Leo strolled around the studio, examining the paintings. When he grew bored, he returned to the office doorway, leaning against the frame with his legs crossed at the ankles. "She really liked to paint the streets of St. Augustine, didn't she? She must have a hundred canvases in there, and all of them are of places downtown."

"Ninety-two, to be exact." She spun around in the chair. "This one's my favorite, though. She reached up and ran her fingertips along the bottom of the frame on the wall behind her. "It's Kitty's house. Do you recognize it?"

As if on cue, Violet Rizzo's spirit flew across the room at Sid. The spirit then flew at Leo, and he felt the sting of the cold breeze as Violet passed right through him. He felt it a second time as she passed back through him again, returning to Sid. Then he watched the spirit try to beat his boss with her fists.

"Don't touch that!" he cried. "She doesn't like that."

Both women turned to look at him.

"Oh?" asked Sid.

"*No!*"

It was a high-pitched scream in his head.

Leo winced, his hands flying reflexively to his ball cap. He uttered the words Mad Hattie had taught him, ordering Violet Rizzo not to talk to him and to stay away from him. The spirit of the dead woman conceded and turned her attention away from him and back to Sid, trying again to slap his boss with her invisible hands.

Leo sighed with relief. "Just don't touch it, okay?"

Sid held up her hands in surrender. "Fine. I won't touch the painting. Sorry."

Violet Rizzo stopped her assault and took up her position, standing guard in front of the blank wall.

"You okay, kid?" Sid whispered.

"Yeah," he whispered back. "She was screaming."

Sid's brow furrowed. "Wanna ask her about it, why she doesn't want me to touch it?" She tilted her head toward the painting.

"Not really, no. I had to tell her not to talk to me just so she'd stop screaming." He shook his head. "And I really don't want her to start screaming again."

Sid smiled at him. "Okay, kid. I understand. We'll wait until she's not so agitated." Lowering her voice even more, she added, "Because, if she was angry before, she's about to get royally pissed off."

"Great." Leo sighed heavily.

"And we'll try to keep her anger focused on me, not you," Sid suggested. "Violet Rizzo can be mad at me all she wants, but she's dead. What's the worst that can happen? She tries to freeze me out of here?" Sid shrugged. "It's not like she can push me down the stairs or anything."

He watched Violet drift a little closer toward Sid, her head tilted to one side and a frown deepening the lines on her face. Leo's pulse quickened as he muttered, "I wouldn't be too sure."

Half an hour later, Leo met his grandfather in Violet Rizzo's driveway and escorted him into the carriage house. They found Sid in the office, seated in the desk chair and staring at the blank wall.

Burt stood in the doorway, toolbox in hand, and asked, "Are you sure about this?"

"Yep," she replied. "The owner's son, who's the executor of her estate, gave me permission, as long as we promise to clean up the mess."

"All right." Burt shrugged and then instructed Leo to help him move some boxes and other items and lay out the tarps.

Once everything was ready, and both Sid and Leo were standing back at a safe distance, Burt rapped his knuckles on the wall a few times, donned his goggles and gloves, and then swung his sledgehammer. A hole opened in the wall, and Burt ripped a piece of the drywall away with his hands. Sid joined him at the wall and shined her phone's flashlight into the hole.

"Nice job, Burt." She patted him on the arm. "Keep going."

Burt made quick work of the demolition, leaving a pile of rubble on the tarp at his feet and a meager wooden frame where the wall had once been. Behind the frame were dozens of file boxes, stacked tightly together from floor to ceiling, each of them marked with a series of dates and initials. The most recent date was nearly fifty years ago, the oldest more than a hundred. The room now smelled stale, like musty cardboard and aged paper, and drywall dust continued to swirl in the air, lit by the late afternoon sunshine.

Leo stood next to the two adults as they surveyed the stash of boxes. "What is all this?"

"That's what we're going to find out," answered Sid. "Right after we clean up this mess."

It took more than an hour to tidy up the office, bag the debris, and haul the garbage bags downstairs to Burt's truck. Before departing, Burt gave Leo strict instructions to head home so he could walk and feed the dog. Leo reluctantly agreed and slumped back to the office to tell Sid he had to leave.

"Is she still here?" Sid asked when Leo shuffled into the room. She knew the answer already but wanted to check to be sure.

Leo nodded. "She is, and she is not happy."

Sid began clearing the desk in order to make room to work. "What's she doing?"

"Crying, I think."

Leo tried to gauge the old woman's demeanor, but she had her back to them. She was leaning on the boxes, and her shoulders were shaking. Even though Leo didn't hear a voice or any other sounds coming from her, he felt her sadness. It rolled off her, buffeting him like waves on a beach.

Sid stopped working and looked up at him. He shrugged, not knowing what to do. Sid motioned for him to follow and led him back into the art studio. It was almost six o'clock. "You should head home."

Leo nodded. "Yeah, Grandpa said I have to go take care of the dog."

Sid smiled and patted him on the shoulder. "Better go do it then. Maybe you can help me tomorrow." He nodded and walked away, looking sadder than she'd seem him look since he first arrived in the Old City a couple of months ago. She wanted to call him back, to tell him it was okay to stay and help, but she wasn't his mother. So she let him go and turned back to the office to face the icy-cold wrath of Violet Rizzo.

She stayed at the dead woman's house for another eight hours. She pulled box after box from the secret stash behind the wall, starting with the box with the most recent date. In between sneezing fits brought on by the swirling dust motes, she conducted a slow and methodical review of the contents. It made for some interesting reading.

Just after three o'clock in the morning, Sid walked home, enjoying the quiet neighborhood streets and the ever-so-slight decrease in temperature and humidity. When she finally reached Burt's house, she entered her office, dumped her bag on the desk, and climbed the metal staircase that spiraled up to her tiny studio apartment on the second floor. She was asleep as soon as her head hit the pillow.

———

Sid was standing over the coffee maker, inhaling the aroma and willing the machine to work faster to brew its liquid magic, when her phone buzzed.

Finished school early

Can I come help?

Too tired to type a response, Sid hit the call button.

Leo picked up on the first ring and didn't bother with a greeting. "Don't say no. I really am done with school. I started early 'cause Grandpa was up at the crack of dawn for his work at the restaurant."

Sid smiled. "And you would rather sort through an old lady's things than help Burt with a remodel job?"

"Definitely," Leo blurted. "He told me that he's doing trim work today. That means he'll be busy, but I would just be standing there, handing him tools and nails and stuff all day. He doesn't let me help much when he's doing trim. Demolition is okay. So is painting. Even putting up drywall isn't so bad. But when he's framing or doing trim—basically all the fun carpentry stuff—he won't let me help with any of it." He paused. "Oh, and I hate laying tile. That sucks, too."

"Certainly sounds like it." Sid yawned and poured herself a cup of coffee, no longer waiting for the pot to finish brewing. Coffee splashed onto the hot plate with an angry sizzle before she could replace the pot, and the smell of burnt coffee now filled the air. She added a splash of cream and lots of sugar to her cup. She was going to need copious amounts of caffeine and sugar to get through the day, she just knew it. "And you're not hanging out with your mom today?"

"No, she has to work." Sid paused mid-yawn, unsure whether she'd heard him right, but he continued. "She's writing blog posts and editing videos and posting stuff. She and Brooklyn are gonna be busy all day."

Sid finished her yawn before asking, "And Eliza Doolittle?"

"You mean Jezebel?" She could practically hear his eyes roll through the phone connection and couldn't help but smile.

"Sure, kid. Whatever."

"Mom said I don't have to watch her today. Brooklyn wanted me to, but Mom said it was okay for me not to."

Sid had a couple of choice words to describe Brooklyn at that moment, but none were appropriate for the kid's ears. She was happy to hear Paizley had stepped up, though. Finally. "Well, as luck would have it, I'm still at home. Give me ten minutes, and we'll head over to Violet's house together."

"Got it."

"Oh, and Leo?"

"Yeah?"

"Make us a couple of sandwiches and toss in whatever else you might want to eat. It's going to be a long day, and we won't have time to stop and go out for lunch." She heard him grumble his assent before hanging up. Sid downed her cup of coffee and a bowl of cereal and poured the rest of the pot into two large travel mugs.

Leo was waiting for her in the driveway when she finally emerged from her office. "Is one of those for me? 'Cause you know I don't drink coffee, don't you?"

"No." She looked down at the two mugs in her hands and shook her head before realizing he was teasing her. She lifted a finger to point at him and raised her eyebrows. "Are other people joining us for lunch?"

"No." His lips curved up in a smile. He was holding the insulated cooler bag in one hand and a plastic shopping bag filled with an entire bag of potato chips and a family-size pack of sandwich cookies in the other. "You look like crap, by the way."

Sid smirked. "Good morning to you, too."

"How late did you stay?"

"Got home at three."

Leo whistled. "Find anything good?"

"If by *good* you mean jewelry, the answer is both yes and no." Sid stifled a yawn. "I also learned a lot about Violet Rizzo."

"Like what?" Leo fell into step beside his boss as they made their way through the neighborhood to Violet's house on Valencia Street.

Sid took a sip of coffee. "Well," she began, "I went through the file boxes."

"All of them?"

"Unfortunately, no." She rolled her shoulders. "I made it

through about half of them and then took a quick glance through some of the others."

Leo shook his head. "No wonder you didn't get home until three."

"Yeah, well, the last file Violet added to her stash before sealing it away behind that fake wall predated her move to St. Augustine almost fifty years ago." Sid yawned again.

She'd been surprised to learn (1) that none of the files in any of the boxes were dated after Violet's southern migration to the Old City and (2) that they contained nothing but order forms, sketches, invoices, receipts, and bookkeeping ledgers. "Those boxes contained a paper trail of business transactions going back more than a hundred years. And even though I haven't looked through all of it yet, I think I've got a pretty good picture of Violet's life before she moved here."

"Um, Sid?" Leo reached up to tug at the brim of his ball cap.

"Is your friend back?" Sid asked.

"Yep," answered Leo. "And he's definitely not my friend. He just started following us. Not sure where he came from."

"Maybe he's been lying in wait."

"Please don't say stuff like that." Leo visibly shivered and snuck a peek over his shoulder. "Crap, he's close. Definitely closer than he's ever been before."

She shrugged. "Maybe he wants to parley."

"What does that mean?"

"Negotiate a truce." When he stared back at her like she had seven heads, she chuckled. "Never mind. As long as he keeps his distance, there shouldn't be anything to worry about."

Sid wished she believed her own words. A sword- and pistol-carrying pirate stalking them through the streets of the Old City was enough to make anyone nervous. The fact that he was dead should have brought her comfort, but she couldn't help worrying for Leo. She saw what the ghosts had done to him at the Oakmire Golf and Country Club. Their invisible golf clubs had left very real bruises on his back and arms. What would a pirate's sword do? Or his pistol? She shuddered at the idea.

They arrived at their destination and went straight through the courtyard to the carriage house and up to Violet's office. "Did he follow us in?"

Leo shook his head as he looked around.

"And Violet?"

"Don't see her."

"Good." Sid placed her travel mugs on the desk and pulled the pink notebook from her bag. "I made a timeline," she explained. "There was so much paperwork in those boxes—and I did some research online as I went along last night—that I was making myself crazy, so I drew up a timeline to try to understand how everything fits together. There are some major unanswered questions, but I've got a pretty good idea of what Violet was doing before she moved here forty-eight years ago."

Leo leaned against the doorframe, arms crossed over his chest and legs crossed at the ankles. "Okay, so what's . . ." His question died on his lips as he tugged again on the brim of his cap. Lowering his voice to a whisper, he said, "She just joined us. Over by the boxes." He shook his head. "She's pacing back and forth."

Sid sat in the desk chair and resisted the urge to turn and stare. "Good to know. Thanks."

She flipped through her notebook, found the relevant pages, and began to tell Leo the story of Violet Rizzo's early life. "She used to be a jeweler in New York City. So were her father and her grandfather. The grandfather's name was Luigi Rizzo, but he changed it—or had it changed for him—to Louis when he immigrated to the United States from Italy. It seems he found a job with a jeweler doing repair work. I found a notebook of his in which he kept details of everything he worked on, how much he was paid, and some sketches of his own designs. Within a few years, he struck out on his own and adopted Americanized names for both him and his business. He became Louis Risso—using *s*'s instead of *z*'s—and he opened a small shop on the edge of the Diamond District in Midtown Manhattan that he called Risso & Co."

"What's a Diamond District?" Leo asked as he continued to watch Violet Rizzo's spirit pace back and forth at the far end of the room.

"Apparently it's a place where people buy and sell diamonds and jewels and whatnot."

"Have you ever been?"

Sid smirked. "Yeah, I go all the time. I just decided to leave my tiara at home today."

Leo snorted a laugh and shook his head. "Why did I even bother to ask?"

"As I was saying," she continued, "it looks likes Louis's business grew modestly over the years. Eventually, Louis's son, Giuseppe, who went by the name Joseph, was made a partner in the business. Louis and Joseph ran the shop together for fifteen years. Then, Louis died, and Joseph ran it by himself."

She flipped a page in her notebook and continued. "At that point, the business really took off. Sales shot through the roof, and so did the value of the pieces Joseph was selling. But, curiously, Joseph remained the sole jeweler, designing and creating everything himself. There are no records of anyone else—no partners, no staff, no one—at least none that I could find so far. That is, until Violet came along.

"I found jewelry sketches made by Violet in the files. Based on their dates, she began designing jewelry when she was just a child. Her designs, even her early ones, are these really intricate creations drawn in colored pencils, and all of them were marked with the same artist signature that is on those canvases stacked up in her studio out there."

Leo had watched Violet slow her pacing and begin to pay closer attention to Sid's story. Now, the dead woman's spirit was standing only a few feet from Sid. Leo cleared his throat and said, "Sounds like she was always an artist."

"It appears that way," Sid replied, pulling a sweatshirt from her bag. When she shot Leo a look, he gave a quick nod in return. "Anyway, when Violet turned twenty, her dad made her a partner in Risso & Co. Business was good, remained steady, and Joseph and Violet continued on like that for eighteen years. But then Joseph died, and Violet was left to carry on the business alone."

Sid looked up from her notes. "And here's where it gets weird. Less than three months later, Violet closed the shop. Practically overnight, she cancelled orders, broke her lease on the building, and sold her entire inventory in a single lot. That was the end of Risso & Co." She slumped down in the chair. "All that happened right before Violet Risso packed up and moved to Florida. She began using the original family name of Rizzo with the z's and purchased this house. Three months after she moved here, Buddy was born.

"Everything else for the past forty-eight years, all other documents, files, and paperwork in the rest of these boxes"— she waved her arms around, gesturing to everything that had been stored in the office in plain sight—"is nothing but school photos and report cards and finger-paint masterpieces from her son and her granddaughter. There is no evidence that Violet ever worked again as a jeweler."

She leaned forward, resting her elbows on the desk. "And there is absolutely no mention anywhere of where she might have hidden her own jewels. From what I can tell, she sold the inventory in her shop before moving down here. The only mention of any personal pieces that I was able to find were some wedding rings and a few other modest pieces that both Louis and Joseph must have made for their wives. I didn't find any mention of Violet designing or making things for herself."

Violet Rizzo ran her fingers over the elaborate necklace fastened around her throat.

Leo frowned. "But what about the ruby necklace? It's definitely real, and it's definitely, uh . . . somewhere."

Sid held up her index finger. "Funny you should ask about that. I found a file with drawings, receipts, and valuations for several ruby and diamond necklaces, but this one caught my eye." One of Violet's old files lay on the desk, and Sid slid it toward her, opened it, and spun it around for Leo to see.

"That's it!" Leo exclaimed, crossing to the desk. He glanced quickly from the photograph and sketches in the file to Violet Rizzo's spirit and back again. "That's the necklace she's—I mean, that's the one that's missing."

Sid nodded. "I thought maybe it was." She shuffled the papers in the file until she found what she was looking for. "This is the appraisal of the necklace that was done at the time, which was nearly sixty years ago now." She pointed to a line on the paper. "It was valued at just over $98,000."

His eyes widened. "What's it worth now?"

She shrugged. "More. Probably a lot more. Which explains why Buddy's wife is so desperate to find it." Leo nodded as Sid pulled another piece of paper from the file. "What's interesting is that the necklace was sold to someone in New York almost sixty years ago, right after the appraisal was done. See the date on this receipt?" She tapped the page. "So that begs the question: What is Violet Rizzo doing with the necklace if she sold it to a customer all those years ago?"

He shook his head. "I don't know. Maybe she bought it back? Or maybe someone gave it to her?"

"Maybe," Sid responded. "I haven't made it through all the boxes yet. As for the ones I have been through, I found some things that don't make sense. Discrepancies, I guess you'd call them, some of them going all the way back to when Violet's father, Joseph, ran the business all by himself."

Leo pushed aside the appraisal and receipt in order to have another look at the photo of the necklace. "What kind of discrepancies?"

"Just . . . things that don't make sense. I've got some work to do still to figure it all out." She swiveled back and forth in the chair, staring at the open file on the desk in front of her.

Violet Rizzo now hovered next to Sid, her fingers still resting on the necklace.

Sid rubbed her arms. Even wearing the sweatshirt, she was feeling the further drop in temperature. "So, why did Violet Rizzo have a necklace that she made and sold to a customer nearly sixty years ago? And why bury it rather than give it to her son or her daughter-in-law or even her granddaughter?"

Sid glanced up at Leo, who shrugged in return. She tapped the folder in front of her. "And what the hell happened to make Violet close down a thriving jewelry business in New York City, practically overnight, and then all but disappear to St. Augustine, Florida, of all places?"

Chapter Twenty-Four

With Leo's help, the work went faster. Not twice as fast, as Sid had hoped, because the kid spent a lot of time asking questions about what he was reading, but it was still faster than if she had searched the rest of the boxes alone. They walked home together around six o'clock, still no closer to knowing where Violet had hidden her jewels. If Sid didn't find something by the end of Friday, she was going to have to suggest that Buddy exhume his mother's body.

As they turned onto Saragossa Street, her phone rang, and she smiled at the caller ID. "I was beginning to think you were avoiding me," Sid said by way of greeting.

"Not avoiding you, no. Just wanted to get my ducks in a row before I called you." Sid could hear the sound of street traffic through the phone as Dan Murdock spoke. "Any chance you're still free for dinner tonight?"

Why the hell not, thought Sid. "Sure. What time?"

"How about now?"

After Sid hung up, she said goodbye to Leo and went to her apartment to shower and change before heading out again. Thirty minutes later, she found Dan sitting on his boat, sipping a glass of wine.

"I thought we could order from that place across the street," he said as he extended his hand to help her on board. "Is it any good?"

"I thought you were cooking?"

He laughed. "Trust me, you don't want that." He poured a second glass of wine and handed it to her.

"Yeah, the food's pretty good there. As long as you like seafood." Sid took the offered glass. "I don't think they offer much else."

"That's fine with me." Dan nodded. "But before we order, I have something to show you. Come with me." He turned and headed below deck.

Sid remained frozen where she stood, holding her wineglass and listening to her elevated pulse ringing in her ears. Why did they have to go below deck?

After several awkward moments, Dan climbed back up into the companionway. "Coming?" When she didn't answer, he gave her a sad smile. "I just want to show you what I found in the letters, Sid. That's all." He put a hand over his heart. "I promise, I'll be a perfect gentleman."

She nodded, feeling her face heat with embarrassment, and slowly descended the ladder into the cabin. Then she immediately burst out laughing. "I think you may have a serious problem."

"I'm an addict. I freely admit it." He nodded as his gaze swept over the room, and his sad smile turned into a bright grin. "I have a weakness for charts and graphs."

Spread across the galley table, taped to the galley cabinets and stateroom doors, and covering all of the windows were poster-size pieces of paper torn from the easel chart propped up on the navigation table.

"And office supplies." Sid flipped the little pages of a pad of neon orange sticky notes, which sat on top of a pile of a dozen similar pads of various colors. Next to that stack were piles of indexing flags, sorted by color, and eight different plastic cups holding pens—black, blue, and red—and highlighter markers— pink, yellow, green, blue, and orange. "You should probably seek professional help."

He laughed. "I've had years of therapy. Nothing's helped so far." He guided her to the bench seat at the galley table and then stood in front of her rubbing, his hands together. "I cracked it. The code in the love letters. I cracked it."

"The baseball code?" Sid leaned back against the soft, cushioned bench and smiled. "Okay, Murdock. Let's hear it."

His eyes lit up as she said his name, and Sid felt her heart stutter for a split second.

He launched into his presentation as if he were teaching a class in advanced calculus. Within the first five minutes, she had to ask him to repeat himself not less than three times. Immediately after that, she begged him to slow down and speak to her as if she knew absolutely nothing about baseball. Which, to be honest, she didn't.

Ten minutes later, he finally paused and slid onto the bench across from her. "What do you think?"

"I'm not sure." She pinched the bridge of her nose and sighed. The look he was giving her both warmed her heart and broke it in two. He was so excited about all of his hard work, so eager to share it with her, that she didn't want to hurt his feelings. "I . . . um . . . I'm not sure."

"Want to hear it again?"

"No!" The word came out louder than she'd meant it to, and he frowned. "I'm still processing."

She leaned forward and picked up one of Violet's love letters, which was open on the table. Dan had paperclipped it to its corresponding envelope, affixed it with several index flags along the right margin, placed four sticky notes on the back of it, and stacked it on top of a pile of other letters that were organized chronologically. All of the letters were similarly decorated with colorful flags and notes.

Sid put the letter back down on the table. "If I understand you correctly, you believe that in all of these letters"—she swirled her hands over the table—"Violet and her lover were not actually talking about baseball at all."

"Or love," Dan added.

Sid nodded. "Or love." Her gaze slid around the room, taking in all of the work Dan had done over the last couple of days. "You think they were actually talking about the New York *Mafia*."

"Yes." He nodded, the smile returning to his face.

"And why do you think the two of them exchanged letters back and forth for more than forty years discussing the Mob?"

"I haven't worked that part out yet." He rubbed the stubble on his chin.

"Okay," Sid said softly.

"I mentioned on Saturday night that I thought it was weird that a letter from 1986 contained a reference to Billy Martin because he wasn't with the Yankees organization that year." When she nodded, he continued. "Well, after reading all of the letters, I'm convinced that Violet and her boyfriend were talking about the Mob."

He stood up and moved toward a door to what Sid suspected was the captain's stateroom, where Dan slept. "The Yankee players and managers"—he tapped a chart that hung on the door—"are code names for members of the Corsetti crime family in New York. Yankees owner, George Steinbrenner, is actually the family patriarch, Enzo Corsetti. Yankees General Manager Bill Bergesch is Enzo's oldest son, Nico Corsetti. Yankees Manager Billy Martin is Enzo's youngest son, Marco." He moved his finger farther down the chart. "And Enzo's wife is Yogi Berra."

Sid bit down on her bottom lip to keep from laughing. "Yogi Berra, right."

Dan smirked. "Trust me. I'm right about this. Look here." He tapped the same chart. "I think Yankees right fielder Reggie Jackson was the code name of a guy named Gio Segreti, who was one of the Corsetti lieutenants. The letters mention other players like Don Mattingly, Dave Winfield, Rickey Henderson, and Goose Gossage. All of these players represent different members of the Corsetti organization."

"But those guys weren't still managing or playing baseball for forty-something years—"

"No," Dan interrupted her, "but they used the names of whatever player or manager took over for them. The roles or positions stayed the same; only the names changed. For example, when Reggie Jackson left the Yankees after the 1981 season, the letters start referring to Dave Winfield, who took over Jackson's position in right field. Regardless of whether the letters mentioned Jackson or Winfield, it was the right field position that was important because that position was code for Gio Segreti." He placed his hands on his hips and scanned his chart. "And Violet's friend did a pretty good job, too. I only found about ten references where the dates were off. Like Billy Martin in 1986."

"I see," Sid said, even though she really didn't.

"And Yankee Stadium itself was actually a code for New York City, all five boroughs." He moved to a series of maps he'd drawn that were taped to some of the galley cabinets. "The letters mention center field and home plate and the visitor's dugout, things like that. but they were actually code names for places in and around New York City."

Sid nodded along, more confused than ever.

"And whenever they referred to the New York Mets"—he tapped another sheet of paper covering one of the windows—"I think they were referring to law enforcement, like the police or the district attorney's office."

He pointed to another chart. "And there were a couple of mentions of specific games. I think those were supposed to be specific incidents that happened—arrests or a death of someone high up. That kind of thing."

He moved back to the table and picked up a stack of papers. "I started doing some research. The specific games mentioned in the letters were on or about the same dates as events that made the news. There was a whole letter dedicated to a Red Sox game that corresponded with a big bust in New York, in which two of the Corsetti lieutenants were arrested." He dropped the top letter in the stack onto the table.

He waved the remaining letters in the stack. "In 1995, the Yankees got a wild card berth into the American League Division Series. They faced Seattle. There are numerous letters discussing the Mariners games, even continuing for several months afterward. Marco Corsetti was scheduled to go to trial around that same time, but the case was eventually dismissed because two witnesses went missing and a third was found floating in the East River."

He dropped the stack of letters onto the table and picked up another letter off the top of a neighboring pile. "Enzo Corsetti, the head of the family, died in 1990, and his funeral was attended by representatives of all the major crime families in New York. The papers ran stories about it for a week. One whole letter was devoted to a Milwaukee Brewers game that happened around the same time. That game was actually one of the worst-attended Yankees games that season. The stadium was only about a quarter full, but the letter mentions record-breaking crowds. I think that was a reference to the number and . . . familial affiliations, shall we say, of the attendees at Enzo Corsetti's funeral. Interestingly, after that letter, Yankees owner George Steinbrenner isn't mentioned again, despite the fact that he continued to be the principal owner of the New York Yankees until 2010. Enzo Corsetti died, and George Steinbrenner vanished from all future letters."

He waved that page before dropping it as well. "I think Violet was getting news about the Corsetti crime family for almost forty-five years."

"But why?" Sid shook her head as she looked around the room. "Why on earth would someone go through all that trouble of creating a code to keep tabs on the Mob?"

Dan shrugged. "Maybe Violet Rizzo was in hiding."

———

The information Dan had discovered tumbled around in her mind all through dinner. By the time the evening was over, Dan had finally managed to convince her that his wild theory about the Mob was probably true.

The clincher had been the repeated references in the letters to the Yankees' general manager—and there were several of them throughout the relevant forty-four-year period. In each and every letter, the Yankees GM was mentioned, always with a criticism about him lacking some crucial knowledge of one kind or another. Apparently, he didn't know how to win games; he couldn't scout talent effectively; or he wasn't able to set an effective roster, even if his life depended on it. On a few occasions, when the letters were so brief that it seemed the author had been in a rush to finish, there was simply the following sentence: "In my opinion, he's clueless."

Dan had scratched his head at this. Literally. According to him, these statements were unfair. Some of the GMs mentioned were widely considered to be successful, so the criticism in the letters seemed overly harsh.

If Dan's theory was correct, then the various GMs were code names for Nico Corsetti, heir to his family's crime syndicate. The mobster had ascended the throne after Enzo's death thirty-odd years ago and was still alive and kicking in New York City. Dan had found recent news blurbs about the man's eighty-eighth birthday on the internet. Apparently, not even a Mob boss could escape the tangles of the world wide web.

After bidding Dan a good night and making her way home, Sid had sat in her office until well past midnight, conducting her own online research. Though the idea that Nico Corsetti remained in the dark about something piqued Sid's interest, it was the online photos of the Mob boss that hooked her.

Sid had stared at the photos for a long time. In his younger days, Nico Corsetti had been a handsome man of average height and slight build. He had dark brown eyes; thick eyebrows; and a slicked-back mane of dark, wavy hair. He also possessed a long, straight nose and cheekbones that could cut glass. Other than the hair, the resemblance was uncanny. There was no denying that Mafia don Nico Corsetti bore a striking resemblance to Buddy Rizzo.

Chapter Twenty-Five

Sid sat at Violet's desk the next morning and watched Dan as he laid out his sticky notes and flip chart paper, getting ready to crack another code. She couldn't help but smile at his organization and enthusiasm for a job that Sid found tedious and mind-numbing. The sight of him arranging his pens and highlighters by color made Sid feel something she didn't want to admit but was finding harder and harder to deny. She liked him.

"Okay," Dan said, standing up and rubbing his hands together. "Show me what you've got."

She pulled box after box from the stacks behind the wooden frame that had once supported the false wall. Her own sticky notes—unexciting, pale-yellow ones—flagged the relevant pages, and they discussed each one of them in turn. It took all morning.

Lunch was ordered from a diner a couple of blocks away, and both of them sat on the floor eating sandwiches and talking through the discrepancies Sid had flagged.

"None of these weird issues are found in any of the files for the time when the grandfather, Louis, was running the show." Dan picked up a fry and used it as a pointer. "They all began right after he died, when Joseph took over the business." He flipped a page in his notes. "And they continued up until the time that Violet closed the shop."

Sid nodded. "So I'm right that there are discrepancies."

Dan flipped to another page in his notes. "Yes, but they're not in every file. There are a lot of them, and they seem to be steady. Once a calendar quarter, give or take." He flipped back a page. "Yeah, four times per year for most of these years." He pointed to the files now decorated with colorful flags and sticky notes. "There were two years with five of the weird files. And three years with six of them. But it was usually once per quarter like clockwork."

"A regular customer then?"

Dan shrugged. "I would say yes, except that the customer details are never the same. Different names, different addresses. And always payment in cash."

"Sounds like money laundering," Sid offered before taking a sip of her sweet tea.

"Perhaps, and maybe the names are all fictitious."

"Well, I can work on that part." She held out her hand, wiggling her fingers. "I'll see if I can find the customers, at least the most recent ones."

Dan smirked. "I doubt many of them are still alive."

"Probably not. But anyone who buys jewelry this flashy and expensive is no shrinking violet." She smiled. "No pun intended."

———

They worked until after eight o'clock, when they finally broke for dinner. Sid had found no information about any of the people on the list of jewelry customers, and Dan was still elbow-deep in the files.

They met the next morning for a five-mile run, at which point Sid called it quits and went home for a shower. Dan ran another three miles and then met her at Violet's house around ten o'clock. He'd stopped to pick up coffee from Pirate Joe's and donuts from Fire in the Hole.

In Violet's office in the carriage house, Sid sank her teeth into a donut—and nearly choked on it.

"You okay?" Dan held out a cup of coffee for her. "Are they not any good? Based on the line inside the shop, I thought they'd be great."

"They usually are." She took a sip. "They must have given you the wrong box. These are plain."

"Yeah, I know." Dan nodded as he picked a donut out of the box and began to rearrange his notes and office supplies. "That's what I asked for. They tried to sell me some with hot-pepper sauce in them, but I told them no."

"Datil pepper glaze. And it's on them, not in them." Sid shook her head in disbelief as Dan's nose wrinkled in disgust. "You don't like datil-pepper-glazed donuts?"

"God, no. And I don't know anyone who would." He blinked, though, when he looked up and took in her expression.

They stared at each other for a long moment before Sid finally shook her head. "I may have to seriously rethink my original assessment of you."

Dan's mouth quirked up in a smile. "Which is what exactly? And how far have I fallen?"

"Far." Sid felt her cheeks start to flush. "Very, very far. In fact, I'm not sure you can climb out of a hole that deep."

"Try me." He bit into his donut, flashing her one more smile before turning his attention to the file boxes and picking up where he'd left off the night before.

By midafternoon, Sid realized that she had not heard from Leo since Sunday night. She sent him a text, which went unanswered. When she and Dan left Violet's house at quarter past seven that night, there was still no word from Leo. Sid declined Dan's offer to buy her dinner again, much to his disappointment, and went home to check on her missing apprentice.

Burt was cleaning the grill in the backyard when Sid arrived. He greeted her with a sad smile and a sigh.

"What's going on?" Sid set her bag down on the little wrought iron table near the grill and came to stand next to him.

Burt offered her the beer bottle that was sitting on the side shelf. "Haven't drunk any yet," he said. "You may want it."

"Why?" She cocked an eyebrow and took the beer. "What's happened?"

Burt twirled the wire grill brush in his hand. "They're leaving, Sid."

"So it's a celebration?" She tipped the bottle back and took a sip. "About time. When?"

Burt dropped his gaze.

"What?" She pointed to the turquoise-and-white polka-dotted camper still sitting in the drive. "Don't tell me you won't be happy to see the backs of them, especially Brooklyn." She shook her head and took another sip.

Burt resumed brushing the grill grate. "They're leaving Friday. We're having dinner here tomorrow night. I invited Kitty and the band." He glanced sideways at her. "You can invite Dan, too, if you want."

She huffed. "I'm not putting him through that again. Hell, I don't want to put myself through it again." She shook her head. "No, thanks." When he shot her a look, she held up her hands. "Fine, I'll be there."

She turned and picked up her bag, heading for the garage. "Thanks for the beer, Burt. I'll see you tomorrow."

She hadn't made it more than a half dozen yards before she heard Burt call out, "Sidney!"

She turned to face him, and in the anemic glow from the light over the kitchen door, she thought he looked ten years older than he had just a few days ago. He twisted the brush in his hands again as he held her gaze.

"He's leaving with them, Sid."

Chapter Twenty-Six

Sid didn't wait until morning. She left Burt standing at the grill, changed her clothes and shoes, and ran. She ran for hours, back and forth to Anastasia Island, over to Vilano Beach and back again, and so many times in and around the Old City that she was surprised no one had called the cops. The sun was up when she finally stopped running, exhausted and nauseated and angry as hell.

She sat on the steps of the Grace United Methodist Church, a couple of blocks from home, stinky and sweaty and unable to bring herself to head home. She was still so angry that she might just take a sledgehammer to that stupid, turquoise camper. There was a sledgehammer in the garage, right behind the lawnmower, and it was calling her name. So the longer she stayed away from the house, the safer it would be for all concerned parties.

She sent Dan a text, begging off from their plans of a morning run and telling him not to go to Violet's today. She should call him, she knew, but she lacked sufficient strength to give him a proper explanation. She'd call him tomorrow, after Leo left.

And that notion—*after* Leo was gone—had her shoving her head between her knees and taking deep breaths in an effort not to vomit.

"Sid?"

She picked her head up and blinked. Detective Tony Davis stood in front of her, blocking out the sun and holding two cups of coffee and a small paper bag.

"You okay?"

She shook her head. When a tear escaped and rolled down her cheek, he sat down next to her and handed her one of the cups of coffee. "Here. Looks like you need this. My partner can get his own damn coffee."

She swiped her cheek with the back of her hand and took the cup. "Thanks." She felt so small sitting next to him, which was appropriate given how small she felt at that moment.

He removed two bagels from the bag, handing one to her, and said, "You want to tell me about it?"

She accepted the bagel and shook her head again.

"I could arrest you and put you in an interrogation room and make you tell me."

She snorted a laugh. "On what charge?"

"Being a general pain in my ass."

She smiled and turned her head away to wipe her nose on the inside collar of her shirt. "He's leaving." When Tony took a bite of his bagel without saying anything, she added, "Leo's leaving St. Augustine. His mom came back a few days ago with her traveling partner. She's this awful woman with a voice like an ice pick to your brain, and now they're leaving again and, apparently, taking Leo with them."

"Is he happy about it?"

Sid shrugged, breaking off a tiny piece of bagel and placing it on her tongue.

"Have you asked him?"

She shook her head.

"Damn, Sid." He sighed and took a sip of coffee.

"What?!" she asked, spinning a quarter turn to face him. "I'm allowed to be angry. I'm allowed to be disappointed."

He nodded. "You can be all of those things for yourself after he leaves. But perhaps"—he lowered his chin and stared at her over his sunglasses—"you should talk to the kid and make sure he knows you're happy *for him.*"

"But I'm not happy for him," she snarled.

"Clearly." He turned his head away and stared at the passing traffic. "But he shouldn't know that. All that boy needs to know is that you care about him and that you wish him well."

Sid ground her teeth and picked at her bagel. "He's making a mistake. He shouldn't be going. Paizley is too wrapped up in herself, and Brooklyn's just a hot mess. And he's going to spend all of his time playing photographer and dog walker and not being a kid. It's going to be a disaster. I just know it." She shook her head and lowered her voice to a whisper. "He was doing so well here. He really was."

"I'm sure Burt will let him come back if it doesn't work out."

"But how much damage will she do to him in the meantime?!" Sid set the bagel down in its wrapper, unable to eat another bite.

Tony removed his glasses and stared at her. "Is Leo in danger? Is he in harm's way?"

"Uh—"

"Is his mom abusive? Is this Brooklyn person abusive? Are they endangering a minor in any way?

Sid shook her head. "No. At least not like that, not in the way you're asking."

"Then you've got to let him go." He shoved the remainder of his bagel back in the bag, picked up his coffee cup, and stood to leave. "Say your goodbyes and don't interfere. She's his mother, Sid. Not you." He leaned down and placed his big hand on her shoulder. "It sucks, I know, but you're gonna have to let him go."

After Tony left, Sid headed home and stepped into the shower, where she stood for a long time, alternating between trying not to cry and trying not to scream. By the time she got out, her skin had pruned, and there were several texts and a missed call from Dan, all of which she left unanswered.

She could feel the dark specter of grief, the one she knew as well as her own shadow, threatening to grab hold of her once again and not let go. She hadn't felt like this in a long time, not since those tortuous months after her family's deaths, when she was certain she'd found her own personal circle of Hell. Still dripping wet, she slipped between the sheets of her unmade bed and fell asleep.

Her nap was interrupted less than an hour later. When she sat up and glanced around, nothing seemed out of place. There were no missed calls on her phone, no sounds coming from downstairs.

She lay in bed, angry and frustrated and so very, very sad. She should never have agreed to Burt's stupid suggestion of taking Leo under her wing. She should never have agreed to work with him, never gotten to know him or let him into her world. And she sure as hell should never have let herself like him, let herself care about him. It felt like losing a child all over again. He wasn't even hers, but that didn't seem to matter. Short of an actual heart attack, she didn't think her heart could squeeze any tighter or hurt any worse.

The door opened downstairs, followed by footsteps on the metal staircase. "Sid," Burt said as he entered her apartment, "I need you to come with me."

"Fuck you, Burt." She had meant to yell it, to scream it loud enough to shock the neighbors, but all she could manage was a loud whisper.

He said nothing in return, merely sat down on the edge of her bed.

"I blame you," she whispered.

"For Leo leaving?"

She shook her head, pressing her face into the pillow. "For why it hurts so much."

"I know, sweetheart." He sighed. "You can blame me all you want, but helping me with Leo was exactly what you needed. That boy was the best thing to happen to you since Trip Murdock. Need I remind you that I was right about that, too." He shifted his weight on the bed. "You know, Leo's the reason you've found all this success lately, and I don't mean it's because he can see spirits." He shook his head. "It's because he helped you believe in yourself. He gave you that back. You'd lost your spark, and he helped you find it again." He reached out and patted her foot, the one sticking out from under her wine-stained comforter. "Now, get your ass out of bed and come with me."

Sid felt the bed shift as he stood up, and she glared up at him.

He stood in the doorway and motioned for her to follow him. "Come on. Leo's hurt himself, and you're never gonna believe how."

Chapter Twenty-Seven

Leo was sitting in Burt's kitchen, eating his second bowl of cereal that morning, when his grandfather returned with Sid in tow. She looked terrible. The dark bags under her bloodshot eyes looked like bruises, and her long hair was damp and uncombed. The gray strands scattered throughout her dark mane still sparkled like tinsel, though, and she was back to wearing her worn-out yoga pants and a stained, over-size tee.

"You look like crap," Leo said, wondering at her rapid state of decay. He didn't think it was Dan Murdock who was to blame, but if it was, he'd find a way to sic every ghost in the Old City on that guy.

"Thanks, kid." She slumped down in the seat opposite him at the little kitchen table, leaning forward on her elbows. "Let me see."

Leo held up his arm, bending it at the elbow to give Sid a good look at the razor-thin cut. It was three inches long and hurt worse than any papercut he'd ever received. It wasn't deep and hadn't bled much, but it still stung even now.

"Shit," muttered Sid. She reached for his wrist, pulling his arm closer to her to get a better look. "He really did this?"

"Yep."

"With his sword?"

"Yep."

"Does it hurt?"

"Of course it hurts." He pulled his arm away and folded it in his lap, protecting it with his other arm.

"Did you put anything on it?"

Burt grunted from across the kitchen, where he leaned against the counter. "You mind telling me how you treat a wound from an invisible pirate sword? 'Cause I sure as hell would like to know."

Sid shot a quick glance at Burt. "Tell me what happened, Leo." Pointing her finger at him, she added, "Everything. I mean it. I want every last detail, whether you think it's relevant or not."

He rolled his eyes at her. "I got out of bed. Came downstairs and had some juice. Orange. No pulp. Poured myself a bowl of cereal. With milk. Ate it with a spoon."

"Leo," Burt growled, and the teenage boy slumped down in his seat.

"Miss Kitty wanted to give me some money for . . ." He swallowed hard, glanced at his grandfather, and then returned his gaze to Sid. "But Grandpa said no. I could earn the money, but she couldn't just give it to me." He picked up the spoon and swirled the cereal around in his bowl. "I offered to do some yard work for her, and Grandpa said that was okay. So I went over there this morning to get started, and the pirate was sitting on the porch swing, petting the cat."

"Wait." Sid held up her hand. "He was petting a cat?"

Leo nodded.

"Real or dead?"

"Real." He made a face at her like she'd just asked him if he knew how to spell the word *cat*. "Miss Kitty's gray tabby cat? Batman? Remember him?"

Sid ignored the heaping dose of teenage attitude. "And the pirate was petting him?"

"Yes."

"And Batman was just sitting there letting him?"

"Yes." Leo rolled his eyes. "And Mr. Lonigan was there, too."

Sid blinked. "Kitty's husband?"

Another nod.

"The one who died?"

"Yes. Is there another?"

Once again, Sid let the snark slide without comment. "So Kitty's dead husband, the pirate, and Batman were all hanging out on the porch."

"Sounds like the start of a bad joke," mumbled Burt.

Sid ignored him, too. "This pirate . . . he must be friendly then?"

Leo held up his arm, pointing to the three-inch cut. "Apparently not."

Sid pinched the bridge of her nose. "So, what happened next, kid?"

"I held up my hands"—he lifted his arms—"and I told him that I come in peace, that I was only there to do some yard work and weed under the rosebushes." Leo shrugged, hands still in the air. "And then he flew off the porch and swung his sword at me." He crossed his arms in front of him. "I didn't know what to do, so I tried to block him." Pointing to the cut, he added, "But he cut me."

She placed her palms flat on the table, focusing on the feel of the cool, smooth surface while she gathered her thoughts. "So this pirate . . . he came at you when you told him that you were going to be working in the yard. And he was able to cut you with a sword that doesn't exist."

"Well, it exists obviously." He pointed to the cut again. "In his world, at least."

"And because you can . . ." She searched her brain for the right phrase. "Because you can pierce the veil, shall we say, between our world and his"—she pointed to the cut—"he's able to do that to you."

"I guess." He shrugged.

"And what did Jerry Lonigan do?" Sid asked.

"Nothing. He and Batman just watched." Leo shoved a spoonful of cereal into his mouth.

Burt ran a hand down his face. "So, what does this mean, Sid?"

Sid stood and hurried out of the kitchen, calling back over her shoulder. "It means there's something weird going on over at Kitty's."

———

She jogged across the street, pushed open the white picket gate, and launched herself up the porch steps. As she pounded on Kitty's front door, she felt a cold breeze brush across her shoulders. The sensation was strong enough for her hair to sway ever so slightly.

"Hello, Sidney," said Kitty Lonigan when she finally opened the door.

Sid was shivering slightly, despite the temperature on this late October morning reaching the mid-eighties. "Hey, Kitty. I just wanted to check that you're all right. Is everything okay here?" She stood on her tiptoes and peered over the old woman's cottony tuft of white hair.

"Everything's fine, dear." She clasped her hands under her

chin. "Did you hear about our Leo? That he's going away with his mom?" She tutted and shook her head. "That poor boy. I really wish he'd stay here with us. He's such a lovely boy, isn't he? And he seems so happy here. I just hate the thought of him off traveling around—"

"Yes, Kitty, I heard about Leo." She didn't want to stand here and commiserate with this woman, nice as she was. She had neither the time nor the energy for such a conversation. "But are you okay? Is there anything wrong? Has anything weird happened recently?"

"Weird?" The old woman blinked. "I don't know what you mean."

Sid glanced around the porch, wishing Leo was here to translate. This would be so much easier if he were standing on this porch with her, explaining what she could not. "Kitty, by any chance, do you know any pirates?"

She laughed. "Oh, my dear, I've certainly known my share over the years."

"Yes, but any *real* pirates?"

"You mean, like a swashbuckler?"

Sid shrugged. "Sure, okay. Like a swashbuckler."

Kitty gazed up at the porch ceiling for a moment and then back at Sid. "No."

"How about your husband? Did he have any connection to any pirates or . . . or swashbucklers?

The old woman looked up at the porch ceiling again and then answered, "No."

"What about this house? Does it have any connection to pirates or swashbucklers? Any connection at all, that you know of?"

Another glance up at the ceiling followed by, "No."

Sid took a breath, sending up a silent plea for patience, and asked, "Can you think of any reason why a pirate would be interested in your house?"

"Well," the old woman held up a finger, "real estate values have gone up around here."

Sid shook her head, nearly reaching her limit. "No, Kitty, I mean, a dead pirate. Any reason a dead pirate would be interested in your house?"

Kitty's eyes grew wide. "Do I have a pirate ghost, too?"

Sid blinked in surprise. "Too? What do you mean 'too'?"

"I mean, in addition to my Jerry." She shrugged. "Leo told me that I'm always cold because Jerry is always with me." To emphasize the point, she tugged her pink cardigan more tightly around her shoulders.

Sid glanced back over her shoulder. She could see Burt and Leo standing on the porch across the street, waiting for her to return. "I don't know that it's Jerry that you're feeling." She turned back to the old woman. "And I really hate to tell you this, but I think there's a dead pirate hanging around your house."

Kitty's eyes lit up. "Is he handsome?"

"I . . . I don't know," Sid stuttered. "Does it matter?"

Kitty patted her hair and smiled. "I just think it might be nice to have a couple of handsome swashbucklers fighting over me, that's all."

Sid pressed her lips into a thin line, trying to fight a smile. "Well, let's assume he's a good-looking pirate." She felt the breeze on her shoulders again and shivered. "Wait, why did you call Jerry a swashbuckler?"

A sly smile crossed the old woman's lips. "I told you I've known a few in my day." She tapped the side of her nose. "He was a lawyer, after all."

Sid shook her head, at a loss for anything else to say. "Okay,

Kitty, thanks for your help." She said goodbye and walked back across the street.

"Well?" Leo asked as she climbed Burt's porch to join them. "Anything?"

"No." Sid sighed. "Burt, what do you know about Jerry's law practice? Kitty called him a swashbuckler."

Burt groaned. "They used to always joke about that. I heard Jerry call himself a pirate lots of times." He shook his head. "I wouldn't read much into it. Jerry was a tax lawyer. He helped people hide their money—from the government, from their own kids, whatever. Trusts and offshore accounts. Lots of stuff that seemed sketchy as hell to me, but what do I know? It was probably all perfectly legal."

Sid, Leo, and Burt stood in a line on the porch, staring across the street at Kitty Lonigan's pretty yellow house with its white picket fence and the riot of rosebushes in the front yard.

Leo held his injured arm close to his body. "If everything Jerry Lonigan did was so legal, then why is there a pirate with a really sharp sword glaring at us from his porch?"

Chapter Twenty-Eight

An hour later, Sid entered Aviles Street, heading for Fire in the Hole, when she saw a familiar face coming toward her. "Morning, Carleigh."

Carleigh Sutton, looking sleek in a tailored pantsuit the color of spring grass, flashed her a blindingly white smile. "Sidney Stone! I've been meaning to call you."

"Really?"

The two women stopped, facing each other on the sidewalk, and Sid had to tilt her head up just to make eye contact. Carleigh was over six feet on any given day, but today she was wearing four-inch heels.

"Yes, I sent a potential client your way. I hope he made contact. Buddy Rizzo?" A designer handbag swayed on her arm as she held her cup of coffee aloft.

"He did. Thank you." Sid smiled. "It's been quite a job."

Carleigh grinned. "I bet. Sorry about that. But I know they wanted someone discreet and, well, that's practically your middle name these days."

Sid nodded. "Did you know Buddy's mom, Violet?"

"I did. I inherited her, actually." When Sid looked confused, she explained. "Violet was the client of one of the partners at my firm. When I was an associate attorney, just starting out, I worked for two of the partners who practiced family law. On occasion, they brought in one of the tax partners to help with estate planning and whatnot. My third or fourth year there, that partner asked if I could help him on a matter. We got along well, and after that, I helped him out every once in a while. He died not long after I made partner at the firm. It was a terrible shock. He was such a nice man." She shook her head, clearing the memory. "Anyway, Violet Rizzo called me out of the blue shortly after he died and said that she wanted her files transferred over to me. Evidently, he spoke highly of me and told her to call me if anything ever happened to him."

Sid squeezed the straps of her bag, itching to take notes. "Did you think that was odd? I mean, it seems an odd thing to say. If anything ever happened to him? What do you think he meant by that?"

Carleigh waved Sid's questions away. "Oh, not really, no. It's typical succession planning. If someone is going to retire or becomes ill, etcetera, you make plans for others to mind your files or take over for you. There are procedures in place to make sure all bases are covered."

"Was he sick or retiring?"

"Nooo." She shook her head slowly. "He was still working away. No retirement plans that I knew of. And he was healthy. Old but still in good shape, I think." She shrugged. "Then again, I guess he wasn't. Heart attacks aren't usually a sign of peak health, are they?"

Sid frowned. "Did he tell you that you were part of his succession plan?"

"No." Another slow shake of her head. "He didn't leave express instructions. In fact, the firm had made plans to transfer

Violet's file to one of the other partners, someone who'd been there longer, but Violet asked for me. Said that was Jerry's wish."

Sid's breath caught. "Jerry?"

"Yes, Jerry Lonigan. Did you know him?"

She smiled. "I know his wife, Kitty."

Carleigh took a step to the side, as if to end the conversation and walk on, but Sid slid in front of her again. "Was Violet a good client? Did you do a lot of work for her?"

Carleigh smiled. "I'm afraid I can't disclose that."

"Violet's dead."

"Still." Carleigh shrugged.

"What if I told you that I think she was murdered?" Sid lifted her chin. "Does that change things for you?"

Carleigh blinked rapidly and then cleared her throat. "I cannot tell you about any work I performed for my client. However, I don't see a problem with hypotheticals, for instance."

Sid shrugged. "Would you prefer charades?"

Carleigh chuckled. "I can't give you any specifics. That would be unethical." Lowering her voice to a whisper, she added, "And I will deny ever having this conversation with you. You understand?"

Sid nodded once.

Carleigh sighed, took Sid by the elbow, and led her a few yards farther down Aviles Street, out of anyone's earshot. Then she asked, "What do you want to know?"

Chapter Twenty-Nine

"**P**ermission to come aboard?"

Dan Murdock picked his head up from the book he was reading as he lounged on deck and smiled. "Of course, but I thought we weren't meeting today."

"We weren't," Sid replied as she took his hand and allowed him to help her up onto his boat. "But I came here for two reasons. The first is to ask you to reconsider your position."

"About the Corsetti code?"

Sid grinned. That was the nickname he'd given it. "No, you have defended your thesis on that subject most admirably. I am referring to your position on this." She handed him one of the small paper bags she was holding.

He reached inside the bag and pulled it out. "Is this what I think it is?"

"Just try it." She tilted her head to one side. "You can't say you hate it until you've actually tried it."

"And then I can say I hate it?"

"Yes." Sid grinned. "But you won't. You'll love it."

Dan sighed and took a bite of the datil-pepper-glazed

donut. A second later he turned his head away and spat the mouthful back into the paper bag. "Nope. Sorry. Can't do it." He grimaced and shook his head. "That's disgusting."

"It is not!" She plucked the nearly whole donut from his hand. "How dare you. This is quite possibly the world's most perfect food." She held it up, waving it slightly. "And there is something seriously wrong with you for not loving it."

He grabbed his nearby water bottle, swished a mouthful of water around in his mouth, and spat over the side of the boat into the river. "Are you going to hold that against me forever?"

"No." She smiled. "I guess everyone has to have at least one flaw. It's a big one, mind you, but I'll try my best to overlook it."

"Thank you." He smiled, taking another sip of water.

"Here. Peace offering." She held out the second little bag. "It's just plain."

He took it and motioned for her to take a seat, and he joined her on the padded bench in the cockpit. "What was the second thing?"

"To apologize." She stared at the donut she was holding in her hand. "I got some bad news last night, and it really knocked me for a loop." She shook her head. "I don't seem to be handling it well."

"What happened?" He turned to face her, resting his arm on the back of the bench seat so that his fingertips gently brushed her back.

"It's Leo. He's leaving St. Augustine." She sighed. "Paizley's decided to take him with her when she leaves." She squinted against the bright sunlight and the ache building in her chest. "He'll get to travel around and see different places, and that's great, but Paizley's distracted and selfish and doesn't pay any attention to him. I've never seen her ask him what he wants to do. Not once since she's been here." She could feel her pulse quicken. "She dropped him off here a couple of months ago and ran off with that horrible woman, Brooklyn. Barely called or texted. Just left him here. And now she's been back for only a minute, and she's ready to whisk him away. He was broken when he got here. So sad and so lonely and so miserable."

She held Dan's gaze. "You've seen him. He's happy and engaged and getting better every day." She tilted her head to the side, then shrugged one shoulder. "He's still a teenage boy, snarky and moody and all that, but he's so much happier now than when he arrived." She shook her head. "I'm afraid Paizley and Brooklyn are going to undo all of that."

"They might. And he may end up miserable with them." He brushed his fingers gently over her shoulder blades. "But you can't stop him from going. She's his mother, and if he wants to be with her, you have to let him go."

"I know." Sid bent forward, resting her forearms on her thighs and hanging her head. "I really don't want him to go."

"Have you told him that?"

She shook her head.

"I think you should." Dan leaned forward, mimicking her posture. "If I were him, I would want to hear you say that." When she turned her head to look at him, she found him smiling at her. "In fact," he whispered, "I'd like to hear you say it to me."

Sid bolted upright on the bench. It felt like her heart had given her ribs a swift kick. Dan smiled and remained leaning forward. She was still holding the donut, its glaze beginning to melt under her fingers. In all the years she'd been married, and in all the years since, she'd never been attracted to anyone other than Wes. At least, that had been the case until Dan Murdock sailed into town. He somehow felt familiar and foreign at the same time. That mix was intriguing, but he would be sailing off into the sunset very soon, and she was not interested in having her heart crushed yet again by someone special exiting her life.

"Do you believe in ghosts or spirits?" Sid made a quick change of subject. It was a decidedly unromantic topic of conversation, if not necessarily a safe one.

He sat back, sliding away from Sid a little and propping one ankle over the other knee. "I don't know. Maybe. Why do you ask?"

"Just curious," she explained. "We're in the Old City, after all. If all the ghost tours are to be believed, this place is lousy with them."

He stared at the bridge in the distance and was quiet a moment. "I've never seen one." He seemed to weigh his thoughts before continuing. "But I think my mom might have a bit of a gift for that kind of thing."

"Really?" This revelation surprised her. Trip had never mentioned anything of the kind.

He winced. "I'm not saying she sees ghosts. Nothing like that. But she can read people really well. She gets 'vibes,' as she calls them. Feelings. Impressions. Of people or places. And she swears she's heard the doorbell ring when no one is there and seen lights flash on and off without anyone touching the switch." He shrugged. "And she's weirdly right about things. It's like she just knows things. All the time. It can be really irritating."

Sid smiled. "I think a lot of people feel that about their moms."

"Maybe," he conceded, "but she is eerily accurate some-times." He held out his arms, palms up. "She's the one who said I needed to take this trip, and I needed to take it now. And I absolutely needed to stop in St. Augustine and look you up and give you that box of Dad's old stuff."

Sid laughed, and Dan tilted his head toward her. "You didn't really want Dad's old coffee mug, did you?"

"Maybe not." Sid shook her head, still grinning. "But I'm looking forward to reading his old notebooks. Those should be interesting."

"Then it was worth the trip up here." He rested his arm on the back of the bench again, but this time his fingers didn't brush against her.

The absence of his touch made her heart squeeze yet again. All these feelings were really becoming a problem.

———

She helped Dan clean up the mess down in the cabin—all of Violet's coded letters as well as all of his notes and charts and maps. The former went back into their storage bins, and the latter went into Sid's bag. They grabbed lunch at a small café that sold Cuban sandwiches before trekking up Valencia Street to Violet's house.

Back in the carriage house, Sid stacked the love letter bins next to the desk and continued her research on the long list of jewelry customers while Dan resumed his review of the remaining mystery files.

"Why is it always so cold in here?" he asked. "That has to be the most effective air conditioner on the planet." He blew on his hands and rubbed them together. "Do you think we could turn it off, or least turn it up a few degrees, before we freeze in here?"

"Sure. I'll turn it off," Sid said, adding in a mutter, "but it's not likely to help." Two hours later, it was still freezing in the office, even without the air conditioner running.

When the last name on the customer list had been searched, Sid heaved a sigh and closed her laptop. Nothing.

Not a single one of them turned out to be a real person living in New York City at the address specified during the time in question. It was almost as if Risso & Co. had made them all up.

The surface of Violet's handsome desk was a mess of files and notes, so Sid began straightening up. When she placed the last folder on top of the neat pile she'd made, she flipped it open and stared at the photos and sketches of the diamond and ruby necklace. It was too gaudy for Sid's taste, but there was no denying it was a work of art. She snapped a few photos and then flipped through the contents once more, finding the initial order form in the back. The customer was one of those names on her list that she couldn't trace, and there were no other details in the file to indicate who had ordered and purchased the extravagant necklace.

Sid flipped to the certificate and appraisal, and the signature caught her eye: Paul DeLuca. He was a gemologist at a company called Gemology Experts of New York. She'd looked up the business when she first came across the file. GENY did indeed exist and had done so for over a century. In fact, its history was similar to that of Risso & Co.; it had been started by an immigrant patriarch, Pietro DeLuca, who passed it on to his son, Paul. Unlike Risso & Co., GENY was sold twenty years ago to new owners, who kept the business running. Under the DeLuca family, the business had remained small, a boutique shop with one location in the Diamond District. The new owners had expanded to other locations: two in upstate New York, one in Connecticut, and one in Boston.

Nothing about any of that was unusual or suspect. What made Sid pause was the signature itself. The *P*, in particular.

"Oh shit." Sid reached for the storage bin next to the desk and tugged off the lid. Grabbing the first envelope she could lay her hands on, she slid out the letter and studied its closing. "Found him!"

"Who?!" Dan almost tripped over one of the file boxes in his mad dash around the desk to stand next to her.

"Well, I'll be damned," he said after studying the letter himself. He rubbed at the stubble on his chin. "How did I miss that?"

"You weren't looking for it. Neither was I." Sid laid the letter down next to the certificate in the file. "We were so focused on everything else—the code, the Yankees, the discrepancies—that we never looked at the signatures on anything."

"That's the same *P*." Dan blew out a breath and lunged for the nearest box, pulling out one of the files marked with his colorful sticky notes. Finding the certificate, he held it up and pointed to Paul DeLuca's signature. "It's the same *P*. And I bet we'll find it all over these files."

Sid ran a finger under the large, slanted, single initial *P* at the bottom of the coded love letter. "Violet's fake love affair was with the gemologist who certified her jewelry. And she corresponded with him for over forty years about the Corsetti crime family."

Sid looked around the room, taking in the mess they'd made, and felt goose bumps rise on her skin. "Why in the world was she doing that?"

Chapter Thirty

Sid had tried to convince Dan to head back to his boat after he'd finished reviewing the last of the files and stacked all of the boxes back in place behind the wooden frame at the far end of the office, but he'd refused.

"Things are starting to come together," he'd said. "There's no way I'm quitting now."

Instead of leaving, he took a knee next to her in the desk chair and watched as she began to research Paul DeLuca. When the search quickly revealed that the man had died four years ago, Dan got up and busied himself by snooping around Violet's studio.

Sid, on the other hand, sat glued to her chair, trying everything she could think of to hunt down Paul DeLuca. Sid already knew about Paul's father starting the business in New York. All of that history could be found on GENY's own website. Other professional information about the man was reasonably easy to come by—education, credentials, accolades, even details of his speaking engagements at a few industry conferences—and all of it painted a portrait of a man who was a consummate professional.

The personal information was proving more of a challenge. Paul DeLuca had been eighty-seven years old when he died. The funeral notice in the newspaper said very little, except that he was survived by his only child, Paulina. He'd been married once to a woman named Juno Monetti, but Sid found no death certificate and no divorce decree.

Her phone buzzed, and she turned off the timer she'd set for herself earlier that morning. Reluctantly, she packed up her things and went in search of Dan, whom she found lying on the floor of the studio with a kitchen towel folded under his head as a pillow.

"Hey, sleeping beauty," she said as she shook his shoulder gently. He blinked awake, looking a little disoriented by his surroundings. "I need to head out."

"I'll come with you," he offered as he shook himself and stood up.

"No." She'd been firm about this earlier. "I need to make sure I'm focused on Leo tonight. I don't need any other distractions. Believe me, there will be enough of those there already."

"So you find me distracting?" he teased as he followed her out of the carriage house.

"Yes." She bit her lip. "I'm afraid I do."

Sid said goodbye to Dan and walked home by herself. Before she reached the house, though, she made one phone call.

It was answered on the second ring. "Please tell me you haven't found another dead body."

She smiled. "No dead body." She paused. "Well, that's not entirely true. He's dead, but I didn't find him."

"Sid," Detective Tony Davis growled into the phone. Literally growled. If she didn't know him as well as she did, she would have been intimidated by the sound.

"Don't worry. He died years ago." She shook her head, still smiling. "And in New York City."

"And you're calling me to tell me about it, why?"

"Because I need your help." She slowed as she approached Saragossa Street. "I'm trying to find out more about him, the dead guy, but I'm hitting a dead end."

"And you want my help, why?" he persisted.

Now Sid was the one who growled. "Because he's somehow involved in a case I'm working."

"Are there any dead bodies involved in that case?"

"One," she admitted. "But you already know about it. Violet Rizzo. Remember her? I asked you about her death. Eighty-six-year-old woman found dead on her stairs. Death was ruled an accident."

Tony sighed into the phone. "Yeah, I remember. So, what's the connection with the dead guy in New York?"

"I'm not entirely sure yet." Sid shuffled her feet, slowing even more as she neared the house. "His name was Paul DeLuca." The click of a pen on the other end of the phone told her that Tony was paying attention. "He died four years ago. Lived in the West Village for a long time, as far as I could tell. He was married to a Juno Monetti, but I can't find any record of her after the marriage. He has one daughter, Paulina, who survived him, but I can't find anything out about her either. Paul DeLuca worked with Violet Rizzo years ago in New York. We're talking, like, fifty years ago. And the two of them were . . . pen pals, let's say, for a long time." She sighed and pinched the bridge of her nose. "I don't know, Tony. It's just a hunch. I think there is something there, something that I'm not seeing right now, but it could also be nothing." This case felt like one long, wild goose chase.

"Or it might be something that leads to another dead body,"

Tony added. "That's what seems to turn up whenever you ask me to look into something."

"True. But this guy's already dead." She was smiling as she turned into the drive, but her expression changed as she passed by the turquoise camper. "So, can you help me? Any chance you know someone in New York you can call and ask? Maybe someone who owes you a favor?"

Tony huffed. "What makes you think I have contacts in New York City who owe me favors?"

"Do you?"

He paused for a long moment and then said, "Good night, Sid," and hung up.

She dropped her bag in the office, crossed the backyard, and opened the kitchen door without pausing, giving herself no opportunity to chicken out. She found Burt in the kitchen with slabs of marinated ribs laying on the counter next to a roll of aluminum foil and a box of large, resealable bags. As she walked in, he nodded to her and tore off a sheet of foil.

"Ribs, huh?" She smiled. "Must be a special occasion."

He slapped the foil down on the counter. "Change of plans."

"Really?!" Her smile grew wider.

Burt shook his head. "Don't get too excited. The party's just postponed for a day. We're gonna do it tomorrow night."

Sid felt the energy drain from her body. "Why?"

"They're delayed." Burt shook his head. "They'll be back tomorrow evening, so we'll do it then."

Sid glanced into the living room but found it empty. "How's he taking it?"

"Disappointed, as usual." Burt pulled a slab of ribs out of its marinade bag and slapped it down on the foil. "He's upstairs in his room. I spent the whole day helping him pack, trying to figure out what he could take with him given that there won't be much space in the camper. We went over all of his school-work for the rest of the semester. I made him create a calendar and make a study plan so that he wouldn't fall behind." He wrapped the foil around the ribs so tightly it looked like he was trying to squeeze the marinade right out of them. "I'm going to order pizza. You want the usual?"

Sid sagged against the refrigerator, trying to collect her thoughts. "No, thanks. I'm going to take him out, if that's okay. We'll be back later." Burt nodded but didn't look up. Before exiting the kitchen, she turned back. "You okay?"

"Fine." The way he ripped another sheet of foil from the roll indicated that he was anything but fine, but then he muttered, "Thanks, Sid."

Leo's bedroom door was closed, so Sid knocked softly. "Hey, kid. You in there?"

Silence.

She knocked again, louder this time. When there was no response, she pounded on the door. "Leo, open up!"

More silence. Sid was just about to try the knob and barge in when she heard, "It's open."

Leo was lying on his bed. His headphones were over his ears, and he was holding his phone, likely having just silenced the music he'd been blaring.

"Take those off. We're going out." She swung the door all the way open. "Meet me downstairs. You've got one minute."

Chapter Thirty-One

Leo raced down the stairs, catching up to Sid as she reached the bottom. He followed her through the kitchen, where his grandfather was still wrapping the ribs to preserve them for tomorrow night. Burt didn't look up or say anything as they passed, so Leo didn't either. His grandfather probably already knew about whatever was going on with Sid. He hoped it was something to do with the Violet Rizzo case. Or any other case for that matter. He'd even be happy with a missing pet, if that was all it was. He followed her across the yard to the garage, where she picked up her bag before marching off, without saying a word, toward the Old City's historic downtown district.

He kept pace next to her. Since she said nothing to him, just like his grandfather, he kept silent as well. He asked no questions, made no snarky comments. He didn't even shuffle his feet or roll his eyes. He was simply happy to be out of the house and on some sort of mission. It didn't matter what it was. As long as Sid was leading the way, he was content to follow her.

Sid finally came to a halt in front of the takeout window of the Old City Seafood Company, the restaurant next door to Granny Oak's Music Park. She placed their orders without bothering to ask him what he wanted. There was no need. He ordered the same thing every single time, and she knew it: fried shrimp, hush puppies, and datil pepper coleslaw. She always ordered the same thing as well, and he knew that, too.

They listened to the band warming up on stage at Granny Oak's while they waited for their food. Ten minutes later, Sid's name was called. Leo took the bag of food, and she grabbed the drinks.

Still, neither of them said a word to each other.

They left St. George Street and headed across Avenida Menendez to the bayfront walk between the old fort and the Bridge of Lions. Sid chose an empty bench and sat down, motioning for Leo to join her. He did as ordered and placed the bag of food between them. Each of them took one of the takeout containers and one of the drinks. There was nothing but silence for several minutes as they ate their dinner.

Finally, Sid set her container down and took a sip of her sweet tea. "So, what happened?"

He had known it was coming. He was surprised it had taken her this long. When she had banged on his bedroom door tonight, he had thought she would launch into a tirade about his mom being irresponsible or something like that, but she hadn't. He almost wished she'd rant and rave, scream and throw stuff, do all the things that he wanted to do himself but couldn't.

He'd spent these last two months telling everyone that Paizley would return to claim him, and she had. Maybe not in the way he wanted, but it had happened. She'd come back to town, and he'd asked if he was going with her when she left. She'd hemmed and hawed for a few days but finally agreed that he could come along. They were supposed to celebrate tonight with everyone he'd grown to care about.

But his mom had cancelled. Changed her plans yet again. Left him sitting at home, waiting for her to come back from yet another day trip.

When Sid ordered him out of bed, he'd gotten up immediately. He'd followed her through the Old City without resistance because she'd come for him. And they sat here now, eating the food she knew he liked, and she was asking him for his side of the story.

He dropped his hush puppy and set his takeout container down next to hers. Then he pulled his phone from his pocket, opened the Messages app, and handed it over to her. "Here. You can read it." He had nothing to hide. She might as well read it for herself.

Sid reached slowly for the phone and lifted it out of his hand. The texts from his mom were right there on the screen:

> Going to stay in Daytona Beach tonight

> Something's come up. Cool opportunity for pbj

> Tell Burt for me. Will be back tomorrow

> Sorry kiddo. Love you

He hadn't bothered to text her back. There was no need. She wasn't coming back tonight, and she clearly didn't care about cancelling his party or about how that made him feel. Sid sat quietly, holding the phone in her hand and staring at the screen. Part of him wanted her to scroll up to read all the other texts between him and his mom. Maybe that would send her over the edge, make her shout and pace back and forth. Maybe she'd call Paizley herself and . . . and what?

"Well, that sucks." She handed him back the phone. "Did she call you?"

He shook his head.

"Just the texts?"

"Yeah."

She reached over and squeezed his shoulder. "I'm sorry, kid. I really am."

When her hand dropped away, he wanted to reach out for it and put it back on his shoulder, but he didn't. He stared out at the sailboats bobbing in the bay, moored to their buoys, as if they didn't have a care in the world. His world, meanwhile, was turning into a dumpster fire.

"What's the plan?" she asked.

"Mom will come back tomorrow, and we'll have the party then."

There were a few beats of silence before she said, "I mean after that. What's the plan when you leave us?"

The words hit him in the gut, making him sorry he'd eaten as many shrimp as he had. She'd said, "When you leave *us*," rather than simply, "When you leave."

He couldn't turn his head to look at her. He just couldn't. "Savannah. Charleston. A few places in North Carolina, but I can't remember which ones. And then Virginia and Washington, D.C."

"Sounds like quite a trip."

He nodded.

"And after that?"

"We'll come back here for Christmas."

A long pause and then, "Great. It will be nice for Burt if you're home for the holidays."

At the word "home," Leo's stomach flipped again.

She punched him lightly in the arm. "Guess you'll be expecting me to get you a gift?"

He grinned but still couldn't bring himself to look at her. "You don't have to."

"Don't be silly. I give all my employees Christmas gifts." She paused and then added, "Your job will be here for you when you get back. Who knows? Maybe over the holidays we'll uncover a secret Santa smuggling ring. Bet that'll make the news."

He couldn't hold back the laugh that erupted from him.

She chuckled, too. "What am I going to do without your unique skill set, kid? I mean, who's gonna talk to the dead people and get them to spill their secrets?"

He shrugged. "Maybe you can ask Miss Hattie."

Sid barked a laugh. "Can you imagine? Every ghost in the Old City would run for the hills if they saw her coming." They were silent for a long moment, and then she said, "I'm really gonna miss you, Leo."

He nodded, hung his head, and shut his eyes as tightly as he could. He wanted to say the same thing back to her, but he couldn't. His throat no longer worked, and even breathing was painful. Talking was definitely out of the question. He wanted to tell her that he didn't want to go, that he'd been wrong to want to travel around with his mom and Brooklyn. That wasn't where he belonged. He didn't need to see Rainbow Row in Charleston or the Outer Banks of North Carolina or the famous monuments in D.C. Everything he wanted was right here in St. Augustine. Everything except his mom. If he wanted her, he had to go, but leaving meant giving up everything he'd come to need and love.

None of this was fair. None of it. All he wanted right in that moment was for someone to tell him what to do—to tell him what the right thing was and to order him to do it.

He felt a tear roll down his cheek and land on his right hand, which was currently fisted around the hem of his T-shirt. He heard Sid pick up their takeout boxes, move them aside, and slide closer to him.

And then she did the same thing Burt had done less than an hour ago. She pulled him in for a hug.

Chapter Thirty-Two

The next morning, Sid was still in her pajamas, standing in her kitchen sipping a cup of coffee and bemoaning the fact that she needed to go grocery shopping, when someone knocked on her office door. A quick look out the window brought a wave of relief. She threw on a sweatshirt and hurried downstairs.

"Please say you brought donuts."

"Good morning to you, too." Detective Tony Davis stood in her doorway, looking cool, calm, and collected and holding a box of donuts from Fire in the Hole.

"Thank God!" She took the box from him. "I haven't gone grocery shopping in a week."

"You really need to get your shit together, Sid." He sauntered into the office, hooking his sunglasses onto the collar of his slate-gray golf shirt. The muscles bulging in his arms, straining the seams of his shirt, no longer fazed her. To anyone who didn't know him, Detective Antonio Davis was terrifying. To those who did, well, he was still pretty scary. But to Sid, he was a rock, the person she'd come to rely on to help her out of tough spots. And to deal with the dead bodies whenever they popped up.

"Tell me about it." She opened the box, picked a donut at random, and took a bite. How did Dan Murdock find these disgusting? They were heaven. Sugar-coated, fiery-tasting heaven. "Want some coffee?" she asked.

Tony nodded, made himself comfortable in one of her woefully sad-looking guest chairs, and took a donut for himself. A few minutes later, she was back with the nearly full pot of coffee and two mugs. Tony pulled his small notebook from his jeans pocket. "I looked into Paul DeLuca last night."

"I knew you would." She grinned at him over the rim of her mug.

"And you owe me one. I called in a big favor for this. An old buddy of mine who played peewee football with me back in the day is a detective on the Lower East Side now. Naomi introduced him to his wife. He owed me big time for that." He pointed the remaining half of his donut at Sid. "Now *you* owe me big time. And I do mean *big*."

Sid waved his gesture away. "Fine. Whatever. What did you find out?"

He opened his notebook and flipped to the relevant page. "Paul DeLuca died in his home. Aged eighty-seven. Death wasn't found to be suspicious."

"That's disappointing." She frowned and took another sip of coffee.

Tony smirked. "This job has really warped you. You know that?"

She shrugged. "What else?"

"He died sometime during the night but wasn't found until the next day."

"Who found him?"

"His daughter, Paulina DeLuca. She arrived at the house to

take him to lunch. Paulina disappeared after that. Apparently, the PD tried to contact her about some of her father's effects. There was a mix-up in the paperwork, and a watch he'd been wearing when he was found hadn't been returned as originally thought. Anyway, no one could find her. Her landlord said she just disappeared, cleared out her apartment overnight, but the landlord got a letter from her a few weeks after she cleared out with payment in cash for the remainder of the rent she owed on her lease and a forwarding address for any mail. This all happened several months after her father's death. The forwarding address was a P.O. box in the West Village, but it's no longer registered to her. I checked."

Sid took a sip of her coffee and waited for Tony to take another bite of his donut.

"The place where she used to work"—he flipped the page—"was called Gemology Experts of New York. They said she turned in her notice a few weeks after her father died, and they never heard from her after that. Apparently, her father owned the business at one point but had sold it and retired. He called in a favor and got her a job there when she got out of college, though. And that's all I could find out about Paulina."

Sid leaned forward and made some notes herself. "She just disappeared?"

"Looks that way. No death certificate. No tax returns filed. Nothing."

"So . . . missing?"

He shrugged. "No missing persons reports. If she is missing, no one's looking for her."

She sat back, the chair squealing in protest. "What about her mother?"

"Ah, yes." Tony finished the last bite of his donut and flipped another page. "Juno Monetti was only eighteen when she married Paul DeLuca, who was fifty-one at the time."

Sid blanched. "She was just a kid."

"He'd been married twice before. The first time, he was eighteen, and that marriage lasted only two years. Then he remarried that same year, and that marriage lasted twenty-eight years."

"Either of those suspicious deaths?"

Tony shook his head. "The first was an accidental drowning at her parents' house on Long Island. The second was ruled natural causes. No specifics, though."

"Any children from those marriages?"

"I couldn't find any, no."

"And what happened to Juno?"

"Not sure. Her name appears on Paulina's birth certificate, which was filed ten months after Juno's marriage to Paul." He shrugged. "It's possible Juno died in childbirth."

"And someone covered it up? Paid off Paul to keep it quiet?"

Tony paused, his mug halfway to his mouth. "Your mind goes to some really dark places, doesn't it?"

"You have no idea." She shook her head. "So Juno's missing, too. Both mother and daughter just vanish without a trace. Doesn't that strike you as weird?"

"Sid, everything you're involved in strikes me as weird." He flipped another page. "There was one other thing that my buddy in New York told me. Paul DeLuca was questioned in connection with a racketeering case involving one of the big crime syndicates up there."

"The Corsetti family?"

"Yeah. How'd you guess that?"

"Long story." She shrugged. "Why was he questioned?"

"When the cops raided a Corsetti warehouse, they found a couple jewelry valuations among the records but no jewelry. Paul DeLuca's name was on the paperwork. They questioned him, but nothing ever came of it." He shrugged. "In the interview, he claimed that he often certified jewelry without ever knowing who the customers were. He usually dealt directly with the jewelers, not the customers, so he denied knowing that someone in the Corsetti organization was the owner of the jewelry when he did the valuations."

"And who was the jeweler?" Sid was on the edge of her seat now.

"No idea." Tony smirked. "The Corsettis weren't exactly forthcoming, and DeLuca claimed he couldn't remember. Conveniently, a small fire at DeLuca's shop destroyed a lot of his records, so he had no way of knowing who made the pieces in question."

Sid nodded. "That is convenient. How lucky for him." She rubbed her eyes. "And they didn't find the jewelry?"

"No. Probably hidden in a safe somewhere, or some of the wives were wearing it. Or maybe they sold it on to someone else." He selected another donut. "That would be an interesting way to launder money."

She sipped her coffee for a few moments, thinking quietly while the detective ate. She felt like pieces of the puzzle might be falling into place, that connections were finally being made. "What if the Corsettis used their mobster money to buy jewelry? You know, unique, handmade pieces. One-of-a-kind stuff. Someone makes the jewelry and then gets Paul DeLuca to certify it. And what if he inflates the valuations? The Corsettis could then sell the jewelry at those inflated prices, laundering the money and making a profit at the same time."

He nodded. "Could be something like that. And they might not even have to touch the jewels. DeLuca or the jeweler or someone else could act as a broker and sell it for them. The Mob never has to get their hands dirty."

"Well, that is very interesting." Sid sat back and ran her hands through her hair, tugging at the roots.

"That's not all of it. Want one more interesting tidbit?" His mouth quirked up in a sly smile.

She shook her head. "We've got mobsters and money laundering and missing persons. What else do you want to throw into the mix?"

"Paul DeLuca was found dead on the staircase in his home. He died during the night from injuries sustained from a fall."

Sid nearly spat her coffee at him. "Are you serious?!"

"Yeah, I thought you'd like that part." He shook his head and shut his notebook.

Sid's eyes widened. "You're telling me he died in his home, at night, from a fall down the stairs. And I bet the house was locked up tight when his daughter found him the next day. No forced entry, no signs of anything suspicious."

He nodded. "Sounds familiar, doesn't it?" He held up his hands. "To be fair, DeLuca and Rizzo were both old. Rizzo was eighty-six when she died; DeLuca was eighty-seven. And while DeLuca had a possible connection to the Mob, Rizzo did not. At least, not that we know of. He died in New York four years ago. She died here only recently. It seems purely coincidental." He smirked. "But I've learned to assume nothing is a coincidence whenever you're involved."

She grinned.

He picked up his mug and took a sip of coffee. "I don't know if the two deaths are connected, and I'll look into it further, but—"

"But we're adding two murders to the mix." Sid sighed.

"Possible murders." Tony held up a finger, correcting her. "And it will be damn hard to prove."

Sid tore a sheet of paper from her notepad and scribbled

something on it. "Can you check on one more name for me? It's just a hunch, but I think there's a connection."

She handed the page to Tony, who read it, folded it up, and tucked it into his pocket. "You want to tell me what's going on?"

"Yes, I do. Very much so." She nodded. "But I need to know what you find out first. This may lead to a whole lotta nothing, and I may be looking in the wrong place."

"And if it's not? If it turns out to be something?"

She grimaced. "Then it will be something big enough to kill for."

Chapter Thirty-Three

Leo waited until Detective Davis left before knocking on Sid's door. He was still feeling a bit raw and wrung out after dinner with her last night, and he didn't want to have to brave a conversation with the big detective. If the man said anything nice to him, any mention of missing him, he might just start bawling all over again. It had been embarrassing enough to have done it in front of Sid; there's no way he wanted it to happen in front of someone like Detective Davis.

As he and Sid headed over to Violet Rizzo's house, she made two phone calls. One was to Buddy to ask for a little more time to wrap up the case, telling him she was close to finding something but didn't want to reveal what it was until she was absolutely certain. He agreed to give her the weekend to finish her investigation. The second call was to Dan Murdock.

Leo liked Dan. The guy was cool and laid-back and didn't treat him like a little kid. Dan was a lot like the Geezers and Detective Davis in that way. And Dan liked Sid. He seemed to like her a lot, judging by the way he looked at her. Whether Sid liked him back was anyone's guess, and Leo suspected she hadn't even noticed how Dan stared at her and laughed at her jokes and opened doors for her. Sid was really smart, but she could be completely clueless about some things.

"Any sign of our pirate friend?" Sid asked after she hung up with Dan.

"He's right behind us." Leo didn't bother to turn around. The pirate was still tailing them. He'd been standing watch at Kitty's house and had fallen in behind them as they headed to Valencia Street. Fortunately, he was out of sword-striking distance, but he could probably still reach them with his pistol.

"Just ignore him. He'll go away eventually."

"Easy for you to say," muttered Leo.

She fidgeted with the bag on her shoulder. "I can't believe Burt let you take the day off from school."

Leo shrugged.

"Well, I'm glad you're here. I'm going to need your help."

He simply nodded, not wanting to risk having to talk about leaving town with his mom. He'd done enough of that already, and nothing anyone said could change the inevitable.

They went straight to the carriage house and upstairs to Violet's office. Sid grabbed one of the boxes marked with one of Dan's sticky notes and carried it over to the desk. Leo noticed at least half of the boxes had similar notes attached to the outside. How long had it been since he'd been here? When was the last time he'd helped Sid with the case? So much had happened this week that Leo no longer knew which way was up.

Violet Rizzo materialized in front of the wooden frame that had once supported the wall hiding her secret stash of boxes. She stood in a wide stance, arms folded across her chest, glaring at them both. Given the fact that she didn't appear to be carrying a weapon, he decided to ignore her and turned his attention to Sid. He pulled the sticky note off the file box and read it. "What's going on? What's with all the crazy notes?"

"Remember I mentioned that there were some things in the files that didn't make sense to me? Discrepancies?" When he nodded, she added, "I asked Dan to take a look at them."

Leo felt a cold sensation come over him, which had nothing to do with the proximity of Violet's spirit and everything to do with the fact that she'd found someone to replace him while he'd been playing paparazzo for his mother. "Oh?" He dropped the sticky note on the desk, and Sid picked it up and put it back on the box.

"Yeah, he's good at deciphering codes and working on problems that, frankly, make my brain hurt." She pointed to the piles of notepads and flags and markers. "We've been at it for days now, and something Detective Davis said this morning made me think that I found the key to this mess." She flipped through one of the files, her brow furrowed in concentration.

He leaned against the desk and crossed his arms, feeling a bit jealous that Dan had been asked to work on the case while he'd been left out of the loop. "What is it, then? This key?"

The knock on the door downstairs interrupted them.

Sid didn't even glance up from the file when she asked, "Can you let him in?"

"Who?" Leo stayed where he was, leaning against the desk. He knew who was downstairs. He'd overheard her phone conversation this morning.

"Dan. Go let him in, please."

It was less of a request and more of a demand, so Leo got up and took his time making his way to the door. "Hey," was all he said by way of greeting.

"Leo!" Dan stood there holding a box of donuts, two cups of coffee, and a bottle of orange juice. "I'm happy to see you. I hear you're heading out today for a big road trip with your mom."

He stared at the man, feeling both anger at Sid for telling

Dan that he was leaving and sadness at the reality that he would be leaving her alone. Well, not all alone. Apparently, Dan was still here. He shook his head. "I leave tomorrow."

"Oh." Dan's brow creased. "I must have gotten the day wrong." He shrugged. "Anyway, I'm here to help you both. This is for you." He held out the box for Leo to take. "And I got you orange juice. You didn't strike me as a coffee drinker."

Leo fought the reflex to smile at the notion that Dan had thought of him when ordering. "Thanks." He took the box and the orange juice and headed upstairs. "We're up here." He left Dan to close the door and follow him.

Once they were all back in the office—the three of them with their donuts and drinks, and Violet Rizzo glaring at them from her guard post in front of the boxes—Sid began pacing back and forth.

"I have a theory," she began. "And bear with me while I talk it through."

"Okay," Dan said. "Let me get comfortable." He sat down on the floor, leaning against one of the tall windows and crossing his ankles. As Sid continued to pace, he sipped his coffee. "Have a seat, Leo." He patted the floor next to him. "Looks like this is going to be big. We may be here a while."

Given that Sid was still pacing and hadn't said anything, Leo tended to agree. But he didn't sit next to Dan. Instead, he took a seat on the floor, leaning against the next window over.

Finally, Sid stopped in front of them, placed her hands on her hips, and blew out a breath. "Here's what I think." She paused for a moment, biting her lip, and then continued. "I think Violet Rizzo was helping the Mob launder money."

"Well, that is interesting." Dan's eyes narrowed as he nodded slowly.

Out of the corner of his eye, Leo saw Violet Rizzo stiffen.

"Here's what we know so far," began Sid. "Violet Rizzo

made jewelry. Fancy, expensive, bespoke pieces that she designed herself. Just like her father and his father before him. Risso & Co. was successful for a small shop in the Diamond District, but something happened after her grandfather died and her father took over. Business picked up markedly, but, as far as we can tell from these records, they hadn't expanded. No additional staff, no opening of a second storefront. Nothing to indicate why. Just a lot more business all of a sudden, and it continues like that for three decades."

"But Violet joined her dad about halfway into that," Dan added. "That could explain some of the increase, or at least how they sustained it."

Sid nodded. "I think Violet was making jewelry long before she was made a partner in the business. We know she was designing pieces when she was a little kid. Her drawings are all over those files. But I think Joseph had her helping him make the stuff, too."

"So?" Leo shrugged. "What's the big deal about Violet helping her dad? I help you."

Sid smiled at him and nodded. "True. And like us, I think they kept a secret."

Leo squirmed in his seat and glanced quickly at Dan, but the man merely took a sip of his coffee, looking unfazed by her comment. Had she told him about Leo's ability to see spirits? Clearly that was what she was talking about. Did Dan know, too?

Sid returned to her pacing. "I think whatever Joseph was doing was something he didn't want anyone else to know about, so he brought Violet in to help. She'd keep his secret. Keep it in the family, so to speak." She began rubbing her arms, and Leo noticed that she was pacing very close to where Violet stood guard over her boxes. "I think what they were doing wasn't entirely above board. They made jewelry and had it certified and appraised at a shop called Gemology Experts of New York, which was run by the DeLuca family. Their names appear on the certificates in the files, especially Paul DeLuca's."

She stopped and selected one of Violet's love letters, handing it over to Leo. "Open it up. Check the signature."

Leo really didn't want to read another love letter, but he did as he was told. "It's just an initial. P. That's it. No name."

She picked up the open file on the desk, flipped to the certificate, and held it out for him to see. "Look. It's the same *P*."

Leo blinked in surprise. The *P* in Paul DeLuca's signature was large and slanted, with a big, curly flourish where the pen lifted from the page. It was the same as the initial at the bottom of the love letter. "Okay. So Violet was in love with this guy, this Paul DeLuca, who wrote these certificates. How is that a big deal?"

"It's a big deal for two reasons." She closed the file and set it back down on the desk. "One, I think they were running a scam."

Violet Rizzo's spirit flinched at Sid's words. Visibly flinched. Her fingers fluttered up to her neck, and she clutched at the ruby necklace.

Sid took the letter back from Leo. "I think Joseph Rizzo had Paul DeLuca falsify the certificates to inflate the valuations. That way the pieces could be sold at a profit."

Leo watched Violet's grip on the necklace relax. "What's the other reason?" he asked, addressing Sid but keeping his eyes on the spirit. "You said there were two reasons that guy's signature was important? What's the other?"

"I don't think Violet Rizzo and Paul DeLuca were having an affair."

"But—" Leo shifted his gaze back to Sid, frowning.

"I know, I know." She held up her hands. "That's a lot of

letters written over a lot of years, but I don't think the two of them were in love at all." She crossed her arms and leaned back against the desk. "Dan and I think they were corresponding in code."

Leo glanced between Sid and Dan and then back over to Violet. "Code?"

Dan nodded. "All those baseball references in the letters." He leaned sideways toward Leo. "You and I both know that men who write letters to their girlfriends don't go on for pages and pages about baseball, certainly not if they're madly in love. Right?" He gave Leo a knowing nod and then shifted back against the window.

Leo nodded along with him, although, in truth, he had no idea what men in love wrote about in their love letters. Did men do that? Write letters? Would he have to write a love letter someday? He frowned slightly as he studied Dan. Was this man writing love letters to Sid? Did Detective Davis write letters to his wife, Naomi? Had his dad written love letters to his mom before he died? Did Grandpa ever write them to Grandma when she was alive? And what about the Geezers? Was Cesar Hernandez writing any love letters to those women who were always hanging around the stage when Recent Geezer played at Granny Oak's? He wanted to know, but he didn't really want to ask.

Sid cleared her throat. "Anyway, we think Paul was passing information to Violet. Information about someone back in New York."

"Who?" Leo asked, keeping one eye on Violet's spirit, which had drifted a little closer to Sid.

"I think it was the same person she made the jewelry for. Or maybe he was just one of the people. Regardless, I think she made the jewelry for him and his family."

Leo watched Violet closely. Her hands were no longer on the necklace but balled up in fists by her side. "Um, Sid—"

But Sid spoke right over him. "I think Violet Rizzo was making jewelry for the Corsetti Mafia family as a way to launder money, and I think Paul DeLuca was writing to Violet to keep her apprised of the Mob's goings-on." Sid held up her index finger. "And she was very interested in one member of the family in particular: Nico Corsetti, the oldest son and the man who eventually took over the business when his father died."

Leo squirmed in his seat as Violet circled around behind his boss. "Sid—"

Again, she spoke over him. "I think Violet wanted to make sure that Nico Corsetti remained in the dark about her biggest secret of all."

When she paused, Dan leaned forward. "Well, don't keep us in suspense, Sid."

She smiled. "I think Nico Corsetti is Buddy Rizzo's father."

Chapter Thirty-Four

The voice was so loud that Leo reflexively covered his ears. It did no good, however, because the sound wasn't entering his ears. It was inside his head and his head alone. No one else could hear it. The woman screaming at the top of her lungs was dead and currently trying to strangle Sid.

His boss, however, was merely leaning against the desk with her arms folded, smiling at him. "I'm right, aren't I?"

"No!"

The word was repeating over and over again in Leo's head at a volume and octave that he worried might split his skull. "Stop it!" Leo screamed. He tucked his head between his knees and covered his head with hands. "Make it stop!"

Dan was up in a flash, lunging for him and wrapping his arms around him. "I've got you, Leo." He whispered the words, and Leo was amazed that he was able to hear it over Violet's screeching.

Sid moved to stand in front of him and bellowed,

"Enough!" It was her angry teacher voice, the same one she'd used on the ghosts at the Oakmire Golf and Country Club. She clapped her hands together in that way that makes them sound like a whip being cracked. "Violet Rizzo, you stop it right now! He's only a boy. He's just a kid, like Josephina."

At the mention of her granddaughter's name, Violet Rizzo went silent. She was still trying to beat Sid with her invisible fists, but at least she was no longer in danger of making Leo's head explode. As soon as he relaxed, Dan released him, gave his shoulder a squeeze, and returned to his seat against the window.

Sid moved back to the desk. "Better?"

Leo glanced over at Dan, who had picked up his coffee again. There was no point in pretending that he hadn't already known. If, by chance, he hadn't, he would certainly figure it out now. Leo looked up at Sid and nodded. "She's still trying to beat you up, but at least she's not screaming anymore."

Sid sighed. "Sorry about that, kid. I didn't know she'd react like that."

He shrugged. "It's okay. It happens." Leo had to smile as he watched the dead woman continue her relentless yet fruitless beating of his boss.

Sid shivered. "Guess I'm right then, huh?"

"Guess so."

She rubbed her arms. "Violet, you can stop now. I'm not going to tell Buddy."

The spirit gave up her fight and floated back to her post in front of the stacks of file boxes. For his part, Dan didn't bat an eye. He simply sat there, silently sipping his coffee and paying attention to the conversation.

"That's better." Sid shivered a final time and then picked up a file. "What I want to know is how. How did they do it? What was the game exactly? Can we figure out who was ordering the jewelry and who they were selling it to? Can we determine just how inflated the valuations were? It's got to be important because Violet Rizzo kept these secrets buried behind that wall for nearly fifty years." Sid pointed to the stacks of boxes stored on the other side of the wooden frame. "I think she did it because she and her father spent decades laundering money for the Mob. They wouldn't have done it for so long if they hadn't been very, very good at it. I want to know just how good they were, and"—she waved the folder she was holding—"I want to know what her cut was. She bought this house for cash when she moved here, and she never worked a paying job in all the years she lived here. How did she do that? We know how much she sold the business for when she closed up shop and left town, and it certainly wasn't enough to allow her to live so comfortably for nearly fifty years."

She dropped the folder onto the desk. "We are missing something. There's some clue buried in all these files. There has to be." She sighed. "I know there is more to this than we're seeing. There just is. I can feel it. And I want to find out what it is."

The three of them got to work and, once again, went over every single file in Violet's secret stash. By the end of the day, however, they still had no proof of money laundering. No names of the Corsettis or their known associates appeared in the files, and none of the valuations seemed inflated to any significant degree. Frankly, there was no evidence to suggest that Risso & Co. had engaged in anything suspicious, let alone illegal—unless, of course, one considered it suspicious that all those files had been hidden behind a false wall in Violet's office. They were also no closer to finding any so-called missing jewelry, which was the original reason Sid had been hired. Defeated, they left the office, locked the carriage house, and headed for home while Violet Rizzo stared smugly down at them from her office window.

As they turned onto Saragossa Street, Kitty Lonigan greeted them from the sidewalk in front of her house, a chocolate cake in tow. "Hello there. Where have you three been? You look like you've been through the wringer."

"We have," Sid said. "We've been working all day."

Leo took the glass cake stand from Kitty.

"Thank you, my dear." She wrapped her bony hand around his elbow and let him walk her across the street to his grandfather's house. "I made a fresh cake today." She leaned in and whispered, "But I've got yesterday's cake boxed up in the fridge for you to take with you. Come by in the morning before you leave, and I'll give it to you." She winked at him.

He swallowed hard and managed to mumble, "Thanks, Miss Kitty," before he felt his throat constrict to the point where more words were not possible.

Brooklyn's white Jeep was back in the drive, hooked up to the camper and ready to go. Leo recognized Guppy's van parked on the street, so that meant the Geezers were here as well. The heavenly scent of Burt's spareribs cooking on the grill out back wafted across the yard. Leo wanted to slow his pace, drag his feet, and not actually go inside, but Kitty was tugging him along, heading for Burt's front porch.

Sid called out to him as she and Dan veered off toward the backyard. "Leo, I'm going to drop my stuff off in the office, and we'll be over in a few minutes."

He and Kitty climbed the porch steps to Recent Geezer's version of "Runnin' Down a Dream" by Tom Petty. Fitting, he thought.

As he opened the front door and followed Kitty inside, the music ceased, and he heard her chirp, "Look who I found!"

"Leo!" A chorus of voices sang out his name in greeting, and Kitty managed to snatch the cake away from him just before the members of Recent Geezer crushed him in a round of bear hugs.

"There you are!" Paizley glided toward him and wrapped her arms around him, kissing him on the cheek. "We've been waiting for you."

He knew that wasn't true. The others might have been waiting for him, but she hadn't. She'd only recently arrived at the house. She wasn't wearing makeup, and her hair was still damp. It smelled like that new shampoo she'd started using. It was strong and floral. He liked her old shampoo better, the kind that smelled like green apple candy. "Hi, Mom."

"Leo, there you are," cooed Brooklyn as she sauntered down the stairs. Her hair wasn't damp, and her face was thickly coated in makeup, so she hadn't raced to get ready for his party like his mom had. "We have big news. I hope you didn't tell him without me, Paiz."

She threw her arm around Paizley and started to guide her into the living room. Paizley in turn grabbed Leo's arm and dragged him with her. He took a seat on the sofa between Kitty and Eli, and the other Geezers returned to the chairs they'd dragged in from the dining room. Brooklyn and Paizley stood facing them all, Brooklyn looking like the cat who'd just swallowed the canary and Paizley looking decidedly less smug and more nervous.

"Well, as you all know," Brooklyn began, gesturing wildly with her hands, "we spent the last two days in Daytona Beach for Biketoberfest. And it was amazing."

No one said a word. Leo didn't know what Biketoberfest

was, nor did he care. He was also pretty sure that no one else in the room cared that they'd been there either.

Brooklyn continued, looking slightly disappointed that her audience hadn't oohed and aahed at her revelation. "Anyway, we met a guy there who is the head of marketing for this new leather goods company called Hide & Chic. They make purses and bags and stuff, but they are trying to break into the biker market. You know, jackets and chaps. That sort of thing. He was in Daytona doing some marketing, and well . . ." She glanced over at Paizley, eyebrows raised. "Go on. Tell 'em."

Paizley shook her head. "You go ahead."

"He saw our girl here"—she squeezed Paizley's waist— "taking a photo of me on some old guy's bike—"

Leo felt both Eli and Kitty shift in their seats next to him at Brooklyn's utterance of the words "old guy."

"—and he walked up to us and said we were exactly what he was looking for." Paizley's gaze dropped to her feet as Brooklyn prattled on. "Turns out he's looking for a few select influencers—people who are a little bit older and more sophisticated, not these teenagers who are all over social media who haven't actually lived a life yet." Her lip curled in disgust. "Anyway, he loved our look, our whole brand, and he wants us to market Hide & Chic's new line of leather clothing. He took us to dinner and outlined a proposal, and we agreed on a deal."

She bounced up and down, taking Paizley right along with her. "Hide & Chic are going to pay us to wear their clothes and post about it as we travel around. We're going to start in Southern California where they're based and then work our way up to L.A. around Christmas and New Year's." She squealed and hugged Paizley even tighter. "After New Year's, we'll start traveling around the rest of California, and if all goes well, we'll be all up and down the West Coast by the middle of next year. Isn't that exciting?!"

There was silence for a moment before someone asked, "What about Savannah?"

It was Sid, standing in the doorway to the kitchen. She had chosen that moment to arrive, having entered from the back of the house. "And Charleston? And North Carolina and Virginia and Washington, D.C.?" She crossed the dining room and stood at the edge of the living room.

Paizley spun around, breaking free from Brooklyn's hold around her waist. "Oh, well, we'll get there eventually. It's just that we need to be in California as soon as possible to get started."

Sid tilted her head to one side and stared at the two women. She'd changed clothes for his party. Put on a dress and those sandals of hers with the turquoise stones and even brushed her hair. Leo smiled at the effort she'd made, choosing to assume it really was for him and not for Dan, who now stood a few feet behind her.

"What about Christmas?" she asked. "I thought you were coming back here for the holidays?" Raising her voice a little, she added, "I thought Leo was going to get to spend Christmas here, at home, with his grandfather."

"Well, plans changed." Brooklyn tossed her head slightly, and her platinum-blonde hair swished against her shoulders.

Sid pursed her lips and paused a moment, and Leo knew she was trying to rein in her anger. Finally, she asked, "When are you coming back to St. Augustine?"

Brooklyn shrugged. "Who knows?"

"We're not sure," Paizley added. "It may be a while before we can get back here. If things go well in California, it could mean a lot more opportunities for us. The company is eyeing the Canadian market. Maybe Europe as well. This could be our big break." She threw a pleading glance at Leo. "It's going to be great. Really."

"So, what does that mean for Leo?" Sid growled. There was no denying the frustration in her voice.

"Oh, we have big plans for him," Brooklyn agreed. "We're really going to need his help now. Both of us will need to be in the shots when we're wearing the Hide & Chic clothes, and someone has to be there to take the photos." She swept her arm toward him in a big arch. "And that's where Leo comes in. Besides, he's so awesome with Jezzie, and she just loves him. Leo's gonna be a really big help to us."

Leo's heart sank. This was not what his mother had promised. She'd told him he wouldn't be stuck minding the dog while they went off sightseeing, and he wouldn't have to always act as their photographer. Sometimes, yes, but not all the time, not every day. And he would be back in St. Augustine for Christmas. Maybe even Thanksgiving. He stared at his mom, willing her to correct Brooklyn, to deny that this was really their new plan, but she simply stared back at him with that pleading look and said nothing. He felt Kitty's bony, cardigan-covered shoulder brush his arm as she slid closer to him on the sofa.

Sid crossed her arms and stared at both women. "Are you fucking kidding me?!"

Brooklyn blinked in surprise.

Paizley's head spun back around toward Sid. "What do you mean?"

Sid's nostrils flared. "I mean," she nearly growled, "Leo is a fifteen-year-old boy who deserves to spend his time enjoying high school and making friends and doing all the things that teenage boys do. He does not deserve to be dragged all over God-knows-where, taking photos of you two all damn day." She took a step forward, glaring at Paizley. "He deserves to go on dates and make plans for his future. He deserves a stable home and time to grow up and the ability to count on the people he loves to protect him. And he's not going to be able to do any of that stuff if he's stuck being a glorified purse holder and dog walker."

"But he's doing all that stuff now, isn't he?" Brooklyn cocked her head to the side, her hair swishing again. "Isn't he just a glorified errand boy for you?"

Sid ignored Brooklyn and kept her gaze on Paizley, stepping forward until they were only a few feet away from each other. In a low voice that was even scarier than the teacher voice she used with ghosts and spirits, Sid snarled, "You and me. Outside. Right now." Then she stomped forward, forcing Paizley to leap to the side to avoid getting run over.

"What are you talking about?" Paizley's voice shook. "I'm not—"

Sid didn't bother to slow down. "Get your bony ass outside, or I'll drag it out there myself."

Chapter Thirty-Five

By the time Leo got outside, Sid was already pacing back and forth in the front yard, yelling at his mom, and his mom was yelling back. Burt had tried to keep him in the house, but he'd given his grandfather the slip. Now, he stood on the porch steps with Burt on one side of him, arm wrapped tightly around his shoulders, and Dan on the other. It was difficult to concentrate on the actual words over the pounding of his frantic heartbeat, his pulse was so loud in his ears, but he knew they were arguing about him.

Part of him was elated. These two women who cared about him were arguing over who would get to keep him, over who wanted him more, and he had never felt so loved in his life. If he was completely honest with himself, it was mostly Sid arguing and his mom defending herself, but still. The argument was about him. Because they both loved him.

He'd never seen Sid like this. The flush in her cheeks and neck, the anger in her eyes, the arm waving and finger pointing. She was stomping on the grass so hard Leo was afraid she'd kill it. In fact, he was afraid she might kill his mother if she actually got her hands on Paizley. Fighting for him was one thing. Actually punching his mother in the face for him was quite another.

Leo lunged forward, trying to launch himself down the porch steps and across the lawn in time to come between them and avoid an actual physical confrontation, but Dan stepped in front of him, pressing his hands to Leo's chest.

"Stay here," Dan said softly. "They're just talking."

"They're fighting!"

He shook his head. "It's just words. They're not going to fight. It won't come to that."

"You don't know that." Leo struggled against Dan's palms and his grandfather's vise grip on his shoulders.

"Leo, trust me." Dan shifted to block his view. "Let them hash this out."

Leo felt his energy draining away, and tears pricked his eyes. "They're fighting over me," he whispered. This was everything he'd ever wanted—to be loved this much—and yet he just wanted it to stop.

"I know." Dan nodded. "Must be nice. I don't think I've ever had two women fighting over me." He looked over at Burt. "You?"

Burt shook his head. "Can't say that I have."

"I have," Cesar admitted from where he sat on the porch railing, watching the argument. He was swinging one leg, trying to appear very nonchalant about the whole thing, but Leo saw the tension in his muscles. He was like a coiled spring, ready to launch himself off the porch the moment things turned really ugly. "Several times." He glanced over at Leo and winked. "And it was glorious."

Guppy, who stood next to Cesar, shook his head. "You would say that." He, too, looked poised to vault over the railing if necessary.

Brooklyn was noticeably absent from the fracas on the front

lawn. She stood on the porch between the imposing Eli and the diminutive Kitty, chewing her thumbnail. Leo wasn't sure whether her hesitancy to come to her friend's defense was due to her own reluctance to risk physical injury or if it was due to Kitty's warning. Leo had heard the old woman growl, "Don't even think about it, deary," and her words had even made Leo hesitate for a moment.

He stood there helplessly and watched as Sid shouted at Paizley about being selfish and Paizley yelled back that Sid didn't understand what it was like. But Sid did understand. Leo knew that. As put-together as she looked right now with her clean hair and nice sundress, she'd been an absolute mess only a few months ago. She'd lost everything, and it had taken her years to claw her way back to something resembling normal. His mom, on the other hand, was still a mess, still grieving. He knew that her dyed hair, trendy clothes, and constant travel were just her way of dealing with his dad's death. Maybe going to California and wearing leather jackets was her way of clawing back to normal, too. He had no idea. All he knew was that he didn't want to go with her.

Leo felt completely helpless, standing there with Burt's arm around him and Dan's hands pressed to his chest, but as he watched Sid and Paizley square off in the yard, he saw a dark SUV pull up in front of the house. Detective Tony Davis got out, slammed the door, and was through the iron gate in seconds. Leo had never seen the big man move so fast and guessed he must have been scary as hell on the football field when he was young.

"I lost my kid! So I do understand!" Sid screamed, her arms flailing wildly. "And I would give anything in this world to have her back with me. Anything! What I don't understand is how you can just abandon your kid when he needs you most."

"I'm not abandoning him!" Paizley yelled back. "I'm taking him with me."

"To be your photographer! To walk that damn dog!" Sid's eyes appeared ready to bug right out of her skull. "He's your son! Your only son! And he needs you. He needs his mother. He doesn't need this!" She waved a hand at his mom. "He doesn't need this 'Paizley with a Z' nonsense. He doesn't need the posts and the brand and the constant chaos that is your life right now. He needs a home! He needs to be taken care of and protected and made to feel safe."

"I can't protect him!" Paizley flung out her arms. "He sees ghosts! Did he tell you that?! I've had to deal with that his whole life—him seeing things that weren't there, and all the nightmares and the imaginary friends. He was called a freak! My little boy!" She pounded her chest with her fist. "We were shunned by everyone. We had no friends. No one!"

"But you had him! You had Leo!" Sid screamed.

"You don't understand!"

"I don't understand you! That's what I don't fucking understand!"

And that's when Tony Davis, with one arm wrapped around Sid's waist, picked her up and deposited her on the driveway about ten yards away. "Stay there!" he ordered and then marched back over to Paizley. Pulling his badge off his belt and holding it up for her to see, he barked, "Is that yours?" He pointed to the polka-dotted trailer.

"Um . . ." Paizley stared wide-eyed at the hulking detective, at a complete loss for words despite having just hurled a whole flurry of them at Sid.

"It's mine, officer." Brooklyn descended the porch steps, having given Eli and Kitty the slip, and approached Detective Davis with a broad smile. "Actually, it's ours. We both own it."

She pointed to Paizley and then back to herself. "We're travel bloggers and social media influencers."

Leo almost let out a groan, and he heard Kitty huff in disgust.

"Oh, please!" Sid barked. "You two couldn't influence jack shit." She crossed her arms but didn't leave her spot on the driveway.

Brooklyn gave her the middle finger.

Tony clipped his badge back onto his belt. "I'm going to need to see your driver's licenses and the registrations for both vehicles. And I'll ask you to wait inside, please." He looked up at the audience gathered on the porch and pointed to the house. "All of you, back inside now."

No one moved for a second.

"Now!" The detective's voice boomed, hitting them like a nuclear blast wave.

Cesar and Guppy jumped to attention and headed back inside. Eli took Kitty by the arm and escorted her toward the door. Leo heard her say, "I like him. So handsome."

Leo watched as Paizley dashed over to the camper and Brooklyn made for the Jeep, trying to collect the registration certificates. They both gave Sid a wide berth. Less than a minute later they launched themselves up the porch steps past Leo and ducked into the house. While all this was happening, Burt and Dan didn't move. They simply stood there, holding Leo in place. Once his mother and Brooklyn were inside, Burt finally released his hold, patted Leo on the shoulder, and whispered, "It's okay if you want to stay out here."

Leo nodded. He didn't want to listen to his mother rant about Sid, nor did he want to hear Sid rant about his mother. Staying right where he was seemed like the best option.

Dan stayed put as well. He moved to stand next to Leo,

folded his arms across his chest, and sighed. "I think this might be the weirdest party I've ever been invited to."

Leo let loose a small laugh. "Me too."

"At the house earlier today," Dan began, "who was it? Was it Violet?"

Leo nodded.

"Thought so."

He glanced over at the man. "Did Sid tell you?"

"No." He shook his head. "She and I had a discussion about spirits and the afterlife and whatnot. My mom has a bit of the gift. Nothing as amazing as yours, by the way, but enough that she thinks she can boss me around when she wants to."

Leo bit his lip to keep from smiling.

"I figured the rest out for myself at Violet's house." He nodded toward the front door behind them. "Guess everyone else knows now, huh?"

"Yeah." Leo hung his head and ran the toe of his sneaker along a groove in the porch's floorboards. "I wish she hadn't done that. Just told everyone like that. I try to keep it a secret. It's just . . . easier."

"I get that," Dan agreed. "Sometimes it's easier to bury our secrets so that no one can use them against us. Because people will, won't they? They'll try to hurt you with them or use them for their own gain."

Leo nodded.

"Yeah, keeping secrets seems easier than sharing the truth sometimes, especially if you've been burned before." He sighed. "It's a tough choice, especially when you're young. You want to trust people to do the right thing, but they don't always do it. Do they?"

Leo shook his head. After a few moments of silence, he looked up at Dan. "What do I do now?"

Dan rubbed his chin. "I don't know, Leo. But the truth is

out now, at least with everyone here." He hooked his thumb over his shoulder toward the door. "You're lucky to have nice people around who care about you, so I don't think you'll have much of a problem with this group."

Leo bit his lip and nodded.

"Besides, sometimes burying secrets does more harm than good. Look at Violet Rizzo. She spent fifty years burying her secrets, and where did that get her? She lived her whole life constantly worried that someone would learn the truth of what she'd done. Fifty years guarding that hoard of files. Fifty years of writing letters, waiting to learn if someone had figured out the truth." He shook his head. "Keeping your secrets buried, being vigilant like that every moment of every day, must be exhausting. It's no way to live."

He reached over and squeezed Leo's shoulder. "You know what they say, Leo. Sometimes, the truth can set you free."

Chapter Thirty-Six

"What the hell was all that about?" Tony stood in Sid's office, blocking the door.

He needn't have bothered, though. She'd had enough. She'd said her piece. Finally. Shouted it, actually. Now she felt both better and worse, worse because she'd done it in front of Leo. The rest of the gang, all of them watching them from the porch, hadn't bothered her, but poor Leo. He'd seen her lose her cool with Paizley. No, that was an understatement. He'd watched her go ballistic, all but accusing the woman of being a bad mother. How she'd managed not to shout those exact words was a mystery, but at least she hadn't. Saying that phrase seemed like a step too far. But judging by the way Tony was looking at her now, maybe she'd gone well past "too far" without even realizing it. What exactly had she said out there? She suddenly couldn't remember. Whatever it had been, hopefully Leo would forgive her.

She grabbed a bottle of water from the mini fridge and took a sip. Her throat was killing her. "It's a long story."

"I got time," Tony shot back. "Now, what the hell happened?"

She sighed and told him everything—about Leo's struggles when he first arrived in St. Augustine, about him starting to come into his own, and about her growing fondness for the kid. She told him about their dinner on the bayfront walk when Leo had told her all about his and his mother's plans to travel around the Southeast and eventually head to D.C. She told him about Leo crying on her shoulder when she told him she'd miss him and how she didn't think he really wanted to go with Paizley now that the moment had arrived. And she told him about the big announcement tonight in Burt's living room—that PB&J were the new face of some pissant startup from California that made leather chaps, of all things, and that they were bringing Leo with them so that he could carry their makeup bag and pick up dog shit.

"I lost it," she admitted as she paced back and forth. She was still vibrating with anger, or perhaps it was the post-adrenaline shakes. Either way, she didn't stop moving. If she did, she might just curl into a ball and sink into that deep, dark hole once again. "And I know that you and Burt and Dan and everyone told me that I should just shut up about it and let the kid go with his mother, but damn it, Tony! Someone needs to fight for that kid!" Her voice broke. She'd heard it break, so she knew he'd heard it, too.

He walked over to her, wrapped his big hands gently around her upper arms, and held her in place. "You did good."

And she broke. The anger at Paizley, the frustration with her own feelings, and the fear regarding Leo's safety and well-being all came rushing out of her in one giant sob. Tony wrapped her up in a hug, and she cried into his chest, soaking his shirt. The pain wasn't as sharp as it had been when she lost Wes and Iris. No, this was more of a deep, endless ache.

Regardless, it was still pain, and she vowed to never feel this way again. Not ever, not about anyone.

Tony held her tight and let her cry. "You're okay, Sid. And Leo's gonna be okay, too. He knows you love him. That's what matters. And if he didn't know before tonight, he certainly knows now that you can be mean as hell as well."

She would have laughed, but there was no room for amusement in her current swirl of emotions. He held her until her crying ceased and the fight left her body. Then he eased her over to the green velvet guest chair with the sagging bottom. He took the other one, reaching for the stack of napkins on the shelf behind him and handing her several.

"I should arrest you for disturbing the peace."

Sid snorted a laugh as she dried her eyes and wiped her nose.

"But you put on quite a show. Naomi would have been proud." He grinned at her. "She's a big fan of those reality TV shows where everyone's always yelling at each other." He shook his head. "She's gonna be sorry she missed your performance tonight."

"Well, if we're lucky, someone caught it on video and will post it online. She can watch it along with everyone else in the world. Maybe I'll go viral."

"Maybe." He waited for her to blow her nose before saying, "You know you have to let him go."

Sid nodded. "I know."

"When does he leave?"

"Tomorrow morning."

Tony blew out a breath. "Please don't make me come out here tomorrow and arrest you for the murder of Leo's mother."

She managed a weak half smile. "What makes you think you'll be able to prove it's me?"

He folded his thick arms across his broad chest. "I'm very good at my job."

Sid cocked an eyebrow. "With my help."

"Oh, please. You got lucky a couple of times."

"It's hardly luck, Detective. I'm very good at my job, too."

He nodded slowly. "And it has nothing to do with the kid being able to talk to dead people? Let me guess, the ghosts tell him who the murderer is."

"For the record"—she held up her index finger, when it was really the middle one she wanted to wave at him—"Leo never spoke to the spirits of Cameron Chase or Dru Chase. We solved that on our own."

"No ghosts?"

Sid hesitated, biting her lip. "Not exactly." He huffed, and she added, "There were two dead golfers out at Oakmire. They saw Dru Chase's murder, so we knew who did that. We just had to prove it. But they didn't see Cameron's murder. That one, we solved on our own."

"And the sheriff?"

Sid nodded and slumped in her chair, the last of her energy ebbing away. "Wes showed Leo what happened." She tapped the side of her head. "He can see things that spirits show him. Wes showed him the accident and the sheriff and how it all played out."

"Shit," hissed Tony, sitting forward. "That must have been horrible."

Sid shut her eyes, squeezing them tight, and shook her head once before opening them again. "It was. He was battered and bruised from the experience. Apparently, spirits and ghosts can harm him. It's . . . it's tricky. He wants to use his gift. He likes being able to help people with it, and he has a woman in town who's helping him learn how to control it, but he's still just a kid, and he needs to be protected. He needs to be kept safe."

She shook her head again. "Paizley's not going to do it. She can't or doesn't want to, I don't know. But—"

"But she's his mother." Tony patted her arm. "And you will let him go tomorrow. You'll say goodbye and wave as he drives away, and you will be sad and angry and everything else you're feeling. But you will not slash her tires or beat her up, and you will not stop that woman from taking her son with her." Sid inhaled, nostrils flaring, but Tony cut her off. "I mean it, Sid. Don't make me come back here and arrest you."

"Fine." She closed her eyes and let her head fall back against the chair. "Why are you here, anyway? Did someone actually call the police on me?"

"I looked into that name you gave me: Joseph Rizzo. Also went by Risso with two s's?"

Sid sat up. "He was Violet Rizzo's father." If anything would keep her from sliding into a deep depression at this point, it was her work. "And?"

"Nothing." He shrugged. "My buddy told me that Joseph Rizzo died of a heart attack. He went into cardiac arrest at home. Paramedics were called, but the guy died on the way to the hospital. Nothing suspicious."

"Huh." She frowned. "You're sure."

"You sound disappointed? Hoping for something more exotic?"

"Mob hit." She shrugged.

He sat back and studied her for a long moment. "You better start at the beginning."

"I can't discuss my client's—"

"Bullshit, Sid." Tony crossed his ankle over his knee. "When you start talking about Mob hits, you better know that I'm gonna demand that you tell me everything. I ain't leavin' here until you do."

She shook her head.

"Don't make me call Naomi." He raised an eyebrow. "The last thing you want is my wife comin' in here. She'll make you talk, believe me."

Sid couldn't help but grin. "All right." And, for the second time that night, Sid told Detective Tony Davis everything.

———

Only a few minutes after Tony left, there was a knock on her door. She was still sitting in the sagging guest chair, feeling completely spent and unable to move. Her plan had been to just fall asleep right where she sat, assuming sleep would come. Apparently, that was not in the cards for her tonight.

She took a deep breath and hoisted herself up out of the chair, but she lacked the energy to cross the floor and open the door. Leaning back against the desk, she braced herself for what was sure to be a tongue-lashing from an angry Burt Roberts, come to chide her for opening her big mouth and hurting Leo's feelings.

"It's open," she called out.

Dan Murdock opened the door and stepped into the office.

She blinked in surprise. "You're still here?"

"I'm still here." He nodded. "I sat with Leo on the porch for a while, and we waited for things to calm down in the house." Sid winced, but he simply smiled at her. "He's okay. Tough kid. He'll be fine."

She nodded, grateful to him for saying that. "Is everyone still in the house?"

"No. The band went home, and Burt had to escort Kitty back to her house because she didn't want to leave Leo alone with his mother."

Sid frowned. "Where's Brooklyn?" Her heart skipped a

beat, hoping he'd say that the woman had left town for good without taking Paizley and Leo with her.

"She got into it with Paizley and then stormed out. I think she's still holed up in her camper."

"Why? What were they fighting about?"

Dan pursed his lips and rubbed at the stubble on his chin. "I'm afraid they were fighting about Leo." He walked toward her. "Evidently, Brooklyn didn't know about Leo's gift. She said that he couldn't come with them, but Paizley insisted. There was shouting back and forth, but Paizley promised her that Leo would keep his gift under wraps and not tell anyone."

Sid huffed. "That's rich, coming from the woman who outed him in front of everyone this evening."

"Yeah." He crossed his arms. "I think she feels really bad about that."

"So he's not going?" she asked, finally seeing a ray of hope in all this darkness.

But he shook his head. "No. I think he's still going. Paizley and Brooklyn reached a compromise. Paizley promised her that Leo wouldn't mention anything to them about seeing ghosts or anything like that, and she and Brooklyn agreed not to talk about it anymore."

Sid felt like screaming all over again. Instead, she ran her hands down her face and blew out a long, slow breath. "What did Leo say?"

"Nothing." Dan shrugged. "He and I were sitting on the porch, so he wasn't involved in their conversation."

"But he heard it all?"

"Yeah, he did. And he was pretty upset."

Sid nodded. "He has every right to be." She forced herself to a standing position. Despite feeling exhausted, there was more than enough anger coursing through her right then to propel her back into the house and probably give Tony Davis a very good reason to come back and arrest her. She moved toward the door, but Dan stepped in front of her.

Placing his hands gently on her upper arms, he said, "Let him be, Sid. He needs some time with his mom."

"But I—"

"He knows, Sid." He held her gaze and rubbed her arms. "He knows. Trust me."

She let him hold her. His hug was much different from Tony's, and Sid didn't feel compelled to soak his shirt with her tears. It was also much different from Wes's, because she still remembered how it felt to be in her husband's arms. Nevertheless, some small part of her felt compelled to take his hand and lead him upstairs.

But she wouldn't. First of all, the idea of being intimate with someone new frightened her. She was still mourning Wes, at least on some level. She might have made peace with her husband's death, but that peace had only recently arrived. And her feelings for Wes had not yet subsided to the point where there was enough room for an entanglement with someone else. Second, she'd only spent a few days in Dan's company, and while she had no doubt that she could fall for this man—eventually, down the line, after some respectable amount of time— the reality was that he would be leaving soon, sailing off into the sunset, bound for other ports of call, and she would be left here by herself. Left all alone, missing him. She couldn't add that loss to the lingering grief she still felt over losing her husband and daughter, not to mention the fresh grief she was experiencing over Leo's departure.

So getting closer to Dan was a terrible idea. Tantalizing but terrible. She'd just vowed not to get close to anyone ever again— a promise she had made to herself while crying in Tony's arms.

She wasn't about to break that vow a mere ten minutes later, while in Dan's arms.

So she stepped out of his embrace. "Thanks for staying. I'm sorry for tonight and for, well, everything."

"Sid—"

She shook her head. "I think you should go."

Chapter Thirty-Seven

L eo lay on his bed, staring at the ceiling, not knowing what to do. Everything had gone so wrong tonight. One moment he'd been walking home with Sid and Dan, talking about Violet Rizzo and the Mob, and the next Sid was yelling at his mom for, well, being a bad mom. And Sid was right. Paizley was being a bad mom.

He curled onto his side, facing the wall, and hugged his pillow tightly. He didn't want to go to California, at least not like this. He didn't want to be the official PB&J photographer, following the two women around every day and handling cameras and lighting and whatever other nonsense they made him do. And he didn't want to take care of Jezebel. The dog wasn't his; it shouldn't be his responsibility to feed it and walk it and pick up its poop. And that wasn't even the worst of it. His mom had told him the camper wasn't big enough to fit another adult, so he'd have to sleep outside in a tent. In a sleeping bag. On the ground. In the wild. He hadn't even told Sid about that part because he worried that she'd lose her mind.

Well, she'd done that anyway, and he'd simply stood there

like an idiot and watched as she ranted about all the things he needed, all the things he should have in his life. Truth was, he did want those things—to have a home and make friends and go on dates and plan for his future. When would he get to do any of that? Certainly not while living in a tent and moving around every few days. His mom had promised it wouldn't be like this. She'd promised him.

He pressed his face into the pillow, wanting to scream just like Sid had, but he kept quiet. It wouldn't matter anyway. He had no say in the matter, not that anyone but Sid was listening.

Someone knocked on his door.

"Go away." He was in no mood to see anyone. He just wanted this horrible night to be over.

The door opened, and the person entered. The bed shifted with their weight as they sat. He knew it was his mom by the flowery scent of her shampoo.

"Leo," she whispered.

He didn't respond.

"Leo, I want to say something, and I hope you'll listen." She sighed. "I loved your dad so much."

Leo's heart felt like someone was squeezing it with both hands.

"You know the story. We never kept it from you. I got pregnant, he and I got married, and you came along. And while I don't regret a single minute of my life before, I finally have a chance to do what I've always wanted to do."

She placed a hand on his arm and gently rubbed it. "I love being your mom. I love it so much. And I loved being Gunner's wife. But that's all I was for so many years. I had to drop out of high school my senior year. My parents disowned me. I worked two jobs, sometimes three, just to help pay rent and put food on the table. I studied and took a class to finally get my GED, but I never went to college. I never joined a sorority or went to frat parties. By that time, I was raising a toddler and waiting tables and cleaning offices at night while the woman who lived next door babysat you."

She removed her hand from Leo's arm, and the sensation, the lack of touch, was like being doused with ice. He wanted her to put her hand back and keep rubbing his arm, but he remained silent.

She sighed. "I know everyone thinks I'm being really selfish, and I suppose I am. But I feel like for the first time in so, so long, I am finally something other than just your mom or Gunner's wife. I'm me. I'm Paizley Roberts. And when I write something or post something, people see it. And they like it. And I finally feel like I'm doing something for me, like I'm myself again. And I haven't felt that way in such a long time."

She shifted on the bed, and Leo felt her knee brush against his back. "Leo, I wish you'd talk to me. I want to talk about this. I know our plans changed last minute, but this is really important to me. This is my job now. People are paying me to do something I really love. Something I'm good at. Really, *really* good at. And I think this could turn into something big."

She reached out and rubbed his arm again, and Leo almost sighed with relief.

"I hoped you would be happy for me," Paizley added.

Leo immediately stiffened at her comment.

She sighed again. "I hoped you'd be excited about all of this. You've been saying you wanted to come with us, and now you can. Maybe it's not what we originally talked about, but it's going to be great. You'll see."

He squeezed his eyes tight and fisted his hands in the pillow. He shook his head. He couldn't say what he wanted to say.

"Leo." Her voice took on a sterner tone. "Leo, roll over and look at me. I want to talk about this."

"Why?" he grumbled, gripping the pillow so tightly he was afraid he'd tear it. "So you can just make more promises you don't plan on keeping?"

"That's not fair."

Leo had had enough. "Fair!" he barked, throwing the pillow off the bed. "You know what's not fair?"

He rolled over and stood up, beginning to pace like he'd seen Sid do so many times. "It's not fair that you moved me out of Norfolk without asking me. It's not fair that you drove me all the way down here and then left me with Grandpa without even asking me. It's not fair that you told me we're going to Charleston and D.C. and all those other places, and then you change your mind and announce that we're going to California instead. We didn't talk about any of that, now, did we?!"

"Leo—"

But he wasn't done. "It's not fair that you told me that I don't have to take pictures and watch the dog all the time, but now you're telling me that I do." He ran his hands through his hair, tugging at his curls. "And it's not fair that you promised Brooklyn that I'll keep quiet about seeing spirits or hearing them talk to me. That I'll just walk around pretending that all those things aren't happening to me. All. The. Time." He wanted to throw something, to hit something. Hard. "It's not fair that you promised her I'll keep all of this a secret. That I'll pretend to be something that I'm not. That you didn't even ask me." He stopped pacing. "I'm so tired of keeping secrets, Mom. I'm so tired of always hiding, always lying about what I see and hear. Lying about who I am."

He threw his arms out wide. "What about what I want, Mom? What about *me*?!" The dam broke, the tears began to fall, and Leo sank to his knees.

Paizley kneeled next to him and wrapped her arms around him. He closed his eyes and cried on his mother's shoulder, and she rubbed his back and rocked him like she used to do when he was little. But he wasn't little anymore. He was grown-up now. Much more grown-up than he'd been when she'd left him here a few months ago.

"I'm sorry, kiddo. I'm so sorry." She kept rocking him, and he let her. "You're right. I never asked what you wanted, not really. I came back for you because you said you wanted me to. You said you wanted to come with us, but maybe that's not really true." She took him by the shoulders and leaned back, forcing him to meet her gaze. "Is it?"

He shook his head.

"You want to stay here in St. Augustine?"

He nodded, wiping his nose with the back of his hand.

"You're happy here?"

"Yes." It was only a whisper, but he meant it.

"Do you want me to stay here, too?"

Her eyes searched his, and Leo's heart nearly broke in two.

Chapter Thirty-Eight

When Sid emerged the next day, she stepped out of her office into the bright, midmorning sunshine to find the Jeep and camper gone. Her stomach twisted, the coffee she'd drunk earlier now feeling like molten lava in its pit. "Damn it." She hung her head, closed her eyes, and took a slow, steadying breath. She should have come down to see him off. She should have gone to the house last night and hugged him and said goodbye. She should have done a lot of things. But she'd done none of them.

"You look like crap."

Her eyes flew open, and she found Leo standing in front of her, wearing his Jacksonville Suns baseball cap, his father's old Incubus T-shirt, and that familiar, cheeky grin. She'd never been so happy to see anyone smirk at her. Ever. "So do you, kid."

His grin grew wider. "What's on the agenda today, boss?"

She pressed her lips together and held up her hand to her brow, pretending to shield her eyes from the sun. The reality was that she just wanted to look at him without him meeting her gaze, without him being able to see the complete and total relief she felt in that moment written all over her face. "Nice T-shirt," she said, to buy herself a moment to gather her composure.

"Thanks." He ran a hand down the front of it. "I can wear them again, now that Mom's gone."

She nodded. "You're not needed elsewhere today?"

"Nope." He shook his head. "Grandpa said I can help you if you need me. But we have to be back tonight in time to get dressed for the gig. The band's playing at Granny Oak's."

"Well, let's get going." She began walking, heading back to Violet Rizzo's house, and Leo fell in step beside her. "Are you going to tell me what happened, or do I have to drag it out of you?"

He shrugged, shoving his hands into his pockets. "They left this morning."

"I figured that much out for myself, kid. The absence of the polka-dotted camper kind of gave it away." Sid shook her head. "I mean, why aren't you with them?"

He stared at his feet as they walked, remaining quiet for a few moments. "Mom and I talked last night. I yelled a lot. Seems I learned a thing or two from you, after all."

She reached for his arm, tugging him to a stop. "About that, Leo—"

He threw his arms around her neck in a tight hug and whispered, "Thanks, Sid."

She hugged him, patted his back, and then they released each other and stepped away. "And your mom? She's okay with you staying?"

He nodded. "She offered to stay here with me." He looked away from her, down the empty street. "But I told her she should go." He shrugged. "She really wants to do this travel blogger thing. It makes her happy, happier than I've ever seen her. She talked a lot about that last night. About how she finally feels like a real person again. Like, she's finally back to living again."

Sid fought the lump in her throat and swallowed. "I get that."

"Yeah, I know." He knew she understood.

They turned and continued along the sidewalk, and Leo added, "We made plans to talk on the phone every Sunday and at least one night every week. Probably Wednesdays, but we agreed to be flexible. And I have to text her every day with an update on school and work and everything."

"So she's okay with you still working with me?"

He nodded.

"Good." Sid's heart leaped. "I'm glad." She nudged him with her elbow. "Because I'm going to need your help today."

———

They arrived at Violet's house and went straight to the office. Violet was nowhere to be found. They searched the rest of the carriage house, the main house, and the courtyard, calling her name the entire time, but the dead woman's spirit never appeared.

"She's always here, freezing us out, whenever we don't want her around, but when we do need her, she's nowhere to be seen." Sid opened the carriage house door and, once more, ushered Leo inside. "Why are spirits so damn finicky?"

Leo shrugged. He looked around the garage, lifted the cover on the big Cadillac, and checked inside the car for the second time that morning. No Violet Rizzo.

"Why does she still have this old car?" he asked, tucking the cover back into place.

"Huh?" asked Sid, checking the little bathroom under the staircase for that telltale drop in temperature. No such luck.

"Why didn't she just sell it? She wasn't driving it anymore. Why keep it?" He spun around, checking one more time for any signs of the dead woman.

Sid emerged from the bathroom and stared at the car. "Interesting." She grabbed the front of the cover and lifted it. "Help me get this off."

The Cadillac was still shiny. No dents and only a handful of tiny scratches. It was unlocked, and Sid slid into the driver's seat. The leather was pristine; the dash and console were dusty but unmarred. The odometer showed less than twenty thousand miles on the vehicle. She ran her hand over the smooth leather of the steering wheel. "She must have driven to church and the grocery store and that's it." She reached for the glove box, but it was locked.

Fishing out the set of keys that Buddy had loaned her, she confirmed what she already knew. There were no car keys on the ring. She checked the console and under the seat, and then she flipped down the sun visor. A set of keys dropped into her lap. "Could it be that easy?" she whispered to herself.

The glove box contained the car's manual, a vehicle registration that was nearly four years out of date, and a packet of tissues. She popped the trunk and instructed Leo to check inside, including the spare tire compartment.

"It's empty." He shut the trunk, the sound echoing around the bare bones of the garage.

Sid popped the hood and checked underneath it, but having no idea what she was looking at, she let it fall back into place. "I think we'll have to give up." She kneeled to check under the car.

"Um, Sid—"

"Yeah?" She activated the flashlight on her phone and lay

down on her stomach, happy to have chosen to wear an old tee and pair of shorts today.

"Sid!"

The temperature dropped sharply, and Sid felt a slight breeze across the crown of her head. She looked up at Leo. "I guess we found her. What's she doing? Sitting on my head?"

"Kicking it."

"Really?" Sid tried not to laugh. "Well, that's a first."

"That you know of," Leo muttered.

"True." She turned her attention back to the task at hand, shining her flashlight at the car's undercarriage. "It could have been happening on and off for years. Lots of spirits and ghosts, all of them taking turns trying to beat me up."

The light snagged on something on the floor. Sid crawled around the side of the car to get a better look. There was definitely something under the vehicle. "Help me get this garage door open."

It took several minutes and a fair bit of WD-40 to get the garage door's manual slide lock to open. Once the door was up, Sid tried and failed to start the car, but with the brake released and the gearshift in neutral, they were able to push it out, into the sunshine.

"Well, what do you know?" Sid stood next to Leo, wiping the dirt off her T-shirt and staring down at a small safe built into the floor of the garage.

He kneeled and spun the dial back and forth. "Why didn't Mr. Rizzo tell us about this?"

Sid kneeled next to him and squeezed his shoulder. "I don't think he knew."

Half an hour later, she was no longer smiling. They'd tried every combination she could think of. Leo was pretty handy with the dial combination. His teenage hearing was much better at picking up the clicks of the tumblers than her forty-something ears were, so he lay down with his head close to the dial and spun it to whatever number she called out. For her part, she combed through her endless pages of notes and lists and logs. All they had to show for their efforts was the very first number: 6.

"Okay," said Sid, laying her notes aside. "It's probably three or four numbers. Starting with 6."

Her phone rang in her bag, and Sid fished it out and answered it. "Hey."

"Hey, yourself. How are you?" Dan's voice was low and soft, and Sid wished for the hundredth time that she hadn't sent him away last night.

"I'm good." And she was, except where he was concerned. "I'm at Violet's house, and guess who's here with me."

"The spirit of the recently departed Violet Rizzo."

She giggled. Yep, actually giggled. The sound was foreign even to her own ears. Leo frowned at her like she'd farted. "No, Leo's here. He decided not to go on a walkabout after all."

"That's awesome! Ah, Sid. I'm really happy to hear that. Happy for you both."

Dan sounded genuine, and Sid's heart fluttered, a feeling like beating wings inside her rib cage.

"Listen, I won't keep you. I'm sure you and Leo have a lot to talk about, but I wanted to let you know that I thought of something, and I'm kicking myself for not remembering it sooner, but we got so caught up in those files in Violet's office that I just put the Corsetti code out of my mind."

Sid frowned. They hadn't talked about the code in any detail since he'd convinced her it made sense, and that was days ago. "What is it?"

"There was a letter that Paul wrote to Violet almost seven years ago that mentioned the subway."

"Wait." Sid shook her head. "Are you telling me that you remember what's in every one of Violet's letters?"

"No, but I made a spreadsheet."

"Of course you did." She grinned.

"I made a spreadsheet of the information in Violet's letters—dates, players' names, locations, key words, etcetera. That's how I began to see patterns." Dan cleared his throat. "I can't remember the exact wording, but he mentioned something about Violet seeing one of the Yankees, Bobby Bonds, on the subway. Paul wrote to her that she must have been mistaken because the guy was long dead. Bonds died in 2003."

"Okay . . ."

"Well, I came back from my run this morning—I missed you, by the way." His voice dropped low with that latter comment. "And I saw one of those red trolleys go by. You know the ones I'm talking about? You can ride them around town and see all the sights. They seem to be everywhere, frankly. And I thought: What if Violet saw one of the old mobsters on a trolley tour in St. Augustine?"

"Okay . . ."

"Hear me out. What if she mentioned the subway, and not the trolley, because their code was always based on people and places in New York City. And what if she simply used the wrong player's name?" He began talking faster, clearly excited about his new theory. "She mentioned Bobby Bonds. but what if she got the name wrong? Maybe she was in a rush, maybe she was rattled, and she couldn't remember the correct name for the Yankees' current right fielder, so she used one she did remember. Bonds played for the Yankees in 1975 and had been dead for years. Wrong player's name, but correct player's position. If my code is correct, I think she was trying to point to a Corsetti mobster named Gio Segreti." He paused to take a breath. "Sid, what if Violet really did see someone from her past? What if she saw Gio Segreti right here in St. Augustine?"

Sid was quiet, chewing her bottom lip as her mind spun. "Maybe she got spooked."

"Exactly. What if she thought the Corsettis had finally found her?"

"That would certainly make anyone flustered."

"Enough to mess up the code," Dan agreed. "But I think Paul must have figured it out because, in the next letter he wrote, he mentioned the guy who was actually the right fielder for the Yankees that year. And that player's name appeared in three more letters right after that."

"So you think Paul was keeping tabs on Gio Segreti or whichever mobster Violet saw in St. Augustine and was reporting back to her?" Sid pinched the bridge of her nose. "Shit," she hissed. "Maybe you're right."

"Usually am." She could practically hear him grinning through the phone. "You might want to check the letter. It'll have a February date from seven years ago. See if I'm remembering it correctly. But I think Violet Rizzo saw a ghost from her past, and she told Paul DeLuca about it."

"DeLuca died the same way Violet did," Sid blurted out. "In his house, at night, on the stairs."

There was no hesitation on Dan's part. "I'm coming right over."

The line went dead, and Sid pointed to the stairs. "Leo, I need you to go upstairs and find the February letter from seven years ago. I organized them all in reverse chronological order, so it should be in the top box. I need to see it." He wrinkled his nose at the idea of having to even touch the love letters. "Just go!"

He grumbled but jogged up the staircase to retrieve the letter. She stared down at the phone in her lap, debating whether to call Buddy Rizzo. If she did, he would probably come right over, take one look at the safe, assume the missing jewelry was inside, and send her home. And that would be the end of the job.

But Sid didn't want it to be over. Yes, she wanted to know what was in the safe, but she also wanted to know the details of Violet Rizzo's grift against the Corsetti Mafia. And most of all, she wanted to know if the old woman's death was really a Mob hit. Paul DeLuca died three years after Violet mentioned seeing a familiar mafioso's face in the Old City, and he died in the exact same way as Violet had. Granted, Violet died four years after him, but still. What were the odds?

Sid tried to rein in her anxiety, which was starting to buck and kick like a wild horse. This could all be just one long series of coincidences. Nothing more. But she no longer believed in coincidences.

And if she called Buddy now, she would never get any of the answers she sought. So she wouldn't call him yet. Soon, but not yet.

She stretched forward to put her phone back in her bag and was struck by a thought. She tapped the screen and brought up the phone's keypad. Violet Rizzo was old-school. She stored a hundred years' worth of paper files in her office, for crying out loud. What if her safe's combination was a word, not a number? Studying the keypad, Sid saw the number 6 stood for the letters M, N, and O.

"Could it be that simple?" she whispered to herself.

Sid turned the dial slowly: 6, 4, 6, and 2. A loud click echoed in the now-empty garage, and Sid opened the safe.

Chapter Thirty-Nine

Sid had just finished snapping half a dozen date-stamped photos of the safe and its untouched contents and was donning a pair of latex gloves when Leo came downstairs with Violet's love letter.

"You got it open? How?" He rushed over and stood staring down into the safe. "Well, that's disappointing."

"Don't be so sure, kid." Sid carefully lifted the manilla envelope out of the safe. Its contents were too thin and smooth to be jewelry. "Not every buried treasure has to be gold and jewels."

"Maybe it's a map!" Leo's eyes blazed with excitement. "Maybe she drew a map to show where the treasure is buried."

"I doubt any treasure is actually buried, kid. It's just a figure of speech. I think it's much more likely that Violet's missing jewelry is in a safe deposit box somewhere. Or maybe she sold it all, and the cash is sitting in a Swiss bank account. Although I'm still not convinced there is an actual stash of missing jewelry."

"You mean other than the ruby necklace?" Leo added.

She nodded. "Yeah, kid. Other than the ruby necklace."

The envelope looked new and clean, unmarked except for "Attn: Carleigh Sutton" written across the front in Violet's now-familiar handwriting. Sid unfastened the clasps and slid out a stapled set of handwritten pages.

"Whatcha got there?"

Sid and Leo both jumped. Dan Murdock strolled in through the open garage door. Sweat glistened on his brow and dampened his shirt, so he must have sprinted all the way here.

"Don't do that!" Sid chided. Thankfully, she hadn't dropped the envelope or its contents.

"Sorry, didn't mean to scare you." He approached with his hands raised and a guilty grin on his face. "The door was open."

"You're just in time." She held up the stapled document, turning it so he could read the first page.

His eyebrows shot up. "Interesting."

"Let's go upstairs." Sid picked her bag up from the floor and led the way. "I don't want to do this down here."

They left the safe open but closed the garage door, leaving Violet's Cadillac still parked outside, and went upstairs to the office. Dan and Leo cleared off the desk so that Sid could set down the envelope and the stapled pages.

Sid read the first page, waiting until the two men standing next to her nodded, and then turned to the second page. She blew out a breath, and Dan let out a long, low whistle.

Leo rubbed the back of his neck. "So, what is all this?"

Sid hovered her gloved finger over the first line of hand-written text and began to read the words out loud:

1. 18K Gold Ring – Center Stone: 4.25-ct Asscher-cut Emerald – Side Stones: 2 x 0.05-ct Asscher-cut Diamonds

> 2. *Platinum Tennis Bracelet – TCW: 3.00-ct –*
>   *Diamonds: Round Brilliant-Cut, 0.05-ct each*
>
> 3. *18K Gold Necklace – Center Stone: 5.00-ct Emerald-*
>   *Cut Sapphire – Side Stones: 2 x 1.00-ct Round-Cut*
>   *Sapphires – Accent Stones: 10 x 0.05-ct Round-Cut*
>   *Diamonds*

She smiled. "I think we're looking at Violet's missing treasure." She scanned the rest of Violet's detailed list, looking for one item in particular. "Huh," she said, upon reaching the end of the list.

"What?" asked Leo, no longer paying attention to the document.

"I don't see the ruby necklace." She flipped back to the first page of the list and scanned it again.

Dan pointed to an item on the second page listed as number 11. "There's a ruby necklace."

"I don't think that's it." Sid shook her head. "Hey, Leo, is she here?"

"Yeah." He'd been watching Violet Rizzo out of the corner of his eye, but now the old woman held his full attention. Her shoulders sagged, her posture slumped, and she looked like all the fight had gone out of her, but she still clutched the necklace at her throat.

"Still wearing the necklace?"

"Yeah."

"Is it"—she read from the list—"the eighteen-karat gold tennis necklace, with a total of 11.6-carats in round-cut rubies and diamonds, a tenth of a carat each?"

Leo shrugged. "How would I know?"

"Well, you're looking at it."

"Yeah, but I don't know anything about jewelry. What does all that even mean?"

"All right." Sid took a breath. "It should be a thin necklace with lots of tiny, little diamonds and rubies."

He shook his head. "No. The one she's wearing has kind of a big ruby in the middle and some other smaller rubies around it, and there's a bunch of little diamonds." He twirled his fingers in front of his throat. "They're kind of bunched together. Not sure what it's supposed to look like, though. Some kind of weird flower, maybe?" He shrugged. "I don't know."

"That's okay," Sid patted his shoulder. "That's helpful, Leo. Really helpful." She pointed to the item in Violet's list. "This ruby necklace—number 11—isn't the same one that's around Violet's neck. In fact, I think I've seen this number 11 necklace before." She bit her lip and swung her gaze to the stacks of file boxes. "It's somewhere in there." She glanced down at the list again. "I think all of these are in there."

She grabbed her bag from the floor where she'd dropped it and rummaged around for her notes on the mystery customers. She ran her finger down the list of names. "Here." She turned the page around so the guys could see it. "Number 11 was a piece bought by one of the fictitious customers. You know, the customers listed in the files with the weird discrepancies." She tapped the page and then pointed to Violet's handwritten list on the desk. "I'm willing to bet that all of that jewelry will be found in those discrepancy files."

"Okay." Dan nodded slowly. "Then they should be easy enough to find. We still have all those files marked in the boxes." He grinned at Sid. "Bet you're glad I went nuts with all the color-coded flags, now, aren't you?"

Everyone took photos of Violet's handwritten pages with their phones. Dan and Leo got to work pulling files to try to find all of the jewelry on Violet's list, and Sid left the office and headed downstairs, placing a phone call as she went.

When the call went straight to voicemail, she fired off a quick text that included two photos: one of the in-ground safe and one of the first page of Violet's handwritten document. Less than a minute later, her phone rang.

"What exactly am I looking at here, Sidney?!" Carleigh Sutton's voice sounded frantic, and Sid heard the din of traffic in the background.

"I found the document this morning," Sid explained. "Violet had an in-ground safe hidden under her old car in her garage. I managed to get it open and found the document inside."

"How . . . what . . . how . . ." Carleigh stammered before blowing out a loud, steadying breath into the phone. "Okay. First of all, how on earth did you manage to get the safe open?"

"I'm very good at my job." Sid couldn't help but smile.

"How do I know it's real? How do I know—"

"I took photos. I wore gloves. You can have it dusted for fingerprints, if you want."

The lawyer blew out another long breath. "I'm having brunch on St. George Street. I'll leave now and be there—"

"Carleigh, there's no need. I just put it back in the safe. No one will be able to get to it." She stared down at the safe, which was now locked and keeping Violet's list securely buried. "I'll keep the combination a secret until you and I can sit down and do a proper handover on Monday morning. Draft up whatever legal documents you want me to sign, and I'll hand over the combination to you then. You can take it from there."

"We should do it today—"

Sid interrupted once more. There was no way she was going to let anyone else dictate the pace of her investigation; she didn't care what was at stake. "No, we'll do it Monday. I have some work to do to wrap up my job for Buddy, and he's only given me through the end of the weekend to finish. You and I can meet on Monday, and then you and Buddy can do whatever you want after that."

There was a long silence on the other end. "Fine." Carleigh heaved a sigh. "Monday, nine o'clock. My office. Does that work for you?"

"That will be fine." Sid grinned, pleased with herself for standing her ground. "I assume this changes things for everyone. Otherwise, why would Violet have gone through all this trouble to keep the document safe?"

Carleigh sighed. "It might. It depends on what's listed on the next page. I assume you didn't send me that on purpose."

"You'd be correct. That is part of my case." She sat down on the bottom step of the staircase. "And you'll thank me for delaying until Monday if my hunch pans out."

"In light of your discovery today, I guess I can share a few things with you, given what you know already." Carleigh paused, and Sid heard the background noise quiet a little. In a loud whisper, Carleigh said, "About four years ago, I was contacted by a lawyer in New York. He called looking for Jerry Lonigan, but Jerry had passed away by then, so the call was transferred to me. The lawyer needed to get in touch with Violet Rizzo, and Jerry was listed as her point of contact on his client's will. Violet was supposed to receive a settlement payout. Half of his client's estate, actually."

"Was the client a man named Paul DeLuca?"

"Yes! How did you know?"

"Like I said, I'm good at my job." Sid grinned again. "Who got the other half?"

"DeLuca's daughter," Carleigh replied. "When I called Violet to tell her, she came in immediately and changed her own will. Jerry had originally drawn up a will that divided her estate into two equal parts. Half to her son, and half to DeLuca. Since DeLuca was now dead, she changed it so that all of it went to her son. But if Buddy predeceased her, half went to Violet's daughter-in-law, who was Buddy's first wife at that time, and half to her granddaughter, Joey.

"But less than a year later, Violet came back to see me and changed her will yet again. Until this morning, when you found what you found in that safe, Violet's estate was to be divided evenly between Buddy and Joey, and if Buddy died first, then all of it went to Joey. Given Joey's young age, all but fifty thousand of Joey's inheritance goes into trust until she turns twenty-five."

"So Violet's current will leaves someone out," Sid noted.

"Yes," Carleigh agreed. "Nothing at all goes to Violet's daughter-in-law."

Sid frowned. "Why change the will to cut out her daughter-in-law?"

"Well, Buddy remarried," Carleigh explained. "Buddy's first wife was still alive when Violet changed her will the first time. The second change came right before Buddy's wedding to his second wife."

"So Violet didn't like Penny," Sid suggested.

"I don't know about that," Carleigh replied, "but she definitely didn't want Penny to get any of her money."

"And the document I found this morning? How does it factor into all of this?"

Carleigh sighed. "What you found this morning is called a codicil, and it was dated after the current will. So if the codicil you found today is valid, it modifies Violet's will to the extent that anything listed in the codicil is governed by the terms of that document. Everything else will be governed by the will."

Sid remained silent, staring at the safe dial poking up from the garage floor.

"Sid, you there?"

"Yeah."

"What's listed in the codicil?"

"You'll find out Monday morning, Carleigh."

The woman heaved another sigh of exasperation. "Can you at least give me a hint? What am I going to be dealing with here?"

Sid squeezed her eyes shut. "Potentially something worth killing for."

Chapter Forty

Sid hung up with Carleigh Sutton, refusing to give the lawyer any more information despite her repeated protests, and sat quietly for several minutes with her eyes shut and her head resting on her arms, which were folded across her knees. When she heard keys turning in the lock on the carriage house door, she looked up to find Penelope Rizzo waltzing in.

The woman jumped when she saw Sid sitting on the stairs. "I . . . I thought no one was here." She adjusted her designer handbag on her shoulder and flashed Sid a tight smile, but Sid caught the slight twitch of her left eye. "There was no one in the house when I arrived to clear out the old flowers and take out the garbage, so I assumed you were finished with your work."

"Nope. Still working." Sid stayed where she was, effectively blocking the only avenue into Violet's office. "Just taking a short break. Had to make a phone call."

Penny nodded, both hands gripping the handles of her purse. Her eyes flicked around the garage, likely taking in the absence of the old Cadillac. When her gaze narrowed on the safe dial, clearly visible in the middle of the floor, her eyes widened. Sid watched her carefully as she walked over to it.

"What's that?" Penny pointed to the safe. "When did she get this?"

She. Not Mom, not Violet. *She.*

"No idea." Sid shrugged. "I take it you didn't know about it."

"No." Penny frowned, staring down at the safe.

"Do you think your husband knew about it?"

"Of course not! He would have told me." She kneeled and tugged on the handle. "How do we get in?"

Sid shrugged.

"We'll have to get someone out here to cut into it." Penelope stood, hands on her hips.

"Don't know the combination then?" Sid asked, still not getting up from her seat on the stairs.

"Of course I don't know it. There must be a million possible combinations."

"Ten thousand," Sid replied. Leo had looked it up for her. "Wanna venture a guess?"

Penny bit her lip, thinking. "Shall I assume you've tried already?"

Sid nodded. "All the obvious combinations. Everyone's birthdays. Anniversaries. Addresses. Various numbers I found in the house and upstairs. Everything I could think of."

"Well, I'll take care of it." Penny hoisted her bag higher up on her shoulder and headed toward the door. "So I assume you'll be out of here by the end of the day."

Sid shook her head. "Tomorrow. Late. Very late. Your husband gave me an extension through the weekend. Perhaps he forgot to mention it. I'll be out of here by Monday morning, and then the house will be all yours. I'll let Buddy know."

"Don't bother," Penny sniffed. "I'll tell him."

"Feel free." Sid smiled. "But *he's* my client, so I'll be calling him to give him my report." She held the woman's glare. "My full report."

Penny's left eye twitched again. "Fine."

The woman turned to leave, but Sid called her back. "I'm curious, Penny. Why do you think Violet cut you out of the will?"

Penny stiffened. "She did nothing of the sort."

"Yes, she did." Sid nodded slowly. "She changed her will right before your wedding day. Now, Buddy and Joey get everything. But, if Buddy had died first, then Joey would be getting it all." Sid tilted her head to one side. "Do you think that's strange, that she made sure none of it went to you?"

Penny pursed her lips. "Did Carleigh tell you that?"

Sid shook her head. "Let's just say that I'm very good at my job." She gave the woman another wide grin. "Very, very good."

The other woman huffed, spun on her heels, and stormed off, slamming the carriage house door in Sid's face. Sid glanced over at the safe. Penny hadn't bothered to ask if she'd been successful at opening it. The woman had assumed that she'd failed. She shook her head. Should have asked the follow-up question, thought Sid.

"Hey, Sid? Everything okay down there?" Dan stood at the top of the stairs.

"Fine." She turned and nodded up at him.

"Friend of yours?"

"What gave it away?" She smiled. "The slamming door?"

He grinned. "Come on up here. I think we figured it out."

Sid scrambled up the stairs after him. When they entered the office, Leo was standing in the center of the room, both of his hands squeezing the brim of his baseball cap.

———

"Leo!" Sid flew to his side, grabbing him by the arms. "What's going on?"

"Violet's just mad." He lowered his hands and grinned. "She started screaming, but I got her to stop. Now she's just stomping around the room, trying to kick things and throw stuff." He leaned in closer and whispered, "It's actually kind of funny to see."

She smiled at him, gently squeezed his arms once, and let go. "Good job, kid. Now, show me what you guys found."

The three of them sat on the floor in the midst of a dozen tidy little stacks of files. Leo took the lead and opened file after file, pointed to the relevant information, and explained to Sid what he and Dan had found. Sid had been correct. Each of the items on Violet's handwritten codicil did indeed match one of the files Sid had initially flagged for discrepancies.

Dan sat quietly next to him, only jumping in to clarify a point or offer help when Leo struggled with an explanation. And Leo was grateful that Dan seemed content to sit back and let him do most of the talking. Working on the case today made him feel useful, like he was contributing, even if most of the complicated stuff had been done by Dan. And with Sid's gaze on him, seeing her smile at him as he talked, he was convinced that he'd made the right decision to stay. This was where he really, truly belonged.

"So the customers in these files really were fictitious?" Sid asked as she stared at the photo of a diamond and opal ring that appeared in Violet's codicil. "She didn't sell these pieces to anyone. She kept them. She simply made up the names in order to create a paper trail."

Leo looked to Dan for confirmation before saying, "Yeah, that's right. So no one would think she still had them."

While Leo had been talking, Violet Rizzo had continued her tantrum. She'd slapped him several times, but it hadn't hurt much. There'd be no bruises, certainly nothing like he'd suffered from the beating the ghosts on the Oakmire golf course had given him. But in the last few minutes, her anger seemed to have waned. She was no longer storming around the room, throwing a hissy fit. Now, she floated slowly around the perimeter of the office, not looking at them. Her shoulders sagged, her gaze was downcast, but she still held tightly to the necklace with one hand.

Sid nodded, closed the file she was studying, and placed it back on the nearest pile. "But wouldn't Violet's accounts have been off? If she never sold these pieces, then she never received any money for them. These files show that the pieces were sold. Even if the documents were falsified, she wouldn't have been able to explain the missing money. And all of those pieces on her list were expensive. How would she have explained the shortfall?"

"There wasn't one," Dan answered. Sid's brow furrowed, and he raised a finger. "Let me explain."

He stood, reached for the file Sid had just been reviewing, checked the date, and then plucked another half dozen files from other boxes before sitting back down again. He opened the file with the photo of the diamond and opal ring and laid it down in front of Sid. The file was marked with two of Dan's colored index flags: one white and one green, with an "O" written on it.

Then he laid the other files out in front of him, all of which were marked with flags of the same color. Inside each of the files was a photo of a piece of diamond and opal jewelry. Dan glanced over at Leo, eyebrows raised.

Leo nodded. "You go ahead." He knew what was coming next. Dan had tried to explain it all to him earlier when they were elbow-deep in file boxes, and he'd marveled at how the man had been able to tease evidence out of numbers and words that were, to him at least, only slightly more comprehensible than hieroglyphics. As such, he was content to sit back now and watch Dan try to explain it all to Sid.

Dan gave him a quick nod in return and then launched into his explanation. "I didn't pay close attention to this the first time I went through everything because I didn't know to look for it, but once we started pulling these files"—he pointed to the stacks that corresponded to Violet's codicil—"things started to fall into place. This one, for example." He tapped the photo of an intricate diamond and opal necklace. "Fifteen gemstones in total, all various sizes." He flipped to the order forms in the back. "I matched that against the invoices from her suppliers and found seventeen gemstones." He looked up at her, one eyebrow raised. "Violet ordered more than she used."

"Okay." Sid's brow remained furrowed. "You're saying she had extra gems."

"Yes. But the exact right number of extra gems across all these files"—he waved his hand over the six in front of him—"to make that ring." He pointed to the photo of the diamond and opal ring in the file in front of Sid.

"But how would she hide that?" Sid asked. "If she was skimming gems, wouldn't someone notice that they were missing?"

"Obviously not. I mean, it went on for years, and she had the perfect way to hide it." Dan held up one of the certificates from Gemology Experts of New York. "Paul DeLuca's valuations. I think he inflated his valuations just enough to cover the pocketed gemstones without raising suspicion."

"Tell her what you told me," Leo suggested. "You know, the example." Turning to Sid, he added, "His example helped."

Sid grinned. "Go ahead, professor. I'm listening."

Dan smiled, put the certificate back in the file, and reached for a legal pad, flipping to a blank page. "Let's pretend that someone, we'll call him Mr. X, comes to Violet and gives her fifty thousand dollars to launder for him. Mr. X lets her keep a small percentage as a fee for helping him. Say, a thousand dollars. Violet then turns around and buys forty-nine thousand dollars' worth of gold and gemstones. She pockets a bit of the gold and a few of the gems for herself. Maybe four thousand dollars' worth. That leaves her with forty-five thousand dollars' worth of gold and jewels, which she uses to make a necklace. When it's done, she has Paul DeLuca certify that the necklace is worth forty-nine grand—exactly what Mr. X expects it to be."

"And then what?" Sid chewed her bottom lip, staring at Dan's scribbled handwriting.

"Then she gives the necklace to Mr. X, but she doctors up a sales slip for her own records, showing the necklace was 'sold' to a phony customer." He added air quotes for emphasis. "Mr. X keeps the necklace or sells it to someone else. Doesn't really matter. What's important is that he thinks his money has been successfully laundered.

"But what Mr. X doesn't know is that he's actually getting something that is worth less than he paid for it. The valuation is inflated, true, but not ridiculously so." Dan rubbed his chin. "At least the valuations weren't ridiculous in the earlier years." He held up a finger. "I think she got greedy toward the end. She seemed to be pocketing larger and larger stones and keeping more and more gold, so DeLuca's valuations were becoming more and more inflated in order to cover her theft. She was definitely taking much bigger risks at the end."

He swept his hand over the files in front of them. "And she does this same thing over and over again. Once she's skimmed off enough gold and gemstones, she makes a necklace for herself, or a ring or whatever, and then drafts a file of fake documents in order to cover her tracks. That way, her official record books show that everything—every dollar, every gemstone, every ounce of gold—has been accounted for. It makes it all look legitimate, even though what she's really done is steal from her own customers."

He flipped to the order form in one of the files. "The customers, like Mr. X, paid for a finished product—a necklace, a ring, a bracelet—so I don't think they knew Violet was buying more than she needed for each piece. I don't think the customers had that level of visibility. And speaking of customers"—once again, he passed his hands over the six open files in front of him—"all of these pieces of jewelry were all made for the same customer. Someone named Nathan Cohen."

He reached over and pulled another file from a nearby box. This one bore one white tape flag and one blue tape flag marked with an "S." Inside was a photo of a diamond and sapphire necklace. "This one, and four others like it, have extra gems that I think make up one of the bracelets on that new list you found. And they were all made for the same customer, one Mrs. Nell Coughlan." He held the file out to her. "Different names. But the same initials."

She took the form, glancing down at the customer details. "N. C."

"N. C., yes." Dan nodded. "And for the files that go back even earlier, the customers all had the initials E. C."

"E. C. and N. C." Sid set the file down on the floor. "In other words, Enzo Corsetti and Nico Corsetti."

Dan held up his phone, a photo of one of the pages from Violet's codicil visible on its screen. "You might be interested to know that all of the items on Violet's handwritten list that you found in the safe had phony customer names with one of two sets of initials—J. R. and V. R."

Sid blinked.

Dan nodded. "I'm guessing those are for Joseph Rizzo and Violet Rizzo."

"Seriously?!" How had she not realized that? As many times as she'd stared at her list of mysterious customers, she'd still not seen that pattern.

"Now, I will say," Dan added, holding up his index finger, "there are some files that you originally flagged that are missing from Violet's list from the safe."

Sid frowned. "How many?"

"Well, there's the one with the ruby necklace that you were interested in." Dan glanced at the list and then around at the stacks of files, and Leo could almost see the calculations being run in his head. Finally, Dan answered, "Maybe another twenty-five percent."

"That's a lot." Sid sighed. "She couldn't have forgotten about them. Surely, she remembered making those pieces. Why would she have left them off the list?"

"Maybe she sold them," Leo suggested. "You know, hocked them for the cash."

"Could be." Dan grinned. "Another possibility is that she gave them away."

Leo frowned. "Why would she just give them away?"

"As payment," Dan replied. He plucked a file with an orange sticky note out of another box. "This is one that doesn't appear on the list from the safe." The file contained a photo of a diamond ring. "This ring went to a customer named Pedro Diaz."

"P. D.!" Leo exclaimed.

Dan nodded. "For Paul DeLuca."

Sid ran her hands down her face and blew out a breath. "And all of this goes back to when Violet's grandfather died and her dad, Joseph, took over the business?"

"Yes." Dan nodded. "It appears to have started within months of the grandfather's death."

"And it all ended when Joseph died and Violet closed up

the shop." Sid shook her head. "So Joseph and Violet Rizzo were stealing from the Corsettis for almost twenty years."

"Looks like it."

"No wonder Violet kept a low profile when she moved here to St. Augustine." Sid glanced over at the wooden frame that had once supported the false wall, behind which lay decades' worth of evidence of the Rizzos' grift. "She must have been so scared they'd find out."

The spirit of Violet Rizzo drifted closer, the old woman staring at Leo with pleading eyes, and then she pointed to her head.

Reluctantly, Leo reached up and removed his baseball cap. "Okay," he whispered.

"Terrified."

The female voice, if you could call it that, was shaky and high-pitched as it filled his head.

He swallowed hard. "She says she was terrified."

Both Sid and Dan turned to look at him. Sid reached over and placed a hand on his arm. "She's talking to you?"

"Apparently." He shrugged and then glanced over at Dan. "Sorry, but this could get weird."

Dan smirked. "I'm beginning to think you two specialize in weird." The man leaned toward him and lowered his voice. "What do you need me to do? How can I help you?"

Leo blinked in surprise. "I . . . I'm okay, thanks. Just . . . just try not to freak out."

"Freak out? Me?" Dan winked and leaned back on his hands, stretching his legs out among the stacks of files. "Never."

Leo grinned and turned back to Violet.

"Papa."

The word sounded in his head. "Your dad?" Leo asked. "What about him?"

In his head, the scene changed. He was peering out from behind a curtain, looking at four men and a boy standing in a small jewelry store. He could tell from the angle of the scene—close to the floor, so that all the men loomed above her—that Violet was showing him something that happened when she was just a child.

Diamonds sparkled in glass cases that were lit with bright, white lights. The slender man with dark, thinning hair standing behind the counter spoke animatedly, waving his hands about and pointing to the jewelry in the cases. Leo couldn't hear what was being said—it was all just muffled noise—but the man was clearly excited, much more so than anyone else in the shop. Two men stood by the door, their backs to Leo, staring out at the street. The fourth man stood in front of the counter. He had broad shoulders; a barrel chest; and a shock of thick, dark, wavy hair. Unlike the thin man behind the counter, the big man stood quietly, listening, with his hand on the boy's shoulder. Suddenly, the boy looked Leo's way.

And then the vision was gone. Leo was back in Violet Rizzo's office.

Leo stared up at the spirit. "Was that Enzo Corsetti?"

"Yes."

Leo winced when the word came sharp and quick into his mind, and a wave of fear hit him like a punch to the gut. Clearly, Violet was not a fan of Enzo Corsetti. "And the boy? Was that Nico?"

"*Yes.*"

This time, Violet's reaction was altogether different. Her voice was soft and quiet, and he felt waves of yearning and sadness coming from the old woman. He rubbed the center of his chest, trying to ease the heartache he was feeling. He needed to distract her. "Whose idea was it to launder money with the jewelry?"

"*Papa.*"

There it was again. A flash of the scene in the jewelry shop. Leo nodded to Violet and then turned to look at Sid. "She says it was her dad's idea about the jewelry. He met with Enzo and Nico in his shop. Nico and Violet were just kids then. I think she was in love with him. Nico, I mean."

"That's good, Leo." Sid nodded. "Why did she stop?"

Leo glanced up at Violet again, and the scene in his head changed once more. The image lasted no more than a second, but the message was clear. A cemetery. A black veil over his eyes.

He shook his head, trying to clear the image. "Her dad died. She just showed me his grave site."

"But why didn't she keep going with the business?" Sid asked.

"*Enough.*"

Once again, fear speared Leo in the chest. "I think she'd had enough. She wanted out. She seemed really scared."

"He let me go."

Leo frowned up at the old woman. "Who let you go?"

In his head, the scene changed. Leo was standing in a bedroom—not Violet's over in the main house, but a different one that was smaller and more modestly decorated. He was hugging someone tall and broad. Strong arms wrapped around him, and he could feel soft cotton against his cheek. The scent of someone's cologne—musk and spice—filled his sinuses. When the person pulled away, Leo stared up into the face of Nico Corsetti. He was older, sadder, much more tired than the boy he'd seen in the jewelry shop, but he had the same dark eyes; the same long, straight nose; the same prominent cheekbones. Leo felt a crushing mix of heartbreak and relief. Were the emotions coming from Nico or Violet? He couldn't be sure. But as Nico left the room and closed the door, there was no doubt in Leo's mind that he had just witnessed their goodbye.

He rubbed his chest again and swallowed hard, trying to force a separation between Violet's emotions and his own. "I think Nico let Violet leave. She just showed me their goodbye. I think he loved her, too."

"So that's how she got out." Sid whispered. "Nico Corsetti let her go."

"Yes."

Leo nodded. "Yes, she says that's right."
"Did Nico know about the grift?" Sid asked.

"No."

Leo shook his head. "Nico didn't know."

Sid raised an eyebrow. "Did Nico know that Buddy was his son?"

Leo felt his jaw drop open, and he waited for Violet's reply. Several heartbeats passed before he finally heard the answer in his head, the voice shaky, the accompanying pang of fear so sharp that it felt like he'd been run through with a bayonet.

"No."

Chapter Forty-One

"Where is she now?" Sid asked.

Leo knew the temperature of the air in their immediate vicinity was no longer subzero because Violet had drifted away and was no longer hovering beside him. "She's over there, behind the desk." He nodded in Violet's direction.

Sid reached over and placed a hand on his arm. "Are you up for chatting with her some more?"

Leo studied the old woman's spirit. It was fading, no longer as clear as it had been when he'd first seen her two weeks ago, floating through the house with a finger pressed to her lips. She was translucent now, less solid. He nodded to his boss. "I can try, but I'm not sure if she's willing to talk anymore. What do you want to know?"

She spun toward him, sitting cross-legged, and chewed her bottom lip for a moment. "I want to know more about how she died. I want to know if the Corsettis were behind it."

"But I already told you," he whispered. "The person had pink hair." He was careful not to say Joey's name. Deep down, he didn't want to believe that the pretty girl in the goth makeup and the kick-ass boots, the one who wrote songs and liked his concert T-shirts, was capable of killing her own grandmother.

"I know, I know." Sid held up a hand. "But I'd like you to ask her all the same."

He nodded and stood up, slowly approaching the spirit of Violet Rizzo. When he was within a few feet of her, he stopped and ran one hand through his messy curls.

Violet watched him, still clutching her necklace.

"Mrs. Rizzo," he said softly, "can you tell me how you died?"

Violet Rizzo backed away from him, fading partially into the wall.

"Wait! Don't go, please!" Leo reached for her, and his hand passed right through her arm. It felt like he'd just plunged it into a bucket of ice. "We need your help, Mrs. Rizzo."

Violet froze, one arm and shoulder vanishing into the wall.

"What you might not know is that Joey hired us."

The spirit glanced around the room and then returned her gaze to Leo.

"She thinks someone killed you. She doesn't know who, but she's sure that you didn't fall on your own."

The old woman drifted back into the office, all of her limbs now visible if still translucent.

"I know a little about what happened to you. I know there was someone standing at the top of the stairs that night." Leo swallowed hard and wrung the ball cap in his hands. "Can you show me what happened?"

There was no hesitation on Violet Rizzo's part.

The scene in Leo's head changed again, and he was standing in Violet Rizzo's bedroom in the main house. It was night. All of the lights were off except for one small lamp on the nightstand. He moved toward the bed, reaching to pull back the covers. The hand he used was bony and covered with age spots, and Leo flinched at the sight. He caught a glimpse of himself in the mirror over the dresser. The person staring back at him was Violet Rizzo. He shuddered again, not enjoying seeing himself as an eighty-six-year-old woman dressed in a pale-yellow nightgown.

"She's showing me where she was, I think," Leo said. "I'll tell you what I see. Just let her show me, and don't ask questions."

"Okay, kid." Sid's voice was soft. Dan stayed silent.

Leo heard a noise, the scrape of heavy furniture on a wood floor. It was immediately followed by the clang of something metal. The spike of fear that pierced his sternum told him that it was Violet's reaction, not his own. The sound he'd just heard had come from somewhere in her house that night. Furniture moved. Probably bumped into. Something got knocked over in the process.

He watched Violet's hand reach for her robe at the foot of the bed, and then he was drifting down the hall toward the staircase. There were no lights on in any of the upstairs rooms, no lights coming from downstairs either, but the small windows in the foyer, the one over the front door and the few high up on the wall above the stairs, let in some ambient light from outside. It was just enough to make out the shape of furniture and the top few steps so he could see where he was going, but the rest of the staircase and the first floor remained bathed in darkness.

"She heard something. Something being knocked over, I think. Not sure. She's going to investigate."

He watched through Violet's eyes as she reached into each of the other upstairs rooms, flicked on their light switches, glanced around quickly, and shut off the lights again. From Leo's perspective, nothing appeared out of place. Everything looked to be exactly where he'd seen it that day he'd inventoried the contents of Buddy's bedroom.

He scratched his head. "She's checked all the bedrooms. Just a quick glance, but I don't think she saw anything unusual. I think she's heading back to bed."

He felt himself drift back along the hallway toward the master bedroom, but a creak of the floorboards behind him made him stop. Another spike of fear hit his sternum.

"Someone's behind her," he whispered. "She stopped right at the top of the stairs." He squeezed the ball cap in his hands even more tightly.

He felt Violet Rizzo begin to turn.

"She's gonna look." His whisper sounded panicky even to his own ears.

But before Violet could complete her turn, a pair of gloved hands shot forward and shoved her. Hard. Violet's slippered feet lost purchase on the wooden floor, and Leo felt himself begin to fall backward.

That weightless sensation, falling backward into the darkness, had his stomach threatening to revolt. It was only seconds in reality, but Violet slowed time for him, so the nauseating feeling of his free fall seemed to last forever. Finally, Leo felt a crack on the back of his head, as if someone had hit him with a baseball bat, and the world went black.

"Leo!"

Sid was standing right behind him, there to catch him as he fell, but his momentum knocked her off her feet as well. She landed hard, the jolt of the impact rattling his bones as he fell on top of her. Everything was still black when Dan lifted him up in his arms and set him down gently in the desk chair. Someone brushed the hair out of his face and gently tapped his cheek.

"Open your eyes, Leo." It was Sid, her voice gentle. "Damn it, Leo! Open your eyes!" Not quite as gentle that time.

It took all of his energy to open his eyes and blink against the early afternoon sunlight shining in through the office windows. As soon as he did, his energy returned and the pain in his head disappeared. But so had Violet Rizzo.

"She's gone." He looked around, feeling silly for having fainted.

"What happened, kid?" Sid was kneeling in front of him, and she brushed a stray curl off his forehead. "What did you see?"

"It was the same as before." He shrugged. "Someone kind of small, not much bigger than Violet, dressed in all black. They were wearing gloves. I couldn't see their face." His heart squeezed, a dull ache this time, not the sharp sting of fear that he'd felt from Violet. "But they had pink hair, Sid."

She nodded, squeezing his arm gently. "Okay, Leo. It's okay."

He shook his head and closed his eyes again, recalling that image Violet had shared with him, the one where she'd slowed time. He scoured it in his mind, looking for anything he might have missed. The person standing at the top of the stairs. Arms cloaked in black and hands outstretched. Pink hair cut to their shoulders. A diamond glinting in the pale light from the window.

Leo's eyes flew open. "She was wearing a necklace."

Chapter Forty-Two

"Tell me about it," Sid ordered. "Describe it to me."

Leo shrugged. "It was a necklace. A chain with a diamond."

"Are you sure it was a diamond?"

He shook his head. "No, it was dark. But whatever it was, it wasn't a dark color, like a sapphire or that black one."

"Onyx?"

"Whatever. I just know it was clear. Or maybe a really light color. And it sparkled." He closed his eyes again. "Yeah, just a real thin chain and one stone. I can see it sparkle even though I can't see much else. Violet must have noticed it and really focused on it because I can see the diamond, but I can't see the woman's face. It's almost as if she stopped trying to see anything once she saw the necklace."

"Or maybe that's all she had time to see before she struck her head on the stairs," Dan suggested.

Leo nodded. "Maybe, yeah."

Sid picked up a stack of files and plopped them down on the desk. She searched through them until she found one with a photo of a necklace made of diamonds and pale blue stones. The design was sort of frilly-looking, like lace. Sid held out the photo to Leo. "What size was the diamond?"

"I don't know."

He tried to push the photo away, but she shoved it back in front of him. "Look at it, Leo. Remember what Violet showed you, and then point to a diamond in the photo that looks like it's the same size."

Leo studied the photo. "It's too hard to tell. This photo is close-up, but Violet wasn't that close to the necklace when she saw it. I can't tell which one is the right size."

Sid huffed and tossed the file onto the desk. Rifling through the drawers, she pulled out a pair of scissors, a roll of gift wrap tape, and some of Violet's personal stationery. Leo and Dan watched as she engaged in some arts and crafts over Violet's desk, bits of creamy paper falling away as she cut.

"Okay, how far away was the person with pink hair?" she asked. "Show me. You be Violet, and I'll be the mystery woman."

Leo stood up but then sat back down again. Sitting gave him a better angle, closer to the angle at which Violet had seen the necklace when she fell. He rolled back a few feet, then forward, then back again until he was satisfied. "Okay. Right about there."

Sid nodded, cut a small piece of tape from the roll, and taped a small circle of stationery paper to her skin just below the dip at the base of her neck. "Is this the right size?"

Leo frowned. "Too big."

Sid tried the next size down.

"Um, maybe," he said with a shrug.

She tried the next smaller circle.

"No, I think that's a little too small."

She tried the smallest one.

"No, that's definitely too small." He shook his head. "I like the second one best. That's closest to what I saw."

Sid ripped the tape off her skin, which was now a little red with irritation, and pressed it onto a clean, uncut sheet of stationery. Right below that piece of tape with circle number two, she placed the tape with circle number four. "Thanks, kid. That's really helpful."

She looked at her watch and then reached down and pulled her wallet out of her bag. She held out some cash to Dan. "Would you do me a favor and run over to the diner and bring back some sandwiches?"

He took the cash. "Happy to." Then he turned to Leo. "Feel like getting some fresh air?"

Leo nodded.

"You sure you're feeling up to it, kid?" Sid asked. "Not dizzy or anything?"

"No, I'm fine," he said. "I could use a break."

Dan touched Sid gently on the arm. "You sure you want to be here by yourself?"

She nodded. "I'll be fine."

He smiled and then swept an arm toward the door. "After you, my good man."

"And bring back the receipt!" Sid barked as Leo and Dan left the office. "I'm going to be billing Buddy Rizzo for this lunch."

———

Sid watched Leo and Dan walk across the courtyard and disappear around the house as they headed off to pick up lunch. She pulled her notebook from her bag and dialed Joey Rizzo's number.

"Hello?"

"Joey, it's Sidney Stone." There was a lot of noise wherever Joey currently was, lots of conversation with punches of laughter. "Do you have a minute to chat?" The sound of a dish breaking rang through the phone.

"Sure, let me step outside." Sid heard rustling, more voices, and then the noise dimmed. "Sorry about that. I'm outside the restaurant now."

"That's great. Sorry for the interruption. I won't keep you long." She pulled the sheet of stationery with the two taped circles toward her. "I'm working on your case. No answers for you yet, but I do have a few questions for you. This may sound strange, but I want to ask you about your necklace."

"Okay . . ." It came out as a question rather than a statement.

"Can you tell me about it?" Her pen hovered over her notebook. "When did you get it? Who gave it to you? That sort of thing."

"Right, okay, sure." Sid could picture the young woman standing on the sidewalk in her kohl eyeliner and combat boots, sliding the small diamond back and forth along the thin gold chain. "Penny gave it to me when she married my dad. She asked me to be her maid of honor because she didn't have any family or any friends she was really close to. She gave me the necklace on the day of the wedding. It was sort of a thank-you gift for being her maid of honor and for welcoming her into the family."

Sid wrote it all down. "And how big is the diamond, if you don't mind me asking?"

"It's about three-fourths of a carat. At least, that's what Penny told me."

Sid made a note next to the smaller taped circle on the sheet of stationery. "Correct me if I'm wrong, but your necklace looks a lot like Penny's necklace."

"Yeah, it does. They're the same, in fact. We both wore them at the wedding. She never takes hers off."

"How big is hers?"

Joey laughed. "Oh gosh, hers is like three and a half carats, I think. Much bigger than mine."

Sid made a note next to the bigger of the two circles taped to the sheet of stationery. "And was her necklace a wedding present, too?"

"Oh, no, uh-uh," Joey said. "She told me she inherited it from her dad when he died."

"Her dad?" The tip of her pen slid across the page.

"Yeah, he died about a year or so before the wedding." Again, it sounded like she was asking a question rather than answering one. "Apparently, she was really close to him. Her mom had died years before, so she and I have that in common. You know, being raised just by our dads. Yeah, she got the necklace from him. Part of her inheritance, I guess."

"Joey, where are you right now?"

"I'm downtown. That pizza place off of Charlotte Street," Joey answered, although the lilt at the end of the sentence made it seem like she wasn't entirely sure.

"Are you with anyone?"

"Yeah, my roommate and some friends from school. There's about eight of us. It's my roommate's birthday." She paused. "Why?"

"Joey, I hate to do this to you, but I'm going to need you to cut the celebration short." Sid worked to keep her voice steady so as not to alarm the young woman. It was not an easy feat, given that her heart was banging against her ribs like it was trying to break free. "Now, I need you to do something for me. This is very important, so listen very carefully."

A minute later, she hung up with Joey and was on the phone with Burt Roberts. She let him know that Joey would be stopping by the restaurant he was renovating, which was luckily only two blocks west of the pizza joint. He should expect to see the young woman in a few minutes, and he needed to keep her there and not let her out of his sight until he heard from Sid again. He agreed without question, asking only if she and Leo were safe, and then he hung up.

The final phone call Sid made was to Detective Tony Davis.

"I hope to God you are not calling to tell me there's another dead body."

Sid smirked. Apparently, they no longer bothered with pleasantries. "Nope, no dead body. Not yet anyway."

"Sid," he growled in warning.

"Look, Detective, I'm trying my best to prevent anyone else from dying. Okay? So just cut me some slack."

He sighed loudly. "What's going on?"

"I can't tell you everything over the phone. Can you come by my office later this afternoon? I can tell you all about it then. Trust me, you'll want to hear it."

A long pause. "All right, but I'll have to bring Dante. Naomi's working a weekend shift, and my mom has to fill in for someone at the museum this afternoon."

Sid bit her lip. "That's fine. He'll be okay. Leo can watch him."

"Leo?" Tony asked. "I thought he left this morning."

With all that had happened so far today, she had forgotten that the whole world hadn't yet heard about Leo's decision to remain in the Old City. "They left. He stayed."

"That's great, Sid. I'm happy to hear it." He chuckled. "I like having the kid around. He does a pretty good job of keeping you in line."

"I beg your pardon?" Sid tried sounding offended, but it was hard to do given that she was smiling.

"You know you're much better behaved with him around, last night's theatrics notwithstanding." There was no laughter in his voice, and Sid realized he was serious. "I was really dreading what was going to happen around here after he left. Lord knows what kinds of calls I'd be getting from you. Dead bodies would probably be the least of my worries."

"Well, speaking of weird calls," Sid said, "can you run a check on someone for me?"

"And there it is." Tony sighed. "Here I thought you were calling to give me the good news about Leo, not demand something from me."

"Ask. Not demand. Pretty please?" Sid replied. "You'll understand why when I see you later."

Chapter Forty-Three

While Sid waited for the guys to return with lunch, she tidied up the office, putting all the files back in their appropriate boxes and stacking up the boxes in chronological order. All of Dan's sticky notes and color-coded index flags were left in place. They'd be needed later, when she had to explain everything to others. It was an impressive feat, his sifting through a century of information to find clues buried in the chaos. She was grateful to him for all of his help and for his unhealthy obsession with office supplies. She wasn't sure she could have done it on her own.

Once the office had been returned to a state of reasonable tidiness, Sid drifted around, running her fingertips over various surfaces and thinking through what her next moves would be. She paused in front of the painting of Kitty Lonigan's house and admired its riot of color; she was nearly able to smell the heady scent of Kitty's roses. Sid spun the chair around and sat down, gazing up at the pretty painting. Violet really should have put this one in the Lightner Museum rather than the one hanging there right now. This one was much more colorful, much cheerier than the other one. It was probably her best painting out of the lot.

She stood back up and gently touched the intricate, gold frame with one finger, waiting for the expected drop in temperature. Nothing happened. "Huh," she muttered and slid her fingertips along the bottom length of the frame. No temperature change. "Strange." She called out, "Violet? Where are you?"

Nothing.

She gripped the painting with both hands and lifted it from the wall. It was heavier than she thought, so she set it down on the desk and tilted one side up in order to have a look at the back. The painting had no backing, so the canvas's underside was visible. Sid searched it for markings, shining her flashlight over every square inch of it, but found nothing.

It took some wrangling, but the painting was finally returned to its hanging place, and Sid fussed with it until it looked straight. Stepping as far back as she could, right in front of the windows, she studied the painting again, double-checking that it wasn't hanging lopsided. Her gaze snagged on the porch steps. Something wasn't right. She stood frozen in place, staring at the painting for another couple of minutes, but the problem eluded her.

It wasn't until she heard the knock downstairs on the carriage house door that she finally struck upon it. Violet had painted four steps leading up to Kitty's porch, but Kitty Lonigan only had three steps. Sid grabbed her bag, shut off the overhead light, and raced downstairs.

"We have to go!" she shouted as she threw open the door.

"But what about lunch?" Leo mumbled through a mouth full of french fries.

"It can wait." She shut the door, turning the knob to make sure it was locked, and began moving toward home.

Dan took her by the elbow and spun her toward the little café table in the courtyard. "Whatever it is, it can wait ten minutes while we eat lunch."

"No, it can't—"

"Yes, Sid. It can." He leaned in and whispered in her ear. "You have a teenage boy here who just ate half a bag of fries on the walk over here, and I'm pretty sure he is still faint with hunger. Let him eat lunch with you before you go running off to solve whatever mystery is up next." He stepped back and raised an eyebrow. "Seriously. Sit down and eat something. Ten minutes. That's all we need. Then we'll both follow you wherever you want to go."

She held his earnest gaze for a moment and then glanced over at Leo. The boy was staring at her wide-eyed while shoveling fries into his mouth by the handful.

"Okay," she said, nodding her head. "Let's eat."

———

They only needed nine minutes for lunch and would have finished even sooner than that but for Dan's stubbornness in eating every bite of his meal. Leo was done in no time, and Sid ate only half of her sandwich before offering him the rest. Then she sat fidgeting in her chair, waiting for Dan to finish.

Leo and Dan followed Sid back to Saragossa Street. On the way, she called Burt, told him they were heading back to the house, and then hung up.

"I can't go over there," Leo said as he stood with Sid and Dan on the sidewalk in front of Burt's house. They all stared across the street at Kitty Lonigan's pretty yellow house with its white picket fence and scores of rosebushes. He was the only one who saw the others. "They're standing on the porch, and they don't look happy."

"They?" Sid asked.

He nodded. "The pirate and Jerry Lonigan."

"Interesting." Sid pointed back and forth between him and Dan. "Stay here. Both of you." Dan cocked an eyebrow, and Sid paused, giving him a smile. "Please."

"Since you asked so nicely." Dan leaned back against Burt's wrought iron fence that bordered the sidewalk and crossed his arms over his chest. As Sid marched across the street, Dan turned to Leo and asked, "Is she always this bossy?"

He shook his head. "She's usually worse. I think she's being nice because you're around."

Dan sighed dramatically. "You've got it rough, kid."

He leaned back against the fence and crossed his arms, too. "You have no idea."

Kitty answered the door when Sid knocked, and the two women disappeared inside the house, leaving Dan and Leo standing in the bright afternoon sun and waiting for them to return. Burt's truck rumbled past and pulled into the drive.

Joey Rizzo got out of the truck and waved at Leo. "Hi!"

"Hi." He waved back, and after catching a glimpse of Dan smirking at him, he lowered his hand. "What are you doing here?"

She crossed the lawn and met him at the fence. "I don't know." She shrugged. "Sid sounded worried. She told me I had to find your grandfather at his jobsite and stay with him until she called. That I'd be safe there."

"Where is Sid anyway?" Burt asked as he arrived to join their little party.

"She's over at Miss Kitty's." He hooked a finger over his shoulder. "She ordered us to wait here."

"Did she now?" Burt flashed Dan a look.

Dan nodded back. "It was definitely an order."

"Well, all right then. I guess we wait here." He crossed his arms over his chest, resting them on his big belly, and the four of them stared at Kitty's front door.

A dark SUV drove past and pulled into the driveway behind Burt's truck. Detective Tony Davis got out, lifted Dante from the back seat, and slung a little blue-and-red backpack with a yellow dinosaur on the front over one shoulder. The sight was so comical—the enormous detective in his tight, black T-shirt and mirrored sunglasses, sporting the child-size backpack—that Leo almost laughed. But the man was the size of a mountain and carried a gun, so Leo kept this amusement to himself.

"Leo!" Dante waved to him, his well-loved, stuffed bunny dangling from his tiny fist.

"Hey, Dante." Leo smiled, pleased that the kid remembered his name.

The four-year-old squirmed in his dad's arms until the detective finally set him down. The moment Dante's feet touched the ground, he took off running in Leo's direction. The little boy stopped in front of Joey and looked up at her. "I like your hair."

Joey smiled and twirled a section of pink hair around her finger. "Thanks. I like your rabbit."

"His name's Hopper. He's my favorite." He held the rabbit out to Joey, who took it for closer inspection. "Catch me!" Dante shouted and took off running in the yard.

Joey looked up at the adults, blinking in surprise.

"I'll go," Leo offered. He moved to open the gate, but Joey held out a hand to stop him.

"That's okay. I got this." She pushed up the sleeves of her mesh top, winked at him, and took off running after Dante. The two of them disappeared around the back of the house.

Tony hoisted the tiny backpack farther up on his shoulder. "I take it you all were called to this meeting, too."

"Yep." Burt nodded in the direction of the yellow house. "She's inside with Kitty."

Tony sighed. "Is she coming out any time soon?"

The others shrugged in unison, and all four men took up their positions, standing by or leaning against the wrought iron fence with their arms crossed in front of them.

Sid finally emerged with Kitty on her arm, and the two women descended the porch steps and wove their way around the roses to reach the picket fence. Sid waved them over, and all four men crossed the street. Leo lagged behind the others.

"Nice backpack, Detective," Kitty said, beaming up at him.

"Thank you kindly." He nodded to her and removed his sunglasses, hooking them on the collar of his shirt. Turning to Sid, he said, "You mind telling me what's going on?"

Sid held up a hand. "I will. Give me a minute." She turned to Kitty. "Why don't you tell them what you just told me?"

"About the roses?" Kitty pulled her cardigan more tightly around her shoulder.

Leo knew that the reason for her sudden chill was the spirit of her husband, Jerry, who had just drifted down from the porch to stand beside her. The pirate remained on the porch, one hand on his sword and the other on his pistol.

"Well, my Jerry planted all these roses for me. He gave me a new one every year for our anniversary. Every once in a while, one of them would die, but he'd always replace it with a new one of the same color." Kitty beamed proudly at her rose-bushes, and Leo felt waves of love emanating from Jerry's spirit.

"Tell them the other part," Sid urged.

"Yes, dear." She patted Sid's shoulder. "My Jerry was always out here, tinkering in the garden. A couple of years before he died, he took a whole week off from work. I thought he was going to surprise me and take me on one of those fancy cruises"—her shoulders sagged—"but he said he just wanted to stay home and rest. He spent all his time on that vacation gardening and doing house repairs. I made him a long list of things that needed doing, but he hardly got around to any of them.”

“What was he doing instead?” Sid prompted. Leo recognized that her fidgeting and pursed lips meant her patience was growing thin.

Kitty swept her arm out wide. “He just worked out here! Said the roses needed to be fertilized and whatnot. I don’t know. And he did some repairs on the porch. He told me we had one step that was ready to just fall apart. He said I might step on it and fall right through it at any minute, so he fixed it up for me.” She nodded and smiled, clearly pleased with her husband’s gallantry despite the fact that he hadn’t surprised her with a Caribbean cruise like she’d hoped.

Sid patted the woman’s arm. “That’s great, Kitty. Thanks.” She turned to the guys, her eyes wide. “See?”

They stared back at her like she’d just delivered the punch line but forgotten to tell them the whole joke.

Dan leaned forward. “I think you might need to help us out here, Sid. It seems like you jumped ahead, and we’re still back on the first page. Maybe you can give us the abridged version.”

Sid placed her hands on her hips and nodded once. “Okay, in a nutshell.” She heaved a sigh and then continued, “Violet Rizzo was running a grift on the Corsetti crime family.”

“She what?!” Tony shook his head, like he’d just been sucker punched.

Sid held up a hand. “I’ll explain the details later. It’s all in the files at her house. Just . . . just let me get through this.” She took another breath. “She and her dad were jewelers who were helping the Corsettis launder their Mob money by making and selling jewelry. Violet pocketed a few gems from every Corsetti order and pooled them to make her own pieces. When her dad died, Nico Corsetti allowed her to close the shop and leave New York, so she fled and hid out here in St. Augustine."

She crossed her arms, mimicking her audience. "Buddy Rizzo knew his mom had some jewelry. He wasn't sure how much or what it looked like, except for one necklace. All he knew was that the jewelry was missing, and he hired me to find it. What I found instead were hidden files dating back decades, evidencing the scam Violet and her dad had been running."

She turned to Kitty. "We know that Jerry had been Violet's lawyer for a long time."

"Almost since the beginning." Kitty smiled. "She was one of Jerry's early clients, when he was just starting out in the law."

"She must have trusted him, then, if she stuck with him all those years."

"Oh, yes. My Jerry was a good lawyer." The old woman nodded, and Leo was once again assailed with a strong wave of love coming from Jerry.

"And a year before he died, he did some work on your porch steps," Sid said.

"Yes." Kitty nodded.

Sid held Kitty's gaze. "I'm afraid we're going to need to look under your porch steps, Kitty."

"Why?" Kitty blinked, and Jerry stiffened beside her.

"Because I think your Jerry hid something for one of his best clients." She turned to look at Dan. "About seven years ago."

Dan's eyebrows shot up.

Sid nodded. "Right after she'd seen Yankees right fielder Bobby Bonds riding an Old City trolley."

Chapter Forty-Four

"Did you fall and hit your head, Sidney?!" Burt bellowed. "What on earth are you talking about? Bobby Bonds died twenty or so years ago."

Dan leaned forward. "She knows that. Bonds is a code name for a mafioso."

Burt frowned. "Which one?"

"We're not positive, but we think it's a man named Gio Segreti." Dan shrugged. "One of the Corsetti lieutenants and an all-around scary guy. He wasn't a member of the C-suite, though. We're pretty sure we've identified their code names. If Bobby Bonds wasn't Gio Segreti, then he was someone heavy enough to have scared Violet Rizzo."

"Huh." Burt thought for a moment and then nodded. "Okay, Sid, go ahead."

"Thanks, Burt." She huffed in frustration. "And you wouldn't happen to have a crowbar in your truck, would you? We need to take up that porch step."

"Be right back." He strode back across the street to get his tools.

Burt came back with a crowbar, his tool belt, and Joey Rizzo, who toted a tired and sweaty Dante on her hip. The little boy had his head on her shoulder and was clutching Hopper to his chest.

"Did you run her ragged, little man?" Tony asked, sweeping his big hand across the boy's small forehead.

Dante yawned. "Yeah, she's tired."

"I can see that." Tony smiled, and Joey bit her lip to keep from laughing. He lifted his son from her arms, and Dante snuggled against him.

"Pirate," Dante muttered. With his tiny finger, he pointed to the porch.

Everyone froze.

"What did you say, little man?" Tony swayed gently back and forth, rubbing the boy's back.

"He's got a sword." The little boy yawned and pressed Hopper under his chin.

"Can he see them?" Sid asked.

"See what?" Tony frowned.

"Leo?" Sid turned to him. The others followed suit.

"Some kids can." He shrugged. "They usually grow out of it."

"You didn't." Burt smirked. "Neither did your father."

"I think it runs in families."

Tony cleared his throat. "Are we talkin' about what I think we're talkin' about?"

Leo nodded. "I wouldn't worry about it. I'm sure he'll grow out of it. Besides, the pirate is really old. His spirit is probably strong if it's been roaming around here for hundreds of years. That's probably why Dante's able to see him."

"You're tellin' me there's actually a pirate ghost here?"

Leo nodded. "Pirate spirit. Not a ghost." When Tony cocked an eyebrow, Leo added, "I'll explain later." In a lower voice, he stated, "Not that I have a good explanation, though."

Tony ran a hand down his face. "Wait 'til Naomi hears about this."

"Right, well, no sense in debating the whys and wherefores of the spirit realm," Burt interjected, "when we have porch steps to dismantle." He swung his crowbar up onto his shoulder.

"Oh, do be careful, Burt." Kitty wrung her hands as he carried his tools through the gate in the little picket fence. "And you'll put it back, right? I'm going to need to have my porch steps put back where they were."

"I'll take care of it, Kitty. Don't worry." Burt strode past her, heading toward the porch.

As he walked away, Leo saw Jerry Lonigan lunge and pass right through him. Burt shivered. As he reached the steps, the pirate took several swings at him with his sword. Leo shut his eyes at the first swing, but when he heard no reaction, he opened them again. The pirate tried his best to take down Burt, but his grandfather simply got down on one knee and began inspecting the steps.

"I don't think I can bear to watch," Kitty moaned. She turned to Dante. "I have some lovely chocolate cake inside. Would you like to come inside and have a slice with me?" Dante nodded and wriggled in his father's arms, trying to get down. She turned to Joey. "You're welcome to join us. It's too hot to be standing out here, anyway. Come on inside."

"I think that's a good idea, Joey." Sid nodded. "Probably best if you stay inside. I'll come get you when we're done."

Joey gave Kitty a bright smile. "I'll never turn down an offer of chocolate cake. Thank you." She took Dante's hand, and the two of them followed Kitty toward the house.

"I like your hair, by the way," Kitty said. She patted her own white, cottony coif. "How do you think I'd look in pink?"

"I think you'd look great." Joey swung Dante up onto her hip as they climbed the steps, bypassing Burt, and went inside.

Once they were out of sight, Sid turned to the others. "Okay, let's see what we've got."

She crossed the yard to where Burt kneeled by the steps. Dan and Tony followed, but Leo hesitated for a moment. The pirate and Jerry were flying back and forth, one swinging his sword and the other swinging his fists. Sid stood rubbing her upper arms, but the men seemed unfazed. Leo took a deep breath, tugged at the brim of his baseball cap, and stepped forward.

As soon as he got within ten feet of the porch, the pirate flew at him and sliced Leo across his left cheek.

"Fuck!" Leo cried, his hand flying to his face. A second slice, this one to the right side of his neck, had him dropping to the ground and curling into a ball with his arms over his head to protect himself. He felt the skin on his arms being cut over and over again. "Stop! Make him stop!"

He heard Sid yell for the pirate to cease his bullying. She clapped her hands and shouted her demands, but Leo still felt the sting of the sword as it made fine lacerations on the bare skin of his arms and legs.

The next thing he knew, Dan Murdock was on the ground, covering Leo with his own body and shielding him from the worst of it. He still felt the occasional jab, but it was now more like getting pricked with a needle than being tortured with paper cuts. Leo shifted one arm and tilted his head so he could take a peek at what was happening. Tony, Sid, and Burt had formed a defensive circle around him. He could hear Sid yelling. Tony was standing with his hands on his hips, making himself as big as possible, and Burt was swinging his crowbar at the ether.

"Hang in there, Leo," Dan said, picking his head up and looking around. Otherwise, Dan didn't budge. He continued to lean over Leo, his arms forming a cage over his head, providing cover from the attack.

The pirate was still flying around the circle, swinging his sword at anyone and everyone, trying to reach him, and Jerry Lonigan was right there with him, punching and kicking and attempting to inflict whatever modest damage he could.

"Jerome Lonigan! You and your pirate friend stop your fighting this instant! Do you hear me?!"

Everyone froze. Leo peeked through his arms to see Kitty Lonigan standing on the top porch step with her hands on her hips and her pink cardigan sliding off one shoulder.

Chapter Forty-Five

"Does it hurt?" Joey asked as she dabbed a cotton ball soaked in antiseptic cleanser against the cut on his cheek.

Leo winced. "A little."

"Sorry. I'll try to be quick." She cringed. "The good news is there's very little blood, and none of the cuts look very deep, so you shouldn't have any scars." He nodded. "Of course," she continued, "if you do have a scar, you can always tell people you got it in a sword fight with a pirate." She smiled at him.

Leo shook his head. "Yeah, that'll go over well."

"Are you going to tell your mom?"

She moved the cotton ball to the cut on his neck next, and Leo nearly jumped off the porch swing. That gash felt deeper than the one on his face. "I don't know." It was an honest answer. He wanted to tell his mom all about how he'd been in a fight with a dead pirate, but he knew she wouldn't want to hear any of it. He shrugged. "We'll see."

Joey nodded and worked to clean the wounds on his arms.

Leo had been forced to tell her about his ability to see dead people. She'd rushed to the window when she heard him scream at that first slash from the sword, and she'd been the one to alert Kitty, who came scurrying out to the porch to find the brouhaha in her front garden. Kitty, sharp as ever, had surveyed the battlefield, released her battle cry, and launched an attack of her own.

Jerry Lonigan had been brought to heel at the sound of his wife's raised voice. When she told him he should be ashamed of himself for picking on a lad whom she considered to be the grandson she had never had and then further threatened to ban him from the house for the rest of her days, Jerry called off the pirate. The fight was over. Kitty emerged the victor. And while Leo was the only casualty with any physical injuries, the others were shell-shocked from the experience.

Kitty had assumed command of the situation. Jerry and the pirate were ordered to the far end of the porch, where they both stood sulking. Everyone else was given a glass of sweet tea and a slice of cake, which Kitty promised would soothe their nerves, and Joey was tasked with triage duty and given the bottle of antiseptic cleanser and a bag of cotton balls. With all of that sorted, Kitty went back inside to finish watching the Disney movie she was streaming for Dante. Fortunately, the little boy had fallen asleep on the sofa before finishing his piece of cake and had missed seeing any of the battle in the front yard.

"Are we gonna do this or what?" Burt set his empty plate and iced tea glass aside and went to fetch his crowbar from where he'd dropped it in the yard.

The rest of them ate their cake and sipped their tea as they watched Burt get to work loosening the plank on the top step.

Tony leaned toward Sid. "You and I are going to have a very long chat later."

"Understood." Sid nodded. "I'll explain everything."

"You keep saying that," he growled.

Sid glanced quickly over at Dan, who was leaning against the porch railing with a cheeky grin on his face, eating his cake in silence. She sighed and turned back to the detective. "I know, Tony. I know. But if I'm right, what we find under that porch step will make all of this worthwhile."

Tony stacked his empty plate on top of Burt's and then stood up, offering Sid his hand to help her to her feet. "And what exactly do you expect to find under there?"

Sid's eyes sparkled. "Treasure, Detective. I expect to find treasure."

There was a loud crack as the board was pried free, and Leo saw Jerry Lonigan and his pirate friend begin to buzz with annoyance.

"Hate to disappoint you, Sid." Burt stood back, set one end of the long board on the ground, and held the board upright. "Nothing but dirt and weeds under there. Maybe a few earthworms."

She kneeled at the edge of the porch and stared into the gap in the steps. He was right. Nothing but dirt and weeds. "Well, we'll have to dig. Can you get the rest of these boards off? I bet Kitty has a shovel somewhere."

Burt sighed. "Fine." He moved the board to the side so he could lay it flat without disturbing the rosebushes.

"What's that?" Joey asked. She pointed to the board. "There's writing on it." She then went back to swabbing at a cut on Leo's knee, causing his leg to jerk reflexively.

Sid launched herself over the gap in the steps and grabbed the board in both hands. "Well, I'll be damned." She laughed out loud and then glanced over at Leo. "Please tell Jerry thank you."

"Why?" Leo stood up from the swing and stood at the porch railing.

Sid swiveled the board so that Leo could see it. "Because Jerry Lonigan left us a treasure map."

———

Over the next hour, there was nothing but chaos in Kitty's front garden. The board was laid in the grass, and everyone took turns inspecting the map that Jerry had drawn on the underside. Then, garden tools were gathered from Burt's and Kitty's garages, Sid barked out orders, and everyone took up a position next to one of the rosebushes. Kitty, who'd emerged from the house when the request for garden tools had been made, now went back inside. She claimed she was unable to bear seeing the destruction of her beloved roses and was happy to take solace in minding Dante while he napped.

Sid's instructions were clear: They were to dig, trying their best not to damage the plants, and shout out if they found anything, but under no circumstances were they to open anything they found. Pretty soon, everyone was shouting, and Sid ran around snapping photos and taking notes as, slowly and carefully, small, black boxes were unearthed from beneath the roots of Kitty's roses. Each little box bore the stylized "R" logo of Risso & Co. jewelers.

The boxes were stacked on the porch, more photos were taken, and the garden was returned to a state as close to normal as possible. Burt and Joey sat inside with Kitty and Dante while Sid, Dan, and Tony began hauling the boxes over to Sid's office. Tony wanted to call it in to the sheriff's department, but Sid managed to convince him not to after pulling him aside and whispering a few details about the providence of the boxes' contents and the possibility that Joey might be in danger.

Leo stayed behind on the porch, guarding the remaining boxes. Jerry Lonigan and the pirate hovered at the far end of the porch, their legs wide and their arms folded across their chests. Leo shuffled a bit closer to them. He removed his baseball cap and whispered to Jerry. "Why is he here, Mr. Lonigan? What does he have to do with all of this?"

"Protection."

Jerry's voice came through as a bright tenor, a bit musical and definitely male.

Leo nodded. "So he was supposed to watch over the . . . the treasure?"

"Yes."

"Did you hire him because you called yourself a pirate, too? Miss Kitty called you a swashbuckler."

Leo was hit by that familiar wave of love that emanated from Jerry whenever Kitty was around. He sighed. "I'm sorry we dug it all up, but we had to do it. We think someone killed Mrs. Rizzo in order to get her out of the way and take the jewelry for themselves."

"Will."

Leo frowned. "Wait. Do you think she was killed because of her will?" He stiffened, glancing back over his shoulder to the front door. He lowered his voice even more. "She left all the jewelry to Joey. We found her list in the safe in her garage. Joey's dad and stepmom won't get any of it."

"Will."

He shook his head. "I don't understand. What about the will?"

But Jerry Lonigan had said all he had to say.

Leo sighed and ran a hand through his sweaty hair. As he did so, his gaze landed on the potted rosebush in the corner of the porch behind the pirate, who was currently staring him down. The pirate had one hand on his sword and one hand on his pistol.

He cleared his throat. "Mr. Lonigan, may I take a look under that rosebush, please?"

The pirate drew his pistol and cocked the hammer, aiming for the middle of Leo's chest. Leo was pretty sure that a bullet from an invisible gun wouldn't kill him, but he was also fairly certain that it would hurt like hell.

He raised his hands. "Please don't shoot me!" He glanced quickly at Jerry. "Mr. Lonigan, please! I know you gave that rosebush to Miss Kitty for your anniversary. You told me yourself. It was the last one you ever gave her, so I know how special it is to her." He swallowed past the lump of fear that had lodged in his throat. "I know whatever it is you buried in that pot, it's not the diamond and ruby necklace. That one is buried with Mrs. Rizzo. I just want to take a look. I promise I won't say anything to anyone. I'll let it stay buried right here. You can keep it. Or he can keep it"—Leo nodded toward the pirate—"if that's what you paid him. That's fine. I'll keep quiet about it, I promise."

Nothing happened for a long moment, and he stared at the pistol pointed at his chest, but then the pirate lowered his weapon and drifted aside, and Leo almost sank to his knees in relief. Instead, he slowly lowered his hands and kneeled next to the pot. He carefully pulled back the soil around the base of the rosebush until his fingers touched a smooth surface. Very carefully, Leo removed the box from the pot, brushed off the soil, and took a peek inside.

"Whoa!" Leo stared down at a beautiful emerald necklace. It was simple in design: one large emerald surrounded by tiny diamonds on a triple strand of shiny, white pearls. "It's the nicest one." Leo looked up at the pirate. "I can see why you like it so much."

Leo felt an overwhelming wave of sadness hit him. The force of it was so great that it almost knocked him over. In his head, he saw an image of a woman with dark, thick, wavy hair; olive skin; and deep green eyes. Just as quickly as the image came, it left him again, and he was hit by another wave of emotion. This one brought him to tears.

He wiped his eyes with the hem of his T-shirt. "You loved her," he said, staring up at the pirate in wonder. Leo wasn't asking. The emotions rolling off the pirate were as big as tidal waves and left no room for doubt. He closed the box, maneuvered it under the roots of the rosebush, and pushed the soil back into place.

"Hey, kid," Sid said as she climbed the porch steps to collect the last of the boxes. "Whatcha doin'?"

He cleared his throat again before answering, "Just checking this one. We missed it before." He patted the soil and kept his face averted, not wanting to look at her. Tears still stung his eyes, and he knew she would take one look at him and realize something was up.

"And?"

"Nope." He shook his head. "Nothing in here. Just a rosebush."

"Okay, well, come on. You can help me carry the last of these."

He nodded and slowly got to his feet. Sid filled her arms with boxes and headed to her office. Leo picked up the remaining few and turned back to Jerry and the pirate. "Don't worry. You're secret's safe with me."

Chapter Forty-Six

"Can we open them now?" Tony stood in front of Sid's desk, legs wide and arms on his hips, taking up more than his fair share of room in the office. The rest of them had to crowd around the other side of the desk. "Or do you want to invite someone else to your little party?"

Sid smirked and was about to fire back at him when his phone rang.

"Hey, Ma." Tony shot Sid a look that warned her not to make fun.

She almost wanted to laugh, but she wouldn't dare make fun of Virginia Davis. Tony? Sure. Virginia? Absolutely not.

"Yeah, Ma. I'm at Sidney Stone's office." A pause. "That'd be great." He recited the address, thanked her, and hung up. "She's coming to get Dante and take him home."

Sid smiled. "I'm not sure Kitty will be ready to let him go."

"She will when he starts getting cranky." He raised an eyebrow. "Just wait." He nodded to the stacks of boxes. "Can we get on with this?"

"Guess that crankiness is hereditary," she huffed. She

pulled up the photo of Violet Rizzo's codicil on her phone and started at the beginning. She explained what they'd found in the safe at Violet's house and what Carleigh had told her over the phone.

Tony surveyed the stacks of boxes. "You think this is the missing jewelry? The stuff she cobbled together from the gems she skimmed off the top?"

"Yes," replied the three of them in unison.

He scrolled through the photos on Sid's phone, handed it back to her, and picked up one of the boxes. "Actual buried treasure." He shook his head and huffed. "Fuck me."

They opened each of the boxes and compared the contents to the photos of Violet's handwritten list. Each piece of jewelry was more stunning than the next, diamonds and pearls and a rainbow of gemstones. They sparkled, even under Sid's cheap, overhead lighting, and Sid didn't think she'd ever seen, ever held, anything more beautiful. When the last box was opened and compared to the items listed on the codicil, all of the jewelry was accounted for except for one piece: an emerald, diamond, and pearl choker.

"Where's the emerald one?" Sid asked as she scanned the boxes, which were laid out on every flat surface in Sid's office.

"Lost, maybe," Leo suggested. "Or maybe she had to sell that one."

Sid nodded. "Could be. But maybe we should look again."

"No!" he blurted out. She glanced over at him, and he stared back at her with wide eyes and gave her a slight shake of his head. "Let's not. I mean, we dug up everything already today."

Sid sighed and then opened her mouth to speak, but Leo pursed his lips and shook his head at her again. She relented for the moment, but as to the whereabouts of the missing emerald necklace, she would have a long talk with him later.

"I think Leo may be right," she said slowly. "Violet probably sold whatever's missing. We've been over every square inch of her property, and it isn't there."

"And what about the ruby necklace? I saw the photo of it on your phone," Tony added, referring to the fancy necklace Violet's spirit had been wearing these past couple of weeks. "It's missing, right?" He picked up the ruby and diamond tennis necklace—number 11 on Violet's codicil—and frowned. "This isn't it."

"No. That one's not on the list from the safe," Sid answered. "And it's nowhere to be found. Trust me, we've looked."

After all, the ruby necklace wasn't in Violet's house, nor was it still buried in Kitty Lonigan's front garden. Sid was now certain that Leo was correct. The missing ruby necklace was actually draped around Violet's neck, which was lying in a coffin six feet underground. Sid sincerely hoped she'd never have to say that out loud to anyone, though. Given all of the treasure they'd found today, perhaps Violet's ruby necklace could stay buried with her.

There was a knock on the door, and everyone froze.

"Tony?"

"It's my mom," Tony hissed. He looked like an oversize, panic-stricken teenager who'd just been caught doing something he shouldn't.

He grabbed the nearest box, shut it, and moved on to the next. Sid, Leo, and Dan did the same, and they stacked all the boxes out of view under Sid's desk. Tony went to answer the door while the others took up poses of varying degrees of nonchalance around the office.

Tony opened the door to a rather annoyed-looking Virginia Davis.

"Antonio." All four of them flinched as if she was scolding

them all, not just Tony. "I've been standing out here for ten minutes."

"It wasn't that long, Ma." Tony stood back and let her in. "You know Sid and Leo." He pointed to Dan. "And this is Sid's friend, Dan Murdock."

Virginia smiled and offered Dan her hand, which he shook with a smile, adding, "Nice to meet you, Mrs. Davis."

"You, too." She turned from him to Sid, flashing her a smirk and a raised eyebrow.

The woman's gaze swept over the office and landed on a small, black ring box that had been left on one of the shelves in Sid's makeshift kitchen. Sid caught the flare of surprise in the woman's eyes upon seeing it, and Sid breathed a sigh of relief that the box was closed. Virginia turned back to Tony. "And where is my grandson?"

"He's across the street." Tony swept his arm toward the open door. "I'll walk you over."

Virginia waved him off. "Are you really going to make an old woman walk all the way over there in this heat, only to walk all the way back here again? I'm parked right outside. I don't want to have to do all that walking."

Tony sighed. "You're not old, Ma. And you walk around that museum all day—"

"Which is why I don't want to do all that walking now." She waved him off again. "Just go get my grandson, Antonio. I'll stay right here with Sidney and wait for you."

Tony stared up at the ceiling for a beat and then turned and left the office, shutting the door behind him.

Virginia turned to Sid next. "If we could have a word, Sidney." She glanced over at Dan. "In private."

Dan pushed off the wall he'd been leaning against and smiled. "Of course." He moved toward the door, but Leo stayed where he was next to the mini fridge. Dan changed course, put a hand on the back of Leo's neck, and gently steered him toward the exit.

"But—" Leo began.

"Let's go, Leo." Dan opened the door and guided the teenager outside.

Alone in the office, Sid and Virginia smiled at one another. Virginia placed her handbag down on the green guest chair and walked over to the kitchenette.

"You asked me about Violet Rizzo last weekend." She picked up the ring box. "We knew each other for a lot of years. Been best friends for almost as many. But I never once asked about her life before she came here. She didn't want to tell me, so I didn't want to know." She turned the box over in her hand, inspecting it from all angles. "All I knew was that the life she had before must have been a bad one. A very, very bad one. And I knew that she would have done anything to protect her son and granddaughter from the bad things in that other life." She rubbed at a small smudge of dirt on the bottom of the box. "She once told me that the life she made for herself here was balanced on the edge of a knife." Virginia glanced over at Sid. "Am I correct in assuming that you know what she was talking about?"

Sid nodded. "Yes."

Virginia sighed. "I thought so." She opened the ring box and removed a stunning ruby and diamond ring. Smiling, she rotated it back and forth, causing the jewels to twinkle under the lights. "So when Violet asked me if I would do her a favor, I said yes. No questions asked."

Virginia turned to Sid, still holding the ring, and waited.

Sid realized the woman wasn't going to volunteer anything on her own. "What was the favor?"

Virginia smiled. "To hold on to something for her and give it back to her when the time was right."

Sid's mind raced with possible questions. "When was this? The favor, I mean. When did she ask you?"

"The day before Buddy's wedding."

Sid felt her mouth drop open, but Virginia continued to smile at her as she twirled the ring, causing little flashes of light to appear on the walls. Sid watched the flashes of light. "This thing she had you hold for her, was it valuable?"

"Yes." Virginia nodded. "In more ways than one, I think."

"And you returned it to her after she died?"

"I did."

Sid blanched. "She asked you to hold a ruby necklace for her. And when she died, you put it around her neck while she was laid out in the coffin."

Virginia tapped the collar of her silky blouse, right at the base of her throat. "I slipped it under the collar of her dress so no one would notice." She huffed. "Not an easy feat, I can tell you that. I almost had to get hysterical just to get a moment alone with her after the funeral Mass, before they took the coffin away. But Buddy saw sense. Gave me some privacy."

"I can't imagine anyone refusing you anything, Virginia."

The older woman put the ring back in the box. "I think that's what Violet was counting on." She shook her head at the memory. "Never thought I'd ever have to do anything like that ever. Hope I never have to again." She closed the lid and passed the box back to Sid. "Not every secret has to be shared, Sidney. Sometimes its best just to leave 'em buried. They do less harm that way."

Virginia picked up her handbag and headed for the door. "Violet told me that someone may come snooping around someday. If they did, I was to tell them about a painting in the Lightner Museum. Violet visited it every time she came to the museum."

"Her painting?" Sid asked.

"No." Virginia shook her head again. "A different one."

"What was the painting?"

"It's a small canvas. Not more than ten inches by twelve, I'd say. It depicts a Roman temple on a hill at sunrise."

Sid frowned. "Why was Violet so interested in it?"

The woman shrugged. "I have no idea. It's not a particularly nice painting, if you ask me."

Sid reached for a pen and leaned over the desk to jot down some notes on a scrap piece of paper. "What was it called?"

"*The Temple of Juno Moneta.*"

Sid bolted upright only to find Virginia Davis closing the door behind her as she left.

Sid collapsed into her desk chair, feeling a bit sick to her stomach. She opened the little black box, took out the ring, and placed it on her finger. The blood-red ruby almost glowed, and Sid wondered exactly how much of the Corsettis' Mob money had been spent to purchase that single stone.

Scrolling through her phone, she found the photo of the missing diamond and ruby necklace and let out a low whistle. If the ring on her finger was likely worth a small fortune, she shuddered to think how much that necklace was worth. "No wonder you wanted to keep it, Violet," Sid muttered.

She removed the ring and put it back in the box. She knew perfectly well that not everyone would agree to hide an expensive diamond and ruby necklace for their best friend without asking any questions at all, and far fewer would agree to fasten that necklace around the dead body of their friend before her casket was lowered into the ground.

"Virginia must have been a damn good friend." Sid shook her head, staring at the photo on her phone. "But why keep that particular necklace, Violet?" she asked aloud, though she knew that Violet was not around, nor could she have answered if she was. "You had dozens of pieces to choose from." She rolled the chair back and stared at the boxes stacked at her feet. "What made that ruby necklace so special that you had to be buried with it?"

Sid twisted the end of her ponytail around her fingers and sighed, wondering where to go from here. Then, she swung her monitor toward her and began to type out a search for *The Temple of Juno Moneta*.

Chapter Forty-Seven

One click on one article from one website was all it took for Sid to leap up from her chair, grab her bag, and go charging out of the office. She found Tony, Dan, and Leo standing in the driveway, waving to Virginia and Dante as they drove away.

"We need to go back to Violet's house," Sid announced as she slammed her office door.

The three men spun to face her.

"Why?" Leo asked.

"Because we need to talk to Violet Rizzo." She searched her bag for the set of spare keys.

"Um, Sid." Tony crossed his arms. "Violet Rizzo's dead."

"Yeah, I know." She set the bag down on the hood of her car and kept searching for the keys.

"So, how exactly do you expect to talk to her?" Tony asked.

Leo slowly raised his hand, and the big detective rolled his eyes and blew out a breath.

Finding the keys, she picked up her bag again and walked over to Tony. "I want to ask her about Juno Moneta."

"DeLuca's missing wife?"

"No." Sid shook her head. "That's Juno Monetti. I want to ask Violet about Juno Moneta. With an *A*, not an *I*."

Dan rubbed his chin. "Can we ask why?"

"Because Violet was interested in a painting in the Lightner Museum that depicted the Temple of Juno Moneta." Sid hoisted her bag onto her shoulder. "Did you know that Juno Moneta was the Roman goddess of money?"

"I did not know that." Dan smiled at her. "And that's important because?"

"Because I think Violet knew what happened to Paul DeLuca's missing daughter, Paulina."

Tony held up a hand. "You lost me. What does a Roman goddess have to do with DeLuca's daughter?"

"If I'm right, everything." Sid began bouncing on her toes. "By the way, what happened to that name I asked you to check out earlier?"

"A number of hits throughout the country." Tony patted his pockets and pulled a folded piece of paper from one of them. "Only one in New York and one in Florida. Found a death certificate for the one in New York. Died more than twenty years ago. And the one in Florida, well, I couldn't find any record going back more than four years." He handed the paper to Sid.

She scanned the page, her eyes finding the incongruity almost immediately. "They have the same Social Security number."

"Yep." Tony nodded. "I called my buddy in New York, and he's having someone look into it up there. Meanwhile, we'll pick her up here and bring her in for questioning."

"Soon, Tony." Sid shoved the paper into her bag. "Do it soon. And hold her as long as you can. I'm hoping we can tie her to two murders." She nodded to Leo. "Let's go, kid."

When they all turned to follow Sid, she put a hand on Tony's chest. "Not you, Detective. You have to stay here."

"Excuse me?"

Sid pointed to the garage. "There's a gazillion dollars' worth of jewelry in there right now. Someone has to guard it."

Tony placed his hands on his hips and raised an eyebrow. "And you expect me to play security guard?"

"Yes," Sid answered. "You're the one with the gun."

"Sid," he growled, which seemed to be the way he always said her name these days. "I'll give you half an hour. If you're not back by then, I'm hauling all this loot to the station."

"I need an hour."

"Sid." Another growl.

"An hour. Maybe more. We have to find the spirit and then get her to talk to us. I can't promise it will be quick." She shrugged. "It might take a while."

He heaved a sigh and ran his hand down his face. "Fine. One hour. No more."

Sid smiled. "Thanks, Detective." She took Leo by the arm, nodded to Dan, and began walking away. "We'll call you if we need you."

———

Sid, Dan, and Leo arrived at Violet Rizzo's house to find a panel van parked behind Violet's black Cadillac. "Sunshine Locksmiths" was written across the van's side in big, orange letters. The three of them crept up alongside the carriage house and stood under the shade of the bougainvillea, listening through the open garage door to the conversation inside.

"Just drill into it!" Penny's voice was shrill with desperation.

"Ma'am, as I just told you, I can't drill into a safe simply because you want me to. You are not the owner of this house." A man's voice, strained to the point of anger.

"I'm the owner now."

"I need to see proof of that. Right now, I just have your word."

"Oh, for heaven's sake, just open it!"

Sid fired off a text to Tony, heaved her bag up onto her shoulder, and left the cover of the bougainvillea. Dan and Leo scrambled to keep up with her as she strode into the garage.

"Hello, Penny," Sid said.

Penny's posture went rigid, and her nostrils flared. "Get out."

"Are you the owner?" The man was wearing olive cargo pants and a black golf shirt with the Sunshine Locksmiths' logo on the breast pocket.

Sid held Penny's gaze. "No, I'm a private investigator. I've been hired by this woman's husband." Sid tilted her head a little. "Most likely, her soon-to-be ex-husband." She turned to the man, nodding toward the open garage door. "Probably best if you don't stick around."

The man took a few steps back, shook his head at Penny, and left the garage.

"Now, what's all this?" Sid asked, eyes wide, arms held out from her sides. "I leave for a couple of hours and come back to find you trying to con a man into breaking and entering."

"It's not breaking and entering if I own it," Penny spat. "Now, I'd like you to leave."

Sid held up a finger. "One, you don't own it yet. The estate is still in probate. You probably never will own it, if Buddy's as smart as I hope he is." She held up another finger. "And two, I don't work for you. I work for Buddy, and he has given me permission to be here." She smiled. "So, Penelope Draper, unless I hear it from his mouth, I will not be going anywhere."

"It's Penelope Rizzo."

"Not for long, I'm sure." Sid pulled the sheet of paper Tony had given her from her bag. "And, frankly, it's not even Penelope Draper, is it?" She held up the sheet of paper. "It's Paulina DeLuca, isn't it?"

The woman's reaction was subtle, a twitch of her left eye, and if Sid hadn't been looking for it, she would have missed it. "I don't know what you're talking about. My name is Penelope—"

"Juno Monetti."

Penny froze when Sid uttered the name.

"She was your mother, yes?" Penny's eye twitched again, so Sid kept going. "She died in childbirth, didn't she?" Sid didn't actually know if this was true, but the dates seemed to indicate that was the case. "I'm very sorry about that."

Penny remained silent but continued to glare at Sid.

"I recently learned that there is a Roman goddess called Juno Moneta. Did you know that?" Sid huffed. "Of course you did. She was the goddess of money, apparently." She shrugged. "I didn't know that. Had to look it up. Anyway, there is a painting of the Temple of Juno Moneta hanging in the Lightner Museum, right here in town. And that painting, which is not a particularly nice one, so I hear, was one of Violet Rizzo's special favorites. She used to visit it all the time. Why do you think that is?"

"I have no idea," Penny answered through gritted teeth.

"I think I do." Sid nodded. "I think the Temple of Juno Moneta reminded Violet of Juno Monetti. She was the wife of a close friend and colleague. The friend's name was Paul DeLuca." Sid tapped a finger on her chin. "See, Violet worked with Paul DeLuca for years. Decades, actually. He was your dad, wasn't he?"

"I don't know—"

"Oh, come off it, Penny!" Sid had had enough. She was not interested in playing games with this woman any longer. She was tired and dirty and wanted a shower. "I know he was your father." She waved her arms around the room, pointing to Dan and Leo. "We all know he was your father."

Penny folded her arms across her chest and lifted her chin. "I'm not saying anything."

"Fine, I'll do the talking." Sid pinched the bridge of her nose. "Here's what I know. What we all know. *And* what the *police* now know." She exaggerated a little bit with that last fact. And since she was about to bluff even more, she said a quick prayer that Penny wouldn't call her on any of the rest. "Violet and your dad were running a grift on the Corsetti crime family. Violet pocketed a few gems from every Corsetti order, and she had your dad inflate their valuations to cover it. Then, she cobbled those extra gems together to create her own pieces. Some of those pieces she gave to your father as payment for his services. You learned what had happened, or maybe you knew all along. I don't know, and I don't care."

Sid glanced quickly at Leo, making sure he was standing close to Dan and well back from Penny. Then she took a deep breath before continuing. "What I do know is that, after your father died, you disappeared from New York. You came down here, sought out Violet, and learned that the best way to get to her was through her son. So you married Buddy. How you convinced him to do it so quickly is a testament to your powers of persuasion, Penny. Really, it was the perfect plan."

Sid shrugged. "Violet was old. You didn't think she'd know who you were. She'd never met you. She'd escaped New York before you were even born, and it was easy for you to take a fake name. Probably one of your dad's old clients. I bet your dad kept very good records, didn't he?" She winked at Penny.

"Fire or no fire, I bet he had a secret stash of records that spelled out everything."

Penny's eye twitched again.

"So you showed up here as Penelope Draper. Penny, for short. Nice touch, by the way. Penny—an homage to the goddess of money, Juno Moneta, which was so similar to your mother's name. Very cute. But Violet knew who you were. Of course she did." Sid tapped her temple and grinned. "She figured it out before you even married her son. She changed her will and made sure you were cut out of everything."

Sid pulled her phone from her bag, scrolled through the photos, and held it up for Penny to see. "You're the one who knew about this necklace."

Penny's eyes flashed with surprise upon seeing the photo of the ruby and diamond necklace.

"I bet you found out about it from your dad's records. Am I right?" Sid asked. "See, Buddy wouldn't have known anything about it. He didn't know about his mother's life in New York. Violet made very sure of that. And yet he hired me to look for it because *you* told him it was missing. I don't know what web of lies you spun for him, but he believed you enough to hire me." Sid waggled the phone again. "So, tell me, why is this one so important?"

Penny's gaze drifted over to the safe.

"It's not in there, by the way."

"You've opened it?!" The woman staggered back half a step.

"Of course I opened it. I told you, I'm very good at my job." She huffed. "Now, tell me why this necklace is so important."

"Have you found it?" Penny straightened again, trying to regain her composure.

Sid sighed in exasperation.

"So that's a no then." A grin slid across Penny's face.

"I didn't say that." Sid smiled as Penny's grin faded. "Tell me, Penny."

Penny's nostrils flared. "Because it's the most valuable piece."

Sid nearly dropped her phone. She hadn't actually expected Penny to confirm any of the suppositions she'd been spewing. She'd only been trying to keep the woman there long enough for the police to arrive. "More than all of the other pieces Violet made?" She took another look at the photo of the missing diamond and ruby necklace. "More valuable than the diamond and sapphire necklace? Or the diamond and opal ring? Or the emerald bracelet? Or the ruby tennis necklace?"

Penny's gaze flew once more to the safe.

"Sorry to disappoint you, but they aren't in there either." She scrolled to the photos of the codicil. "Want to see what is in there?" She strolled over to Penny and passed her the phone.

Penny's eyes went wide as she read the words in Violet's handwriting on the first page. She scrolled back and forth, skimming every page.

"That hurts a little, doesn't it? Joey getting everything?" Sid tutted. "Violet cut Buddy out, too. Probably couldn't risk you getting your hands on any of it."

Penny tapped the screen a few times and then handed the phone back to Sid with a smug, satisfied look on her face.

Sid glanced down at the screen. "Seriously? You deleted the pictures?" She chuckled. "There are three other people who have copies of those photos. Probably even more than that by now. Not to mention the original document, which is tucked safely away." She pointed to the in-ground safe. "You think deleting my photos changes anything?"

"She owed me," Penny hissed.

"Violet?" Sid snorted a laugh. "She didn't owe you jack shit. Violet was the one taking all the risks. She was the one doing the actual stealing. Your father merely helped with the paper trail. He could have denied the whole thing if he had to. And besides, she paid him off. Your father got his cut, fair and square."

"And he blew it!" Penny's eye was twitching much more noticeably now. "My father was a nice man, a trusting man, and the Rizzos took advantage of him. They got him in too deep, and he couldn't get out. He started drinking. His hands shook so much that he couldn't work. He had to sell the business. My family's business!" She pounded her chest. "It was my birthright, that business, and he had to sell it. He had to sell everything. All the jewels that the Rizzos had paid him with, everything. All he had left was the house. That's all I got when he died, and half of it went to her!"

Sid remembered Carleigh telling her that Violet got a payout from DeLuca. She'd assumed it was millions, but that hadn't been the case, if Penny was to be believed. "So you came down here to exact your revenge."

"I came down her to get my fair share!"

"Oh, Penny, please—"

"I found her letters!" Penny's eye was twitching uncontrollably by this point. "My father loved her! He loved her, but she abandoned him."

"He didn't love her, Penny."

"Yes, he did! I've read the letters. Years and years' worth of letters."

Sid shook her head at the woman. "No, Penny. It was all a ruse. The letters were all in code. Violet and your father were keeping tabs on the Corsetti family, making sure no one had caught on to what they'd done. They weren't having an affair. They were keeping each other's secrets."

Penny blinked in surprise, a difficult feat given that one eye was twitching so much that she was barely able to keep it open.

"It must have been very frustrating, believing all these years that your dad pined for another woman. Even after he married your mom and she died in childbirth, he still kept writing letters to Violet Rizzo." Sid shrugged. "And that old woman was so stubborn, wasn't she? You came all the way down here, married her son, became stepmother to her granddaughter, and she just didn't have the common decency to die already. Very rude." Sid shook her head. "All those years that you took her to her hair appointments and sat through Sunday dinners, and she still wouldn't kick the bucket." Sid tutted. "So you helped her along, didn't you? You simply pushed her down the stairs one night."

Despite her twisted, spasming countenance, Penny managed to sneer. "She deserved it."

Sid pretended to wince and then heaved a loud sigh. "But, Penny, you forgot about the slippers." Penny's expression faltered ever so slightly, and Sid nodded. "Yeah, the slippers. She was wearing her upstairs slippers when you pushed her." Sid wagged her finger. "Violet never wore slippers on the stairs. You should've remembered that."

The sneer slid away, and Penny shook her head. "Stupid fucking slippers."

"Yeah," Sid agreed. "What I don't understand is why you had to wear the pink wig to do it."

Penny stood there, wide-eyed and slack-jawed, her eye spasming uncontrollably.

Sid grinned. "And if you thought your dad was such a great guy, why did you kill him, too?"

Chapter Forty-Eight

P enny Rizzo wasn't the only one standing in the garage wide-eyed and slack-jawed. Leo and Dan remained in the open doorway, watching as Sid spun her tale of mischief and murder while Penny twitched and spasmed before ultimately admitting it was all true.

Sheriff's deputies arrived soon after Sid accused Penny of wearing a pink wig to murder her mother-in-law, and the woman almost looked relieved when the deputies hauled her away in handcuffs. Anything to get out of further verbal torture from Sid.

Luckily for Sid, Dan had had the wherewithal to hit record on his phone and slip the phone into the front pocket of his Hawaiian shirt as soon as Sid strolled into the garage to confront Penny. He sent her the video as Penny was being loaded into the deputies' car. Sid sent the video immediately to Detective Davis.

Throughout the whole ordeal, the spirit of Violet Rizzo had hovered on the carriage house staircase, leading up to her studio and office. She said nothing and flashed no images into Leo's head despite him removing his baseball cap and nodding to her, trying to convey to her that it was all right to do so. When the deputies arrived, Violet floated upstairs and disappeared from view.

Now the three of them—Dan, Sid, and Leo—stood side by side in the garage and watched the patrol car pull out of the driveway with Penny sitting in the back seat. Once they were gone, Sid doubled over, hands on her knees and head hanging low.

Dan reached over and gently rubbed her back. "You've had quite a day."

She nodded, blew out a breath, and rolled slowly up to a standing position. "And it's not over yet." She turned to Leo. "Where is she?"

"Upstairs."

Leo led them to the studio, where they found Violet Rizzo sitting at her easel, trying desperately to finish her final painting. She kept attempting to pick up her paintbrush, but it passed through her ghostly fingers. When she reached out to touch the canvas, her hand passed straight through it. He approached her slowly, not wanting to spook her. The old woman seemed so frail, almost completely transparent now, but the diamond and ruby necklace still glittered around her neck.

Sid whispered in Leo's ear. "Ask her about the necklace. Why was it so important?"

"*No.*"

Leo hadn't even opened his mouth when the answer came. He glanced over at Sid. "She doesn't want to tell us."

Sid set her bag on the floor, ran her hands down her face, and tugged at her ponytail. "Okay, how about this?" She didn't bother whispering this time, nor did she need to have Leo act as translator. "Tell us about the necklace, Violet. Tell me why it's so important to you, and maybe I'll let you keep it."

They waited for several moments before Sid finally whispered, "Anything?"

Leo shook his head. "Nothing. She's not talking."

"Fine, you leave me no choice, Violet." Sid picked up her bag and slung it over her shoulder. "I'm going to have to tell Buddy that the necklace is buried with you. He can dig you up, for all I care."

"No!"

It was an eardrum-piercing, skull-cracking shriek, and it nearly brought Leo to his knees. He clutched at his ears and shut his eyes as tightly as he could, willing the wailing to stop.

"Sid!" Dan yelled, wrapping his arms around him. "Sid, make it stop!"

"Stop hurting him, you bitch!" Sid screamed. "Your beef is with me! If you want to keep that damn necklace, then convince me it's worth leaving buried! Otherwise, we're digging it up!"

Inside Leo's head, the world went quiet, save for the soft crackle of a fire. When Leo opened his eyes, he saw a bedroom decorated in wood paneling. The only real light was that from the fire in the hearth set into the wall opposite a big bed, where he sat perched on the end. A suitcase stood open on a luggage stand near the bathroom, and Leo realized he was in a hotel room. He also realized he was wearing a nightgown and holding a Risso & Co. box in his lap. His hands were smooth, his fingernails painted with bright, red polish. This was Violet Rizzo's memory.

Next to her sat Nico Corsetti. Leo recognized him from the

earlier memory Violet had shared with him. He looked exactly the same, so both memories were very close in time; except in this memory, Nico wasn't wearing a shirt. Leo cringed as he stared at the man's broad, hairy chest.

Violet opened the box and presented it to him. The diamond and ruby necklace had an otherworldly glow as Nico lifted it from the satin tufted pillow on which it rested and held it up to the firelight. The rubies blazed, a deeper red than Leo had ever seen before, and the diamonds shone so brightly that Leo almost needed to shut his eyes. This was how Violet saw the piece—brilliant and blazing and practically beating with life.

Nico said something, but Leo couldn't hear. Violet was muffling his words. Hers, too. Leo quickly understood why, based on what he was feeling from either Nico or Violet or both —a longing so deep, a desire so great, that he wanted to shut his eyes and run from the room. Instead, he slowly moved his hands to cover the front of his shorts, and in his head, he begged Violet to stop.

But she forced him to watch as Nico unfastened the clasp of the beautiful necklace and draped it around Violet's neck.

When Leo next blinked, he found himself back in Violet's studio. Violet was gone, her stool vacated, but the effects of her memory were still very much alive in Leo's teenage body.

Dan stood on one side of him with his lips pressed together, and Sid stood on the other with her hand over her mouth, likely biting her tongue.

"Nico gave her the necklace!" Leo barked. He didn't dare move his hands.

"You sure?" Sid asked. She didn't move her hand either.

"Yes!" he growled. "She loved him. He loved her. End of story."

He turned and stomped off, leaving Sid and Dan in the studio. Once outside, he crossed the courtyard to the big, stone fountain and plunged his whole head under the waterfall of cool water.

Chapter Forty-Nine

On the walk home, Leo made Sid and Dan walk ahead of him. The two of them had pulled the car back into the garage, shut the garage door, and locked the carriage house, but he hadn't bothered to offer to help. Instead, he'd splashed himself with water until he was soaking wet, and he'd paced around the courtyard until the feelings, and everything else, began to shrink. But he was still too embarrassed to look Sid in the eye, hence the need for her to walk on ahead.

Before they reached Saragossa Street, Sid had exchanged a series of phone calls and texts with Carleigh Sutton. The result of that exchange was Carleigh calling in a favor with a branch manager of a local bank and securing a large safe deposit box to be available first thing Monday morning. Until then, it was agreed that Violet Rizzo's jewelry would remain in Sid's possession, under her vigilant watch.

Dan offered to stand watch with Sid for the next thirty-six hours, which she'd politely declined, though she made him a counteroffer: She would order pizza, and he could stay for dinner tonight; then he could visit her tomorrow provided he brought more food, since she still hadn't gone grocery shopping; and finally, he could accompany her to the bank on Monday morning. He'd smiled at her, accepted the counteroffer, and told her that he liked pepperoni and mushrooms on his pizza.

Leo watched the two of them as he walked a few steps behind them. Unlike spirits, he couldn't feel the emotions of living people, but the slight blush on Sid's cheek when she turned to look at Dan as well as his smile and constant glances at her gave Leo a pretty good impression of how they felt about each other. Mercifully, it was nowhere near as embarrassing as the feelings that had passed between Nico Corsetti and Violet Rizzo.

When they reached Burt's house, Leo could hear music coming from inside—Fleetwood Mac's "Don't Stop." Unlike the usual Recent Geezer jam sessions, this one included a piano and a female voice.

"I thought the Geezers had a concert tonight," Sid said as they stood in the driveway, listening. "Why are they practicing here?"

Leo shook his head and checked his watch. "They shouldn't be. They should be leaving now for Granny Oak's."

"Well, you better get going." Sid punched him lightly in the shoulder. "You're the roadie. Assuming you still have the job, that is."

He rolled his eyes. "Yes, I still have the job." But then he glanced up at the house, listening to the music, so lively and upbeat, and he chewed his bottom lip. "Wait, do you think they replaced me?"

Sid smiled. "Not a chance, kid. My guess is they're in there waiting for you."

"Hope so." He nodded. "You guys coming tonight?" He included Dan in his question. He liked the man, hoped he'd stick around for a while. Dan was a good influence on Sid, and

Leo was grateful he'd been around today, ready to jump in and save him from swashbuckling pirates and old ladies who screamed like banshees.

"Can't." She grinned. "We're babysitting until Monday morning, remember?"

Leo grinned when she said "we."

She pointed to Tony Davis's SUV, which was still parked in the drive. "Besides, I believe I have some explaining to do."

Leo grimaced. "Good luck with that."

She grimaced, too. "Thanks. I'm gonna need it."

Dan held out his hand to Leo. "Nice work today."

"Thanks," Leo said as he shook it. "And thanks for your help with . . . well, you know."

"Anytime." Dan nodded at him and then followed Sid to the garage.

"Check in with me tomorrow, kid," Sid called out. "Just not too early."

Leo bit his lip to keep from smiling and jogged up the porch steps and into the house.

"Leo!"

This time, when the chorus of voices hit him, he was over-joyed to hear it. So much had happened in the last twenty-four hours, and yet the Geezers were still here, sitting in the living room, drinking beer with their best groupie, Kitty Lonigan, and waiting for him to join them.

The only change to this typical scene was the addition of Joey Rizzo, who sat at his grandmother's upright piano in the corner. According to Burt, no one had played that piano since Camille died, and yet every year, Burt had it tuned just in case. He'd never specified what that case actually was, but appar-ently a young, pink-haired keyboardist was all the reason he needed to set aside the family photos, dust off the keys, and let someone finally play it.

Leo felt his stomach twist as he stood there, staring at Joey while she smiled back at him. She had no idea that her step-mother had just been arrested. No idea that Penny had admitted to killing Violet Rizzo, explaining that she donned the black clothes and pink wig in case she was caught on any of the neighbors' security cameras.

Joey also had no idea that her grandmother had left her the buried treasure that they'd dug up that afternoon or that the jewelry was the product of a grift pulled on one of the biggest crime families in New York City. And the young woman definitely had no idea that she was actually the granddaughter of a Mafia don. Leo had no idea who would break all that news to her, but he certainly didn't envy them the task.

"It's about time you got here," Burt said, pulling him into a big bear hug. "We've been waiting for you."

His grandfather released him after a long while but kept hold of his shoulders. His gaze roamed over Leo's face and body, likely checking for more cuts and bruises and other signs of scuffles with the afterlife.

Leo smiled. "I'm okay, Grandpa."

Burt patted his cheek with his big paw of a hand. "Then go grab a shower. We leave in ten."

"Got it."

Leo dashed past him and up the stairs, taking them two at a time. He went straight to the bathroom and jumped into the shower. The soap stung the cuts on his body, and memories of the pirate swinging his sword at him flashed unbidden into his mind. He washed and dried himself as quickly and carefully as he could, wrapped a towel around his waist, and went to his bedroom.

He made it two whole strides into the room before stopping short. Laying open on his bed was a beat-up guitar case cradling the most beautiful bass guitar he'd ever seen. It had a simple, chocolate-brown body with a faux-wood pickguard, and it was obviously secondhand, but it was absolutely beautiful. He picked it up, holding it gingerly, and strummed. The sound the instrument emitted was glorious, albeit a little out of tune. Easily remedied, he thought, as he hugged it close.

"Leo!" Burt shouted from downstairs. "You've got two minutes, or we're leaving without you!"

He returned the guitar to its case and dressed quickly in the nicest of his dad's old Tom Petty and the Heartbreakers T-shirts and a clean pair of cargo shorts.

Then he fired off some texts to his mom:

> Helped Sid solve a big case today

> Can't talk about it but it's really big

> Heading to granny oaks to hear the geezers

He put the phone in his pocket but quickly pulled it out again and typed:

> Hope you're having fun

> Love you

Leo checked his appearance in the mirror one last time. Then, he rushed downstairs for a night of rock and roll with his favorite band and an evening with his new family.

Acknowledgments

The idea for this book has been with me for a very long time and is very loosely based on a bit of family folklore. It was fun to take a single story about a (not so) distant relative and turn it into a puzzle with a bit of murder thrown in for good measure. To everyone who helped bring this story to life, thank you so much. In particular, I offer special thanks:

To my mother and grandmother, whose wild family stories served as the inspiration for this book.

To my family, for loving and supporting me, even as I kept talking and writing about murder and the paranormal.

To my editor, Jessica Hatch, for all of her expertise, advice, and patience, and for being such an enthusiastic supporter of my characters and stories.

To James at Bookfly, whose cover designs perfectly capture the spooky essence of St. Augustine that I strive to reflect in my books.

To the members of the Reading Between the Wines Book Club, who are not only wonderful friends but also excellent readers—especially Cathy Klein, Tracy Tripp, Meg Balke, Charmaine Brooks, Leah Maltz, Donna Nuckols, Christine Schmitt, Renee Schreck, and Cecile Spiegel, all of whom were early beta readers and provided outstanding feedback.

And last, but always first in my heart, to my husband, Matt, for being my first and most important reader, as well as my best friend. Thank you for always believing in me.

About the Author

Stacey Horan writes about things that scare her, and her goal is to keep writing until nothing scares her anymore. Stacey is the author of the *Old City Mysteries*, an adult paranormal mystery series set in St. Augustine, FL. Additionally, she has penned seven young adult novels, including two paranormal thrillers and an adventure/mystery series. Stacey also hosts *The Bookshop at the End of the Internet* podcast, which is dedicated to helping book lovers discover new authors.

You can learn more about Stacey at her website (www.staceyhoran.com) or on social media (@staceyleehoran).

www.ingramcontent.com/pod-product-compliance
Lightning Source LLC
Chambersburg PA
CBHW031202310726
48969CB00001B/189